# Amore Lost

## Bernadette Carson

Copyright © 2008 by Bernadette Carson

ISBN  0-7414-4790-8

*Cover photo by Mark Pacoe.*

*Published by:*

**INFINITY**
PUBLISHING.COM

*1094 New DeHaven Street, Suite 100*
*West Conshohocken, PA 19428-2713*
*Info@buybooksontheweb.com*
*www.buybooksontheweb.com*
*Toll-free  (877) BUY BOOK*
*Local Phone (610) 941-9999*
*Fax  (610) 941-9959*

*Printed in the United States of America*

*Printed on Recycled Paper*

*Published  May 2008*

# Acknowledgments

From the time I began *Morning Glory,* the first in my Ogunquit trilogy, through *Some Kind of Miracle* and *Amore Lost,* I have had to impose on many people to answer countless questions that arose as the plots developed. Without hesitation, all of them had agreed to help—and some had even volunteered—unaware of how time-consuming their involvement might be.

I am humbly grateful for the efforts of all those individuals who contributed to the success of *Morning Glory* and *Some Kind of Miracle.* Although their names appear on the acknowledgment pages of those novels, I wish to thank them again for their courtesies. Without their help, publication would not have been possible.

I also wish to thank the following individuals who have assisted me with *Amore Lost:*

Fellow writer E.P. (Betty) Vallone and Grace McGannon, who both reviewed chapters pertaining to my new Italian character, Sergio Giannetta.

My friend and attorney Thomas E. Walsh II, Esq., and Jeanne Finan, paralegal.

I also thank my entire family—my four children and their spouses, my eight grandchildren and my extended family, whose praise, pride and enthusiasm pulled me over the rough spots.

Web site: BernadetteCarson.com
e-mail: Bernadette057@optonline.net

# Dedication

This book is dedicated to all the people of Ogunquit, its residents and tourists, who welcome me every year and enthusiastically support my novels. May I sincerely say it's been my pleasure to entertain you through my characters.

There are three people, however, who hold a special place in my heart and I dedicate *Amore Lost* primarily to them:

Leanne Cusimano (a/k/a "Frannie Oliveri"), whose excellent restaurant, Amore Breakfast, coupled with her warm personality, provided the plot for *Morning Glory,* the first novel in my trilogy. Her guidance has been invaluable.

Donna and Gordon Lewis, whose generosity knows no boundaries.

*I can never thank you enough, dear friends.*

# Prologue

For a fifty-something woman, she still looked damn good. Her sandy blonde hair was pulled high on her head, fastened with a huge tortoise shell clip. Although sunglasses covered her eyes now, he had seen her without them and definitely liked what he saw.

At a popular Pocono Mountains resort in Pennsylvania, he sat on a park bench in the village square. People around him were admiring the colorful clusters of flowers that adorned the park along with statues and plaques commemorating fallen war heroes.

His target de jour was one of a large family assembled there for a reunion. How touching. She wore a pink cotton knit jogging suit with a white tank top underneath, revealing generous breasts that made him forget how old she was. Not that he ever entertained the thought of sex with an older woman. There were plenty of young ones, ripe and ready.

His lady in pink had a tight and trim figure with a rear that looked sweet and round as a peach. Shame, he thought, that he had to stay focused on business. Visualizing again that face and body, he allowed his imagination to amuse him. But when Oliver Linden had seen her on the resort grounds, he had no doubt that despite her great packaging, this one had plenty of mileage behind her. Especially when he saw her husband. Fortunately for Oliver, the guy liked to use the resort's state-of-the-art equipment in the exercise room while his wife browsed and did her thing, with or without her relatives, in and around the resort.

Today she had taken off alone, and Oliver kept a close, but discreet, distance behind. He sighed when she went inside the gift shop, knowing this could take awhile. But a smug smile curled at his lips recalling how his patience had paid off so often this past year. At twenty-three years old, he was proud of how nicely his business had developed. Short hours, excellent working conditions and a sizeable tax-free income.

He sat there quietly content, sipping his coffee, reading a newspaper through designer sunglasses while keeping a watchful eye on the gift shop, waiting for his lady in pink to emerge. Just like all the other idiot husbands who waited patiently while their wives shopped.

The newspaper held his attention awhile, but his mind kept drifting back to the lady in pink with the peachy ass. His loins came alive. But Oliver couldn't let sexual urges interfere with his work. He had been making a nice income simply robbing these tourists, enabling him to travel from one city to another, all over the country. It had worked for him over a year now with no mishaps. His only regret was that he hadn't thought of it sooner. Unfortunately, most women used credit cards and checking accounts to pay for their items, but many still paid cash, or had a healthy wad of bills stashed somewhere in their purses.

After a half hour, his patience was wearing thin. He was tempted to go inside the shop and yank her out, but suddenly there she was, carrying a shopping bag full of purchases.

If his instincts served him correctly, this job would be easier than most. When he had followed her earlier, the poor little darling had a tough time finding a decent parking space. Since the sun wasn't due to make its debut for hours, the cool weather and hazy sky drove throngs of people to the shops, to the delight of their proprietors. Hot, sunny days kept the tourists flocked around the pools and lakes; so, from a business sense, gray skies and cool temperatures were the merchants' sunniest days.

Maintaining a safe distance behind, he watched her walk to her car, which she had been forced to park in the last section. Poor thing. She looked exhausted from the long walk. The weight of her shopping bag was apparently too much for the poor woman because she kept shifting it from one hand to the other. He laughed at the sight but was almost tempted to help her. She looked so pathetic. But he shrugged it off. She should have thought of that before she bought all that stuff.

Oliver's car was in the row behind hers and so far, so good. Not a single person was walking towards or driving into this remote section.

He seized the moment. "Oh, ma'am? Excuse me," he said politely, feigning shyness. Only steps away from her, he waved a finger and smiled, as though to assure her he was harmless.

Her body tensed as he approached her. Her sunglasses slipped down her nose a bit and he could see her furrowed brows. On the lid of the open trunk, her hand remained frozen.

Still Oliver smiled his boyish smile. "I'm sorry. I didn't mean to scare you, ma'am, but I only want to help. There's a huge bee crawling in your hair, and I—"

Repulsed by the thought, she shook her head violently. "Oh, God! Is it still there?" She looked at him pleadingly and Oliver was happy to oblige.

"If you stay perfectly still, ma'am, I'll get it out. But don't move. I wouldn't want it to sting you."

A second later he was inches away. In that fleeting moment she sensed this was no good samaritan. His sinister smile told her otherwise. She shrieked when she saw the flash of his knife as it slashed the strap of her shoulder bag. Instinctively, she made a desperate attempt to defend herself by digging her nails into his neck.

But the sudden stinging pain fueled Oliver's anger. This was the first time any of his victims dared to fight back. "What the hell are you, *crazy*?" he yelled out. Then he too acted instinctively. His left hand gripped her throat, his thumb squeezing her larynx, and his right hand thrust the knife into her neck. He stared at the fear in her eyes, almost as shocked as she was, while her body crumbled. With his heart pumping wildly, he shoved her body into the trunk and slammed the lid, cursing her with every breath he took. Trembling from the shock of what he had done for a damn handbag, he jumped in his own car, pulled a towel out from under his seat and made a futile attempt to wipe her blood off his hands and clothing.

It killed him not to scream out all the profanities locked inside him, but he clenched his teeth instead. If ever there was a time to stay in complete control, this was it. Right now he had to concentrate on getting out of the area slowly and calmly. Once he got over that hurdle, he'd have to find the ways and means of cleaning up the blood and getting rid of the knife before he could return to the resort. The knife could easily be tossed into the lake. The clothes he could burn somehow, but the bloodstains on the car seat . . . well, he'd have to figure that out later. For now, he'd improvise.

He reached back, grabbed his sweatshirt from the back seat and used it to cover the white shoulder bag and the upholstered passenger seat, both stained with blood. While he struggled to drive slowly and appear calm, he eyed the lump under his sweatshirt. That white bag better have enough cash in it to make this f---in' mess worthwhile, Oliver thought.

* * *

In The Shoppes at Twin Lakes parking lot, a female police officer did her best to calm the hysterical young woman who witnessed the horrific crime. But because of a dead cell phone, she had lost precious time in calling 9-1-1.

The parking lot was flooded with crime scene teams and uniformed officers. All of them worked in concert to seal off the area while technicians from the medical examiner's office examined the body of the lady in pink who might still be alive if only the sun had shined.

* * *

Twelve miles away, two local detectives walked across the grounds of The Twin Lakes Resort. For the first time in their law enforcement careers, they had the grim task of informing the victim's husband of his wife's brutal murder.

At the registration desk, they showed their badges and spoke to the manager. "We need to see one of your guests, please," the older detective said.

The manager gazed at them cautiously. "Is there a problem, detective?"

"I'm afraid so, but we have to speak to a particular guest first, if you don't mind."

"Certainly, sir. I'm sorry. What is the guest's name, please?"

"Daniel Madison."

# Chapter One

The first year is the worst to get through, everyone tells him. The first Thanksgiving. The first Christmas. The first New Year's. The first everything. Are they all implying the pain will ease, dulled by the passage of twelve months? Is it some kind of apprenticeship the grievant must struggle through before crawling out of a cold dark tunnel into warm sunshine?

What do they know? They can't possibly know a damn thing until they too have that ax fall down on their lives, splitting them apart with such finality that it seems impossible to survive without the half of you that's been sliced away.

Dan's eyes welled up again remembering how excited his Louise was when the invitation came. "Wow, what a great idea!" she had said. "A three day family reunion at a Pennsylvania resort. I'm so glad my cousins arranged this." He could still hear her voice and visualize her beaming face when they finished loading the car and took off. "I've been looking forward to this weekend since the invitation came two months ago."

Dan had smiled at her as they drove away, but couldn't share her enthusiasm. He had met some of her relatives only occasionally during their thirty-six years of marriage, and most of them not at all. But there was no way he could have said no to her, so he pretended to be just as delighted that September morning.

Little did he know that his reluctant acquiescence would lead his wife to her untimely and violent death.

Almost ten months had passed since that horrifying day. Dan knew he shouldn't complain, but his four children were relentless in their quest to get him to "move on," an expression he had come to detest.

This June night his son Todd was working on him again while they waited for the rest of the family. "Dad, we know you didn't want to celebrate your birthday; neither were we in the mood, to tell you the truth. But we all have to go through the motions of getting on with life as best we can without Mom. And we couldn't just ignore your birthday. We wanted to be with you, for this one especially. And don't think it hasn't been hell for us, too. Not only losing our mother so suddenly, but the *way* we lost her."

"Stop it, Todd," Dan snapped. "I've told you before and I never want to say it again—" He leaned forward and pointed a finger. "Don't ever say a word about the way your mother died. Not one single word, you hear me?"

Todd stared at his father in disbelief. It was as though the face and body were familiar but the person a stranger. "Okay, Dad, calm down. I'm sorry. You know we never bring that up. It just slipped out. I'm sorry."

Dan nodded dismissively, but never made eye contact with his son. He shoved his hands in his pockets and went out on the porch to be alone with his thoughts. Anger stirred inside him as he stared down at the colorful flower beds and clay pots all neatly arranged and radiant in the sunlight.

Did Vanessa and Wanda, his daughter and her partner, really believe their efforts to keep Louise's garden alive would give him pleasure? He had an urge to run down there and rip them all out. It was Louise he wanted alive, not her damn garden.

He covered his mouth with his hands to hold back the screams and sobs that wanted out. If only he could have squeezed the life out of the degenerate bastard who took her life, maybe he could have expunged all this rage inside him.

Then he'd have only the grief to deal with. But before he got the chance, the police had shot him dead.

While Dan was pumping up his heart rate on a treadmill, trying to stay healthy, his wife fought for her life with the only weapon she had—her fingernails. A mournful sound escaped Dan's throat as a memory flashed before him. He recalled the day before their Pennsylvania trip, when she came back from having her nails done. He had teased her about her attempts to protect them; how she used gloves for everything she did. She had looked at him pleadingly when she asked him to handle all the minor chores that might chip her polish. As he unloaded the dishwasher, he had given her a slanted smile. "Isn't this a little overkill?" he asked. She had laughed, knowing he was absolutely right, then said, "It is, but indulge me, okay? How often do I get my nails done? I want them to last through the weekend."

She had looked so beautiful—so happy and healthy. Her only concern was that her *nails* should survive the weekend.

He was so lost in his thoughts of Louise that he never heard footsteps behind him, but when he felt the brush of a kiss on his cheek, the fragrance was familiar. Mechanically, he stood up to greet his daughter, Glory, his love child, born of a summer romance long before he had met Louise. An old romance so clouded by time that the memories had faded into oblivion.

"Why did you come? I told you guys—"

"We know what you told us, Dad, but we're your children and we want to be with you today, so do it for us, okay? We're just going to barbecue steaks and have an ice cream cake for dessert. We won't sing Happy Birthday and we didn't buy any gifts. But that's only for *this* birthday," she admonished. "We're not going to watch you curl up and die. You can't expect us to put blinders on and let that happen."

"I'm not asking any of you to do that. Just don't push me. At this stage, all I want to do is think about her . . . reminisce about all the happy years." He lifted his gaze and looked at her, then changed the subject. "Where's Alex? Did he close yet on Ratherbee?" he asked, referring to the family estate Alex had inherited, albeit tragically.

"Almost. The lawyers scheduled it for Thursday. He'll be here later. I came with my own car because I brought some of the food for today. He's busy at the restaurant, in the office."

"And why aren't you with him? Don't you have plenty of work yourself at Amore Evenings?"

Glory eyed him sideways. "Are you trying to get rid of me?" She said it with a half smile and his face softened.

"No way," Dan said. He squeezed her hand, then sighed. "I'm sorry I haven't been easy to live with these last ten months, but that doesn't mean that I love my children any less than I did before. It's just so tough . . ."

Glory dragged her chair closer, wrapped her hands around his arm and leaned her head on his shoulder. "Dad, if we could share that pain with you, we would. But please, Dad . . . for Vanessa, Todd and Amy, please try to pull yourself out of this somehow. Louise was their mother and their grief is very painful, too. They try not to show it, but when they look at you and see that distant, unreachable look in your eyes, they feel like they lost two parents, not one. Help them, Dad. Help them help you."

Dan nodded silently because a million words were stuck in his throat, and as much as he loved his Glory, the person he wanted to say them to was gone. No matter how much he called out to her day or night, awake or asleep, he'd never again see her face or hear her voice.

Never. Never. Never.

Glory spotted the family behind the sliding door, raised a finger and shot them a *not-yet* glance. She allowed her smile to break through, then turned his face towards hers.

"Dad," she whispered, "everyone's here now. Vanessa and Wanda, Amy and Mitch are waiting in the kitchen with Todd."

Dan turned to call them out, but Glory touched his face once more. "No, Dad, they're waiting for me to give them the okay."

Dan gave her a quizzical look. "What's going on? Something good, I hope."

Glory relaxed with a laugh. "It certainly is good news, Dad. I'm hoping it'll let me see you smile again." She folded her arms and grinned while he studied her. "Well, did you figure it out yet?"

"Don't tell me you're pregnant!"

"Okay, I won't tell you," she said teasingly, then threw her shoulders back and her stomach forward. "Here. Meet your grandchild. It's either Daniel Steven Howard or Danielle Stephanie Howard."

Stunned, Dan hugged his daughter and his eyes welled with happy tears for the first time since Louise's death. He pulled away and gazed at her with the same surge of love he felt that summer day three years ago, when she—a total stranger then—announced she was his daughter. "I wouldn't have been offended, Glory, if you had chosen Steven or Stephanie for a first name. After all, he raised you from birth and loved you as much as I do, so if you want to—"

She put a finger on his lips, cutting him off. "I knew you'd say that, but you *are* my real father and that's what I wanted. And Alex totally agreed. He never knew my other father . . ." She paused, made a sour face. "I hate saying 'my other father'; it makes him sound so insignificant, and I loved him too—so much." Vivid images of her father's smiling face flashed in her mind, but she blinked them away. This was a special moment with Dan, her real father. Seeing how the news put the light in his eyes again, this was not the time to mourn again for Steven, the only father she had known for thirty-five years.

"Of course you loved him. He *was* your father all those years. And in a way I love him too for doing such a great job raising you." His emotions surfaced again, but he fought them off and smiled wide. "But let's not get teary-eyed again. This is such wonderful news, Glory. It'll be so great for me—for all of us—to have a baby to look forward to. And Glory, one more thing before the family comes out— don't postpone your wedding any longer. I know you cancelled all your plans after Louise died, but no matter how tragic life can be sometimes, we can't stop living. More than ever, we need to celebrate happy occasions. Whenever and wherever people can find happiness, they should seek it out and embrace it; the catch-all phrase being, life is too short."

Glory's arms were crossed while she listened. She grinned at him now, playfully. "I can't believe I'm hearing this, Dad. Do you hear yourself? You're preaching the exact sermon we've been trying on you all these months. And you let it all go in one ear and out the other."

Dan recognized the humor in her words and found himself laughing. It felt good to laugh. Damn good. But it didn't feel *right*.

He looked at his daughter and threw his hands up in defeat. "Okay, you got me there. But be patient with me. I'm trying." He lifted her hand and kissed her fingertips. "Not go get the gang out here and call Alex. Tell him to take a break and get his ass here ASAP. Today is definitely a day to celebrate. What better gift could I get than a grandchild?" The smile dropped from his face as he silently answered his own question, but he forced it back on.

When Glory signaled the others, they all came out beaming with arms opened wide to embrace Dan. It was a relief for everyone, particularly his four children, to smile and laugh again in his presence. And especially to see their dad smiling again, if only for the moment.

Amy, his youngest, got to him first. "Gee, Daddy, I almost forgot how handsome you are. Your face lights up when you smile. You look so much younger."

He gave her a forlorn look. "Yeah, well, grief can age a person something fierce, but at least for today, I'm going to fight it. Today is about life, not death. A baby in the family is just what we need, right?" He kissed her forehead and his smile came easier this time. Although he'd never share the thought with his children, he was glad it was Glory who would make him a grandpa first. Glory was not Louise's daughter. It would have been bittersweet if Vanessa, Todd or Amy had announced this happy news. Dan had no doubt that Louise would have been thrilled to take on the role of grandma to Glory's baby, but not to be compared to the joy she would have felt for the baby born to one of her own children.

Vanessa hugged him next, smiling wide, though her eyes were glazed with tears. "Congratulations, Grandpa!" she said.

Wanda took the bottle of champagne from Todd and poured the first glass. She lifted it and looked at Dan. "And I want to congratulate you too, Dan. You'll make the best grandpa any child could ask for," she said, then softened her voice and added, "And I'm sorry, but I have to say happy birthday too, because today it *is* a happy birthday, isn't it?"

"It sure is," Dan said and meant it, but silently he felt strangely grateful that his daughter Vanessa would never bear a child. He didn't have to think about Louise missing that joyous event. Plans to adopt a child were already in motion for Vanessa and Wanda.

Todd was next in line for a bear hug. Both father and son exchanged tight-lipped smiles. Since his mom died, Todd had spent more time with his dad than any of his sisters. Grieving for his mother himself and coming out of a relationship gone sour with a girl he had loved and still did, he knew well the pain of loss. But he had only loved Holly for two years. He couldn't imagine the intensity of his dad's heartaches after thirty-six years with his mom.

And the *way* she died. Although today, when he was stunned by the fire in his father's eyes, Todd resolved never to bring it up again.

With furrowed brows, he put his hand on Dan's shoulders and tried to see beyond his facial expression. "So is this an act for Glory's sake, Dad, or is that happy face genuine?"

Dan's hand went up. "No, it's genuine, all right! I can't wait to hold that baby in my arms. I'm going to spoil it like crazy if Glory and Alex let me."

"That's great, Dad. I hope—we all hope—that this puts you on the right track. So is it safe to say happy birthday now?"

Dan laughed and squeezed the back of his son's neck. "Sure, I can't promise it'll last forever, but today I *am* happy," he said, then whispered, "I would have been even happier if they were *married* and pregnant, but I know they would have been if . . ." He waved it off, determined now to allow grief to overshadow the joy he was feeling today.

Todd patted his back assuringly. "It'll happen, Dad. And I'll bet it'll be sometime soon, before the baby is born."

Dan's face brightened. "Oh? And did you get that information from a reliable source or are you making an assumption?"

Todd laughed. "Neither, actually. Knowing Glory and Alex, I'm guessing that's what they'd want, don't you?"

Dan considered it a moment. "I think so. I *hope* so," he answered, then took a moment to watch his family. A smile crossed his face again. Everyone was bubbling with energy, huddled around Glory, throwing questions about the baby. His heart swelled with pleasure seeing them all so animated and happy. He hadn't realized how selfish he had been all these months, shutting them out while he buried himself in grief.

*I have to try, Louise. For their sake . . . and yes, for mine, too. I'll never stop loving you, but mourning you every hour of every day is agonizing. I can't go on like this.*

Dan's ruminations were interrupted when he overheard part of Glory's telephone conversation. She was speaking to Alex, trying to convince him that joining the family here was more important than what he was doing at Amore Evenings.

*Why should she have to talk him into it?* Dan wondered. *It's his baby, too. Why weren't they together to share their good news?*

# Chapter Two

Glory drove back to Amore Evenings *seething*. At her father's house, she had been mortified trying to make excuses for Alex's absence. Since Louise died, this should have been the first happy day for the entire family— particularly for her dad. And it was, except for the fact that the baby's father chose not to attend the celebration.

Her finger tapped the steering wheel while she sucked in deep breaths. It couldn't be good for the baby to be this upset, but her mind couldn't shake away her anger-provoking thoughts.

Last summer, after she and Alex had talked out their problems and finally planned their wedding, she had put it all behind her. But his streak of jealousy refused to die. Every now and then it flared up again to flame another argument. Some scenes were worse than others, but even the milder ones left an icy wall between them. And every time they argued, Alex would vehemently deny that Dan was the crux of their problems. Then he'd soften and apologize. His anger would dissipate as quickly as it had escalated. In took only seconds of warm kisses and traveling hands to send sparks rippling through Glory's body, melting her resolve.

Down went the icy wall.

Flashing lights sobered her thoughts the moment Amore Evenings came into view. Glory's stomach flipped over and her body went numb at the sight. Police cars, an ambulance, EMS vehicles and a crowd of stunned onlookers surrounded the restaurant. She froze momentarily in her car, afraid to get out and face whatever tragic news awaited her.

She laced her fingers over her stomach, as though to protect her unborn child from impending shock.

*Take a deep breath and stay calm,* she told herself. *Maybe someone got deathly ill; maybe someone had a heart attack; maybe someone died. A total stranger you'll feel bad for tonight, but tomorrow life will go on as usual.*

"What happened?" she asked, scanning the crowd for answers.

Pete Fowler, an officer with the Ogunquit Police Department, was first to spot her and rushed to her side. "Glory, we called you at your dad's, but you had already left. We chose not to call you while you were driving."

"Why? What happened here? Who is it?" Panic gripped her, especially when she saw Frannie breaking through the crowd to reach her.

"Come inside, Glory," Frannie said, leading her by the arm. She threw a dismissive eye wink to Pete, indicating that she'd handle telling her friend.

"Don't ignore me, Frannie!" Glory shouted.

But Frannie did ignore her until they were in the vestibule of the restaurant with some degree of privacy. "It's Alex, Glory. There's been an accident."

Glory's heart thundered in her chest and her mouth went dry, but she couldn't cry; couldn't speak.

"We had a party of six we should never have seated. They were already drunk when they came in, but no one noticed. At least not until two of the men got into a heated argument. I was headed for their table to ask them to simmer down or leave when Alex stopped me. He insisted he'd handle the disturbance." Frannie paused, struggling to get the words out. "The guy went ballistic when Alex interfered. He pulled out a gun . . ." Her tears said it all.

Glory gripped her shoulders and screamed at Frannie, horrified. "What are you telling me? Where is he?" She didn't wait for an answer, just made a dash for the dining room, but one of the detectives blocked her. "I'm sorry, Miss English. We can't let you in there. It's a crime scene."

"But I have to see him! I know he's in there. The ambulance is still outside!"

The detective heaved a sigh. "Again, I'm sorry, Miss English, but they couldn't save Mr. Howard. They tried; they worked on him, but . . ." He shook his head.

Frannie steeled herself to be strong and pulled her back to the sofa in the vestibule. Numbed by the news, Glory gave no resistance. Frannie held her like a child in pain, rocking and rubbing her back while her friend sobbed through the shock and agony. Silent tears stained Frannie's cheeks as she thought of the baby—Alex's baby—who would never know the father who gave him life.

"I was so mad at him, Frannie . . . all steamed up for an argument because he never showed up at my father's house. It was supposed to be a happy day . . . telling my dad about the baby . . . Oh, Frannie, my poor baby, my poor baby!"

"I know, Glory, but your baby will never be wanting for love. You have family and you have me. We'll all be around for both of you."

"But it'll never have its father's love," she cried. "I loved him so much, Frannie. Maybe sometimes I didn't *like* him, but I always loved him."

Another detective leaned down and whispered in Glory's ear. The voice was familiar. It belonged to Detective Sergeant Tony Gerard, who had seen Frannie and Glory through tragedies before. "Glory, I'm so, so sorry. I got here as fast as I could."

"Oh, Tony, can you believe this? What else can possibly happen to us?" She couldn't go on; just buried her face in her hands.

"Hang in there, Glory," Tony said. "Your family will be here soon. They've been notified."

Glory nodded, as though it wouldn't make much difference. All the love and comfort she could get from family and friends would never bring Alex back.

Tony excused himself to attend to his unpleasant business in the dining room, leaving the two women alone. Frannie listened to Glory ramble on, crying out her grief; her guilt for feeling anger while Alex was probably struggling for his last breath on this insane planet; for postponing the wedding after Louise died.

With Frannie at her side, Glory waited in her apartment above Amore Evenings for her family to arrive. She sat there dry-eyed now, staring out the living room window. Tonight the foamy white waves crashing against the black rocks took on a different meaning. Endless life. Infinity, she thought. Nothing would ever stop the racing water from reaching its destination. It would remain forever in motion; forever alive. Although sometimes calm and serene, seemingly at peace with the world it invades but allows to exist, in one violent split-second, could swallow up our entire earth and all its inhabitants.

"I have such dark thoughts tonight," she told Frannie. "Not only because I lost Alex, but about life itself. How it can tease you with tastes of happiness and then snatch it away in the blink of an eye."

"No one is spared grief in this life, Glory. Some suffer more than others, but no one who lives long enough can escape it. Look at us—we're only in our thirties and tragedy is no stranger to us. You never forget or stop loving the person you lost, but somehow we get through it, one day at a time. Another cliché, yes, but there's some truth in all of them, although we hate listening to everyone repeating those same words we've heard over and over again. Especially when you're the one grieving and they're not."

*And sometimes your loss isn't caused by death,* Frannie wanted to say, but didn't. She and Glory had both suffered through loss by betrayal. A different kind of emotional pain, but a stinging, relentless pain, nevertheless.

Glory's thoughts mirrored Frannie's, but once she had begun a new life here in Ogunquit, Maine, she vowed never to waste another tear on Jason. She had wasted twelve years in a marriage that only she had honored.

The sound of soft footsteps behind her interrupted Glory's thoughts. She turned to see her father's outstretched arms and ran to them, prompting another rush of tears.

A breath caught in Dan's throat as he hugged his daughter, but he struggled to control himself for her sake. She would need his love and support more than ever now and he couldn't allow himself to fall apart.

"Tell me this is just a nightmare, Dad. Tell me I'll wake up to tell Alex how real it was. Tell me, Dad . . ."

Of course Dan could tell her none of those things, but reached for the tissue box on her end table and blotted her eyes. "I wish I could, sweetheart. I'd give anything to be able to say those words to you."

The rest of the family was behind him, waiting. Glory hugged Amy first. She had always had a special affection for Amy, the youngest of her siblings. She was the first to accept her as family and was instrumental in bringing them all together. "Isn't this unbelievable, Amy? Only an hour ago I was so happy to see Dad smiling again, and now look. And on his birthday, too. What a horrible memory it will always be for him—for all of us."

Frannie stepped aside, allowing Glory time alone with her family. It was bittersweet to watch the love that enveloped them; how tragedy once again unites a family and strengthens their bond.

Perhaps the one slice of light that could break through this darkness would be for Dan to find a reason to go on. Knowing Dan, he would put his daughter's grief before his own and do everything he possibly could to ease her burden. And once Glory's baby is born, he would step in as both father and grandfather. No doubt about that. There was some comfort knowing that, but Frannie silently threw a quick prayer up to God that Dan would live a long and healthy life. If Glory lost Dan, her grief would be far worse than what she was feeling now for Alex.

Yes, she believed Glory had loved Alex. But she also believed that Glory was so vulnerable at the time she met Alex that she might have been more in love with *being loved* than *loving.* Jason's betrayal had been a tremendous blow to her confidence as a woman. Her wounds were raw and Alex had patched that hole in her heart with little effort. No matter how much she wanted to resist, his debonair charm and knock 'em dead good looks melted her faster than ice cream under a blazing sun.

*Look who's talking about vulnerability!* In retrospect, Frannie had to admit that if someone had extended a hand to her after the shocking discovery of Wade's double life, she would have grabbed hold like a drowning person reaching for her rescuer's hand.

But somehow she had survived and grown stronger. She chose her friends more carefully now. It had taken awhile, but she learned to trust her own judgment again. It had been like pulling yourself out of quicksand. Once you're safe, you never, ever take that path again.

She intended to keep a close eye on her friend. There would be no quicksand traps for Glory, Frannie resolved. She had been through enough. They *both* had been through enough.

From now on, there was no place to go but up.

# Chapter Three

Their names were Oliver Linden and Austin Beckerle. Two human beings, one dead and buried; one dead and cremated. One by a police officer's bullet; one by a seizure while crying to his lawyer. Two men that neither Dan nor Glory had ever laid eyes on, but who had buried them in sorrow.

On this day in particular, Dan tried to push them out of his mind. Although he had only seen their photographed faces on TV screens and newspapers, he could never obliterate their ugly, evil images from his memory.

But today he would not dwell on hatred. Today his daughter was in labor with Frannie and Amy at her side; her friend and sister, when it should have been Alex who shared in the birth of his child. But life throws you wild pitches sometimes, Dan thought. There's isn't a damn thing you can do about them.

Glory had been in labor almost three hours when Amy emerged from the labor room. "It shouldn't be too long now, Dad. They just checked her again and she's fully dilated." She laced her fingers through her father's. "I'm glad Glory decided not to find out the sex of the baby while she was pregnant. It's so much more exciting this way. Do you want something from the machine—water? coffee?"

Dan frowned, then laughed. "No way. If I drink any more coffee, I'll float out of here."

Amy came back with a coffee for herself and two granola bars. Dan downed his in two bites. "Thanks. That'll hold me," he said while he munched away. "I didn't realize how hungry I was until—" He stopped short when a female doctor came out of Glory's room. She was dressed in scrubs and her face broke into a friendly smile when she extended a hand to Dan. "Hi, I'm Dr. Jessica Branson. I understand you're the baby's grandfather?"

"Yes," Dan answered, his eyes dancing with anticipation.

"Well, congratulations. You have a seven-pound grandson eager to meet you." Her smile faded. "And your daughter came through it pretty well, considering . . . you know, the tragic loss of her baby's father."

Dan's proud smile was tainted with sadness. "Yes, my Glory's a fighter. She was determined not to bring her child into this world under a 'cloak of darkness,' as she put it." No tears, she made him promise. Alex would have agreed, she'd said, that their baby's birth should not be shadowed by grief.

He beamed suddenly when the doctor's words sunk in. A grandson! His eyes welled with tears again—happy tears like the day Glory had brightened his saddest birthday when she surprised him with her pregnancy, and the day he first met her that memorable summer afternoon at Perkins Cove. He had shed buckets since Louise's senseless death, but now with these tears came a swelling in his heart rather than an ache, like sunshine peeking out from behind charcoal-colored clouds.

He licked his dry lips and felt a catch in his throat the moment he stepped inside her room. There she sat, his glorious Glory, looking worn and weary after her hours of labor. But despite her disheveled hair and perspired face, she looked radiant.

"Well, don't just stand there, Dad. Come in and take a look at your grandson. Did you ever see such a head of hair?"

Dan basked in the pleasure of seeing the joy on his daughter's face. Her pregnancy had been fraught with grief, but right now she seemed to lock it all out. He stood there, in a dream-like daze, staring at the baby cradled in his mother's arms. A reddened, wrinkled face crowned with a light blue cap on his tiny head. He licked his lips again, afraid to speak, knowing for sure any words would be flooded with emotion.

Glory laughed. "It's okay to cry, Dad. As long as they're happy tears." She gently lifted the baby. "Here, hold him."

Dan took the baby from his daughter's arms and kissed his forehead. A soaring feeling enveloped him; love like he'd never known before. Completely unlike what he felt when his children were born. No, this was entirely different. This little grandson of his had already captured his heart and would cling to it forever. He brushed a finger over his little hand. "Hey, little man, say hi to your grandpa. You and I are going to be great pals. You wait and see."

Glory's smile stretched across her face as she looked at the two most precious people in her life. But unexpectedly Alex's handsome face flashed before her eyes and she felt a stab in her heart, thinking of the joy he had been denied. She blinked away the images of him holding his son for the first time, but swallowed hard thinking instead of what her baby would be denied in his lifetime. No matter how much love and attention Dan would give him, he'd never know his father. Never feel his touch or hear his voice. She succumbed to a few escaping tears, then wiped them away at the sound of familiar voices outside her door.

Her wide smile returned. "Hey, Daniel, can you open your eyes again? It's time to meet your aunts and uncle." After kissing each of them, she looked towards the door. "Where's Frannie?" she asked, but everyone's attention was on the baby and no one answered. "Where's Frannie?" she repeated.

Amy laughed, apologetically. "Oh, sorry," she said. "We didn't mean to ignore you. We were all so anxious to hold our little nephew. Frannie's out in the lounge. She'll come in later, she said. She wanted to give us some family time."

"Family time? Is she crazy?" Glory turned to Dan. "Dad, would you go out there and drag her in, please?"

Dan acquiesced gladly and returned with Frannie. "I was coming in a few minutes," she started to explain. "I just—"

Glory cut her off. "You just nothing. Get over here and say hello to your godson."

Frannie arched her brows in surprise. "Godson? You want me to be godmother?"

"Of course. Why should you be surprised?"

"I don't know. I had no idea. You never said a word while you were pregnant, but, hey, I'm thrilled!" She didn't mention, of course, that she had assumed Glory planned to ask Vanessa or Amy.

"Frannie, after I watched you take care of Heather during that crisis," she said, referring to Frannie's cousin Suzanne's baby, "I couldn't think of a better candidate." She glanced over at her sisters. "I already discussed it with Vanessa and Amy and they absolutely agreed that you'd be the perfect godmother. Right, guys?"

Frannie gave their faces a quick study and recognized that the two sisters were truly pleased that Glory had chosen her. "Well, since there are no objections," she said, "all I can say is I'm thrilled and honored to be Daniel's godmother." She lowered her head and kissed Glory on the forehead. "Thanks for asking. I'll try to do a good job." She gave a slight laugh and shook her head. "I guess I'd better stop saying 'I don't do babies.' Now, with Heather and Daniel in my life, I can enjoy feeling like a grandmother—give them lots of love and kisses, then give them back when they wear me out."

"And with no labor pains and no sleepless nights," Glory quickly added. She winced at the memory. Getting through labor had been worse than she imagined. She laughed then and waved her hand in a *never again* gesture, before turning her gaze to Todd. "And if it's okay with you, Todd, I'd like you to be godfather." A mix of sentiment and guilt watered Todd's eyes. He had given her such a hard time, unwilling to accept her into their family. Glory read his thoughts. "It's okay," Todd, she said. "Wipe the guilt off your face. I know you used to hate me, but you love me now, and that's all that matters."

Todd squeezed his sister's hand. "You're easy to love, Glory. I was being a stupid jackass at the time. Only someone with your big heart could forgive a jerk like me."

Glory yanked at his shirt to pull him closer, then kissed him on the cheek and smiled wide. "Yes, you were a stupid jackass—and a jerk too—but that's all past tense, so let's forget it."

*Good advice,* Frannie thought, but could Glory apply it to herself as well? Every time she glanced down at the baby's face, she could already see traces of Alex. On a daily basis, Glory would see in her son a haunting resemblance to the love she lost. Right now she was doing a fine job of masking her grief, but Frannie couldn't help but wonder if she'd crack when she and little Daniel were alone together.

# Chapter Four

So far the month of May had been good to New Englanders. It brought warmth and sunshine, a welcome relief after a wintry March and rainy April. Nothing like waking up to sounds of birds singing in the trees, Frannie thought.

She heard the crunching sound of tires on her graveled driveway and went to greet her company. All smiles, she reached for Heather as soon as Suzanne took her from the car seat, but Heather wiggled herself free and ran for the backyard swing set.

"We're never going to get her inside without a fight anymore," Suzanne told her cousin. "Ever since you put up that set for her, I can't drive past your house. She cries, 'F'annie, seesaw, F'annie, seesaw!'"

Frannie laughed. "Well, that makes the money well spent. Anything that makes our little darling happy is okay by me." She dragged two cushioned chairs off her patio. "Let her enjoy the swing for a while. We can always bribe her inside with cookies and milk."

After they secured Heather in the swing, they sat in the chairs and took turns pushing her. "So what's new since I last saw you? How's Rob doing?"

Suzanne wrinkled her nose. "Good, I guess, but his life is so busy, we don't get to spend much time together. With both of us busy taking classes and working different hours, it's rough. Then, of course, Heather is going through this 'terrible two' stage." She gave a rueful laugh. "He also got into volunteer counseling, visiting and talking with other amputees. He feels good about that and so do I, but it takes another bite of time away from us."

Frannie merely nodded in response, as though acknowledging Suzanne and Rob's problem. *A dangerous sign,* she mused. *Love has to be nurtured or it dies.* The couple's friendship had developed when they were both hospitalized with injuries resulting from near-fatal accidents. Although Suzanne's injuries were extensive, she had recovered fully. Rob, conversely, was left without his right foot. He seemed to have adjusted to his prosthesis well, though, physically and emotionally. That didn't necessarily mean that he didn't struggle with bouts of depression once in a while. But if that were the case, no one would ever know. Rob would never reveal that side of himself.

After a brief pause while Frannie exchanged baby talk with Heather, she turned her attention back to her cousin. "As I've told you before, I'd be happy to babysit Heather occasionally in the afternoon so you two can enjoy some time alone. As long as you don't ask at the last minute. I have a busy life too—always running somewhere."

"Oh, I know that, Frannie. I'd never impose on you like that, except for an emergency." Their eyes locked at the word *emergency,* both recalling the horrific night when Suzanne had left Heather alone in Frannie's house, with a one-line note about an "emergency."

While Frannie entertained Heather, tickling her belly with every forward swing, Suzanne was exceptionally quiet. She seemed lost in her thoughts and apparently oblivious to her daughter's attempts to get her attention. "Your turn, Mommy, your turn!" she yelled.

Frannie stepped aside. "Guess your little break is over. Your turn to push, the princess says." She laughed when she said it, but Suzanne remained distant. Frannie curled her brows and stooped down for a closer look. "Are you all right?"

Suzanne avoided her gaze. She wasn't sure herself if she was or not, but her cousin's concern brought her emotions to the surface. She tightened her lips and drew a breath before she spoke. "I'm fine. Just didn't sleep much last night."

"That alone makes me suspicious," Frannie said. "I know what a deep sleeper you are. You always say a bomb couldn't wake you. When Heather was born, you were afraid you wouldn't hear her during the night." She folded her arms. "So what's wrong? Talk to me. I can see you need to. Your face looks like it's about to explode."

As though Frannie's words had burst a dam, Suzanne sobbed into her hands.

"Oh, Suzanne, something *is* wrong! What is it?" Frannie leaned over her and tried to lift her face to meet her gaze while Heather grew restless in her swing. "Out, out, Mommy," she cried.

Suzanne stood up, stopped the swing and unbuckled her daughter. She wiped her tears with a baby wipe and put an instant lock on her emotions. "Forget it, Frannie. This isn't a good time. Heather won't let us get through an uninterrupted conversation."

Frannie conceded with a nod, then asked, "So how about tonight? It's Glory's turn to stay late and close Amore Evenings. I'll be out of there by eight."

Suzanne had every intention of refusing the offer, but different words spilled from her lips. "I'm not sure, Frannie."

"You're not sure of what?" Frannie prodded.

Suzanne avoided Frannie's gaze, focusing instead on freeing Heather's grip from the gold locket Rob had given her last Christmas.

Observing her cousin's troubled face, Frannie refused to give up. "You're not sure of what, Suzanne?" she repeated.

"I'm not sure it's something I can discuss with anyone," she answered, still carefully avoiding eye contact.

Frannie arched a brow and lowered her voice. "After what we've been through together since the night of your accident, I'd like to think you'd consider me more than just 'anyone.'"

Suzanne squeezed her eyes shut and erased her words with a sweep of her hand. "Sorry. That didn't come out right. I meant I'm not sure I should discuss this particular problem at all—with you or anyone."

"But maybe I can help," Frannie persisted.

Suzanne laughed, but her tone was laced with bitterness. "Oh, I would definitely say it's too late for that!"

Heather interrupted again, whimpering for a drink. Suzanne picked up the baby's empty sippy cup. "I'd better go, Frannie. She's thirsty and tired."

Frannie took the empty cup from her hand. "Well, come inside first. No sense letting her cry all the way home. I have orange juice and milk, so take your pick."

Heather drank the milk with her eyes half-closed. Frannie put her on the loveseat in her living room and she was asleep in seconds. "Oh, damn," Suzanne mumbled. "I guess you're stuck with us for a while. If I wake her up now, she'll be a nightmare. You know how cranky she gets when she's tired."

"I guess I am. And you can't use Heather as an excuse to avoid talking to me." She folded her arms and grinned.

Suzanne responded with only a defeated smile.

Frannie's grin faded. "I don't mean to squeeze anything too personal out of you. Only you can decide what to say or not say. But sometimes when we bottle things up inside us too long, the problems reach explosive proportions. Talking doesn't necessarily solve them, but it helps to pour out the emotions. Believe me, I speak from experience. My sonofabitch bigamist husband sent me to hell and back. So if

29

you need to talk, I'm here. And I promise you," she said, raising her hand, "it'll never reach anyone else's ears."

With her fingers steepled over her mouth, Suzanne blew a breath. Her eyes were glazed with tears. "You're going to hate me!" she cried.

Frannie wanted to hug her cousin and comfort her, but the loveseat was too small to accommodate all three of them. She rolled the ottoman over, sat on it and held Suzanne's hand. "Talk to me, Suzanne. There's no way I can hate you. My love for you and Heather is *stuck* there," she said, patting her heart. "I could never get it out."

"But I don't deserve your love, Frannie." She put a hand up as Frannie was about to protest. "No, don't stop me. I might lose courage to go on." She inhaled deeply and fixed her gaze on her sleeping daughter. "I'll start with the good news: Rob asked me to marry him."

Frannie let out a yell and her face lit up like a Christmas tree, but Suzanne cut her off. "No, don't get excited. I said that's the good part. The bad part is he wants to adopt Heather if that's possible."

"And is it?" Frannie asked, a sense of foreboding filling her. Everyone, including Suzanne, had assumed Tyler Keaton was Heather's father, but DNA tests performed after his murder at The Admiral's Inn revealed otherwise. Suzanne had given Detective Sergeant Tony Gerard a made up story about a one night stand with someone she met in a bar. They had been drinking heavily and she had no memory of anything about him; not even his name. It was strictly a hit and run night of sex fueled by too much alcohol, she'd said. She suspected that Tony Gerard never believed a word, but she held to that story and refused to discuss the subject again with him or anyone else.

"Sure, it would be possible and no problem at all if her father was dead or had signed off that he wanted no part of her."

"Or if you had no name or any recollection of him from the night Heather was conceived, I would assume." Frannie darted her cousin a slanted look. Her eyes and twisted mouth revealed that she too never swallowed that story.

"But I *do* know his name, and I *do* have recollection. I wish I *could* forget that night; it's been tormenting me since it happened." She winced as the images flashed in her mind, choosing not to include the scene in the car when Greg impulsively pulled over and tried to kiss her. In her heart she knew that should have been forewarning, but when he called her that night in New York, she had allowed herself to wave it off like one crazy, isolated incident that would never be repeated. "It's funny, but I was able to handle it much better before Rob and I got serious. Once we did, I knew it would come to this. I always feared it would blow up in my face someday."

Suzanne choked and paused to wipe her tears, but Frannie didn't prompt her to continue. She suddenly had a sickening feeling she was about to learn something she'd be better off not knowing. But Suzanne had already unlocked the door to her secret and there was no stopping her now.

"The baby's father is married, Frannie. Happily married."

Frannie stood up and peered down at her. "*Happily* married? How can he be happily married and make another woman pregnant? And how and why did you get involved with him in the first place? Did you know from day one that he was married?"

A mournful cry escaped Suzanne's lips. Frannie already had fire in her eyes asking the *how* and *why.* She cringed anticipating her reaction to the *who.* Her body chilled and she shivered. She kept her gaze cast downward and rubbed her arms. "Yes, I knew," she admitted, "but we were just supposed to have an innocent dinner, like two old friends. It was never supposed to end like this! Don't you think at least one of us would have come equipped with something to prevent pregnancy if we had known?"

31

Frannie was stunned and angered by Suzanne's confession, but since she had encouraged her to open up, she had no choice but to mask her reaction and let her cousin spill out her story. "Was he an old friend? Where was Tyler at the time? You were still living with him, weren't you?"

"He was away, supposedly on business," she said with a smirk, then rubbed her hands that had begun to shake. "I was in bad shape emotionally those days, Frannie. Tyler was so cruel and abusive. Only when we were among his customers or friends did he treat me halfway decently. He had me trapped like a caged animal most of the time. I lived in constant fear of not knowing what would set him off. It didn't take much. And the more depressed I became, the more homesick I was. I wanted so much to just leave him and come home, but if you knew Tyler, you'd know that was not an option. Only when he was ready to dump me did I jump at that chance."

Frannie was truly sorry she had provoked this conversation, but she pressed on. "Tell me about this 'friend,' Suzanne. Was he Tyler's friend?"

"No, he was my friend." She sneaked an upward glance to catch Frannie's reaction, then continued. "As I said, I was so homesick and aching for someone to talk to; someone who truly cared about me." She paused to frown and shake her head, as though still in disbelief that it had all actually happened. But her beautiful daughter was right beside her. So much of her father was reflected in Heather's features and facial expressions, but fortunately, unless people knew, they'd never look for the similarities.

"How did you two manage to become friends? Was he a regular customer or employee at the lounge?"

She shook her head. "No, neither. He was a friend from home who happened to be in New York on business. When he called me, I was so happy to hear his voice—any voice from Ogunquit—that with Tyler away, I couldn't resist the opportunity." She paused again, reflecting on the memory. "It seemed so innocent, but I guess I was so vulnerable . . ."

Her voice cracked and this time she didn't try to hold back her tears.

Frannie, still sitting on the ottoman, rubbed her cousin's back, her gaze a blank stare. There was no turning back; they had come this far, so in a barely audible voice, she asked, "Who is he, Suzanne? Who's Heather's father?"

"Greg Haggarty!" she blurted out while her whole body rocked with sobs.

The words shocked Frannie so profoundly that she felt as if the floor beneath her had collapsed. "Oh, my God!" She put a hand to her temple and stared with disbelief. "Hold on a minute . . . I can't think straight. I'm so stunned I'm shaking." After a frozen moment and with a surge of self-control, she gripped Suzanne's hands and pulled them away from her face. "Look at me, Suzanne, and answer me: Does he know? Does Kim know?"

Unable to control her flood of tears, Suzanne could only shake her head.

Frannie sat there, frozen in silence, not knowing what to say, what to do. Yes, as Glory had said, she was Ogunquit's Oprah. Everyone confided in her. But today she could offer no solution; could find no comforting words.

# Chapter Five

Although she had tried not to crack when her cousin shocked her with the identity of the baby's father, Frannie remained stunned after Suzanne left. Still in tears, she had picked up her sleeping daughter and taken off as fast as she could. Maybe if Frannie hadn't reacted as she did when Suzanne blurted out the name, she might have stayed and told the whole story. But when she heard *Greg Haggarty*, the name had exploded in her mind. The nausea in her stomach was probably smeared across her face.

Frannie's first thought was to call Glory. This was one problem she couldn't handle alone. Not that it was her problem—and not that it was a reversible problem, but since the accident she had unleashed all these inexplicable maternal feelings. Well, maybe not inexplicable, she mused. It's probably some deep-seated emotion inside all women that sprouts to the surface when the need arises.

And the need had arisen the night of Suzanne's horrific accident, from which she miraculously survived. With Suzanne's daughter to care for, Frannie had been thrust into the semblance of motherhood, along with the responsibility of making all medical decisions while she was incapacitated.

The months flew by like pages in a book and after a somber holiday season, little Daniel Steven Howard was born to Glory seven months after his father's death. Another life lost at the hands of a hot-tempered businessman with too much alcohol in his blood.

Yes, with two babies in her life, Frannie had completed her crash course in motherhood, although unsolicited.

She picked up the phone to cancel her golf plans. Her friends would be disappointed, but she was too upset to be energetic and sociable. After making her lame excuses, she grabbed her car keys and took off.

* * *

When Frannie rang her bell, Suzanne was reluctant to let her in. She opened the door only as much as the chain allowed. "You shouldn't have come, Frannie. I made a big mistake telling you—maybe the biggest mistake of my life, so I don't—"

"No, Suzanne. The biggest mistake of your life happened when—" She stopped short realizing this was not a private dwelling; other tenants might overhear. "Open the door, Suzanne," she demanded through clenched teeth.

Suzanne rolled back her eyes, then blew a defeated sigh. She felt like a condemned person surrendering to the hands of her executioner. "I just got Heather back to sleep, so let's try to get through this conversation as calmly as possible, okay?"

"Suzanne, believe me, I *am* trying. I may be a generation older, but don't think for one minute that I'm trying to pull rank on you. I'm not your mother and I'm not your judge or jury. But how the hell did you expect me to react when you dropped a bomb like that?"

Suzanne walked towards her kitchen with Frannie shadowing behind. She responded with a quick head turn over her shoulder. "Well, you asked and I answered. Simple as that. There was no way I could sugarcoat that answer." Dry-eyed now, she shrugged, as if she had hardened her heart to the irreversible fact that Greg Haggarty, her babysitter's husband, had fathered her daughter.

Frannie calmed herself, pulled out a chair, and sat at the kitchen table while her cousin avoided her gaze by folding a load of laundry. She lowered her voice to a whisper—like a priest relaxing a penitent sinner into making a good confession. "I know the *how* doesn't much matter, Suzanne; the end result will always be the same. But this is so unbelievable that I have to admit I'm just plain curious as to how this relationship ever got started." She had chosen her words carefully, but what she really wanted to know was who had initiated their forbidden intimacy. Taunted by memories of her cousin's promiscuity, she had a sneaking suspicion she knew the answer.

"It wasn't a relationship," Suzanne snapped back. "It was one insane night that I wish I could undo for their sake—the Haggartys—but then again, I wouldn't have Heather, so for my sake . . ." She let the rest hang suspended, knowing it needed no further explanation.

Frannie grabbed a handful of clean baby clothes from the laundry basket, smoothed them out to fold. "Tell me, why did you choose not to tell Greg? I can see why you wouldn't want Kim to know, but if he's the father—"

"There's no *if.* Greg is the father. Don't forget, Frannie, until that DNA test was done, I thought Tyler was Heather's father."

"You're absolutely sure it was Greg?" Frannie asked cautiously. "There was no one else that month?"

"Of course I'm sure. Believe me, even if I had wanted someone else, I never had the freedom. I took a huge chance that night, and when I did, it was supposed to be just dinner and conversation. I couldn't resist the temptation of an evening of pleasant conversation with someone who'd treat me like a human being instead of a punching bag."

Frannie took her time with the baby clothes; folding them meticulously so she could avoid looking her cousin in the eye. "I guess I can understand that. But back up a minute. Can you please tell me how you and Greg got together in the first place? During all the time you knew him—from when you babysat for their kids to when that reversed and Kim babysat for Heather—did Greg ever try to hit on you?"

"Never," Suzanne answered without hesitation. "Except one time," she added reluctantly. "An isolated incident when he was driving me home. He tried to kiss me, but when I pushed him away, he apologized over and over again. We agreed to let it die right there. We had no choice. What could I do? I didn't want to lose Kim as my babysitter. She's so good with Heather and Heather loves her."

"Why were you so sure during your pregnancy that Tyler was the father? Why didn't you consider the possibility that it could have been Greg's?"

Suzanne blew a breath and crossed her arms. "Because Greg mentioned that night that they wanted one or two more, but he had the mumps as an adult and that left him sterile— or so he thought."

"And after that one night you never saw him again?"

"Never. Not until I moved back to Ogunquit, and after Heather was born when I went back to work. Thank God for Kim," she said reflecting back, "If she hadn't offered to babysit for practically peanuts, I would have been up the creek!"

*How she had the guts to take advantage of Kim's kindness beats me,* Frannie thought. *How do you accept your lover's wife as the babysitter for her husband's love child? How do you face her every day?*

While Frannie ruminated, Suzanne kept a keen eye on her. "I know exactly what you're thinking, dear cousin," she said with a slight sneer. "I lost plenty of sleep asking myself the same questions that are spinning in your head. I didn't approach Kim, but when she heard I needed a sitter, she offered, and I was pretty desperate for money. What was I supposed to say—'Sorry, not a good idea since your husband is my baby's father?'"

"What about after the DNA results? Don't you think Greg would have been worried sick, knowing he slept with you?"

"Not really. Since he considered himself sterile, he probably assumed I had another lover that month." She shrugged it off as though what he thought didn't matter, but Frannie wasn't fooled by the gesture. "I can just imagine what he's been thinking of me," Suzanne continued. "Like I'm the queen of all pigs. Not that I was a candidate for sainthood before that."

Frannie hoped her thoughts were not transparent since they were almost identical to Suzanne's words. "I'm not so sure of that. He might think that because he wants to, but I can't believe the truth never occurred to him. Let's face it, Suzanne, Heather has a strong resemblance to Greg. Once you know, it stares you in the face. And Kim sees her five days a week."

Suzanne couldn't maintain the pretense of confidence. She broke down again and sobbed into her hands. "I know. It scares me too, I admit. But if you don't look for it, you don't notice." She pointed a finger at Frannie. "You never noticed, right?"

"No, that's true, but it's not me you should worry about—it's Kim."

The short silence that followed was almost palpable as both women battled with their thoughts. Then Frannie pushed aside the little piles of folded baby clothes and looked Suzanne in the eye. "Look, I'm not going to give you any sermons about what you should or shouldn't have done. Everyone has a skeleton in their closet. All you can do is take a look at what *is,* and deal with it. But before you make any decisions, you'd better think long and hard about their long-term effects—not only on yourself, but on all the people affected by your decisions."

Suzanne merely nodded while deep in her own thoughts, then a sad smile touched the corners of her mouth. "Actually, Frannie, that *is* a sermon. It's pretty much what I've been preaching to myself." She turned now to meet Frannie's gaze. "I'm sorry I dumped this on you. I know there's nothing you, my father or anyone else can do for me.

I just couldn't hold it inside any longer. I had to talk to someone or burst."

Frannie brushed away the strands of hair from Suzanne's cheek and tucked them behind her ear. "It's okay. I'm glad you chose me as your confidant. I only wish you had come to me sooner so you wouldn't have suffered alone." She paused, then said, "I think I have to agree that you should never tell Greg. But have you decided what to tell Rob?"

"That I can't marry him. What else can I tell him? As long as he hangs that stipulation on his proposal, our situation is hopeless. Never, ever will I tell him or anyone else that Greg is Heather's father. *No way.*"

# Chapter Six

Sara Baisley arrived for work at Amore Evenings and looked for her boss. "Where's Glory?" she asked Tim Waite, the guy she adored and planned to marry immediately after their college graduation—two years away.

"I haven't seen her since I got here an hour ago. Why?"

"No emergency. I just want to tell her something."

"Tell me what?" came a voice from behind them. "I've been in the office on the phone."

Sara smiled pleasantly, but she wasn't sure how Glory would react to the news. "I met Corrine this afternoon—Tony Gerard's wife. She's pregnant. Isn't that great? So see, Glory, there's another woman who's having her first baby in her late thirties."

Glory waved it off. "Oh, I'm long past that hang-up, Sara, . . . considering."

Sara's smile faded. "I'm sorry," she said, aware that losing the man you love before his child is born can cancel out all other minor problems that seemed monumental at the time.

Glory forced a wide smile, flashing her perfect teeth. "I'm sorry too. I have to get out of the habit of putting Alex into every conversation or situation, silently or otherwise. It makes people uncomfortable, and that's the last thing I want to do. Actually, I'm thrilled for Tony and Corrine. I'll call later and congratulate them."

Sara winced after Glory left them. "She's right about that, Tim. She does sort of put Alex's ghost in the middle of everything, and it does make people uncomfortable."

"Well, at least she's aware of it. Maybe she'll make a real effort to break the habit." He opened his mouth to say something more, but stopped himself. "I'd better get back in the kitchen."

Sara touched his arm. "No, wait. What were you going to say about Glory?"

Tim looked away. "Nothing. Forget it."

"No," Sara persisted. "Don't say nothing. I saw that face. You know I can read right through your expressions, Mr. Timothy Waite." She gave him a devilish smile. "So tell me."

"If you can read through me, Miss Smartypants, you tell me." Tim's smile belied his sarcastic tone.

"C'mon, Tim," she prompted. "We can't stand here all day."

Tim sighed. He knew once his Sara started working on him, it was only a matter of time. She always won. And he loved letting her win. "Okay. I was going to say sometimes I think she's more in love with his memory than she was with *him* when he was alive."

Sara looked shocked. "Really? How can you say that? She was *crazy* about him."

"Yeah, maybe, but not like now." His eyes narrowed. "Pay attention. You'll see what I mean. Now that he's dead she puts him on a pedestal, but when he was alive, he was just . . . I don't know . . . just Alex, I guess."

Sara wrinkled her nose dismissively. "That doesn't mean she didn't love him enough. I think everyone does that when they lose their mate. Even the ones who never got along. Apart they can't fuel new arguments, so the surviving spouse focuses only on the good memories and suddenly all the bad ones are forgotten. They magnify the good and suppress the bad."

Tim pursed his lips and nodded, pretending to give her analysis serious consideration. "That makes sense, I guess." He gave her a mock salute and walked off.

Sara's scowl curled her brows but her annoyance melted into laughter. *I should know better than to get into analytical discussions with Tim,* she thought. *He manages to worm his way out of them every time!*

She put on her uniform and headed for the kitchen, ready for another night of nonstop serving at Glory and Frannie's successful waterfront restaurant. Not that she dared complain. The summer jobs had been a godsend to her and Tim during these college years.

Glory was on her way out just as Sara entered the kitchen. "Hey, Glory, are you okay?" she whispered.

"I'm fine. Why shouldn't I be?"

"I don't know. I'm just asking. You seemed a little distant before. Like you had something on your mind; you know . . . preoccupied. Is little Danny okay? Is he with his grandpa Dan again?"

Glory lifted her brows. "No, actually, he's not. Vanessa and Wanda are sitting tonight. Grandpa Dan has a date. Can you believe it?"

Sara opened her mouth to express her joy for Dan, but closed it faster than a cat catching a fly. "Of course I believe it. And I think it's great. Why? Is that a problem for you?" Sara asked, but felt as if she were walking on raw eggs. "He's been suffering with grief something awful since Louise died."

Glory gave her a reluctant nod. "I know, but he's been much better since Danny was born. Haven't you noticed the difference?"

"Oh, sure. Anyone can see how much he loves his grandson, but it's not as if he can take him to dinner or a movie. Everyone needs adult companionship," she said with emphasis on *companionship* and all it implied.

Glory shot her a sidelong glance. "Not necessarily. You just have to stay busy. Look at me. I lost my 'companion' too, and I'm doing fine, aren't I?"

Sara's silence was the most honest answer she could offer.

# Chapter Seven

Dan had butterflies in his stomach exactly like the night he took Susan Bentley to the junior prom. He remembered vividly the queasy feeling he battled walking up the flagstone path to her front door, corsage in hand. He could still see them—white carnations edged with blue tint and trimmed with blue ribbons. He laughed to himself thinking back to that night; how his fingers fumbled trying to pin the corsage onto her dress. Finally, her mom had come to his rescue, probably fearing his hand would slip onto forbidden territory.

Like most teenagers, he wasn't too crazy about his tuxedo either; especially the baby blue cummerbund which was a *must* to match Susan's dress.

Dan looked himself over in the mirror and grinned at the memory. That junior prom was forty-something years ago and in a way he decided he looked better today than he did then. He wasn't that skinny, scrawny kid anymore. He'd put on a lot of weight over the years, but he had needed it, he mused. His stomach protruded only slightly now and he slapped it with dubious pride. Thanks to all his years working the boats, the rest of his body was still tight and muscular. He gave his image in the mirror a complacent nod. At 62, he felt pretty darn healthy, thanks to daily exercise and a low-fat diet. Although his heart attack three years ago had alerted him to the necessity of maintaining a proper diet, he cheated every now and then and only on special occasions.

Tonight, his dinner date with Dr. Jessica Branson, his daughter's obstetrician, was without a doubt a special occasion. He hadn't been alone in the company of a woman since before he met Louise.

He shook his head and grinned thinking how strangely things take shape sometimes. They had met in the produce aisle of the supermarket in Wells, fingering through the fruit and vegetables. Both were sneaking hooded glances trying to place where they had seen the other's face before. They practically bumped into each other when they reached the peaches.

Jessica was first to laugh. "Okay. I give up. Where have we met before?"

Her warm smile and informal approach put Dan instantly at ease. He returned a friendly smile of his own, then laughed, too. "You caught me staring, didn't you?"

She giggled. "I did. But only because *I* was staring at *you.*"

"Your face is so familiar, it'll drive me crazy until I remember where I saw it before." Dan fingered his chin, then widened his eyes. "Oh, wait a minute! Do you ever dine at Amore Evenings? That's a possibility."

She shook her head. "No, I don't think it was there, although I have eaten there several times." She smiled almost shyly. "I know one of the owners fairly well. I delivered her baby."

Dan punched the air and laughed. "That's it—the hospital! I'm Glory English's father." He slapped his forehead. "And yes, you delivered my grandson!"

Jessica enjoyed his elation. "Yes, I did. And how is the little guy these days?" she asked, without the foggiest recollection of how long ago she delivered Glory's baby. She had brought so many into the world, before and after Glory's, that after awhile you stop counting.

"He's absolutely great. Five months old already and a lot of fun—a good baby, too." His face grew suddenly serious. "Thank God she has him. Little Danny's filled a big hole in my daughter's heart." *And mine,* he thought.

For one fleeting second, their gazes locked. It was common knowledge in and around Ogunquit that both father and daughter had lost their mates by heinous acts of violence.

Dan answered her silent question. "He's done a lot for me, too. For a long time I thought I'd never smile or laugh again, but he's changed all that."

"Yes, I can see you're one proud grandpa," Jessica said with a bright smile, hoping to steer him away from the bad memories at least for the moment.

Dan nodded and an awkward silence fell. He could see she was about to excuse herself and he acted on impulse. He eyed the coffee shop in the rear of the supermarket. "I know this isn't The Ritz, but can I interest you in a cup of coffee?"

Jessica hesitated and Dan was instantly embarrassed. "I'm sorry. I can imagine what a busy schedule you have as an obstetrician."

"No, excuse my 'pregnant pause'; no pun intended. That's true; most of the time there aren't enough hours in the day, but not always. We make a concerted effort to arrange our private lives too. And it happens that I'm not on call today. I had two deliveries this morning and I'm free until tomorrow." She glanced down in her shopping cart. "If I can drop off my perishables, I'd be glad to join you for coffee."

"Wonderful!" Dan said. "In that case, I'll do the same and we can make it a nice, sit-down lunch. Is that okay with you? Wherever you'd like is fine with me."

She thought about it a second, then said, "I haven't been to The Grey Gull Inn in a long time. The food and view are fabulous!"

"Perfect," he answered. "And later we can walk along the ocean path if you'd like."

"Sounds great. How's one o'clock?"

"One o'clock's fine. Where shall I pick you up?"

She gave him her address and Dan walked off beaming.

# Chapter Eight

Frannie pulled into her pebbled driveway and did a double take.

A Land Rover was parked on the shoulder of the road, maybe one hundred feet from her house. Since a thousand feet separated her property from her neighbor's, her curiosity piqued.

If she hadn't gripped the door when she emerged from the car, she would have collapsed. A familiar face and body—with a little less hair and twenty or thirty added pounds—was seated in her Adirondack chair, fingers laced together.

He grinned at her without a trace of discomfort. His mannerisms exuded confidence. "Surprise, surprise!" he said, wiggling all his fingers.

It took a long moment for Frannie to find her voice. Her mouth felt as dry as sun-baked sand. "What the hell sewer did you crawl out of?" The sight of Wade, her bigamist husband, made her feel as if her blood had drained. Now it felt explosively red.

Still seated, he gave her a condescending look. "C'mon, Frannie, get over it," he said with a hand wave. "I could have done worse things than being a loving husband to two women."

"And two children!"

"My sons have nothing to do with you."

"The hell they don't! Not when they were two and four years old when you married me."

Wade held his complacent grin. "But I married Barbara first. We can't forget that."

Still stunned by his presence, Frannie struggled for words. "Don't worry," she sneered. "That's something I will *never* forget. And I still want to know what the hell you're doing in *my* town, on *my* property!"

He lifted a hand. "Now calm down, babe. The town is not exclusively yours, but the property . . ." He wiggled his eyebrows and made a sweeping motion towards the ocean. "I'm very impressed with the property. Amore Breakfast must have been doing quite well for you to buy oceanfront property in Ogunquit. You must be raking it in. And now you have *two* restaurants." He put a hand over his heart. "Well, may I humbly say, I'm damn proud of you, babe."

"I'm not your babe, and I want you off my property and out of my sight. Now!" She pulled out her cell phone. "Don't force me to call the police, Wade. You won't like the repercussions. You don't have many—no, make that *any*—friends in this town."

He furrowed his brows, but held his smile. "That sounds like a threat to me. I hope you're not implying that you'd use your political influence to run me out of town?" He tsked-tsked and shook his head. "Not Miss Holier Than Thou, friend of the people, epitome of integrity."

Frannie didn't have to say a word; her face said it all, but she had to spit out her disdain. "No matter what mistakes I make in my life, nothing will compare to marrying you. My skin crawls every time I think of those years."

He pointed a finger. "Ah, hah! So you *do* still think about me. Good!"

Her eyes fired up. "I think of you with revulsion and nothing else. How dare you even insinuate anything more, you sick bastard!"

The angrier she became, the wider he smiled. "Go ahead, babe—oh, excuse me, *Frannie*—or would you prefer

*Ms. Oliveri* now—well, call me whatever the hell you want. If it makes you feel better, fine. Get it out. Get it all out."

"If I lived two lifetimes, I still couldn't rid myself of the poison you left inside me." She made a fist and punched herself under her breasts. "It's like a ball of rot stuck there."

"Hold it, Frannie, time out," Wade said, making the hand gesture. He dropped the false smile and blew a breath. "Let's declare a truce for a minute. Tell me, can you honestly say that after all the good years we had together, that's all you feel for me now—an ulcer?"

"No, not an ulcer," she countered, "more like a *cancer!* I can't believe you had the audacity to show up here. What the hell do you want?"

He paused just long enough to let her steam settle. She stood there with her arms folded, waiting for an answer. "What I want is you, Frannie." His face went instantly contrite. "I'm sorry I egged you on, but I knew you'd need to release a lot of anger before I confessed why I'm here. But that's the absolute truth. I want back the life we had. We were fine until everything hit the fan, weren't we?" His hand went up before she could blast him again. "No, you don't need to remind me that I made some huge mistakes in my life. And one of them was falling in love with you. I had no right to, but once I did, there was no turning back. But Barbara was—*is*—a good woman and a good mother to our boys. There was no way I would give them up, but I couldn't give you up either, so . . ." He raised his arms in surrender.

Incredulous, Frannie stared at him, unable to digest what she was hearing from this man who had caused her so much pain. Finally, in a voice more subdued, she said, "Oh, and so bigamy was the only solution, huh?"

"I never said it was the right choice. Everyone makes mistakes." Again she opened her mouth for rebuttal and he went palms up. "Don't bother to say it . . . I know, not as big as mine. But when I listen to some men complain about their stale marriages, I wonder how many would do what I did if they could afford it and work out the details."

"Oh! And that makes it right?"

"No, I never said that either. All I said is once I fell in love with you, I couldn't give you up. And that's why I'm here, Frannie. I want to know if we can possibly turn back the clock; if you could possibly forgive me. 'Everyone needs forgiveness in their hearts.' Isn't that a line you used to preach?"

"I can't believe I'm hearing this! Not only do you want total absolution, but you expect me to ignore the existence of your wife and kids?"

"Barbara won't be my wife much longer. She tried; for the sake of our boys, she really tried to forgive me, but she couldn't. They're living with her parents now until she gets a place of her own. Our divorce will be final in a month."

"How nice and tidy! So you think you can move in here and pretend it all never happened? Do you really believe I would subject myself to such public humiliation?"

"Don't let pride get in the way, Frannie. If you have one iota of feeling for me buried inside you—"

A heavy silence fell while she pondered his plea. She allowed the hostility to drain and gave him a weak smile. His eyes brightened with hope. "Wade," she began softly, "get the hell off my property and don't ever show up again!"

When she slammed her door and locked it, she took a deep breath and smiled wide. Satisfaction had never tasted sweeter!

But she cried anyway.

# Chapter Nine

Vanessa had guilt pangs. How awful to call a family gathering for full-blooded Madisons only.

That meant everyone but Glory.

"I wish you had handled this by individual phone calls instead of this clandestine meeting," Wanda said. "I shiver thinking how Glory would react if she knew you intentionally excluded her. She'd be devastated."

Vanessa busied herself preparing a new salad dressing recipe for her impromptu barbecue. "First of all, it's not a *meeting.* That sounds so cold and formal. It's simply that Glory works nights and we work days." She shrugged as if that reason should suffice.

Wanda gave her a sidelong glance, then laughed, making no effort to hide it. "Try that one on somebody else; not me," she said.

Vanessa gave the dressing a vigorous shaking, then put it aside. She laughed too, thinking how idiotic it was to offer Wanda such a lame excuse. "I know it's wrong, but there's no malicious intent. My father wasn't invited either, and you know how we adore *him.* But since their problems are items one and two on our agenda, how could we possibly include them?"

Wanda stopped cutting the melon for her fruit salad and pursed her lips. "It's too soon to tell, but I don't think your dad has a *problem.* He has a *solution* to a problem, I'd say. Glory, on the other hand—now *she* has a problem." She punctuated the statement with a finger in the air. "And truthfully, I don't know what you expect to accomplish tonight by calling in the troops." She lifted her shoulders and sighed. "But it's a good excuse to get together. We've been meaning to invite them anyway."

Vanessa released a delayed laugh and Wanda gave her a perplexed look. "I'm sorry," Vanessa said. "I wasn't laughing at you—that 'calling in the troops' expression struck me funny. But it sounds terrible, as if we're 'ganging up' or conspiring against our own sister."

Wanda completed the last of the melons and arranged the wedges on the platter. She stepped back to admire her work, then returned her attention to her partner. "You're not ganging up or conspiring against Glory. You're all just concerned, and I guess I can understand that. As you said, there's no malicious intent."

The doorbell chimes saved them from belaboring it. Vanessa went to welcome her sister Amy, who arrived with her fiancé, Mitch, and her brother Todd, still single and unattached since his breakup with Holly, much to his regret.

The discussion was already in progress when they were all seated at the patio table, except for Wanda and Mitch, who chose to play it safe and man the grill. It was difficult, though, especially for Wanda, to listen but not comment.

"This rubs me the wrong way," Amy said. "I feel like we're all betraying Glory, talking about her behind her back." Amy was the youngest of the three children born to Dan and Louise, and the first to open her heart to Glory.

Vanessa winced. "Oh, don't use a strong word like *betrayal.* This is just a family get-together to share our thoughts on the turn of events in our family."

Wanda controlled herself from throwing in Vanessa's line about no malicious intent. She kept her back to them so they wouldn't see the smile curling her lips.

"Still," Amy continued, "there's nothing earth-shattering going on here. Ironically, Glory's going through the same phase we went through when Dad announced he had another daughter born of a summer romance before he met Mom." She paused because that wasn't exactly true. She had worked on all three of them—Vanessa, Todd and her mother—to accept Glory into the family. After all, she had pleaded, Glory was just an innocent victim of her parents' affair. Punishing her was cruel. "You've all seen how she's been clinging to Dad since Alex died. And naturally, since he lost Mom too, that commonality brought them even closer."

"Hey," Todd interjected. "Don't make it sound like Dad was the only one suffering the loss. I don't think an hour goes by that I don't think of Mom."

Vanessa cut in before Amy could reply. Todd had used an inflammatory tone. She knew he was still hurting from a broken relationship with the woman he loved, so perhaps his wounds were rawer than his sisters'. And Amy was obviously hurt by Todd's remark, so Vanessa wanted to douse the spark of an argument before it caused irreparable damage. "Todd, that's not at all what Amy meant. I'm sure you misconstrued her words."

Amy lifted her chin and crossed her arms. "You don't have to defend me, Vanessa. "I can speak for myself." She caught the *cool it* look Mitch threw her, acknowledged it with a nod, but had no intention of suppressing her opinions. "It's been the same for all of us, Todd," she said. "You haven't cornered the market on grief."

Vanessa gave Todd a wide-eyed plea. The last thing she wanted from this gathering was a family argument. Todd had the same thought, so he softened his voice and spoke slowly. "Vanessa is right, Amy. I never meant to imply that I felt Mom's death more than you and Vanessa did. If that's the way it sounded, I'm sorry."

Amy drew a breath and exhaled, draining the tension from her face. "Okay. Me too. I shouldn't have shot my mouth off like that. I know—I've *seen* how Mom's death affected all of us. But that's not why we're here. Vanessa is concerned—and I am too—about Glory and Dad. Anyone can see she's not at all pleased that he's dating this woman. To be honest, I'm having a tough time swallowing that myself, but thanks to Mitch," she said, turning to smile at him, "I'm adjusting. He's doing a good job trying to convince me that it's selfish to want to deny Dad that pleasure. He's too young, Mitch says, and too healthy to sit home alone and cry. Bottom line is whatever makes Dad happy should make us happy."

Amy's words left a heavy silence while Todd and Vanessa examined their consciences concerning their father. Todd broke the somber mood by addressing Mitch, who was piling the grilled meat onto a platter. "Hey, Mitch, maybe you ought to counsel me and Vanessa," he said teasingly. "When you're on the outside looking in, anyone can be objective and say yes, that's certainly the right attitude to take. But when it hits home, and it's one of your own parents bringing in a total stranger to replace your mother or father, it's different. Like Amy said, that's a little tough to swallow."

Vanessa noticed her brother's eyes grow watery and jumped in to rescue him from his emotions. "Let's get back to Glory, Todd. Do you think we should sit her down and talk to her? I'm sure you and Amy will agree that her situation is uniquely separate and apart from ours. Since Alex died, Dad has been her rock. Even though he'll always be there for her, it'll never be the same. Not with another woman in his life. She feels lost . . . abandoned."

Todd nodded his agreement through everything his sister said. "Yes, I *do* think we should try talking to her. She needs to know that we love her too, and she can always depend on us. Maybe if we make her aware that we're not too crazy about this other woman—I shouldn't call her that; it's so unfair—about his developing relationship with Dr. Jessica Branson, maybe she'll feel closer to us and let go of Dad a little."

"I agree wholeheartedly," Amy said.

"Well, that's a relief," Vanessa said. "We settled half the problem. Now all we have to figure out is how to gently approach Dad and tell him not to sink too fast."

Wanda couldn't keep her lips sealed another minute. She couldn't resist putting in her two cents worth. "But Vanessa, what you guys have to understand is your dad doesn't feel like he's *sinking*. He feels like he's *floating!*"

Everyone acknowledged the humor—and the wisdom—in Wanda's words. The three children all laughed, although with bittersweet overtones. More like reluctant acceptance.

Mitch carried the platter of meat to the table. The smoky aroma of hickory barbecued beef and chicken wafted through the air. "Before we get too deep into phase two of this gathering, can we eat?"

Everyone speared the meat and passed the cold salads. They took generous portions of food and exchanged small talk while they ate, all aware that "phase two" would surely follow.

# Chapter Ten

Under different circumstances, Suzanne would have been thrilled. Unexpectedly, Rob had managed to get great seats for the Ogunquit Playhouse's production of *The Full Monty*, starring Sally Struthers. The buzz around town was that this was a definite not-to-be-missed performance. Until that opportunity had come up, Rob was supposed to come over for a simple dinner, after she'd put Heather in for the night, and they could talk. *Really* talk, he'd said. Not that either one wanted to; they had been postponing this talk for weeks since both had little hope for positive results.

"You don't have to do this tonight," she told Frannie when she arrived to pick up Heather. "I know you always liked to go out yourself on Friday nights. Now, since Amore Evenings, that chance doesn't come up too often."

"Yes, but how often does Rob get a Friday night off? You might as well take advantage. And believe me, if we didn't have Sara and Tim there on the weekends, Glory and I would both have to work. Those two are not only friends, but our best employees." She waved a hand. "Anyway, I had nothing special planned and one night of babysitting won't kill me. But for you and Rob, tonight is very important, so I *want* to help. You need to relax, enjoy each other's company and do something special before you get into the serious stuff. This way, you'll have a clear head. You won't have to worry about Heather until tomorrow morning. When I leave for Amore, my mom offered to stay until you pick her up, as long as it's not later than ten, okay?"

"Oh, I'll be there long before ten," Suzanne said, then dipped her head and shot Frannie a hooded-eye glance. "You didn't mention anything to your mom, did you?"

"Are you kidding? Never! I promised you I'd never reveal that to *anyone*—not my mother, not Glory, not *anyone*! You have enough troubles, Suzanne; don't worry about things that'll never materialize."

"Well, I appreciate the favor, but I'm in no big hurry to have this discussion. It's more like a showdown. Rob will never understand why I can't tell him about Heather's father, and, of course, only you know why that's impossible." She sighed and cast a downward glance. "It's useless. This whole night will be a waste." Saying the words brought tears to her eyes, but she blinked them away.

After Frannie left with Heather, Suzanne sat staring into space while she waited for Rob. Her love for him so consumed her that she wished they had never met. She had never imagined love could hurt so much. Sure, it's great when you're wrapped up in it, she mused, but you don't measure its worth until you lose it. Then you're left with only regrets for never appreciating the gift when you had it.

A typical example for Suzanne was when her mom died. All the regrets, the *if onlys*, piled up high as a mountain. *Why didn't I ever tell her how much I loved her? Why? She told me often enough.* Suzanne couldn't recall ever saying *I love you, Mom* without her mother's prompting.

*If only I hadn't driven her crazy with my bratty, self-absorbed attitude during my teen years. If only I hadn't defied her simple rules. She asked so little.* A pained smile crossed Suzanne's face as she visualized her mom's pleas. "Don't call me a nag, Suzanne. If you wouldn't give me such a hard time, I wouldn't have to nag. Can't you get it through your thick head that as your mother it's my responsibility? Can't you understand that if I didn't love you, I wouldn't give a damn?"

She cringed recalling how she would answer with that all too familiar smirk; that *here we go again* smirk. "Yes," she had answered, "I know you're trying to be a responsible mother, but you don't have to be a fanatic about it."

The memories were painful because they could never be undone. "I'm sorry, Mom," she murmured now; her eyes filling up again. "Come back, come back . . . we'll do it all over, Mom. I'll be so different . . ."

And now, again, she was blessed with a love she truly didn't deserve, but because of one grave sin in her past, she couldn't embrace it. Her heart ached knowing that tonight she may lose him forever. In her entire life she had never allowed herself to *dream* of someone like Rob. Not even Hollywood would create such a character. In today's world, he'd never pass for "normal" or "realistic."

All she had to do was name Heather's father; knock down this wall between them, he'd said. She laughed bitterly, remembering, then imagined how he'd react when she said the two words: *Greg Haggarty*.

So much for honesty.

It would be like setting off an avalanche.

# Chapter Eleven

Suzanne had suggested Amore Evenings for dinner before the theater. Although they had dined there many times before, the food, the ambiance and the view were great, and it was close to the theater, so why go elsewhere, she reasoned. But she had another reason for choosing Amore Evenings. There's comfort in familiarity. Not only did Frannie and Glory own it, but she knew almost the entire staff and the locals who dined there regularly. Rob had agreed not to discuss their problem until after the theater, when they could have complete privacy in her apartment. There was nothing they could discuss—neither immediate nor long-term—that didn't hinge on the identity of Heather's father.

He made five-thirty reservations at Amore Evenings, and when they arrived the tables were less than half-occupied. Glory had greeted them at the door and she personally served the two glasses of wine they had ordered; merlot for him; white zinfandel for her. "Well, that's what I call service," Rob said with his friendliest grin. "I guess that's an advantage of an early dinner. We get served by the boss lady herself. How have you been, Glory? It's been too many weeks since Suzanne and I have been here."

Glory waved off his subtle apology. "Doesn't matter. You're both here now and it's a pleasure to see you again." She put a hand over Suzanne's. "How's your little darling doing, Suzanne? It's been awhile since I've seen her, too."

Pride brightened Suzanne's mood and her smile came easily. "She's great. Healthy and energetic—maybe too energetic!" She rolled her eyes and laughed. "A handful, exploring everything and always getting in trouble."

Glory grimaced. "Sounds like the onset of 'terrible twos'; I'm not looking forward to that stage with Danny."

The two women exchanged another minute of baby talk until Glory realized Rob was sitting there politely, but bored. "Oh, sorry, Rob. I didn't mean to leave you out. I do get carried away when I talk about Danny. And I always like to compare notes with other mothers so I know what to expect."

"Don't give it a second thought, Glory. I enjoy talking about Heather, too."

It probably lasted only a nanosecond, but Glory could have sworn the couple's eyes locked, sharing something other than pride. It could have been her imagination, but she had learned to trust her instincts, so she stood up. "Okay, I'd better get back to work. Enjoy your dinner and maybe I'll catch you later."

Rob watched Glory walk away, and to fill the silence, he said, "No matter when you see her, that woman always looks gorgeous. Even at Alex's funeral she looked stunning."

"That doesn't mean she wasn't grieving."

"I never said that," Rob answered. He picked up the menu. "Let's see what looks good tonight."

Suzanne gave her menu a cursory glance, then put it aside. "I'll wait to hear tonight's specials before I decide."

Her face brightened again when Timothy Waite came to take their order. She stood up to kiss him. "Hey, Tim, good to see you!" She glanced around the dining room. "Is Sara working tonight?"

"Oh, sure. We always work weekends. She'll be here any minute. I'll be sure to send her over." He yanked his pad from his pocket. "So, we have some really great specials tonight . . ."

Suzanne and Rob sipped their wine and made small talk. They talked about anything and everything except what they had agreed to discuss and settle tonight.

When Tim served their crocks of lobster bisque, she realized her appetite had diminished. She had put up a good pretense of being interested in their conversation, but throbbing away in the back of her mind was what she would say to him later. And what would happen once she said it. Sure, her brief affair with Greg was inexcusable, but it didn't seem fair that she should pay for that one mistake with her own lifetime happiness.

It also didn't seem fair that Rob should corner her like this. If he loved her even half as much as he claimed, his love would be unconditional. It *should* be unconditional.

"Okay, let's change the subject," Rob said. His voice was gentle, his smile soft.

She lifted a brow. "Why?"

Rob grinned, drew a breath and reached for her hand. "Because I can tell your mind is a million miles away—and I can guess why—"

"Don't go there, Rob. You promised. Not here. We still have dinner and the play to get through. I'm so glad it's a comedy; I could use a good laugh."

He squeezed her hand. "I hope you're able to laugh. I'm sorry I put you in this mood. The last thing I want to do is make you unhappy." He lifted her hand and kissed it. "Just remember one thing and then I promise I'll shut up: I love you and I love Heather. But I don't want to be her father figure; I want to be her *father*."

She nodded and swallowed hard, casting her gaze on her soup as though eating it required all her attention.

It was Sara Baisley, not Tim Waite, who brought their entrees. "Hey, you guys! What a treat to see you again!" She served Suzanne's pecan-crusted salmon and Rob's cocoanut-crusted haddock with raspberry sauce. Ordinarily Suzanne devoured her delectable dish, but tonight it looked challenging. "When Tim told me you were here, I grabbed this tray from him so I could say hello. So what's new? Heather okay?"

"We're all fine, thanks," Suzanne said. "Rob surprised me with tickets to *The Full Monty* tonight. We heard it's great."

"Oh, it certainly is. Tim and I saw it last week. It was hilarious! And of course anything Sally Struthers stars in is a guaranteed success."

Suzanne laughed in spite of herself. "You're amazing, Sara. It's a pleasure to watch you. Anyone who's down should spend five minutes with you. You're like a live anti-depressant! Are you always this cheerful?"

She wrinkled her nose. "Not always. Especially not when I watch the news every morning. But that's why I try to appreciate life. It's an ugly world out there, but in my world I'm still surrounded by beautiful people and places. So we shouldn't sweat the small stuff, right? Hey, enjoy your meal. I'll stop by again if I have time." She cupped her mouth as she walked away. "But on a Friday night, there's little chance of that."

Rob watched Sara with admiration as she briskly walked away. "That kid's a sweetheart. Like you said, she's always in an up mood."

"Yes, she's a pleasure to have around. Tim too. They're so cute together. I hope they stay together."

"What makes you think they won't?"

Suzanne took a bite of her salmon and her appetite returned. "I forgot how good this is," she said, then noticed that Rob was still waiting for an answer. "I didn't say they won't. It's just that sometimes everything looks rosy on the surface, but people often have unsolvable problems that drive them apart."

Rob put his fork down. "Suzanne . . ."

Her hand went up like a stop sign. "Eat your fish, Rob. It looks delicious."

Suzanne was determined not to shed another tear. Tonight she would hang tough. *Whatever happens, happens,* she resolved. *I should have known better than to believe in fairy tale romances. I'll get over him if it kills me.*

*And it probably will.*

\* \* \*

When they arrived at The Ogunquit Playhouse, Suzanne doubted that the play could distract her from what would follow. The scene kept playing in her mind, with slight variations, but the end result was always the same.

She licked her dry lips repeatedly while they waited for the curtain to rise, and she felt a sudden restlessness. It took all the will power she could summon to suppress the urge to get up and run out of the theater. But when Brad Kenney, the theater's director, came out to warm the audience, his amiable personality did relax her somewhat and soon after the play had begun, she found herself howling with laughter.

The energy was still electrifying as everyone emerged from the theater. Suzanne's mood was noticeably better. "I'm so glad we came," she said to Rob as they walked to their car. "That's what we needed; 'feel-good entertainment.' I always felt if you spend good money on entertainment, it should leave you smiling, not depressed."

"There you go!" Rob said, glad to see her in a better mood. "Now that sounds like something Sara would say." He opened the car door for her and she slid in.

"Sara, the eternal optimist," Suzanne answered. "I certainly would like to emulate her spirit, but it's easier said than done."

Rob stole an analytical glance. It hadn't taken long for her mood to sink again. He wanted to remind her of how Sara survived and rallied after escaping a violent death, but he chose silence instead. The last thing she needed now was a sermon. Besides, Suzanne had also escaped a violent death, albeit not by a Mr. Nice Guy gone mad.

It troubled him all the way home, when not a single word was exchanged between them. He began doubting his judgment. If he chose to forget his ultimatum, would it be possible to live as a family with the weight of that dark secret hovering over them?

He continued to ruminate as he drove, and his thoughts brought an involuntary frown to his face. Suzanne caught it. "What was that for?" she asked.

"Nothing . . . just thinking."

Suzanne didn't have to ask about *what.*

* * *

Their opportunities for a romantic evening alone were rare. Most of the time, Heather was a good sleeper, but there were no guarantees she wouldn't wake up and cry at the most inopportune time. Tonight, though, they couldn't bring themselves to take advantage of the privacy. Although Rob kissed her the moment he closed the door behind them, their embrace seemed veiled with sadness.

She broke away, went to her refrigerator, popped two Diet Cokes and handed him one. She sat in the club chair facing him rather than curling herself in his arms on the sofa. "Okay, where do we start?" she asked, totally in control. "Where did we leave off the last time?"

"Doesn't matter," Rob answered. "Start wherever you like." He leaned forward, allowing their gazes to meet. "Just keep in mind what I said before in the restaurant."

Suzanne gave him an exaggerated smirk. "Oh, I know, you love me and you love Heather. How did you put it? But you don't want to be her father figure, you want to be her *father.*" The pained look on his face stabbed her with remorse. Mimicking his words was a low blow. He had offered them lovingly and she made a mockery of them. But she couldn't keep the crisp sarcasm out of her voice because she knew how this drama would end. It was like walking up a dead-end street, fully aware that there's no way out.

"Suzanne, I know you're upset, so I'm going to forget you said that, but you're not being fair." Rob spoke slowly and evenly without the slightest trace of anger or impatience.

"Can you honestly say I'm wrong—that I have no right to know—"

Suzanne played with the fringe on her throw pillow. "No, not really wrong," she admitted. "You want to know who he is for all the right reasons . . . and I'm pleased that you want to adopt Heather, but I feel I have rights too." She lifted her gaze. "And Rob, I don't want to mention that name—now or ever."

"Okay, then forget me for a minute. What are you going to tell Heather when she's older? When she wants to know?"

She took a long pause, then inhaled. "I was hoping she'd grow up thinking you were her father." She cringed after she whispered the words. Once they were spoken, they sounded weaker and more ludicrous than when she tossed them around in her head.

Rob's patience had reached its breaking point. He put the Coke can on the end table, sat on her ottoman and grabbed her arms. "Suzanne, *look* at me!" he said, his tone demanding. "Can you honestly tell me you believe that's possible? There's no way in hell that could work! You can't be—" He clenched his teeth and threw his gaze to the ceiling.

"I can't be what—that stupid?"

"Don't put words in my mouth. I was going to say 'you can't be serious,' not stupid. But I *do* think this has you so upset that you're not thinking straight. Suzanne, you know as well as I, the whole world knows we met when Heather was four months old!"

Suzanne didn't answer; just covered her mouth with her hand. She was afraid if she spoke, a flood of tears would spill out.

Rob lowered his voice again and tried to reach her with a gentle approach. "Suzanne, no one has to know this. It'll be strictly between us. I'm sure the adoption records—if I *can* adopt her—will be strictly confidential—"

"Oh, sure. Until she gets older, as you said, and demands to know. Nothing is confidential these days." She turned and looked him in the eye now, pointing a finger. "Look, Rob, understand this: I don't care if my daughter has to believe I slept with a dozen different guys that month—that they were all total strangers I picked up. I'd rather have her hate me than reveal who her father is! Trust me, that's worse." She stood up abruptly and walked into her kitchen. "So you might as well give up trying, Rob. I love you—God knows I do—" She stopped for another deep breath. Her will was about to lose its battle with her tears. "But if you can't accept me for who I am . . ." She trailed off, shaking her head as though the gesture would put her thoughts in order. "Why can't you leave Heather out of this? If you want to marry me, then marry me, not my daughter!"

She had screamed the words while tears rained on her face. Rob stood speechless and crippled, starring at her in disbelief.

"Don't just stand there staring like I'm some kind of mental case! Just say what you have to say then *go*! Because you can wait till hell freezes over, I'll never give you that name!"

*My God, who the heck can it be?* Rob thought, suddenly frightened by it all. Yes, he did stare at her just as she described. Had she snapped? Had he driven her to this sorry state?

His voice cracked when he finally spoke. "It's someone I know, isn't it? Maybe someone everyone knows."

She crossed her arms, said nothing.

Rob grabbed his jacket and cane, went quietly to the door, then turned to her for one more look. "Keep your secret, Suzanne. Maybe I'm better off not knowing anyway. And for whatever it's worth, I'm sorry I caused you all this pain. And don't ever forget, if you or Heather ever need me, I'll always be there for you."

She waited until she heard his footsteps on the stairs, wrapped her arms around her legs and sobbed until daylight peaked through her blinds.

# Chapter Twelve

"Hi, sweetheart, good morning! This is a surprise," Dan said. "What are you doing up and out so early?" He took his grandson from her arms and kissed him till he giggled. "This child is amazing. Such a happy baby. I can't remember if your brother and sisters were this playful. Poor Vanessa was a colicky baby in the beginning, and Todd had a temper Louise and I couldn't believe! Amy, though, was more like little Danny—always pleasant." He kissed the baby's forehead.

"Maybe she realized as number three in the family it would be a waste of time to be too demanding. You guys couldn't give her all your attention."

It took little effort for Dan to recognize the sadness in Glory. For another family this casual conversation would be harmless. For Glory, it hurt knowing neither she nor her father had any memories of her young life. It had taken each of them thirty-five years to learn the other existed. "I'm sorry, Glory," he said. "It hurts me too knowing such a huge chunk of our lives was denied us. I wish I had a memory of bouncing you on my knee, or seeing you take your first steps ... watching you dress up for your high school prom ... but we can't unravel all those years. We can only look ahead and hope we have many more years to build new memories."

He put his free arm around her shoulder and pulled her close, kissed her on the cheek. "You all right?"

"I'm fine, Dad. I had a few errands to run, so I stopped by, that's all."

"Good, as long as everything is okay. I was just surprised that you'd have time for an unexpected visit, this being the Fourth of July weekend. I imagine Amore Evenings will be bursting at the seams for the next few days."

Glory smiled proudly. "Not that Frannie and I would dare complain, but our restaurant 'bursts at the seams' all summer long."

He poured them each a glass of iced tea and they sat out on the deck. Glory drank half of it down in one gulp. "Ah! Nice and cold. I worked up quite a thirst running around the village." She pulled a small bottle from Danny's diaper bag. "Here, feed him, Dad. I'm sure he's thirsty, too," she said, handing him the apple juice. "So tell me," she said, trying unsuccessfully to introduce the subject casually—to slip it in as though she were just trying to make light conversation. "How was your date last night?"

Dan pretended not to notice. He grimaced, then laughed. "Excuse me. I wasn't frowning about Jessica; it was the word *date* that irks me. After a thirty-six year marriage, it's a tough word to get used to." He grew serious and curled his brows thoughtfully. "It was nice, though. It's strange how you don't realize what you're missing until it hits you in the face. I never, ever thought about dating someone else. Louise was everything to me—my life. You don't replace that kind of love; it's a part of you, even after they're gone."

"Tell me about it!"

"I'm sorry, sweetheart. I was selfishly thinking only of myself. You and Alex barely had time to get to know each other . . ." His voice trailed off, and he was momentarily lost in the horror of those surreal memories of how Louise and Alex died; both by senseless, spontaneous acts of violence. But then again, he thought, what kind of violence is sensible?

He flashed a smile and waved off his grim thoughts. No sense dragging them both down to the bowels of that black pit of grief. "But getting back to Dr. Branson—Jessica— she's a really nice person once she sheds her white coat. Not that she was unpleasant when Danny was born, but I only spoke to her for a minute. Once she assured me that you and Danny were fine, all I cared about was getting in to see you and my grandson." He smiled wider, remembering the surge of joy he felt at that moment. "What I'm saying is, when you meet people in their professional environment, you don't visualize them as private individuals, but yesterday I was surprised to discover that Jessica is very pleasant and interesting company."

"Well, you must have surmised that when you met at the supermarket. Otherwise why would you have invited her to lunch?"

Her tone stopped him from answering her question. Instead, he looked down at her, squinting, as though trying to delve deep into her mind.

Despite the heat, a chill ran through Glory, struck by the realization that she had pushed too far. She took the empty juice bottle from his hand and, without eye contact, said, "I'd better get home. I have a million things to do while he naps."

"But you just got here," Dan said, disappointment shadowing his face.

She took the baby from his arms and was about to leave when he stopped her. "Wait, Glory. I'm getting negative vibes. Maybe it's my imagination, but I hope you're not upset that I had dinner with Jessica. I thought you'd all be pleased. For months all of you have been pushing me to get out and socialize."

"Upset? What makes you think I'm upset?" She laughed, pretending to shrug off his assumption as ludicrous, but her facial expression belied her words.

"I'm not sure. I hope I'm wrong."

"You *are* wrong. Trust me, Dad. Why should I resent Dr. Branson? After all, she and I had a brief intimate relationship, you might say. She delivered my baby!" Glory laughed at her futile attempt to infuse levity, but the air was thick with unspoken words. "C'mon, Dad, don't study me like that. I don't resent Dr. Branson at all." She sliced the air for emphasis.

"But I never said *resent*, Glory. I said *upset.*"

She lifted her brows. "Same thing."

"Not really. An *upset* can be easily cured in most cases. A *resentment* is something you harbor inside you; it grows like a cancer. If you let it, it'll kill you. Do you *resent* Jessica, Glory? Be honest."

"Of course not," she answered, trying to be more convincing. "I'm happy for you. Are you going to see her again?"

"Absolutely. Are you okay with that?"

"Would it matter if I weren't?" Glory cringed the moment the words slipped out. She had no idea how they affected her father because she didn't dare look back.

# Chapter Thirteen

Frannie and Glory barely had time to breathe that Saturday night. Ogunquit summers were routinely packed with tourists, but on holiday weekends there wasn't a room available for miles around, especially when the weather reports were favorable. Sandy beaches and a rocky coastline added to its mesmerizing beauty, attracting visitors to the charming village.

It was past ten o'clock when they finally had a chance to put their feet up and sit in the small office they shared. Frannie blew an exhausted sigh and rubbed her aching calves. "Man, if this pace continues year after year, I'll have to work in support hose!"

Glory laughed. "Now there's a pleasant image—both of us still working when we're old and arthritic; you in support hose and me in a back brace."

Frannie tipped her head. "Actually that *is* a pleasant image. It would mean Amore Evenings had survived successfully for decades and we had endured all the years of hard work. Maybe then we can let go of the reins and hire someone else to manage it."

"*Never,*" Glory said adamantly. "This place is my salvation, particularly since Alex died. And now that Marion Landis agreed to take on babysitting Danny on weekend nights, I can come to work with a clear head. She's really great; Danny took to her right away. Not that he was a problem for his other sitters, but most of the time it was Vanessa and Wanda or my dad. True, they never made me feel as though I was burdening them, but they have busy lives, too. Vanessa has her shops, and when school reopens in September, Wanda will be back to work too. So how long can I take advantage?"

"I can understand how you feel, but under the circumstances, everyone was glad to do it for you. When someone has tragedy in their lives, people want to help. And let's face it, everyone who offered was family—or close as family, like me or Sara."

Glory sipped her bottled water and nodded. Yes, when it came to family and friends, she had been blessed all her life.

Before making a move to close up for the night, Frannie took a moment to rest her eyes. When she opened them, she caught a familiar expression on her friend's face. Taut and troubled. "Okay, spill it," she said with a smile, "I can see you have something on your mind and you're not sure you want to get into it, right?"

Glory picked up a pen and pretended to throw it at her. "I hate when you do that. Always analyzing my facial expressions. I never was good at hiding my feelings, I guess," she said with a look of hopeless resignation.

"You do the same with me, so get it out," she said, turning her chair to face Glory. "Unless you need more time. Do you want me to stop at your apartment after we close up? That way Marion can leave and we won't be rushed."

"Marion's a night owl; unusual for a senior citizen, but it works to my advantage." She wrinkled her nose at Frannie. "But it might be too much for you. You have to get up early to be at Amore Breakfast."

"And you have to get up early for Danny, so stop wasting time. Do you want me to come or not?" She folded her arms.

Glory hesitated to answer, but she gave Frannie a pleading gaze.

"Okay, that's my answer; that puppy-dog face that asks 'Would you mind?' And don't you dare throw that pen at me!"

Glory laughed, then stood up and turned serious. "Thanks, Frannie. I do need to dump on you. I'll try not to chew your ears off too long."

"Glory, we're long past that. You don't have to thank me. I don't do much to help solve your problems, except listen. And to be honest, I need to get something off my chest, too." She rolled her eyes upward. "I have a feeling it'll be a long night."

"Maybe we'd better forget it. I feel bad to keep you up late . . . hey, I have an idea! Why don't you go home, grab pajamas and whatever you need, then come back and sleep over on my sofabed. That way you can get comfortable and you won't have to drag yourself home. We can relax with a glass of wine and enjoy some girl talk without interruption. What do you say?"

Frannie smirked negatively while she pondered the thought, then brightened. "Okay. What the hell; I haven't been to a pajama party since I was a teenager!"

\* \* \*

Glory stared at Frannie as if she were seeing her for the first time. And in a way she was. Her baby pink shorty pajamas with ruffled edges were actually adorable and might have made another woman fall into that category, but Frannie's satiny long legs made them look seductive. Another long look reminded Glory that Frannie also started wearing eye makeup—just a hint, nothing overbearing, but enough to call attention to her large almond-shaped eyes. They were the lightest shade of brown Glory had ever seen, which made them uniquely arresting. She had also highlighted her hair, which was usually a cross between light brown or "winter blonde," as she defined light hair that bleak cold winters had turned drab, like a wilted flower longing for sunlight. It was shorter now but the angular cut was definitely more flattering. It framed her face like a halo. Studying her other features with a critical eye, none would be considered exceptionally attractive, but they seemed to complement each other, giving Frannie an exotic kind of beauty—indefinable perhaps, but somehow magnetic.

Frannie was enjoying herself telling Glory a humorous story about an incident in the restaurant. She hadn't thought it was funny when it happened, but now as she recalled the sight, she laughed till her stomach hurt. "The poor woman was dressed like a million dollars, but when she walked back to her table with toilet paper trailing from the heel of her shoe . . ." When she noticed how Glory was watching her without sharing the humor, she stopped short. "What the heck are you staring at?"

Glory broke her concentration and laughed apologetically. "I'm sorry. That was rude but silently complimentary, you might say."

Frannie made a face. "I think that one needs explaining."

"What I meant was I suddenly noticed how great you look lately. I got caught up in observing you, trying to figure out what the difference was. Sorry, I guess I wasn't paying attention to what you were saying. Tell me again."

"Forget it," Frannie answered and laughed. "If you're going to throw compliments my way, that's more important. Well, now that you finished your 'in-depth analysis,' did you make any observations that you want to share with me?"

Glory threw her hands out. "Yes, as long as you asked. Your eyes stand out more now that you accentuated them with a little makeup. And your hair is fabulous—the new cut and the highlights. And don't get any ideas—I love men— but I never noticed what perfect legs you have."

Frannie laughed heartily this time and pointed a finger. "No explanation necessary. There's nothing wrong with a woman admiring another woman. Hey, I've admired gorgeous women celebrities all my life, always wishing I could exchange my face and body for theirs."

Glory waved it off. "Their looks are their number one commodity—you know that. They dump bundles of money on cosmetic surgery and anything else necessary to enhance and maintain whatever they had in the first place."

"Still, some are naturally gorgeous, starting with Elizabeth Taylor and many who followed in her footsteps."

"Okay, I can't disagree with that, but that's not why we're here. Let's get on with whatever we need to talk about. You first."

The smile fell from Frannie's face the instant that scene flashed in her mind. That surprise visit from the bastard she lived with and loved for three years, never questioning the validity of their marriage. Never having *reason* to question it. She'd had the rings on her fingers and the huge wedding portrait; she in her snowy white bridal gown, being caressed by her handsome groom. Yes, tangible items authenticating the memorable day.

That wedding portrait was the first to receive the thundering blows of her rage. Denial had overcome her at first, but once it snaked through, she was left with the raw reality of Wade's deception. She had yanked off her rings and thrown them at the portrait. But that wasn't satisfying enough. That face was still looking back at her, still smiling. She had run to the garage and returned wielding a hammer, pounding it against his face until there was nothing left but shards of glass strewn everywhere and nothing left of that smiling face.

She squeezed her eyes closed and shook away the haunting memory. "I'm sorry. You know how I get whenever I allow myself to think of Wade."

"Well, don't think about him. Why torture yourself? You've got to learn to shake it off. That nightmare is long gone."

Frannie sneered. "Not really. Believe it or not, I found him in my backyard a few days ago relaxing on one of my Adirondack chairs, like he owned the place."

"Are you *serious*?" Glory leaned closer, as if she hadn't heard right. "What did he want?"

Fueled by the flames of anger she had stirred thinking back to that day with the hammer, she repeated what had recently transpired with Wade. The initial ugliness and how it petered out to contrition. She avoided Glory's gaze when she revealed what he really wanted—the display of remorse; how he begged for forgiveness and another chance.

Glory stared at her friend in disbelief. "Frannie, don't tell me—" She erased the thought with a hand wave. "No, I don't even want to entertain the thought."

"No, Glory. I'm not taking him back. Not only because of what he did, but because of something else—but that's Part B of my problem. If Wade decides to stay here permanently—which is unbelievable—I don't know how he can hold his head up in this town. Well, anyway, I think that's his intention. And if it is, I feel this need to make peace. I don't know if I can ever heal that pain unless I do. It's like I have to cut him out." She made a fist and twisted it under her breasts, as though cutting out a tumor.

"And how do you intend to do that?" Glory was having a hard time suppressing her rising anger. She couldn't believe Frannie's resolve could have weakened to this degree.

"I don't know. Maybe I'll meet him in some out of the way restaurant and talk it out. Truthfully, I always wanted to get inside his head—to know what motivated him to marry me when he already had a family. Wade and I never exchanged a single word since I found out. I was so furious, I didn't even want to hear the sound of his voice, so I let the lawyers handle everything. But sometimes . . ." She drew a breath, then said, "Never mind, forget it. We should be talking about your problems, not mine."

"We will, but you're not going to leave me hanging like that! 'But sometimes' what?"

Frannie played with the ring on her finger—the one she had bought to replace her wedding band and engagement ring. "Okay, but don't you scream at me. Remember you're my friend, not my disciplinarian." She cleared the frog in her throat. "I was about to say that sometimes I wonder if what Wade did was some kind of mental disorder—well, maybe that's too strong—maybe it was the daddy of all mid-life crises. In a way, it's pathetic when you think about it. He *did* love me; I'm sure about that—but was his love so consuming, so obsessive, that he was unable to control the feeling? Think about it, Glory." She furrowed her brows and met her friend's gaze. "Don't you think leading a double life like that had to be extremely stressful for him?"

Glory couldn't believe her ears. She threw her head back. "Oh, give me a break! You don't expect me to feel sorry for him, do you? There's no way I can take an objective view, evaluate Wade's actions and conclude they were all caused by some irresistible impulse." She shook her head. "Sorry, Frannie, I'm well aware many crimes are committed that way, but that doesn't mean we should forgive them."

Frannie grimaced with frustration, struggling for the right words to express herself. She put a hand up. "All right, wait. That didn't come out right. No, it's not about forgiveness for *his* sake; it's *peace* I need, for *my* sake. Maybe I need to *listen* to him; maybe I can replace all this poison with pity. That would be easier to live with."

Glory gave Frannie's words serious thought. "Then talk to him," she said with a defeated sigh, "but make sure that's all you do."

That got a laugh out of Frannie. "Oh, forget that! There's absolutely no chance of anything beyond talking."

"How can you be so sure?"

"Because the answer to that question is Part B of my problem." She looked at her wristwatch. "But we might have to save that for another session, because I need to hear what's troubling you." She sat up straight and crossed her arms. "So shoot. I'm all ears."

Glory looked away. "It's funny, now that I have your undivided attention, I feel stupid talking about it. If I were doing the listening, I'd call my problem childish, immature, selfish or whatever, but since I'm not—"

"Glory, let me help you get this out. Is it about your dad and your doctor?"

Glory exhaled quickly, then smiled her relief. "Yes, and before you lecture me about my attitude, let me say I know it's wrong, but I can't help it. I feel as if I'm losing him, a little at a time, and I'm just plain jealous."

"I wouldn't dream of lecturing you," Frannie assured her. "Especially since you didn't lecture me about Wade." She paused to restructure her preplanned sentences. Earlier tonight, Frannie had correctly guessed what was eating away at Glory and she didn't want to pour salt in her wounds by using the same clichéd evaluations.

"Well?" Glory prompted. "What's going on in your head?"

Frannie smiled at her. "Nothing, really. I'm just trying to come up with words to replace *childish, immature* and *selfish.*" She laughed as she said it, but didn't think Glory would be amused, so she quickly added, "But I can certainly understand your jealousy pangs. It may not be right to feel them, but right or wrong, suddenly there they are, and you have to deal with them."

Glory returned an *easier said than done* smirk. "And how do I do that?"

Frannie shrugged, then softly said, "I think it's time to find you a new boyfriend." When she caught Glory's shocked look, she allowed a slight laugh to escape. "I never planned to say that, Glory, but sometimes we lose control— like your involuntary jealousy pangs."

Glory relaxed and laughed too. "It's okay. I would never admit this to anyone else, but sometimes that same thought crosses my mind. Loneliness is a bitch."

Glory's honesty touched Frannie and she didn't know what to say. She had hoped that little Danny would fill Glory's emptiness. Frannie had learned from her own personal experience that it didn't work that way. Long after Suzanne's medical crisis passed, Frannie had met Sergio Giannetta, but he had faded out of her life like an autumn breeze, leaving her with all this love to pour out. She had clung to Heather and Danny, allowing herself to become more attached to the babies than what would be considered normal. But no matter how lovable and adorable the two babies were—and are—baby hugs and kisses could never measure up to what she felt when Sergio kissed her for the first time . . . and the second . . . and the third . . .

Glory's voice broke through her ruminations. "So, c'mon, Frannie, before it gets too late, tell me about Part B."

"Okay. But you'd better prepare yourself. This will shock the hell out of you. Do you remember Sergio Giannetta, my gardener?"

Glory peered at her, waiting for more. "I sure do. Don't tell me you and he—"

"No, but we came pretty damn close."

# Chapter Fourteen

Two hours after she had chased Glory off to bed, Frannie remained wide-eyed, anxiety causing sleep to evade her. Her hands were crossed under her head, and although she tried to concentrate on the steady rhythm of the ocean's roar, her mind raced from one problem to another.

It had felt good to share a heart-to-heart with Glory again. In a way, since Alex died, Frannie had felt that she too had suffered a loss, although not to be compared with Glory's. She had felt so helpless watching her friend's agonizing grief; there was little she could do to comfort her. Thinking back, Frannie realized that she had always avoided speaking to her about anything unrelated to their business or her grief. After seeing the old Glory come back to life tonight, she regretted that now. Listening to those day-to-day trivialities might have been the best medicine for her friend. Frannie had erroneously assumed, however, that she would not be receptive to anything more. Why should she be burdened with anyone else's problems while she was emotionally suffering?

But during those long months she felt the loss of their friendship; the comfortable companionship of the person she could dump her frustrations on, could share her innermost feelings with or simply enjoy a good laugh together. She had put all her own problems aside, allowing them to nest and snowball.

How she had wanted to tell Glory about Sergio! In the beginning, when her business relationship with him began budding into something more, Frannie was euphoric. And then, when she lost him, she'd had to go through it alone. But how could she equate the loss of a lover who is thousands of miles away but alive and well with the loss of a lover who was brutally shot to death? No, for her friend, there were no miles to count, no sky or sea to cross. Unlike Frannie and Sergio, there was no sliver of hope for Glory and Alex; no dreams, no maybes.

It was her dad mostly who helped her pick up the pieces and rebuild her life. Sadly and ironically, for Dan, it was his daughter's grief that helped him cope with his own loss. When Alex died, not even a year had passed since Louise's death. Dan had been like a drowning man. It was as if Alex's death had forced him to swim against the tide to save his daughter. And although Glory was too grief-stricken to notice, she had been his lifeline as well.

Tonight Frannie finally felt comfortable enough to discuss the growing problem with Glory. But only because Glory was finally ready to listen. She felt better after warning her not to give Jessica Branson a dose of what her half-siblings did to her.

And tonight, as far as she herself was concerned, after her talk with Glory, Frannie felt a sense of relief, as though she had punctured a rock-hard ball somewhere in the recesses of her mind.

"Damn, it's almost 2:30!" she mumbled when she got up to use the bathroom. She had to be up and out by 6:30, but at least Amore Breakfast was only a three-minute car trip.

Back in the sofabed, she assumed the same position and kept her gaze on the ocean. Glory's sliding glass doors provided a magnificent view from the living room. She took deep breaths and tried to relax, hoping the ocean would lull her to sleep.

She tried hard not to think of Sergio, but in his place, Wade's shocking visit kept replaying in her mind. She wanted so much to let go of the hatred—even her mother wanted her to forgive him. Way back when it had all hit the fan, Tess had been preaching the same song to her daughter.

"Let it go, Frannie. It's the only way you can put it behind you," she'd said. "Don't you know when you bottle up all that hatred, that rage against someone, *you're* the one who suffers, not the one who caused your suffering. Usually they just go about their business while you, the victim, eat yourself alive holding in all that poison." Frannie could still see her mother's finger wagging at her. "Listen to me, Frannie. You've got to spit it all out and bury that whole damn story once and for all, you hear me? I can't stand to watch you making yourself sick. Can't you see what it's done to you?"

"I know, Mom, and you're probably right," Frannie had answered. "I can't promise anything, but I'll really try because I know I have to."

Blocking her own troubles from her thoughts, she concentrated on the Glory/Dan/Jessica triangle. A tense triangle, to be sure, Frannie mused. If Glory isn't distracted by *Someone Really Special*—and real soon—that could spell disaster.

*I can't think about that now.* She punched the pillow and turned over. *There are no simple solutions. At least not yet.*

She managed to sweep it away a few minutes later, but only until Suzanne's latest problem filled the void. Accepting defeat in her battle with insomnia, she flipped herself over again, cradling her head in her hands.

Now Suzanne's problem, if God forbid it should ever leak out, would make Glory's seem insignificant. She hated to say it—to *think* it, but if Rob stands firm and insists she reveal Heather's father, then she has to let him go, Frannie concluded. The fallout on the Haggarty family would be fatal.

So far she hadn't heard from Suzanne about what happened last night; the showdown, Suzanne had called it. In this case, is no news good news? she wondered.

That too she forced out of her mind and, sure enough, Sergio slipped in.

What the hell, she thought. It seemed her insomnia was here to stay, so why fight it? She pulled the crisp sheet up to her neck and inhaled its fresh lilac fragrance. Considering she wasn't in her own bed, she couldn't have been more comfortable. The mattress was thicker than most sofabeds and the pillows felt soft, like velvet clouds. In its angry voice, the ocean sang its unending song, its rolling waves slapping the shore. Frannie loved to watch them rushing in, like they had a destination with a definite purpose. They'd come tumbling in, melding together into lacy white crescents, blanketing the black rocks like melting snow. And always racing, racing, racing. Like my mind, she thought.

This was going to be one of those nights where she'd just lie there and wait for daybreak. *I might as well close my eyes and dream. I'll think of only the good memories and imagine all the happiness that could have followed if the sudden death of his father hadn't ripped us apart.*

Frannie drew a breath, closed her eyes and allowed the memories to unfold. She didn't want to forget even the tiniest details of their short time together, since memories were all she had left. Her mouth twisted into a sad smile. Sometimes when this mood enveloped her, she'd think of Francesca, the character in *The Bridges of Madison County.* When she had read the book and seen the movie, she was moved by its poignancy and despair; the intensity of the brief affair. *Little did I know that I would experience a similar doomed love story.*

He showed up at her door promptly at three o'clock that dreary afternoon in March. The weather was bleak; the skies gray and the air damp; the kind that penetrates your body and chills your bones. The kind that makes you want to smell soup simmering on your stove. Frannie was pleased by his appearance, but only through the eyes of a businesswoman. At first. Her only concerns were his gardening skills and dependability. The interview was informal and brief. He spoke English well but his Italian accent was heavy and inexplicably intoxicating.

"Thank you so much, Miss Oliveri. This job be good for me. I no mind do carpentry all day. My cousin, he need help, but my hands, they like work in earth, bring life later. Feel good," he said, tapping his heart.

"Yes, I know the feeling, Mr. Giannetta. I enjoy it too, but with two restaurants to manage, I can't find enough time for gardening."

"Please, call me Sergio. In my country, when someone say 'Mr. Giannetta,' they refer to my father. But you, since you be my boss, I call you Miss Oliveri."

She smiled at him and brushed it off. "That won't be necessary. Everyone calls me Frannie and believe me, I won't think you're disrespectful if you use my first name."

Sergio tipped his head. "As you wish, *Frannie*," he said. He widened his smile and flashed a set of teeth that illuminated his bronzed face. The cleft in his chin definitely accentuated his good looks, Frannie thought, and she didn't want to entertain the images showing up in her mind. His accent was doing a number on her in places that had been dormant for too long. She had always been a sucker for accents; as if they coated every word with a silky layer of sensuality.

While they walked around her property, Sergio did most of the talking. She could barely absorb what he was saying. While he made suggestions about which plants, flowers and shrubbery should be where and why, Frannie had a fleeting image of him singing to her—his face and Julio Iglesias' voice. *To all the girls I've loved before . . .*

It was only forty-eight degrees outdoors but Frannie had a sudden urge to shed her jacket. Her thoughts embarrassed her. *Are you out of your friggin' mind, girl? Shake it off!*

She interrupted him although she loved his melodious voice. "Sergio, I'm going to let you do your own thing. I'm sure I'll be pleased. When I heard about your family's restaurant in Italy and how you pride yourself on the gardens there . . . well, that's good enough for me."

He tried to look humble but pride washed over his face. "Yes, I am proud. My family, they handle restaurant mostly; like I say, I enjoy work outdoor."

"Do you have a large family? I know what it takes to run a successful restaurant."

He laughed amiably and his brows shot up. "Yes, I can see that you do. You are smart businesswoman—your partner, too—my family, they could use someone like you. Maybe we open another restaurant. But to answer your question, no, my family not particularly large. I have younger brother, he married with two children, and my sister. She older, but never marry." He lifted his shoulders as if he couldn't understand why. "A pretty lady, my sister," he added. "Big heart, but big temper, too."

Something about the way he said it—something like love in his heart and an apology tugging his lips—gave Frannie the distinct impression there was a family story hidden behind those silvery gray eyes.

If so, it was none of her business, so she let it drop. Instead, she led him towards the back of the house. Benny, her golden retriever, came alive from inside his pen. He gave Sergio one of his *Who the hell are you and what the hell are you doing here?* barks until Frannie calmed him.

Sergio then looked at her with a bemused smile. "I knew you have dog, but children?"

Frannie laughed, realizing Heather's swing set confused him. "Oh, no, that stage passed me by, I'm afraid. I put that set up for my cousin's baby. I take care of her once in a while. She loves it. And soon Glory's baby can enjoy it when he's a few months older."

"Oh, yes, Glory. Nice woman." He shook his head. "Such tragedy for her and baby. But maybe a blessing she has baby, yes?"

Frannie was about to acquiesce, but her innate honesty surfaced. "In a way, yes. She adores that little boy, but sometimes with a blessing comes hardship and sadness. She has the responsibility of raising him alone and knowing that he'll never see his real father—never feel his father's love. That won't be an easy job for Glory; especially when he reaches his teens. Our teenagers are so rebellious—"

Sergio laughed and rolled his eyes. "I'm sorry, but you say 'our' teenagers. I can tell you first-hand that not just here in America. Italy too is same. All over, I think."

"Oh? When you say 'first-hand,' are you saying you were one of those rebellious teens?" she asked teasingly.

He fingered his chin and gave it some thought. "I make my mamma crazy." He gave her a rueful smile circling a finger at his temple. "But pappa," he said, shaking a finger, "we watch out for pappa; he tough man."

She laughed with him this time. "Oh, you don't have to explain. I've seen my share of tough Italian men in my lifetime. But not my father. In his eyes we were angels. But my mother, although she was good—very loving—she would take the clothes off her back for us, but if you gave her a hard time . . ." She wiggled her eyebrows. "You talk about 'tough'; my mother was the tough one!"

"You say was. You mamma and pappa *morte*—die?"

"Oh, no, they're both alive and healthy, thank God." She put her hands together in prayer. "I said 'was' because I meant when my sister and I were growing up."

"Well, they do good job with you. I can tell."

Frannie felt her cheeks flush. "What do you mean? How can you tell? You don't even know me." She knew she was encouraging this conversation and maybe even fishing for compliments, but she felt powerless to stop. All she knew was she was enjoying his company—not to mention the pulsating heat his company triggered off. She felt as if someone had just lit the pilot light inside her body, inflaming all her parts. All the *wrong* parts. Now she had a feathery tickle in her throat that she hadn't felt since she met Wade. Mr. Perfect.

"I know you." He gave her an assuring nod. "In here, I know you." He tapped his heart again. "Like I say, your parents, they do good job. Make good person with kind heart. And pretty face, too." He quickly sliced the air as if to cut away his words. "Forgive me, maybe I say too much. I mean in nice way, believe me."

She waved off his apology. "It's okay. I *do* believe you. And I can say the same about your parents. They raised you to be a respectful, polite man; hard-working and well-mannered. I heard all good things about you before today. If you hadn't been so highly recommended, you wouldn't be here. It's a pleasure to know you, Sergio." She summed it up with a nod and a warm smile, then cupped a hand over her mouth and whispered, "And off the record, we women enjoy a polite compliment once in a while."

He laughed again and when his white teeth flashed those flames inside her shot up awakening more dormant body parts.

"Thank you, Frannie. You be good friend to me, I think, yes?" He offered his hand and she froze, wondering if his last comment was as innocent as it sounded. She also wondered if she *wanted* it to be innocent.

She shook his extended hand, hoping he couldn't read in her eyes what she was feeling elsewhere.

Frannie took her dreams to the next levels—like a stairway to the stars. When she got to the part where his arms were around her for the first time and she felt the sweetness of his kiss, she let the memory linger. She fell asleep with a hint of a smile while one lonely tear stained her face.

# Chapter Fifteen

Glory was pleasantly surprised that Sunday morning. Danny had slept until 7:30, allowing her five hours of uninterrupted sleep. Ordinarily, he was wide awake and bouncing in his crib by 6:00 a.m. She walked through the living room to check on Frannie, but she was long gone, the sheets stripped from the sofabed, the blankets folded, the bed closed. Glory smiled remembering how good it felt to sip wine and have a good heart-to-heart with her best friend. Most of the time they didn't solve anything but felt as if they'd lost a hundred pounds just talking out their problems.

Marion Landis had alleviated a chunk of pressure for Glory when she cheerfully offered to babysit the three weekend nights on an ongoing basis. "You can use the help," she had said, "and I can use the money."

The woman's offer couldn't have come at a more opportune time, but that didn't mean Glory's problem was solved. After Danny was born, people were so sympathetic about Alex's death that babysitting offers came in abundance. And although she had tried a few, some simply didn't work out. She either let them go as tactfully and gracefully as possible, or they grew bored or restless and quit on their own.

It had troubled Glory that Danny so often was in the arms of strangers. When she first learned she was pregnant, her life was already insanely busy juggling the demands of Amore Evenings and her *Glorious Cooking* column at the same time. True, it had been a pleasant challenge and very satisfying knowing that so far all those demands had been met. And she'd had a small taste of infant care—a crash course would more aptly describe it—when she helped

Frannie care for Heather, Suzanne's baby, while Suzanne was hospitalized, but she had no idea how time-consuming a tiny baby could be on a full-time basis.

When Danny was born, as thrilled as Glory was, she was apprehensive about whether she could function successfully with three major responsibilities. But when she first learned of her pregnancy, she had never concerned herself with its ramifications. She was too happy and excited to give much thought to potential problems. And of course she was able to allay her fears knowing she had Alex to depend on. He had been a tremendous help to her and Frannie when Amore Evening's needs became overwhelming. She never dreamed he would die before their baby was born! One small comfort, though, was that when he learned they would soon become parents, Alex had the foresight to make a new will. He provided well for both Glory and Danny. She'd never have to worry about her son's financial security.

It still made her crazy every time she thought of that horrific night—how one second of madness from a loudmouth drunk snuffed out Alex's life. And when the first waves of denial, hysteria and self-pity passed, it was her family—the family she had met only four years ago—that came to her rescue. Mostly her dad. But if Dan's attraction to her obstetrician was to continue, it looked like Danny would be denied his grandpa as well as his daddy.

Danny's big, chubby-cheeked smile and outstretched arms broke Glory's somber mood. "Hey, how's my apple cheeks this morning?" she said as she lifted him out of his crib. How she loved the feel of his cheek against hers! That early morning softness and special baby fragrance no perfume could ever match.

She changed his wet diaper and put him in his highchair for his fruit and cereal breakfast. "So little man, what are we going to do this morning before mommy goes to work? It looks like we're not going to grandpa's house or anywhere else today." She hadn't thought about it before, but realized now that neither her dad nor her sister Vanessa had called yesterday. The family often met on Sunday mornings for an early breakfast at one of their houses or a late one at Amore Breakfast when the crowd thinned out.

The phone rang and she eyed it curiously. No one ever called this early in the morning and a shiver ran through her. She worried abnormally about her father; as though she wanted him to live an extra thirty-five years to make up their loss.

"It's me, Glory, Wanda. Vanessa's in the shower and asked me to call you. We were out with friends last night and came home too late to call. Can you do breakfast today? Are you free?"

"Am I free?" she asked back, mocking the question. "I'll have to check my calendar. I have such a busy social life." Wanda's silence weighed heavily on Glory's conscience. *Here comes that damn self-pity again.* She immediately changed her tone. "I'm sorry, Wanda. My mouth gets ahead of me sometimes. Sure I can do breakfast. Are we eating out or in? Want to come here? Now that I'm a hotshot restaurateur, handling six or seven is a snap for me!"

Wanda paused a few seconds too long. "Well, actually you'll only be four today, but that doesn't include me. Amy and Todd are joining you and Vanessa."

"And not you and Mitch? What is this—a family affair? Our dad's coming too, right?"

"No, your dad can't make it today, Glory."

A snarl slipped out in Glory's voice. "It figures. I don't think I have to ask why."

"C'mon, Glory, be fair." This from Vanessa, who had obviously grabbed the phone from Wanda. "He joined us last week and the week before. And yes, he is seeing Jessica, but only because she has to be at the hospital at 11:00, so he can't see her later."

"He can't see me later either. I have to be in the restaurant at 2:00."

"So he'll see you during the week. You know he always does."

"Yes, he always *did,*" Glory answered curtly.

Vanessa let it slide, knowing this would all come to a head later. Glory needed help big time with this possessive jealousy. "Let's do it here. I have a lot of stuff that'll go to waste if I don't cook it up. I can make a huge omelet and throw it all in. How does ten o'clock sound?"

Glory put the smile back in her voice. "Ten it is. See you later."

# Chapter Sixteen

Jessica Branson's home was nestled in a thickness of pine trees, a good distance away from the hub of the village. Dan was captivated by its tranquility and natural beauty, but surprised that such a gregarious woman would choose to live so isolated.

When she came to the doorway, he felt warm all over. Dressed in a lemon-yellow gauzy slack outfit, the luminous sight of her reminded Dan of glorious daybreaks and lazy summer afternoons.

"I'm sorry. Have you been here long? I was out on the back porch tending to my plants before they die of thirst. Sometimes I don't hear the bell, especially if I'm listening to music."

"No apology necessary. I've only been here about thirty seconds," he said pleasantly," and I like Andrea Bocelli too."

"Oh, good. Then I can leave him on. I love hearing his voice resonate through my house." She lifted a finger. "But let me go lower it so we can talk."

Dan watched her as she walked into the library to turn down the volume. The room was clam-shaped, and a cursory glance revealed that the shelves on all three walls were filled mostly with medical books. There was ample room for the two massive mahogany desks; one of which had obviously belonged to her late husband. Compared to her desk, which was cluttered with several neatly stacked piles of paper, his was highly polished and chillingly devoid of activity. It was as if someone had stamped it "Deceased," like Louise's closet in his bedroom.

Jessica emerged from the library with a hand extended. Dan accepted it as cordially as she had offered it, but he hadn't expected the physical charge that came with it. "Come, I set us up on the back porch," she said. "It's shady and pleasant there in the mornings. You can enjoy the sun without having it cook your skin."

They sat at a glass-topped white wicker table, surrounded by an eclectic mix of potted plants and flowers. The table was set with fine china and snow-white cloth napkins trimmed with lace. She poured orange juice into Waterford crystal glasses and handed him one. A platter of fresh summer fruit served as their centerpiece. She uncovered a stack of waffles that had been warming on a tray.

"Jessica, I feel terrible to have put you to all this trouble," Dan said. "Especially since you have a long day ahead of you at the hospital. You didn't have to fuss for me. I can drink and eat from paper cups and dishes. And you could have fed me two slices of toast instead of waffles. I'm easy, and besides, it's the company I enjoy more than anything."

She pooh-poohed him with a hand wave. "Oh, be quiet and dig in. Believe me, if I didn't want to do it, I wouldn't have. But first of all, you mentioned how you love the waffles at Amore Breakfast and I had this waffle iron taking up space in my cabinet for years! I was glad to put it to use. As for the china . . ." She paused and fingered the delicate tea cup. A sad smile crossed her face. "This is my mother's Limoges. She'd be pleased to see me using it." She lifted her gaze to meet his and brightened her smile. "So which would you prefer on your waffles—blueberries or strawberries?"

Dan glanced indecisively at the berries and pursed his lips. "They both look good . . ."

"Yes, I agree. Why don't we have a little of each?" She topped the waffles with generous portions. Dan's eyes widened in anticipation as he watched the juices drizzle. Jessica laughed. "You look like a kid in a candy shop. I take it you don't treat yourself to this kind of breakfast too often? What do you usually eat?"

Dan wrinkled his nose. "Oh, boring healthy stuff, like bran cereal or oatmeal. I try to watch my weight and eat sensibly," he said, without wanting to discuss why. Since they met, he never once mentioned anything about his heart attack.

But Jessica surprised him. "I'm sorry. As a doctor I should know better, but as a woman I wanted to serve you something you'd enjoy." What she really meant but didn't say was *why* she had decided on waffles. She had based her decision on the old adage, *The way to a man's heart is through his stomach.* "You had a heart attack awhile back, didn't you, Dan? That's why you watch your diet, correct?"

Dan tried to laugh it off. He looked down at his waffles with less enthusiasm now. "Yes, I did, but I have to relax my self-discipline every now and then or I'll crack under the strain. On a daily basis, I'm conscientious about it, though. I try." He broke into a grin. "So let's forget about it for now so we can both enjoy our breakfast without thinking about fat and calories."

"Good idea!" Jessica said, sorry she had mentioned his heart attack. She speared her waffle and he followed her lead. While they ate their conversation was pleasant but impersonal. When it wound down leaving an uncomfortable silence, Dan asked, "Who told you about my heart attack, Jessica?"

"No one told me recently," she said, stressing the *recently.* She didn't want him thinking she might have been warned against getting involved with him. "It was your daughter, actually. I had a sudden flashback of the day your grandson was born. We got into a little conversation in the delivery room before her contractions grabbed all her attention." She gave him a slanted smile implying that men could never fully understand labor pains, being denied the dubious privilege of experiencing childbirth themselves.

Dan laughed. "How did the subject of my health fit into that scene? Do you remember?"

"Sure. She reminded me to keep you posted about her and the baby. She was afraid if it took too long, you'd be stressed out worrying. And that led into the story of how you were hospitalized with injuries sustained in a motorcycle accident and the heart attack that followed."

Dan cut another wedge off his waffle and dipped it in the blueberry syrup that had pooled on his plate. He chewed it in silence, savoring its flavor, then smiled ruefully. "She worries about me too much, my poor daughter. But she has good reason, I guess."

"You mean since she lost Alex?"

"Definitely more so since then, but she worried too much even before that. I'm sure it has something to do with the fact that we were unknown to each other for thirty-five years."

Jessica drew a breath and her gaze was veiled with sentimentality. "Ever since you told me that the other night, I can't stop thinking about it. What a beautiful, touching story! It could have had a tragic ending, with all that happened afterwards. Think about it: your motorcycle accident, your heart attack and the worst of them all—her horrifying experience with that deranged killer. It sounds like a good plot for a novel, but not in real life."

Dan kept his mouth occupied with his food, but he'd eaten enough, so he pushed aside his plate and clasped his hands on the table. "I hate to get into this, Jessica, but maybe we should." He heaved a sigh. "Does it bother you, Jessica, that I had a heart attack? The damage was minimal. My cardiologist is very optimistic. He assures me he sees no indication that I can't live to be an old man as long as I take care of myself."

Jessica's face grew serious. She appeared to be carefully constructing her words before answering. The awkwardness made Dan uncomfortable, so he jumped in. "I apologize if my question is premature or perhaps presumptuous; after all we've only seen each other a few times. But right now all I know is I'd like to continue seeing you. If you don't want to, for whatever reason—"

"Stop, Dan. Don't waste your breath or struggle with words." She reached for his hand and held it. "I enjoy your company very much. Nothing would please me more than to continue this relationship. But I too have concerns—*baggage* as they might label it today. I don't think I need to remind you that I'm a doctor with a busy practice. There will be many occasions when you'll have to take a back seat, so to speak. Can you handle that?"

Dan placed his free hand over hers which was still laced with his. "What's that saying about quality time being better than quantity time?"

The smile she returned seemed so replete with promise that Dan had to summon all his willpower to resist getting up to kiss her.

Instead, he sealed their understanding with a squeeze of her hand.

# Chapter Seventeen

By Monday afternoon, Frannie still hadn't heard from Suzanne. She could only expect the worst. If it had turned out well, she would have called immediately, anxious to share the news.

Frannie had left her mom in charge of Heather after she left for Amore Breakfast Saturday morning, but Tess said Suzanne hadn't said a word other than the play was great and she had enjoyed having a Friday night off.

The suspense was killing Frannie and although she didn't feel optimistic, there was always hope until she heard for sure. Maybe Suzanne never got a chance to call over the weekend. With Frannie working mornings and nights in her restaurants, and Suzanne working evenings along with the demands of a two-year-old, it was possible that the opportunity never presented itself.

She had a million things to do this afternoon, but she couldn't rest wondering what had happened between Suzanne and Rob. As she unlocked her door, she decided that calling Suzanne would be her number one priority. And it wasn't as if she were sticking her nose where it didn't belong. After all, once Suzanne had confided the trouble between them, she couldn't leave her hanging like this!

She took a few minutes to play with Benny before putting him out in his pen. When she returned, she immediately poured herself a glass of iced tea, sat in her kitchen and picked up her phone. "You have two new messages," the recorded voice said.

Frannie pressed the button to listen before making her call. The first message stiffened her:

"Frannie, it's me. I know you're at Amore now, but I've been thinking about you day and night since we spoke. Look babe, I was hoping you cooled off since then, and maybe you'd give me a chance to see you—just to talk, I promise. I won't care if you scream your head off, as long as you give me a chance to speak my piece. What do you say, babe? I know you have a big heart, so use it."

He left his cell number, and as angry as she was at the sound of his voice, she wrote it down, then listened to her next message:

"Frannie, I know you asked me to let you know how everything turned out, but I wasn't in the mood to talk about it, and I'm still not. As you probably guessed, we couldn't work it out. So that's it. It's over. End of story. And you don't have to call me back, there's really nothing to say."

Frannie heard the emotional pain in Suzanne's voice and she cringed imagining her despair. The anger Wade's call had generated only moments ago had dissipated as swiftly as it had risen. She felt an emptiness herself, knowing there wasn't a darn thing she could do to help Suzanne. She and Rob had reached an impasse, and pondering both positions, Frannie saw no possible way they could overcome this hurdle.

Despite the hopelessness of the situation, she picked up the phone anyway, then stopped before completing the call. A minute later Frannie was in her car again, on her way to Suzanne's apartment. "What the hell," she mumbled, "if I can't help her, at least I can hug her."

* * *

Suzanne opened the door with sopping wet hair and a dryer in her hand. She didn't look too eager to let Frannie in. "I figured you'd call me anyway even though I told you not to, but I didn't think you'd show up at my door again like last week." With a defeated sigh, she waved her inside.

"I was about to call, but you would have tried to talk me out of coming. I assumed you'd be home since you have to leave for work soon, right?"

"I start at 5:00 today, but I leave at 4:15 to allow time to drop Heather off at Kim's."

Their eyes locked at the mention of Kim's name.

"If you want to talk, Frannie, you'll have to come into my bedroom. When Heather's napping, that's where I dry my hair. But there's really nothing to say. Rob and I are a dead issue now. Neither one of us would budge and he wanted no part of marriage unless I named the father. To tell you the truth, I don't blame him one bit, but you and I know I have good reason to clam up." She turned off the dryer and lowered her voice. "The whole mess is my own fault. From day one with Rob I knew deep down that it could end like this. But in the beginning who ever thought we'd get serious? We were just friends, had a lot in common in the hospital. We loved being together. Then all of a sudden . . ." She snapped her fingers. "One kiss and the whole scene changes." She paused to brush all her damp hair up and secure it with a pony tail holder. "Like I said, I have no one to blame but myself. I should have stopped it right then and there—from that first kiss when I realized this was more than a great friendship. I loved the guy! In my whole life I never felt for any guy what I felt for Rob—what I *feel* for Rob." She choked up and wiped her eyes with her sleeve. "Don't get me started, Frannie. I can't go to work with bloodshot eyes." She lifted a brow and tried to smile. "And God forbid Kim should notice and ask if I'm okay, I'll really lose it!"

Suzanne had gotten herself so worked up she never realized that she had been doing all the talking. When it dawned on her, she laughed a little. "There I go rambling on again, feeling sorry for myself."

"Forget it. We all have those moments. It's my fault, anyway. Maybe I shouldn't have come. I still have no solutions or ideas . . . I just thought you'd need a hug."

Frannie opened her arms and Suzanne had a good cry on her shoulder. Frannie cried with her, but bit her lip and kept her tears silent.

The rocking sound coming from Heather's room broke their somber mood. "That's her. She always stands up and bounces when she first wakes up. But she'll be calling me before you can count to ten."

Frannie laughed, glad for Heather's interruption. "Finish getting ready. I'll get her."

In Suzanne's cramped kitchen, Frannie sat Heather in her lap and read stories to her while Suzanne got dressed for work. When she came out to join them she seemed calm and her eyes had no tell-tale signs. Frannie studied her a few seconds to make sure she was okay, then said, "Suzanne, I don't want to upset you again, but I never got to ask—how did you leave it off? Peacefully? In anger? Has he called at all since then?" She laughed and shook her head when she realized how she sounded. "Listen to me! Shooting questions faster than flying bullets. You can tell me to mind my business whenever you want, Suzanne, but I can't help it. I care about you—both you and Heather."

Suzanne gave her a twisted smile. "I care about us too! That's why I've been crying so much lately. And to answer your questions, no, he hasn't called nor do I expect him to. When he left that night, he wasn't angry. It was more like defeated. He told me to keep my secret and he was sorry he caused me all this pain. Then he added if we ever need him, he'd always be there for us." She shook her head to knock out the memory. "I swear, Frannie, you should have seen Heather and Rob together all these months. She always went nuts when he showed up. And he adored her . . . was always so affectionate. Anyone looking would have thought he was her father—her real father." Her smile washed away.

Frannie didn't know what to say to her. From what Suzanne had described, their situation didn't sound promising. She didn't want to give her false hopes, but neither did she want to sound cold and insensitive. After a pensive pause, she said, "Look, Suzanne, don't give up yet. Put yourself in Rob's shoes; it can't be easy for him. Give him a little time. Who knows? Maybe after awhile, he'll give in rather than lose you and Heather. So don't speak about him in the past tense yet. I'm still hoping for some kind of miracle."

Suzanne gave her a cynical frown. "How many miracles can we expect God to give me? He already did His thing when that road collapsed."

"Ain't that the truth!" Frannie said. "But we can ask."

# Chapter Eighteen

Rob and his grandpa Dennis had a 7:00 a.m. tee-off time at The Cape Neddick Country Club, but today Rob's heart wasn't into golf. He would never consider, however, disappointing his grandfather. Dennis not only looked forward to getting out on the course, but Rob knew how he loved spending Thursday mornings with him.

As always, Dennis was standing on his front porch wearing his red plaid knee-length shorts, white collared shirt and his signature Sox hat; the same "lucky" hat he wore everywhere except church on Sundays. His golf clubs were already out in the driveway, leaning against the garage door. Dennis greeted his grandson with a great big smile and a mock salute. Rob loved the way his cheeks popped out when he smiled, like two polished apples. It tugged at his heartstrings to watch him and to know the old guy was crazy about him. The feeling was certainly mutual. It did his heart good to know he could give his grandpa pleasure so easily. All he had to do was show up.

"What's going on, Rob? Everything okay?" Dennis asked once they were on their way.

"Sure, I'm okay. Why are you looking at me like that?"

Dennis laughed. "What do you mean 'like that'? You're my grandson and I love you. Can't I look at you if I want to? I haven't seen you for a week and you usually call me in between, but you skipped this week."

"Ah, so that explains the look. I'm sorry, Gramps, I just had a crazy week. It dawned on me only last night that I forgot to call, but I figured I'd see you today—"

Dennis raised a hand. "Don't bother to explain, it's no big deal. As long as you're okay, Robbie, you're allowed to forget once in a while. As long as you don't forget our Thursday morning golf," he kidded.

"Don't worry, Gramps. It'll never happen unless we get rained out. I look forward to it as much as you do."

They got through fifteen holes before the sun pulled a disappearing act behind a string of clouds. By the time they reached the eighteenth hole, they were showered by a faint drizzle, a pleasant respite from the sweltering July heat.

Lunch at the clubhouse topped off their morning where they usually met and joined friends. "The guys are still out, I guess," Rob said. "Want to eat or hang around and wait?"

"No, let's sit down and order. I'm starved! If they come off soon, they can join us."

Without asking, Karen, their waitress, brought over two tall glasses of lemonade, as she did every week. "The seafood salad looks good today, guys, if you ask me."

Dennis handed her the menu, not bothering to look it over. "We always trust your recommendation, Karen. That sounds good to me. I'll take it on rye."

"Same for me," Rob said. "But I'll have it in a wrap with sweet potato fries instead of the usual."

Golf remained the focal point of their conversation while they waited for their food. It shifted from golf to baseball where it stayed until their appetites sated. Dennis pushed his plate aside and reached for his lemonade again. He patted his full stomach and grinned. "That was a great lunch, but I ate too many damn fries."

Rob laughed. "They're hard to resist, I know. Look at me," he said, sweeping a hand over his plate. "I left half of mine, but only because I have to watch myself. Otherwise I could polish them off without a problem. But I don't shed the pounds as easily as I used to."

Dennis felt his heart sink a little and he closed his eyes a second. Although his grandson was still remarkably athletic with the prosthesis that had replaced his right foot, he'd had to accept the limitations of his handicap. He immediately forced the smile back on his face and asked, "So outside of the sports world, what else is new? How's Suzanne and her beautiful little girl?"

Now it was Rob's turn to avoid eye contact. He opened his mouth to say, *They're fine,* and try to cut it off there. But he hated lying to his grandfather. And even if he tried, he'd never get away with it.

Dennis' eyebrows furrowed. "Uh-oh, something's wrong. I can see it written all over your face. What is it—can you tell me?"

Rob glanced around. The place had filled up fast since they came in and he eyed some of their golf buddies outside loading their clubs into their cars. They'd be in for lunch momentarily and he suddenly wasn't in the mood to be sociable. Especially since they'd probably ask the same seemingly innocuous question just to be polite. "Let's get the check. It's too crowded in here," Rob said, signaling Karen.

Dennis was getting bad vibes. *Since when is my Robbie bothered by crowds? He's always been the friendliest guy who can strike up a conversation with anyone.*

They spoke little on the ride back, both keeping their conversation on the safe ground of sports. When they got back to the house, Rob carried his grandfather's clubs back into the garage and was about to make an excuse for a fast exit. "Come in for a few minutes. What's your rush?" Dennis asked, his expression pleading.

Rob blew a breath and gave him a rueful smile. He knew when he was defeated.

"You don't have to talk to me if you really don't want to," Dennis said when they were both seated out on the front porch.

Rob laughed. "Yeah, sure. Why try? You'd squeeze it out of me eventually."

Dennis didn't share the laughter. He face held only concern. "No, not if it's too personal. Sure, I'd worry wondering what's going on, but I'd never push."

"Well, it *is* personal, but—"

"Then don't tell me. Forget it." Dennis reached over and squeezed Rob's hand. "I don't want to invade your privacy. Sometimes I forget that you're not a little boy anymore." He gave Rob a reminiscent smile and raised his eyes to heaven, as if wishing to recapture those childhood years. "I don't have a right to meddle in your affairs anymore. My eyes see you as a grown man, but my heart still sees you as that little boy in his first Little League uniform." He laughed at the memory. "It was so big on you. You were lost in it. They didn't have a size small enough."

Rob nodded and took a sentimental moment to drift back to those early years. His memories were not as vivid as his grandfather's, but he'd always remember how proud he was wearing that baggy uniform.

Reluctantly he let the image fade away, folded his arms and looked up at Dennis. "My body may be full-grown—a little too full grown these days, Gramps, but inside I'm still that little kid who'll always need his grandpa's love and advice. So let me see if I can give you the crux of my problem without going into too much detail."

"Don't spare the details for my sake, Robbie. I have nothing important to do today. So if you need to spill it all out, I'm all ears." He patted Rob's hand. "Just remember, all romances stumble over rocky roads now and then. If you both love each other, you'll get back on the right path eventually."

Rob leaned forward and steepled his fingers, maintaining a downward gaze. "That generalization is usually true, Gramps, if both parties are willing to compromise. That's not the case with me and Suzanne."

Dennis smacked his knee. "Why not? Don't tell me you two are so stubborn you're willing to lose each other instead?"

"It's not that simple, Grandpa. The issue that needs compromise is too important."

Dennis recognized the depth of Rob's problem before hearing it. Worry lines rippled across his forehead. He said nothing, waited for Rob to continue.

"I asked Suzanne to marry me—" He put a hand up to stop the wide-eyed delight that had erased Dennis' worry lines. "Wait, Gramps. Hear me out. As I said, it's not that simple. I also told her I'd want to adopt Heather. Whoever her father is, he obviously doesn't give a damn, but we'd still have to dig him up out of his hole and get him to sign off." Rob took a long pause. The more he thought about it—and now spoke about it—the more hopeless it sounded.

"And?" Without hearing the whole story, Dennis was already growing sick with the realization that this would indeed be a major problem.

"And she absolutely refuses to disclose the SOB's name. She's so adamant that it scares me. Before I proposed, neither one of us ever brought up the subject of the guy's identity. For me it turned my stomach to think that some creep—a stranger she picked up in a bar—" He squeezed his eyes shut to erase the ugly image. "But I tried to get past it. She had her share of hard knocks . . . made plenty of mistakes. But after her mom died she was like a lost soul; a zombie, everyone says, and who did she have? A father who was half-dead himself from alcoholism."

"Is it possible, Robbie, that she *really* doesn't know— doesn't remember the guy? I hate to think it, but if she was stoned at the time, maybe it's all a blur to her."

Rob answered with a painful frown. "I tried to sell myself that scenario, but I always suspected that was not the case. Especially lately. You had to see her face when I was insisting she tell me his name. She was like a brick wall you couldn't penetrate. That's when I got *really* suspicious. I have a feeling it's somebody I might know. Maybe some local guy she's covering for. Who knows?" He waved it off with an air of disdain and hopelessness.

"But she lived in New York when she became pregnant. She never came home. Not that we know of. It had to be somebody there."

"Maybe. I even imagined that it was some politician or celebrity she had a fling with and was trying to protect. But even if she didn't come home—and we can't be sure of that—the guy might have taken a ride down to see her. Either way, the bottom line is, she knows the guy and she's not talking, no matter what price she has to pay." He stood up, stuffed his hands in his pockets and paced. "I'm sorry, Gramps, I might be able to close my eyes to sins of her past, but I can't enter a marriage built on secrets and lies."

Dennis stared out at his garden a few seconds before speaking. "I have a lot of affection for that girl, Robbie. I always felt that she was right for you, despite her history. She's basically a good person and certainly a good mother, but I'm afraid I have to agree. Unless she's totally honest with you, I don't see how you can patch this up."

Dennis' eyes glazed over with tears. He put a hand on Rob's shoulder and squeezed.

Rob hugged him and blinked away his own tears.

# Chapter Nineteen

The Madison children, minus their father, were enjoying breakfast on Glory's deck overlooking Perkin's Cove, comfortably shaded by a flowered umbrella.

Vanessa opened the conversation. "I'm sorry we had to cancel out Sunday at the last minute—"

"Don't share the blame, Vanessa," Wanda said. "It was my fault. Although in fairness to me, how was I supposed to know my two aunts were going to invite themselves for an overnight stay?" She tightened her lips and shook her head. "What nerve! Every time I think of it . . ."

Vanessa cupped her hand over her mouth and laughed. "I guess it's obvious Wanda has no love for these aunts."

"Why should I? As an adult I only saw them at weddings and funerals and I have no recollection of them in my childhood. Believe me, they just planned their surprise visit out of curiosity. They wanted a closer look at our gay relationship. *My dear mother*, too, had no qualms about telling me how they reacted when they heard. They were 'shocked and horrified,' she said." Wanda laughed bitterly. "As if I care what they think. They're the last people in the world anyone should emulate."

Vanessa, surprisingly, was smiling ear-to-ear. "She gets a little worked up," she said to Glory, Amy and Todd. "We have to let her blow off steam."

"I don't blame her," Glory said, then turned to Wanda. "If they were presumptuous enough to show up unexpectedly, why didn't you make an excuse and politely send them away?"

"That's why I'm pissed off! I always have a big mouth after the moment passes, but when it's actually happening, I freeze . . . don't have the guts to react as I should."

Todd kept eating his omelet while the four women got into it. He helped himself to a banana nut muffin until they had exhausted the subject of Wanda's aunts and all other gossip-hungry malcontents who thrive on causing misery for others. He cleared his throat and they got the message. Everyone laughed and apologized for leaving him out.

"You didn't leave me out. I *chose* to exclude myself from the discussion. I'm not going to sit here and butt heads with four women. But actually, I agreed with everything you said, so why bother?" He turned to Glory. "Hey, how long is Danny going to sleep? I'd like to see him before I have to leave."

"He might be good for another half hour or more," Glory answered. "Why? Are you in a hurry today?"

"I have to see somebody later." He glanced at his wristwatch. "I only have about a half hour to spare."

Vanessa caught the look he darted her way and acknowledged the hint with a discreet nod. "I talked to Dad last night," she said, capturing everyone's attention. "Well, there's one thing I'll say for Jessica Branson . . ." She lifted her eyebrows and smiled. "If she's responsible for boosting his spirits like this, she can't be all bad."

"Who said she's bad?" This from Amy, who had tried to cancel out earlier. She was uncomfortable being part of this conspiracy—well-meaning or not—but Todd had presented a good argument and convinced her to come. If Glory was not receptive to their efforts, they'd all back off and hope for the best.

"No one said she's bad. Where did that come from?" Glory said. "Jessica Branson is a respected and well-liked doctor. I chose her to deliver Danny because she was highly recommended. On a professional level, I doubt anyone would have anything *bad* to say about her." Now that Glory had stressed the positives, she cleared her throat and her expression made a swift change. "Whether she's good or bad for Dad, though, is a troubling thought which remains to be seen. I just don't want him hurt. He's been through enough. And I'm afraid he might be walking on thin ice with her." She pursed her lips, making a convincing performance that her concern was strictly limited to her father's vulnerability.

"Why are you looking only at the down side?" Todd asked. "First of all, all this worry is unwarranted at this point. Geez! They only went out a couple of times. It could be over before it amounts to anything. Let's look at the big picture. She's a successful physician with a busy practice. Dad only has his job with Finestkind Scenic Tours. And we all know that's seasonal and subject to weather conditions. He hasn't said anything yet, but maybe this year he'll have the courage to run the Florida tour boat again this year. It'll be tough without Mom at his side, but they had friends there. I could understand why he couldn't deal with it last season; it was so soon after Mom's death. But he might feel up to going down this year. Which would leave this thing with his doctor friend to die a quick death."

Amy didn't like the groundwork being set. Her siblings thought it might work to defuse Glory's jealousy if they all pretended to share her feelings, but in her opinion, that could have adverse effects. Yes, as the saying goes, there's power in numbers, but in this case she feared it would only serve to fan Glory's fire. "That's a strong possibility, Todd," Amy said with a skeptical frown. "*But*—and I stress the word *but*—there's also a strong possibility he won't. That business is something he and Mom built together, along with their four friends." She paused and pursed her lips. "Here comes that *but* again—but how pleasant can it be for him to do it without Mom, working out a schedule with the other two couples. The six of them shared both business and pleasure. No matter how close they were, now that he won't have Mom, Dad would feel like a fifth wheel hanging out with them. He'd ache for Mom more than ever! So what I'm saying is, don't be surprised if he asks them to buy him out and stay here in Ogunquit year-round. At least he has us here and now . . ." She shrugged and left them to fill in the blank. "Who knows?" she said, then blew a dismissive sigh.

Vanessa took the lead again. "We're all aware of the implication of Amy's 'who knows' comment, Todd. But how would you feel—be honest now—how would you feel if Dad's friendship with the doctor really takes off into a serious relationship?"

*Be honest, she says,* Todd mused. *We were supposed to exaggerate our feelings to appear empathetic to Glory. How honest is that?* He raked his long fingers through his unruly hair. "I'd feel pretty lousy, I guess. I keep imagining that one day he'll ask us to meet her, as his *friend*, not Glory's doctor. I cringe just visualizing him holding her hand or resting a hand on her shoulder." A weird feeling washed over Todd as he expressed his anticipated reaction to his dad's budding romance. He had been pouring it on thick, but as the images took shape—especially the image that flew to his parents' bedroom—he realized that he had voiced his innermost feelings. His resolve weakened. Sure, he wanted to see his father happy again; to show enthusiasm for *something*. He'd even given up tennis because, there again, he couldn't cope with pairing off with anyone other than his Louise.

"We've all had those images, Todd," Vanessa said. "I don't like them either, but I'm trying to look at this picture as an adult with an objective view. If this were happening to someone else's grieving parent, we'd be thrilled to hear he'd found someone. Still, it hurts! We keep seeing Mom's face, wondering how she'd react if she knew." She shivered at the thought and when she tried to continue, her voice cracked. One lonesome tear welled in the corner of her eye. She sniffed and pulled in a long breath. The brief display of emotion had hit her by surprise. She had thought she could handle this with complete control.

Amy took over, allowing her sister time to pull herself together. She knew well those surprise attacks of grief. They jump out at you from everywhere—like what had provoked her to break down at the supermarket. "Hey, it's okay, Vanessa," she said. "It happens to all of us, I'm sure." She laughed ruefully. "You should have seen me in the supermarket the other day. All it took to get me going was a sale on asparagus. Remember how Mom would buy several bunches, cook them all, and deliver them to all of us?" The memory prompted faraway smiles from everyone.

A silence fell where everyone seemed to wait for the next person to speak. Glory took that as her cue to fill the void. She kept her gaze lowered while she arranged the words in her mind, toying absently with her silverware. "My dear siblings," she said finally, in the warmest tone she could muster, "I love you all, but I know you well—perhaps too well. Anyone with half a brain could figure out what's happening here." She stopped and laughed. "You're all waiting to hear from me because my case is different. Has to be different. You should see your faces. Shades of that deer in headlights expression." She paused again until the guilt eased off their faces. "Well, I'll be honest. I strongly suspect this was arranged to get me to open up about Dad and *his lady.*"

"We meant well," Vanessa started to say, but Glory put a hand up. She drew a breath, not anxious to continue. "I'm sure all of you are hurting more than I am because Louise was your mother. At least I don't have to agonize over that image," she said, the latter a direct response to Todd's earlier comments about his parents' bed. "But you want the truth and I'm going to throw it out there." She crossed her arms and continued. "I'm jealous; jealous as all hell! And don't hate me for this, but you guys had him for a lifetime. Damn! We were still getting to know each other when your mom died. And please, *please* don't think I'm insensitive to that horrible shocking loss you all suffered. But for me, I felt as if I had lost him. His grief was so profound that I couldn't reach him. We could never talk the way we used to. All of the sunshine had drained from him; his life was then forever clouded. None of us—not only me—could break through. Until tragedy struck one more time." She looked up, her eyes steely, lashing out silently to God. "And let's hope that's the last time this family has to suffer through tragedy." She brought her gaze back to the table and the four attentive faces. "Isn't it ironic that it had to take Alex's death to bring Dad back to life again? Not completely, of course, but once Danny was born, at least we saw him smile again!" She squeezed her eyes closed and paused. "Bear with me. I'm trying not to cry. Don't you see how much more he meant to me after Alex died? Dad's been my crutch. And I don't have to tell you guys what it means to me having him for Danny. He loves the baby so much, and Danny will always need that fatherly love. If he's not around to spend time with him because of *her* . . ." The word slipped out coated with bitterness. She gave a hopeless shrug. "Who's going to love him as much as his grandfather?"

The question hung unanswered, then Todd posed the question, "Would you consider me for the job, Glory?"

"Oh, Todd, I'm sorry!" She got out of her chair and went to hug her brother. "Of course I'd consider you!"

"Good, so go give him a little nudge. We need to get better acquainted."

# Chapter Twenty

Frannie had always found gardening relaxing despite the physical strain on her back. But when the fruits of her labor opened up and burst into color, she forgot her aching back. Although that was way back when she had spare time to nurture her garden; when Amore Breakfast was her only responsibility. But once Amore Evenings was launched, she had to be there five or six nights a week. Spare time was a thing of the past. Not that she was complaining. She loved every insane minute. And yes, financially she was climbing to a level she never would have dreamed possible five years ago.

But they say money doesn't keep your feet warm at night. How true.

She paused at the azalea bushes Sergio had planted and her eyes grew watery. As vibrant as they were in the spring, they were as dead now as their short-lived romance. She smiled remembering how she had tried to convince herself that they were just good friends—two people who had admired and respected each other; who simply enjoyed being together.

Yeah, right! And that's why her insides went bananas at the sight, sound or *smell* of him. That husky, masculine smell that was his alone.

A commercial van pulled up in her driveway, interrupting her thoughts. Bette Jean's Florist. She knew the owner well but not the driver. She approached the van curiously, assuming he was new and somewhat lost. "Looking for someone in the area?" she asked.

The young man smiled politely. "Yes, and I believe it's you. Frannie Oliveri?"

"That's me."

"Well, these are for you." He handed her a huge bouquet of flowers arranged in an exquisite ceramic vase. She barely noticed him driving off because she couldn't wait to read the card. For the life of her, she could think of no reason anyone would send flowers. There had been no recent or upcoming occasion for celebration. Her brows furrowed but her smile widened as her anxious fingers fumbled through the cellophane wrapping. A breath caught in her throat when she pulled off the last of the cellophane, allowing her a closer look at the vase. Not only did it look like fine china, but the pattern had her heart thumping like war drums. A lacy navy blue pattern with clusters of lemons. *Very Italian.*

Her hands were shaking in unison with her thumping heart. She finally got to the card.

*Miss you. Tutti amore, S.G.*

"Oh, my God! Oh, my God!" she gasped, then kissed the card and held it to her cheek. "I miss you too, Sergio. Oh, how I miss you!" she cried aloud, then realized she was still standing in her driveway. Trembling from the shock, she went inside without taking Benny in as she had intended. She wasn't sharing this moment with anyone or any *thing.* After she had placed the flowers gently on her buffet table, she allowed her tears to spill. Like a person half-crazed with grief, she stared at the flowers, stroking them softly as though they were a part of him. She whispered through her tears. "And what is this supposed to mean—'*I miss you*'? You say only that and nothing else? Am I supposed to feel better that you miss me too?" Her voice grew louder as her emotions soared. "You come here and swell my heart with all your promises of everlasting love, then leave me forever with my heart cut out?" She had an urge to fling the vase until it broke into a million pieces. But that kind of anger brought a flashback of when she attacked her wedding photo. Not a pleasant memory. Never again, she had promised herself, would she ever submit to such a maniacal act. Instead, she sat with her head cradled in her hands, staring at the flowers.

A half hour later, her sobs had just begun to ebb when the doorbell rang.

Glory! Damn! Frannie gave her face a cursory glance in the mirror and dabbed at her eyes. They didn't look bad, considering the workout she gave them, but her cheeks and neck were all blotched up. She looked like a dalmation in Technicolor.

With a deep sigh, she opened her front door. "Don't ask," she said with a half smile.

Glory practically pushed her aside and stepped in. Danny was in her arms, sucking on his pacifier. She looked at her friend with deep concern. "What's wrong? Your face is a mess!"

Frannie forced a laugh. "Oh, thanks a lot. That'll make me feel better."

Glory peered at her with concerned curiosity. "Stop it. You know what I mean. What's going on? Why have you been crying?"

With a silent hand gesture, Frannie showed Glory the flowers, then took Danny from her arms.

Glory walked to the buffet table, her worried expression unchanged. "Who sent them?"

"Read the card."

Somewhat relieved, Glory exhaled. She wasn't sure why, but the card spoke only of love. What could be wrong with that? She sat on the edge of the sofa. "You never did finish that story about Sergio, Frannie."

"I know. I couldn't handle getting into it that night. It was late and it needed a lot more time than we had."

"To tell you the truth, I was a little hurt that you hadn't confided in me. Not only that night but right from when your affair started."

"I told you, we never had an affair; not in the true sense of the word. I have no doubt it would have come to that, but we never got the chance. It was over before I could blink my eyes."

"Oh, God, Frannie. I feel awful for you! Why didn't you ever talk to me?"

Frannie lowered her eyes. "Glory, you had so much on your plate—grieving for Alex, trying to raise Danny alone, managing a new business . . . I didn't have the heart to dump my troubles on you. Compared to yours, my problems were miniscule."

Glory shot her a stern look. "That's not the impression I got when you opened that door a few minutes ago." She glanced around the room. "Where's that shoe box you keep with toys for Danny?"

"In the hall closet. Why? He seems perfectly content."

Glory went to fetch the box filled with teething rings and assorted infant toys. "I need a supply of ammunition just in case he acts up." She spread a baby blanket on the sofa, tucked Danny in the corner and sat next to him.

"Okay. We both have to work tonight, so start talking. And no generalizing, no summarizing. So far all you told me about your mystery man—"

Frannie rolled her eyes. "He was never a mystery man. You met him."

"Yeah, right," Glory answered, folding her arms. "I met him like I met the butcher, the baker and the candlestick maker, but that doesn't mean I know the first thing about him. At the time, I never had a clue something was going on between you two. If I had known, I would have been more observant." She gave a slanted smile. "So that was more than just the hots for each other, huh?"

Frannie laughed, short but genuine. Glory had a way of putting things right on target. And her New York style delivery was always amusing. At the restaurant, she conducted herself with eloquence and poise, but when they were alone and their conversation got emotional, anyone could tell where she was born and raised. Out fell The Brooklyn Bridge.

Frannie raked her fingers through her hair and cast her gaze downward into her lap. "I don't know where to begin."

"Begin at the beginning," Glory prompted. "At the part where you first surmised there was something more than business developing between you."

Frannie's smile sweetened at the memory. Sometimes she wondered who had seduced whom that rainy afternoon. Not that it mattered. Like the rain clouds that had darkened the sky and threatened to burst before Sergio could complete the day's planting, it had stormed over them before they could run for safety.

"It hit us like a sudden downpour. Actually it *was* a sudden downpour. It had only been drizzling when I came out with an umbrella and told him to pack it in for the day before the rain got serious and he got soaked. But he laughed it off, insisting he had to get the last shrub in. A little rain never hurt anyone, he said." The image reappeared with amazing clarity and Frannie's eyes lit up while she relived it. She pointed a finger to the sky. "It was as if The Big Guy up there was in a playful mood, saying 'Wanna bet?' And then, faster than a clap of thunder, it *teemed* on us. We ran for the garage, giggling like two kids, but by the time we got there we looked like two drowned rats!"

Glory laughed with her but there was something so sad about watching the joy on Frannie's face, knowing the story was destined for an unhappy ending.

"I left him there and ran inside to grab two towels." Again her eyes seemed to twinkle while she paused to savor the moment. "I threw him one and was blotting up my own hair and face when he unexpectedly yanked my towel away. His naked gray eyes were staring me down, asking all kinds of silent questions." She stepped out of the moment to look at her friend. "Glory, I can never explain how I felt—how *we* felt—in those few seconds. Like we were about to take off on a rocket, not knowing where it would land or if it would land safely."

Glory laughed, then smiled the smile one wears when watching someone else's happiness. "That's a crazy analogy, but I definitely get the picture."

Frannie's gaze returned to the flowers as she continued her story. "But there was just no stopping it. The force was too powerful. When we talked about it later, we both admitted that the feelings had been building since the day we met." She rippled her fingers. "But let me go on."

"Yes, please do. You were about to ride that rocket."

"And ride we did!" she said with a giggle, then sobered again. "I tell you, Glory, I haven't been exactly love-starved all my life, but never—and I mean *never*—" With one finger, she drew an imaginary line over the years. "Never did I experience a feeling like that first kiss. It was as if my body was completely on its own, totally out of my control."

"Complete meltdown, huh?"

"Man, you wouldn't believe how fast and furiously I melted down!" Her gaze shifted towards the garage as if it were some kind of shrine to be revered. "Before that day, who ever dreamed that my messy garage would become the setting for the most romantic experience of my life!"

*And neither did I ever imagine that Amore Evening's exquisite dining room would become the setting for Alex's senseless murder,* Glory thought but avoided Frannie's perceptive eyes.

"You can't imagine how it affects me to walk through that garage now," Frannie continued. "I try to avoid it but of course that's ridiculous. But no matter how I try to blink it away, I always see him there. That vision of him staring at me, kissing me like there was no tomorrow. It's burned in my mind. I'll never forget it—not that I want to. The memories are all I have left."

When her own words bounced back at her, Frannie winced. "Oh, Glory, there I go again. I get so wrapped up in self-pity sometimes that I forget to stop and think of the troubles and sufferings of others. Like you. I'm sorry."

"No, don't be sorry. That's exactly what I *don't* want you to do. It's worse for me if you feel you have to edit every thought and every word you say. Please don't ever hold back what you really want to pour out because you feel none of your problems measure up to Alex's death. Don't you see, Frannie, that if everyone felt that way, they'd all avoid me. And then where would I be?"

Frannie nodded. "I'm glad you see it that way. All these normalities are part of the healing process, I guess." She cleared her throat and looked at her wristwatch. "So should I go on? I'm on a roll."

They both laughed, easing out of the somber mood. "Of course! You can't stop there," Glory said.

"Well, we stood there for I don't know how long. Time gets suspended when love and desire step in without warning. We both had a tough time trying to stop our hands from exploring. I remember grabbing his hair and holding on for dear life when I felt his fingers stroking my sides . . . you know, under my arms." She shook her head. "Wow! Talk about meltdown! As it turned out, it was Sergio, not me, who put the brakes on. He pulled me down onto that antique bench I bought which is still waiting to be refinished." She twisted her face into a *least of my troubles* smirk. "Anyway, he sat there, leaning forward with his head in his hands, apologizing profusely. 'I don't know what came over me,' he said."

Glory arched her brows and grinned. "The same thing that came over you, you should have answered."

Frannie laughed. "That's pretty much what I *did* say. I could have pushed him away or slapped his face, or whatever. But I didn't. I went into his arms like I'd been hungry for them all my life. We were still sitting side by side, struggling not to touch so we could keep our heads on straight and talk it out. That's when he picked up my hand and kissed my fingertips—*every one individually.* Can you imagine? Boy, did that set off shock waves inside me! I felt like I was on fire."

Glory listened with the same anticipatory expression, as though she couldn't wait for more, but so far all the feelings Frannie described were painful reminders of her early days with Alex.

The sparkle faded from Frannie's eyes as she continued. "That day left us dumbfounded. We didn't know how to go on. Our homes were thousands of miles apart, his family, his life, his responsibilities all in Italy; all of mine here. And at that point, we were unsure of what exactly we were feeling. Was it the beginning of an affair between two friends with a strong need to know each other better? I mean physically, of course. Once he went back to Italy, would absence make the heart grow fonder? Or would it be a case of out of sight out of mind? Neither of us knew the answers. We were both groping in the dark, so to speak. All we were certain of was that while he was here, we wanted more of each other."

Glory looked bewildered. "When exactly did it begin, Frannie? How long did you have after that day in the garage before he had to rush home?"

"Only three weeks. Less really, because I didn't see him every day. We talked on the phone every night, though, and I think it was those late night calls that removed the last element of doubt. We were totally convinced after a few of those long conversations that we were deeply in love and the strong sexual feelings were simply part of the package. A normal, natural part. But love had been the catalyst, not sex."

Glory flashed a bemused but devilish smile. "What I can't understand is how you guys never hooked up, especially after the phone calls. Or was that a little white lie?"

Frannie responded with an indignant frown. "Of course not! After all the secrets you and I shared since we met, what would be the purpose?"

"Sometimes you can bare your soul with a friend; tell a whole story replete with sexual situations or innuendos, but when your story reaches the bedroom, you slam the door. Some things are just too personal. No one wants to tell or hear a play-by-play description."

Frannie laughed. "You don't believe me, do you?"

Glory's hand went up. "I didn't say that."

"So what you're saying is I can spare the details, but a simple yes or no would be in order."

Glory nodded with a smug but playful expression. "Correct, my friend. An honest answer."

"Well, the answer is a big fat *no* with a capital N! Why is that so hard to believe? It probably would have happened eventually, and I regret it now, but at the time I was trying to be so damn careful; sensible. Deep down I was afraid that if we got really serious—like marriage talk—it could never work. Not if he expected me to abandon everyone and everything I have here and live in a strange country. Sure, Italy's beautiful, but nothing compares to the good ol' U.S.A.!" She threw her hands up in defeat. "So that's pretty much why I was afraid to get involved sexually. Chances were great the closer we got, the more it would cloud my mind. I didn't want it to influence my decisions."

Glory's eyes widened with surprise. "Why do you think he could have swayed you into giving up your whole life here and moving to Italy?"

It didn't take Frannie long to ponder the question. "I think he might have tried. He always spoke with pride about his beautiful country and how I'd love it. He also alluded to how I'd 'fit right in' with their restaurant business if given the chance. Then, when he came here that night he was grief-stricken and in a state of shock. I felt terrible for him. He said his father just collapsed while working in their vegetable garden—a massive heart attack. He was only sixty. And naturally Sergio was on a guilt trip because his father died doing the job he would have been doing if he hadn't come to America. Anyway, he said he had to leave the next morning and naturally I understood he'd have to stay awhile after the funeral. His mother was in bad shape and needed him, he said. But I assumed he'd come back, not only for me, but to finish the job that brought him here. He had committed to stay with his cousin a few months to gut out and remodel his house. He had been enjoying that project and fussing with my gardens in the late afternoons; said it was like a working vacation in America."

"I imagine everything changed when his father died," Glory said. "But I do believe you're probably right that he would have tried to sway you, and—never mind."

"What?"

Glory sighed. "I was going to say—very selfishly, I admit—that I'm glad that threat is gone now. Not only because of our business partnership, but if I have to lose you too—" Involuntary tears choked her voice but she quickly pulled herself together, waving away Frannie's open arms. "No, I'm okay. I don't know where they came from. It seems I always have a river of tears waiting to gush out when I least expect them."

Frannie leaned forward and held her hand. "Don't worry. You're never going to lose me. Sergio meant a lot to me—he still does. But I'll get over him eventually. At least I hope so. I just can't pay that price for his love. End of story."

# Chapter Twenty-one

Sometimes bad weather is more welcoming than sunshine. At least it was for Dan Madison that Friday afternoon. Much to the dismay of all the tourists who looked forward to an ocean cruise, storm clouds and choppy waters forced Finestkind Scenic Tours to cancel all tours for the day.

Dan picked up the phone grinning like a kid who just won a trip to Disney World. "Hi, Jess," he said, slightly breathless. "Do you still have those three or four free hours this afternoon?"

"Sure do! Why, are you cancelled out? When I saw the weather, I was hoping you'd call."

"And I was hoping I'd get the chance to call. It was the first time I can remember praying for bad weather."

She laughed. Dan loved her adorable giggle. "That's so sweet of you to say, Dan. So what would you like to do? I'm all yours until six."

It wasn't only her suggestive words—said in jest or not—nor was it the sunshine in her voice that always lifted his spirits. This time it was its throaty sound, full of promise, that made him throw apologies up to Louise. It didn't take much to get him going these days. One smile, one sidelong glance, a breeze rippling through her silky brown hair, the sun illuminating her radiant face, the sound of her infectious laughter . . . any of these things. Or simply the thought of her.

"I thought I'd leave that to you. A late lunch, maybe? You pick the restaurant."

She paused while she gave it some thought, then said, "Do you enjoy the beach or are you strictly a sailor?"

"Are you kidding? Why do you think I settled in Maine? I love the ocean, on it or in it. And on the beach, I'm still like a kid—get a real charge out of building sand castles."

"Oh, that's great! I'm glad we have that in common. So, here's my thought: Why don't you pick me up at home about 1:30. And don't bring anything but your bathing suit. I'll grab a blanket and sand chairs."

"Well, let me pick up some sandwiches—"

"No, don't bother. Part of the pleasure of a day at the beach is eating at the food stands. Every now and then I succumb to my insatiable desire for deep fried food. But don't tell anyone; I'll deny it." She giggled a little. "My mouth is already watering."

"I could go for some crab cakes myself, but I'll settle for clam chowder and crackers." Dan said, tapping his foot as he spoke. He couldn't wait to get off the phone and get ready to see her.

"Idiot!" Jessica yelled when she hung up. "Think before you talk!" It annoyed her that as a professional, she could conduct herself with complete control, but in private she was forever tripping up. Mentioning deep fried food to Dan was like offering an ice cream sundae to a diabetic.

Dwelling on his health history dampened her mood for a while, but she shooed it off, reminding herself that he had sustained minimal damage with his heart attack. His cardiologist was impressed with his speedy recovery and gave Dan an excellent prognosis.

Jessica could not blame his health on her hesitancy to get involved.

\* \* \*

She had the firmest, smoothest body he had ever seen on a woman past fifty. Not that he had studied women's bodies while Louise was alive. But a man never loses his appreciation of femininity at its finest. It wasn't easy to hold his gaze on her face, but he managed. Especially since he allowed himself to steal a glance elsewhere every time she turned away.

"It's so darn hot and humid today I might have to brave the icy waves, even if just for a minute to cool off. I wish I had the courage to just plunge in."

"I'm game if you are," Dan said, surprised to find himself admiring the tiny lines fanning out at the corners of her eyes. Every time she laughed or smiled they spread open like the wings of an angel. "Or maybe I could stand with your towel at the shoreline, ready to wrap it around you as soon as you surface."

Again came that deep sexy voice. "That sounds tempting, but I think you should take the plunge with me. Then we can race back to our towels and beach chairs."

"You're on."

The rush of water at their feet was indeed icy and they both ran back to the dry sand. Jessica laughed. "Wow! I haven't ventured into ocean water since last summer and we forget how cold it is in July."

"The initial shock does get to you, true. But if we don't get wet we'll roast in our beach chairs, even with the umbrella shading us."

Jessica grimaced as she stepped forward, allowing the gentle foamy waves to circle her feet. She had always loved the pull of rushing sand sinking her feet. "You're absolutely right. When it's this hot, even a strong ocean breeze isn't enough to cool you. So c'mon, let's take one quick dunk." She took his hand as if it were perfectly natural to do so. Though neither allowed their eyes to meet, they took their dunk together on the count of three. Mopping the wet strands of hair from their eyes, they ran back shivering and laughing, still holding hands.

Rather than sit on the shaded sand chairs, they spread their blanket and sat, basking in the warmth of the sun and the heat generated by the closeness of their bodies. With her right hand, Jessica reached back for her sunglasses. As she turned forward again, Dan's gaze was waiting. He stared at her silently for a long moment, afraid to speak the wrong words. Time seemed suspended while they communicated with their eyes.

Jessica slipped on her sunglasses and threw her gaze out to the sea. "We'll stay awhile and then go back to my house." It was a statement; not an invitation, not a suggestion. For Jessica, as much as she wanted him, it was an admission of defeat. If this were only a sexual need she wouldn't have these haunting concerns. But there was no denying it was more than that. With each passing day, she was falling deeper and more hopelessly in love with Dan Madison.

And she had so little time for love and all the problems that come with it.

* * *

On the ride back to Jessica's house, silence hung thickly between them like fog. It was she who had initiated this—at least verbally—Jessica mused, but if they continued to see each other, how long would it take for sparks to fly, igniting out-of-control passions? Fighting it would be senseless.

"You're so quiet, Jess. You seem introspective," Dan said, darting glances at her while he drove. "Are you having second thoughts? To be honest, my whole body is pulsating just thinking of what we're about to embark on. Not only the physical part, but these strong feelings. I don't know about you, but I feel helpless; like lost in an avalanche!"

A slight smile lifted the corners of her mouth. "Second thoughts? No, just repeats of my first thoughts. Every decision we make—certainly a big one like this—is clouded with fears and anxieties." She shook her head and sighed.

"But I get so darn tired of allowing them to deny me something I want badly." She paused and their gazes locked once again.

Dan licked his dry lips and kept his eyes on the road. There was no need for Jessica to elaborate on what she wanted badly.

"And about the other part," she continued, "the 'avalanche' you described—well, I'm snowed under too. This is not just physical, Dan. Can you handle that? Or is it too much too soon?"

He smiled gently. "Jessica, I never looked forward to anything more."

* * *

Twenty minutes later, they stood at her bedroom door, frozen for the moment as if they were about to step beyond the threshold of the rest of their lives.

"Well, are you going to just stand there?" she said playfully. Her intent was to lighten the mood but her quavering voice betrayed her. "A kiss might be nice before we . . ." She wiggled her eyebrows and thumbed towards the bedroom door.

Dan released his tension with a welcome laugh which lasted only a split-second. He easily lifted her slender body and held her in his arms, lovingly, protectively, possessively. It wasn't until he kissed her that he wondered whether his heart could take it. It was already thumping wildly. He kicked the door open and the troublesome thought flew out of his head.

In the bedroom, when their hungry lips parted, Dan placed her gently on the bed. Her fingers ran through his hair and her white teeth lit up her face in the sunless room.

"Wow! Rhett Butler *hasn't* left the building!" They both laughed until Jessica turned him on his back and smothered his face with kisses.

# Chapter Twenty-two

Suzanne had promised Frannie that she'd call in a day or two, regardless of whether or not she had heard from Rob. She had been putting it off all week, not wanting to rehash it all again. With each passing day, her hopes were rapidly diminishing.

It might have been a noble and self-sacrificing act to give up the man she loved for the sake of others, but it hurt like hell. Frannie couldn't possibly understand what she had been going through without Rob—the pain, the emptiness. Sure Frannie had lost Wade, but that was different. The guy was a bigamist. Whatever love she had for him before that discovery had burned away faster than a raging fire.

She picked up the phone to call Frannie, but changed her mind when she glanced at the kitchen clock. Instead, she scooped Heather into her arms, leaving her toys sprawled on the living room floor. "You can play when we get back, sweetie. Mommy has to see cousin Frannie."

* * *

She was half hoping Frannie would be gone when she reached Amore Breakfast. It was almost two o'clock and the restaurant was obviously closed since not a single person lingered on the porch and the door was locked.

But Frannie's car was in her usual parking space, so Suzanne couldn't simply drive away. She parked and knocked on the door.

"Hey! What a surprise!" Frannie said, truly glad to see her. "I've been thinking about you constantly since Monday, but—" She stopped short and checked the kitchen to make certain the last of her cleanup crew had left. "Okay, we're alone. You just caught me. I was about to leave too. Sit down, Suzanne, and talk to me. How have you been doing? I can see by the look on your face that you haven't heard from him. Am I right?"

"Unfortunately, yes."

Frannie took Heather from her cousin's arms and slipped into a booth table. In desperation, she gave the toddler a pen and allowed her to scribble on the fresh placemats.

"I was half wishing you had left," Suzanne began. "It seems senseless to keep talking about it, but there's some comfort in talking, I guess, so here I am."

"Okay, so talk to me," Frannie urged. "We don't know how long we can keep Heather entertained."

"There's not much to say, actually. I have to accept that it's over, Frannie. Totally, completely and finally over. He won't budge and neither will I."

Maybe it's for the best, Frannie thought. She was sincerely sorry about their breakup, but at least Suzanne's secret will remain securely buried. As it should be. "When I didn't hear from you all week, I sort of figured that out for myself, but I was still hoping for some unexpected turn of events." She shrugged. "I don't know what I was hoping, but I hated to see this happen. You've had such a great relationship. Your love for each other was so strong it radiated in your eyes. Anyone could see that."

"Well, it wasn't strong enough to get past this prob-lem." She waved a hand. "No, I shouldn't say 'problem'; Heather will never be considered my *problem.*"

"I know what you mean. You don't have to explain. What can I say? I'm so sorry you had to go through this, Suzanne."

"No, don't be sorry. It's my own fault. I should have seen it coming. I went into it with my eyes wide open, but in the beginning I never looked too far ahead. We were just two people confined in a hospital who became friends discussing our aches and pains." She laughed without humor. "Let's face it, considering the accidents we survived, we're both lucky to be alive. So it wasn't until later—much later when we were both home and on the mend, that we couldn't ignore our feelings any longer." Her quick laugh was sweetened this time by her reminiscences. "For a while we practically made love with our eyes, but neither of us made a move or dared to say a word about it. By then I knew I was crazy about him, but I also knew someday it would blow up in my face. Still, it's not easy to give up someone you love, Frannie, even when it's crucial that you do."

*Tell me about it,* Frannie thought and cast her gaze aside, but Suzanne was lost in her thoughts. Her words spilled out incessantly, like a dam that had burst. As she went on and on describing the agonies of life without Rob, Frannie considered telling her about Sergio. It would shock the hell out of Suzanne, but she'd probably feel better to know her cousin understood the depth of her sorrow. Misery *does* love company, life experiences had taught Frannie. But still, pouring out her story to Glory had drained her. She didn't want to bring every painful scene to the surface again. So, instead, she chose to simply listen, playing the role of the older, wiser relative, who had never suffered the heartaches of a profound but doomed love.

Frannie waited until Suzanne's emotions were spent, having offered nothing more than comfort and what would pass for sympathy, rather than empathy. "Suzanne, if Rob hadn't made this demand—which he certainly had a right to do—"

"I never said he didn't."

"Yes, I know. Let me go on . . . I was about to ask, do you think you and Rob could ever be truly happy with the weight of that secret hanging between you? He'd always be wondering about Heather's father; who he is, why you can't reveal his name, why you chose to deny Heather the love of her natural father. Is he some kind of brutal beast like Tyler was? Is that the kind of men you've been attracted to and *slept* with? These and similar questions would always be buzzing around in his head like bees."

Suzanne's eyes widened with hope. "So are you saying I should tell him about Greg and swear him to secrecy?"

Frannie sighed. "No, I'm afraid that's not at all what I'm saying. I'm just emphasizing what I said when you first told me. I don't think there are choices. As far as I can see in this very sad situation, there's only one priority. You have to think of Kim and those children. Can you imagine what it would do to them if they found out? I get chills every time I visualize that scene."

Suzanne stared ahead, focused on nothing. She nodded as she digested Frannie's unwelcome advice. "I don't mean to sound cruel, Frannie, and my conscience draws the same conclusions every time I battle with it, but my heart pulls me in a different direction. I can't help but wonder if maybe honesty would work. Isn't it possible if I revealed Heather's father he'd back off on the adoption? Knowing him as I do, he'd never want to see that family hurt either."

Frannie took a long pensive moment, as if considering the possibility. What was actually flowing through her mind were visions of Rob's probable reaction at hearing that the woman he loved had an affair with a married man. A married man whose family she had known well at the time and whose wife still babysat for Heather! She could well imagine the revulsion on his face. The immediate dissolution of all feelings of love. "I wish I could accept that optimistic view, Suzanne, but I can't. Yes, I agree that he'd never want to hurt the Haggarty family, but think about what that revelation would do to his image of you. I know Rob is the epitome of 'nice guys,' but what you're suggesting would be too much to expect of any man."

Suzanne's face soured. "He knows I was no angel before we met. Except for that one night with Greg, I never held anything back from him. When we got serious, I laid it all out on the table. It was his choice to put it all behind us. 'Let's not look back,' he'd said, 'only forward.'"

"Suzanne, you're grasping at straws. Believe me, if I thought it were possible for you and Rob to live happily ever after once you mention Greg's name, I'd say go for it—tell him. But do I think it's possible? No, no way."

Heather began to squirm in Frannie's arms, so Suzanne took her and stood up. "But it could happen, couldn't it? Anything is possible." She arched a brow and pointed a finger. "It dawned on me as I was driving here: What have I got to lose? I already lost him by not naming Heather's father, and if I tell him now, what difference would it make? I can't lose him twice. On the other hand, if there's some remote chance he *is* able to handle it and agrees to give up on the adoption, why shouldn't I try? I have absolutely nothing to lose and everything to gain."

Frannie slid out of the booth shaking her head. When she stood up, inches apart from Suzanne, she put a hand on her shoulder. "Don't do it, Suzanne. Please don't take that chance. The risks are too high."

Suzanne rolled her eyes and avoided Frannie's gaze. "I disagree. I know Rob a lot better than you do. Worst case scenario, he might be furious with me, but he'd never let that cat out of the bag. *Never.*"

Heather became restless in her mother's arms too and struggled to get down. "I have to go," Suzanne said, then wagged a finger at Frannie. "But before I do, I want to say one thing: After the way Wade screwed up your life, I can't blame you for being so cynical. I hope that attitude changes someday, but that won't happen unless and until you fall for some guy so hard that it hurts. That you can't function without him. Right now you focus only on facts because it doesn't touch you emotionally. But wait till Cupid's arrow stabs you in the heart. Boy! Will you change your tune!"

At the moment Frannie already felt stabbed by Suzanne's stinging words and wished she could say so. But she said nothing, stifled by the lump in her throat. As she watched her cousin walk out abruptly, her stomach went queasy. If Suzanne didn't change her mind and assume her first instinctive position, then God help the Haggartys.

# Chapter Twenty-three

Frannie was uncertain as to what caused her gradual dispirited attitude towards her businesses, but she couldn't deny that her enthusiasm had waned. Surely her silent agonies over losing Sergio to the urgencies of his family life had a great deal to do with her depressed moods, but it hadn't affected her so profoundly when he first left. She had thrown herself into her work more than ever and made sure she filled every spare moment with something pleasant.

She had told herself their separation was only temporary. In a few weeks he'd be back. Until then she'd have to settle for his phone calls. She'd survive on the sweetness of his loving words. She'd burn every word in her memory and allow them to drift her into dreamland. They would sustain her and keep her smiling and purring like a kitten.

But that was before all hope had drained. The promised phone calls never came. Not even one. There could be no credible excuse for not calling. She went into a love/hate mode, creating far-fetched possibilities, like an accident or illness that left him hospitalized in a coma or with a breathing tube in his throat.

*Well, it's possible, isn't it?* The voice inside her asked, but that voice belonged to the part of her that still clung to love, faith and happy endings. *And if it did happen, how would I know? Other than Sergio, who in Italy knows I exist?*

But she felt an involuntary twist of her lips. Frannie, the sensible cynic, not Frannie, the romantic dreamer, answered the question with only a sour smirk.

*But what about the flowers? The card that came with them?*

The cynic lifted her shoulders. *So he sent regrets. Big deal.*

Frannie shook her head angrily, hating herself for this obsession with Sergio. It had reduced her to some kind of lunatic who talked to herself.

The doorbell rang and she welcomed the interruption. She opened the door abruptly, the scowl still plastered on her face. Wade stood behind the screened storm door with a cordial smile, but he backed up slightly, shielding his face with a hand. "Still haven't cooled off, huh?" He furrowed his brows, pointed a warning finger in her face and mocked her with his tone. "I suggest you learn to control your angry moods, *Ms. Oliveri.* People will think you're losing it, and I'd be inclined to agree."

She laughed at the absurdity. "*I'm* losing it? Coming from you, that's ludicrous. What are you doing here? Didn't I make myself clear enough the last time you showed up?"

He shot her a disparaging glance. "C'mon, Frannie, grow up and cut all this righteous crap. I think you should invite me in, and for a little while forget about what broke us up. Just think back to the good years. It's not as if you have anything to fear. I never laid a finger on you, right? We need to talk."

"I'm not so sure we do," she said curtly, but she realized her answer had left an opening.

"Okay, so maybe you don't. But I do. What have you got to lose?"

She arched her brows and gave him a defiant look. "Time."

"Ten, fifteen minutes, is all I need."

"Ten or fifteen hours wouldn't be enough to eradicate what you did to me, Wade."

"I'm not expecting you to. I know better. I just want to get some things off my chest. We never really talked after you found out. You went bonkers." He caught her defensive expression and quickly added, "Not that I blame you. I had it coming."

She opened the door wide. "You've got ten minutes."

Frannie extended a hand, directing him to her club chair while she took her usual spot on the sofa. She offered him nothing, squared her shoulders and crossed her arms.

Under hooded brows, he gave her a slanted smile. She remembered that look well; he used it often to entice her to their bedroom at the most inopportune times. She could have spent an hour fussing on her appearance before meeting their friends for dinner, and the next thing she knew she'd be shedding it all. Her hair and makeup would be beyond repair and she'd have to start all over again.

Now, in retrospect, she grimaced remembering what a fool she'd been and how weak she was believing she had to spend her life in his shadow. It blew her mind recalling how she allowed him to control her like a robotic wife. The worst part of all was that she was too starry-eyed doing the love and marriage bit to notice what was happening.

It all flashed through her mind while he tried to work his silent charm. She maintained her impassive expression and sat with her hands clasped. "Well? I have to get to work early tonight, Wade. Amore Evenings is jammed on the weekends."

"So I've noticed. Good for you. Like I said last time, I'm proud. Surprised, but proud."

"Surprised? What's that supposed to mean? You didn't think I was capable?" She lifted her brows with exaggerated complacency. "Actually, now that it's all past tense, I'd like to thank you. You awakened the sleeping giant inside me. I never knew I had it in me to run a business. You were a good provider and I was content knowing you could take care of me." A bitter laugh escaped. "Boy, you were a better salesman than I ever gave you credit for. You conned two women into believing you loved them madly—"

"I *did* love you madly. Still do."

She leaned forward and frowned at him. "Do you really expect me to believe that?"

He shrugged. "No, I guess not, but it happens to be a fact." He leaned forward too, resting his elbows on his knees. Their faces were only two feet apart, the arrogance gone from his face. "I'm serious, Frannie. I don't expect you to forgive what I did. All I'm asking is another chance to make it up to you. Like I said before, it was all about loving you. Sure, I was married; I shouldn't have gotten involved with you in the first place, but I did and there was no turning back. When you're crazy about someone you don't always think rationally. Your heart takes the lead, not your head."

A surge of that aching love for Sergio surfaced and she winced. "How well I know," she said.

Wade gave a hopeful smile, assuming she was recalling the intensity of the love she once had for him. Seeing her resolve melting, he jumped at the opening. He reached for her hands but she pulled away. "Remember, Frannie, how you always used to preach about forgiveness—letting go of bitter memories—"

She put a hand up. "Hold it right there, Wade. At the time I was referring to petty arguments between family and friends, not a bigamist husband with another wife and two kids!"

He rolled his eyes and a defeated smile crossed his face. "True, but the principle is the same." He shook his head ruefully. "I find it so hard to believe that you can forget what we had. In and out of the bedroom, we shared something special, didn't we?"

"Yes, we did," she said. *Not to be compared to what I shared with Sergio Giannetta, though,* she thought, then looked up at him. She was about to speak but he didn't give her the chance.

"So why can't we have a fresh start? If it weren't for your two restaurants, I'd say we'd settle in some other coastal town where we can live a similar life; where no one will know our history."

"That's impossible."

"It's impossible because of your restaurants, so fine. Keep the restaurants, marry me and hold your head up high. Don't worry about what people might think. Who gives a damn what anyone thinks? Just follow your heart, I say."

Frannie wanted to say if she followed her heart she'd be in Italy. She kept her gaze on her lap, her chin resting on her hand. All the anger and hostility had drained. There were moments through Wade's pleas that she actually felt sorry for him. The greater danger, though, was that she felt sorry for herself too. Sergio was all but a dying flame in her life; the flowers his expression of regret, as Glory had suggested.

Wade looked at her with the soft smile that had captured her heart too many years ago. His eyes were hopeful. She sucked in a breath. "You're right, Wade. Forgiveness gives you peace and I'd certainly welcome that. So I do forgive you. I can look at you now without clenching my teeth, but *love . . .*" She shook her head slowly. "My love for you died a fast and furious death." She stood up, opened her front door and spoke softly. "But I'm better now. I'm not going to scream at you to get off my property. I'm simply going to ask you to leave quietly and never try to approach me again—not with reconciliation attempts. If we bump into each other by chance someday, I'll have no qualms saying hello-how-are-you, but it *ends there.*" With her index finger she made an exclamation point in the air.

"You'd better rethink that decision, babe. You'll regret it. I won't wait forever."

"The only decision I'll regret for the rest of my days in marrying you, Wade. Let me correct that—I *thought* I married you. But I hit the bottom of the barrel with that one. So if you'll excuse me . . ."

She smiled politely and held the door open for his exit.

# Chapter Twenty-four

Glory was already briefing the staff when Frannie arrived. They were expecting several celebrity guests, including some star performers appearing in the Ogunquit Playhouse's production of *The Full Monty.*

"Naturally, I don't have to remind you that *every* guest is special to us. You should always give your best performance to everyone. But when celebrities join us, we make an extra effort to ensure their privacy and dining pleasure. And *please*—don't gawk at them or engage in any star-struck conversation. Feel free to tell them how pleased you are to serve them, et cetera, et cetera—that sort of thing—then make yourself scarce once their needs have been met."

They nodded in unison, particularly Carlie and Melina, the two young women assigned to the celebrity tables, who were demonstratively excited about greeting and serving them.

Frannie pored over the reservation list and smiled to herself. It always pleased her to observe Glory on the job. As she bounced from table to table to kitchen to reception area she made certain no guest was neglected or felt neglected in any way. No easy task. But Glory was her omnipresent self and her love for this second career she had chosen radiated on her face.

Even more than little Danny, Amore Evenings had been her rock. It had forced her not to neglect her appearance, to smile till her cheeks hurt and to be sociable with people on a daily basis. No matter what she was suffering inwardly, she masked it well. After Alex died, when she first returned to work, she had resolved that she'd never let the patrons see the grieving side of her. She always appeared strong and optimistic—no one would ever feel uncomfortable in Amore Evenings. It was all about pleasure, not grief.

Immediately after Alex was buried, Frannie's cousin, Mike Duca, had come with a few of his men, along with many volunteers, and completely restructured and remodeled the back section of the restaurant where Alex was shot dead for merely trying to defuse an argument. They had permanently removed the table where his killer had been seated and replaced it with a sixty-inch hutch.

"What are you grinning about? I spotted you from way back there," Glory said, pointing.

"Oh? Did it show? I was trying to hide it. I wouldn't want anyone to think I've gone mental, smiling to myself. But every time I hear or watch you exercising one of your managerial functions, it never ceases to amaze me. I think back to your initial fears and apprehensions. To look at you now, anyone would think you've been in the business all your life."

Glory laughed. "I was a wreck, I know. But we waste so much time and effort worrying about things that never materialize. Hell, we've got enough to cope with over the crap that *does* materialize. Ergo, the old expression, *Don't sweat the small stuff.*"

Frannie lifted her gaze for a cursory glance at Glory's eyes. She hoped her friend hadn't meant to categorize Sergio as *small stuff.*

Glory understood the silent question. "I didn't mean what you're thinking," she said, and they both laughed.

Just as they took off in opposite directions, Glory remembered something and called Frannie back, crooking a finger towards the reception desk, specifically the reservation list. "Have you looked this over yet?"

"Not completely. Why?"

"There's a name there you might be pleased to see. A common name, but I'm hoping it's the same person."

Curiosity curled Frannie's brows and she scanned the list. Her eyes brightened when she reached the name. "Dr. Timothy Quinlan! It has to be him! Unless it's another doctor with the same name. The last time I saw him, when Suzanne was discharged from the hospital, he said he might surprise us someday, so maybe it is him."

Glory nodded in agreement. "Strong possibility, I'd say, considering I remember you telling me Dr. Quinlan lives and practices in Portland. But don't you think he would have called Suzanne or Rob to join him or stop by to say hello?"

Frannie's smile thinned into a hopeless smirk. "Most likely, but if he did, whichever one he spoke to would have told him about their breakup."

"Maybe he couldn't call them. Look, his reservation is for two. He's probably bringing a date or whoever is special to him these days. Maybe even a wife! It's been a long time since you've seen him, so who knows? Things change in everyone's life." She was about to add, *As we well know,* but that was just the sort of comment that made people squirm. She had been making a sincere effort to break the habit.

"Well, we haven't got time for guessing games," Frannie said, glancing at her wristwatch. "He has an 8:30 reservation, so we'll soon find out." She was about to walk away again, but stopped short. "Now that I think about it," she said, her eyes squinted, trying to jar her memory. "Since he was Suzanne's doctor, I spoke about him often, but you never met him, did you?"

"No, but I look forward to being introduced. After all the accolades you and Suzanne showered on him, he must be special."

"He is. And not only because he's an excellent surgeon, but he has a great bedside manner."

Glory teased her with a sexy smile and wiggled her eyebrows.

Frannie laughed. "Yes, he's gorgeous too. And if his looks don't get you, his personality will."

Glory nodded, digesting the image. "I'm impressed. Find me when he shows up."

*Wouldn't that be a gas!* Frannie thought. She grinned imagining the sight of Glory arm-in-arm with Tim Quinlan. What a gorgeous couple they'd make! But if it's meant to be that Glory should find love again someday, whoever he is will have to fall in love with Danny too. *Really* love him, not merely accept him.

Once the dining room opened for the evening, Frannie got so busy meeting and greeting their guests that she and Glory barely exchanged a word. She realized that there were short intermittent periods of time when Sergio never entered her mind. But when he did, she couldn't shake the habit of eyeing the door, always hoping to see him there, looking for her.

The stabs of despair those false images prompted were temporarily obliterated when the strikingly handsome Dr. Quinlan appeared. His presence jolted Frannie; she had only seen him in scrubs or smart-casual clothing in a hospital setting. Tonight he wore a dark blue suit, the quality of which could be spotted a mile away, with an azure blue shirt that complemented his tanned face.

His hand rested on the shoulder of a woman in her early twenties, Frannie guessed. If that. A little young for him, but hey, when you're a successful surgeon with a gorgeous face and a six-foot frame that exudes masculinity from the toes up, graying temples are not an issue.

Frannie dropped what she was doing and welcomed him with a bear hug. "What a wonderful surprise!" she said, then broke her embrace to look at him; admiration lighting her eyes. During Suzanne's hospitalization, not only had he extended himself professionally beyond Frannie's expectations, but he was amazingly supportive to her as well, despite the sporadic angry outbursts of her alcoholic uncle Jerry, Suzanne's father.

"It's a wonderful surprise for me, too." He winked at the stunning young girl and looked at her proudly. "Frannie, this is my daughter, Emma. She turned twenty-one this week and we're celebrating tonight."

"Congratulations, Emma! I'm so pleased to meet you and I'm delighted that your dad chose Amore Evenings to celebrate."

Emma laughed. "Actually, *I* brought *him* here. When he asked me to choose a restaurant, I chose this one. Friends of mine had been here recently and raved about it."

"Coincidence, huh?" Tim said. "I've wanted to come to Ogunquit to check out your restaurants since you piqued my interest at the hospital, but never got around to it."

"So here you are now," Frannie said with a broad smile. "And thank you, Emma, for bringing your dad here. It's so great to see him again. You must be very proud of him."

"That's a two-way street," Tim said before Emma could answer. He gave his daughter a feathery kiss on her forehead.

Frannie glanced around for Glory, but she was nowhere in sight. A new wave of people came in with and without reservations. When she finally found Glory, they were both too busy to chat, but Frannie caught her eye and pointed to the reception area. "When you get a minute," she mouthed.

Fifteen minutes later, Frannie approached Tim Quinlan and his daughter again, full of apologies. "I'm so sorry I had to abandon you. Things get insane here sometimes. But your table is ready now. I'll take you myself," she said, taking the menus from the hostess.

She led them to an outdoor table surrounded by candles flickering against a midnight blue sky. Whitecaps rolled in, dancing to the music of a roaring sea; the crashing waves against the black rocks as captivating as fireworks on The Fourth of July.

With one sweeping glance, Tim soaked it all in. "Magnificent view, Frannie! If your food is half as good, you've hit the jackpot."

In the glow of the candlelight, he shot her a look and a shrug while Emma studied the menu. Frannie gave him a sympathetic smile and nodded, silently agreeing that tonight the romantic ambiance would be wasted.

"I can say now with confidence that our food will more than please you. We've already had several excellent reviews published by reputable food critics." She curled her brows thoughtfully. "I might have mentioned this before, but my partner, Glory English, is also a syndicated food columnist. That alone gave us a boost."

"Oh, Glory English? That's *Glorious Cooking,* isn't it?" Emma chirped up. "I love that column!"

"Yes, it's very successful." She looked around again. "As a matter of fact, when I can steal her away for a minute, I'll bring her over and introduce you."

"Oh, please do! I'd love to meet her," Emma said.

While they waited for their desserts to be served, Tim Waite approached their table with a wide smile. "Excuse me, Miss Quinlan, this is for you." He placed before her an eight-inch birthday cake smothered with whipped cream, blueberries and strawberries. Delighted with the surprise, she looked at her dad, who put a hand up.

"No, I wish I had thought of it, but sorry, no."

She gazed up questioningly.

"I'm Tim, by the way. I've been with Frannie and Glory since they opened here. The cake comes with their compliments and best wishes for a happy birthday."

"Well, thank them both for me. That's so sweet! And thank you too, Tim, for bringing it. Now that's two Tims who made tonight special." She extended a hand towards her father. "You and my dad have the same name."

Tim Waite grinned amiably. "See that? I knew there was something special about him."

The doctor laughed and shook his hand. "Same here, Tim. And please tell the ladies that we'd love to thank them personally if they can spare the time."

"Absolutely. I'm sure they will." Tim served them each a generous slice, then tipped his head and excused himself.

They were still eating it when their regular waitress brought the desserts they had originally ordered. Emma looked wide-eyed at the rich French pastries. "This is like a mountain to climb. I don't think I can squeeze this in too."

Frannie had seen Emma's expression as she approached their table again. "You don't have to eat that if it's too much after the cake."

Emma cut a small piece of the pastry while her father pushed aside his empty cake dish. "No challenge for me," he said, biting into his second dessert.

They both thanked her graciously and Tim said, "We'd like to thank Glory, too, if possible, but if not—"

"She's coming now," Frannie said, turning her gaze. Glory had emerged from the indoor dining room and waved as she walked towards their table.

Tim stood up when they were introduced and both father and daughter thanked her for the cake. "I feel as if I know you, Glory," Tim said. "Frannie and I had many conversations during Suzanne's hospitalization and your name came up often. Nothing but praise, of course."

Glory's quick laugh softened to a humble smile. "And if I had your ear, you'd hear those same praises—and more—about her." She eyed her partner affectionately.

Tim wanted to say, *She never told me what a beautiful woman you are,* but swallowed the urge. Instead, he said, "It would be my pleasure to listen."

It took only a fleeting second for Frannie's perceptive eyes to catch the meaning behind Tim's polite words. The doctor was obviously dazzled by Glory's face and figure. It had become a common occurrence at the restaurant to see that reaction in people who saw her for the first time. Every time Frannie teased Glory about it, she'd wave it off as imaginative nonsense. The funny part of it was that Glory wasn't feigning modesty; she was truly oblivious to her stunning appearance.

After Glory and Frannie left the table, Tim and Emma lingered over a second cup of coffee. "What nice women they are, Dad. And both so attractive—especially Glory; she's a knockout! Is she single—do you know?" She laughed and waved a finger playfully. "You can't fool me, Dad. I could see how impressed you were. Your eyes popped out!"

Tim smiled and didn't try to deny it. "I was more surprised than anything. You know how it is. When you know *of* someone without ever having met, you conjure up an image. Well, that's what I did whenever Frannie talked about her, and I never visualized her like that!" He widened his eyes. "Yes, *very, very,* pretty woman."

"If you're interested, Dad, why don't you talk to Frannie? You're friendly with her; ask her if she thinks Glory might be receptive."

Tim's smile faded. "I doubt it. I guess you never heard the story about Alex Howard, the guy she was engaged to?"

"When your college is in New York, you hear mostly New York news." She wrinkled her brows. "Why? What about him? From the look on your face, I suspect it's a sad story."

"Very sad. Tragic." He patted her hand and forced a smile. "But not a story for a happy occasion. I'll tell you some other time."

Emma leaned forward, gripped by the mystery, particularly since she had just met Glory English. "No, Dad. Forget my birthday. Tell me now."

Tim sighed. "It's not really a story; just an incident. It lasted only a minute or two. A deadly, horrific incident . . ."

# Chapter Twenty-five

It was after eleven when everyone was finally gone, the entire place vacuumed, the tables stripped and the kitchen scrupulously clean, ready for the next night's business.

The quiet, the soft music that usually relaxed her at the end of a long day, and the thought of going home to an empty bed had Frannie sinking into another night of depression. She felt like the smoldering embers of a dying fire.

With an angry flip of one finger, she turned off the music. Before Sergio, she loved to sing along as she worked. Now every lyric was meaningful; she knew well the pain of every broken heart. She didn't need to be reminded by violins and sweet melodious voices.

Glory wasn't in the office when Frannie popped her head in to say goodnight. She had seen her there only minutes ago, feeding information into the computer, as she did every night.

Now she was nowhere to be seen. Curiously, Frannie called out to her and got no response. There's no way she would have left without saying goodnight, she thought, and swung open the kitchen doors. A stream of light splashed across the darkened room, illuminating the stainless steel appliances.

She was about to turn and leave. What would she be doing there? Glory had no business in the kitchen, she reasoned. They had a reliable staff to handle the nightly routine of cleaning and closing up the kitchen.

But she heard a weird sound. A wail, like an animal, who also had no business in their kitchen. A remote possibility since they paid good money monthly to prevent such an unwelcome occurrence.

Just in case, though, she stayed put at the doors and flipped on the light.

"Glory! What's wrong?" She discovered her friend at the sink, her hands bracing her while suppressed sobs rocked her shoulders. Frannie grabbed her arms and turned her around, thinking the worst—that she had some kind of accident or had been stricken by a sudden illness.

But there were no signs of either.

"I'm sorry, I'm okay," Glory said through her tears. "It just hit me suddenly. I've been trying to be good . . . don't want to burden anyone with my troubles, but I didn't want to hold it in and cry when I walked into my apartment. Not until Marion Landis leaves."

A wave of guilt snaked through Frannie. She had underestimated the intensity of the love Glory felt for Alex. She hugged her friend, let her cry a few silent minutes while she soothed her with whispered words. "I had hoped your pain was easing up a little after all this time. When I watch you run around here, you always seem in an up mood; always so animated and cheerful." She laughed ruefully. "You were becoming my role model. I figured if you could rise above everything you went through, I should certainly be able to get over Sergio. Our love was so brief . . . strong, but brief." She didn't have to add *And he's still alive. Nor had he left me alone with a child to raise.*

Frannie had no doubt Glory's hurt would last forever. The passage of time would never erase the memories or fill the void in her son's life.

Glory wiped her eyes. "It's all an act," she said. "I force myself to appear in control for the sake of our business. No one wants to be around depressed people. Sometimes I can even fool myself for a while. I find myself enjoying conversations with strangers, feeling myself smile . . . you know what I mean." She shook her head. "But it isn't just

Alex. Sure, I'll always miss him. How can I forget him? Every time I look in Danny's eyes, I'll see certain expressions and mannerisms that'll remind me. Alex left a part of himself in our son, but—" Glory covered her face with her hands. "Don't say anything—*please*. As I've told you before, I know it's wrong, it's selfish, but I can't help myself. I keep thinking if I had known it would come to this, I never would have chosen Jessica Branson as my obstetrician."

Frannie released a hopeless sigh. "Glory, you've got to let go of this. You're tormenting yourself over something that should make you happy, not depressed. And let's face it, if it hadn't happened with Jessica Branson, it would have been someone else eventually. Your dad is a good-looking man with a lovable personality—at least it was lovable before Louise died. He's been walking around in a trance since then—"

Glory pulled away and looked her in the eye. "Not anymore. Not since he took up with *her*. Not one of us was able to pull him out of his grief—not even Danny. But you should see him now! You'd never know he was so in love with his wife." She twisted her lips to accentuate the sarcasm of her words.

Frannie's patience ran out. She slapped the counter. "Don't say that! He *did* love Louise—very much. I think deep down you know that. You saw it for yourself all those months before she died." She paused to calm herself. "You know, Glory, my grandmother used to have a saying to describe her grief when my grandfather died. It always stood out in my mind: *The greater the gift, the greater the grief,* she'd say. And later, when a widower we knew well was getting married again, everyone was shocked. He and his wife had seemed so happy together. But my grandma explained that when a man has a truly happy marriage, he takes an optimistic view towards marriage in general. When someone else enters his life, it's *because* he had been so happy that he takes the chance again. He wants back a piece of what he had, even if it's only crumbs."

Glory widened her bloodshot eyes. "Are you saying he's thinking marriage? Do you know something I don't know? That would be ludicrous at this point. They barely know each other!"

"No, I'm not saying that at all; only my grandmother's theory on how a man's attitude can change once he becomes a lonely widower. It seems to fit here in the case of your father." She made a *who knows* face, then continued. "In any event, you should prepare yourself. It could happen eventually. You can't let yourself fall apart like this. You've got to let go. It's not as if you're losing him like you lost Alex."

"Maybe not. But once she gets her grips in him permanently, he'll be as good as dead to me."

Frannie cringed at the harsh words. She couldn't believe what she was hearing. Glory's obsessive love for her father had set her on a self-destructive path. Her jealousy of Jessica Branson had soared to abnormal heights. If she didn't shake it off fast, she'd be the one to suffer the greatest losses.

"C'mon, Glory, I'll walk you inside your apartment. You can run off to the bathroom or something. I can pay Marion and see her out."

"No, don't bother. I pay her on Sunday nights."

"Fine. If you need to talk awhile, I'll stay a half hour or so. We can have a good cry together. I'm not in such good shape either. It never bothered me before, but since Sergio left, I hate going home to an empty house, an empty bed."

Glory stepped out of her own troubles and took a close look at Frannie. Her voice sobered. "I thought he never occupied your bed?"

Frannie raised her hand. "No lie. He never did. That's why I dread getting into that bed now. At least I would have had the memory." She put a hand on Glory's shoulder. "Let's go. We'll have a fast cup of tea, shed a few more tears. Then I'm going home. We both have to deal with our heartaches on our own."

# Chapter Twenty-six

Dan fixed himself a mug of coffee and brought it out on his porch. It was time to face the facts. He should have known it was coming. All the signs had been rushing down on him like a roller coaster. Up until that day at the beach, he had tried to convince himself that all he really wanted from Jessica was a social life. Someone from his own generation who shared his attitudes, his kind of music, his history. Life as it was in the sixties. His children had tried everything possible to snap him out of his dark moods. Sometimes he was so sympathetic to their efforts that he'd succumb to their pleadings. But despite their efforts, sitting through dinner in a restaurant with only his children might have made him feel loved, but it also made him feel *old.* And superfluous.

He never meant to fall in love with her—never dreamed it was possible. All he ever wanted—or *thought* he ever wanted—was the pleasure of her company. And yes, pleasure indeed was what he got Friday afternoon when they had joined hands in the ocean, when their bodies lay side by side intoxicated by the warmth of the sun and salty sea breezes. The thickness of desire had enveloped them. Silently, their eyes conceded to what their hearts and bodies could no longer ignore.

So now what? For Dan and Jessica, the answer was uncomplicated. They could simply coast along, seeing each other whenever their busy schedules allowed. Once the summer passed, though, and Finestkind closed for the season, Dan would be free almost anytime. As much as he had loved running the tour boats in Florida, with Louise gone, his days as a snowbird were over.

How they had loved their Florida winters! Those months had become like a honeymoon haven they looked forward to each year. But now, the memories were too painful. Dan had no desire to subject himself to the agony of being there without her. What purpose would it serve? Other than the milder weather, there was nothing to entice him now. Knowing Louise wouldn't be home at their condo waiting for him, the pleasure had been sucked away like quicksand.

Even here in Ogunquit, where he had family and lifelong friends, after his days on the Finestkind, he hated the deafening silence at home. He'd walk around from room to room, always searching for her, hoping, as if she would miraculously float down from wherever she is just to say hello and give him a hug.

Dan shook his head vigorously. The last thing he wanted was to drag himself down again. He sipped the coffee that had now cooled enough to drink. Jessica's gentle face flashed in his mind, overshadowing Louise's. He captured it and held it there, vivid and strong, because in Jessica he saw joy and life; in Louise, death and grief.

His insides melted as he remembered her face on the pillow in her bedroom, her arms outstretched. No matter what was in store for them down the road, that moment was a sight he'd never forget.

The phone rang and he cursed it. First because he had forgotten to take it outside with him, and secondly because it interrupted a beautiful memory. But the caller ID sobered his dreams; returned him to reality. *Glory.* He didn't want to entertain the thought—chased it out of his head every time—but it kept creeping back in. She, more than his other three children, was uncomfortable with his relationship with Jessica. To say *uncomfortable* was putting it mildly. No matter how she had tried to deny it, there was something glaringly unnatural about her smile that morning. She had stopped by with Danny the morning after his first dinner date with Jessica, and he believed that was the only reason she stopped by.

Her last words that morning had removed all doubt. He had asked her if she was okay with his dating Jessica. Her biting words stung him to this day. "Would it matter if I weren't?" she'd said.

He picked up the phone reluctantly. As much as he loved his daughter, he had no intention of telling her what she wanted to hear. Jessica was part of his life now and he wasn't about to listen to any of his children tell him all the reasons why she shouldn't be.

He drew a breath. "Hi, sweetheart. How are you and Danny?"

We're fine. We both miss you."

Dan cringed, hearing the bite in his daughter's voice. It was a side of her he'd never seen. But he loved her regardless and let it pass. "I wanted to babysit and enjoy my grandson Friday night, but you have Marion Landis now."

"I do, and she depends on the income. Besides, I only got Marion so that you could be free for Jessica."

Dan rolled his eyes, sent a quick prayer for patience. "Glory, I'm not always with Jessica," he said softly. "I'm free plenty of nights and I'd love to spend some with Danny."

Glory paused before answering. "I don't know, Dad. I have a workable schedule with babysitters now. Maybe I shouldn't rock the boat. If I switch things around to give you one or two nights, what happens when Jessica's schedule changes? Then I'm screwed up too."

Dan paused too while he plucked at the imaginary arrows in his heart. "But where does that leave me?"

"Free for Jessica, I guess."

She said it with such mocked cheerfulness that Dan's calm collapsed. "Okay, Glory. I get the message. I think we need to talk, just the two of us. Why don't I come over one morning while Danny takes his nap? What day is good?"

"You can come almost any morning, Dad. But there's not much to talk about. As I said, it's all settled. I'm in good shape with babysitters. I realized I have no right to tie you down now that you're dating Dr. Branson. It wouldn't be fair."

The words were okay, but the tone definitely was not. Dan fought for control. "Glory, I'm his grandfather. I never considered my time with Danny as being *tied down*."

"I never said you did, but—look, Dad, it's almost ten. I have to meet Vanessa and Wanda at Amore Breakfast at eleven. Todd and Amy can't make it today, but are you joining us?"

"Of course. But I want to talk to you alone. How's tomorrow? Can I come early—say nine-thirty or ten? I'm working the afternoon and evening tours."

"Sure. Why not?"

* * *

Dan was restless after his brief conversation with Glory. His heart was troubled; his mind confused. Sure, he loved her still and always would. She was his flesh and blood. But lately he didn't like her. Especially today.

He left his coffee and glanced at his wristwatch. He had plenty of time before breakfast for a walk on The Marginal Way. Today he needed it more than ever. Nothing cleared his head more than a brisk walk along the narrow path overlooking one of God's masterpieces. The panoramic ocean view was breathtaking. No matter how many times he walked it, he never tired of its captivating beauty. Its serenity enveloped him every time.

* * *

An hour later, Dan headed for Amore Breakfast with a whole new evaluation of his daughter's distasteful attitude.

He wondered if maybe she was on the brink of a nervous breakdown. Considering all she'd been through—first her husband's betrayal, then learning that the father she had loved for thirty-five years was not her real father; the trauma she went through when she found me and my family refused to accept her. Then, what could be worse than being held captive by a madman with a gun at your head?

Yet, with the help of her therapists and all who loved her, she had fought it through and survived.

Until a drunk with a temper killed Alex, the man she loved and the father of her unborn child.

And now . . . he winced at the irony. Now the woman who brought Danny into the world was the very woman who unknowingly threatened to take Glory's place in her father's heart. If that's what his daughter had concluded, maybe she *was* on the verge of a breakdown.

He shivered at the thought. *Dear God in heaven! Don't ask me to give up Jessica for Glory's sake!*

*No way! I can't give her up. There has to be another way.*

* * *

At Amore Breakfast, Frannie greeted Dan with a hug. "Your ladies are already seated," she said, pointing to a corner table. "They're waiting for you to join them."

He greeted them with a kiss, including Wanda, Vanessa's partner, who had surprisingly become like another daughter. It had taken some getting used to, this gay relationship, but Wanda was one of those "beautiful inside and outside" people—impossible to dislike. Dan caught the wink she sneaked him; the kind that says, "Hang in there. It'll all iron out."

It was comforting to know he had someone in his corner. Although Glory's reaction concerned him most, he doubted the others were thrilled. With the exception of Amy, his "baby," who always looked for a bright side, Dan suspected if Jessica suddenly vanished from their family picture, his other children would shed no tears.

*I would, though,* he thought.

"Who's with Danny?" he asked Glory.

"Sara volunteered to sit and I gladly accepted."

Dan sighed. "Guess I can't blame you. You can eat and talk in peace. But I was looking forward to holding him."

"You can hold him tomorrow—or even today when we leave here. Whatever you prefer."

Dan froze for a long second. He had two o'clock plans with Jessica today, but didn't dare say so. He had worked longer hours yesterday to get today off. For the entire summer, they'd probably never catch another Sunday afternoon when both were free. It would be sinful to waste the opportunity. "No, I have a bunch of repairs around the house I've been putting off too long." *Well, at least that part's true.* "So I'll come tomorrow, okay?"

"Sure," she said, feigning indifference.

"We can help you for an hour or so, Dad," Vanessa offered. "Wanda won't mind."

Wanda's silent smile was transparent. Dan lowered his gaze before his daughters caught the communication between them. Wanda never said a word because she had locked eyes with Dan. She knew damn well he had lied.

And, sadly, she knew why.

# Chapter Twenty-seven

On a regular basis, many of the locals came for break-fast at lunchtime. They enjoyed socializing and picking up the latest buzz around town. Frannie too often chose this time for her own breakfast, taking pleasure in the relaxed and congenial atmosphere after the crowds had dispersed.

She dropped her fork when she spotted the familiar face of an old friend. "Well, Detective Sergeant Tony Gerard! What a nice surprise! We haven't seen you since your wedding." She patted the empty stool next to her. "Park your behind here and tell me what's going on. But first let me congratulate you." She smacked a kiss on his cheek then poured him a cup of coffee. "I just recently heard about Corrine's pregnancy. Boy, you guys sure work fast!"

The detective laughed. "Hey, when you look in the mirror and start seeing more gray than black, you know you'd better get a move on. And Corrine just turned thirty-eight, so we agreed to try." He cupped a hand over his mouth and wiggled his eyebrows. "It gave us a *great* honeymoon."

"I'm sure you did!" she said and laughed. "I have to call to congratulate Corrine. Is she still working?"

"Oh, yes," Tony said, but a twist of his mouth revealed his displeasure. "Before the pregnancy, I worried about her every hour she was on the job. Now with the baby to worry about too, I'm a basket case until she's off duty." He shook his head. "You wouldn't believe the crazies we deal with out there."

"Oh, yes I do. I read the newspapers and watch the news. I keep saying I'm going to give up both. I get sick to my stomach over some of those stories." She rolled her eyes.

"Don't get me started." She handed him a menu. "So what would you like to eat?"

He pushed the menu aside. "I can't decide. Surprise me."

"Fine. You'll get today's special."

They chatted amiably through her breakfast and he beamed when she served him the walnut-apple-cinnamon waffles topped with mixed berries. "So what are you up to today? You working?"

"Later, yes, but I just came from my friend's house in York. His power saw busted and he needed to borrow mine. He has a cousin staying with him who's been helping with his house renovations. The guy lives in Italy and has responsibilities there, so I guess he's in a hurry to get the job done and go back."

Frannie's knees went weak. "Are you talking about Eddie Pisano? Is he your friend?"

Tony turned to her. "He sure is. Great guy. Why? Do you know him?"

"Not directly, no. I know *of* him, though. That cousin you mentioned—Sergio? He did some gardening work for me, but his father died and he had to rush back to Italy. I didn't know he was back." She lifted her brows, feigning indifference. "I had to finish the job myself, not saying how. I don't have his skills. The guy was like an artist in the garden."

"Well, if you still need him, maybe he can give you a few hours while he's here. Why don't you give him a call?" Before Frannie could respond, he laughed and said, "On second thought, maybe you'd better not. The guy, Sergio, dragged his mother back with him. Eddie had felt sorry for her, and after all, she was his aunt, he said, so he told Sergio to bring her. He figured she was probably crazy with grief and the trip to America might be a good distraction for her. But once he had a taste of her personality, he regretted having extended the invitation." He laughed again and gave

Frannie a *better him than me* grin. "Eddie said she's driving him nuts. The only consolation is that she's a great cook."

Frannie's heart was pounding. There was so much she wanted to ask, but she faked a laugh instead. "I can see why Eddie would want to get rid of them as soon as possible. How long has he had them for house guests?"

"I'm not sure. A week or so. Aside from his help with the renovations, Eddie had been enjoying Sergio's company, but now that he brought his mother, it's another story. He didn't really know her before, he said, but his aunt is one of those domineering matriarchs who came in like a storm and took over more than his kitchen. Supposedly, she wasn't always that way—not while her husband was around. But now that he's gone, she's probably drunk with power."

"But as I recall, Sergio's family owns a restaurant in Italy. The mother did a lot of the cooking, I think he said. So what's she doing here?"

"Off the record, I think the family begged Sergio to bring her here. According to Eddie, she wasn't as grief-stricken as she pretended to be. Now that her husband is dead, she can call all the shots."

Frannie sipped the last of her orange juice, then said, "If that's the case, I'm surprised she came. You would think she'd want to stay and put her own plans in motion."

Tony's lips parted to speak, but he laughed instead and waved off the thought.

"What?" Frannie asked curiously.

Tony paused to eat the last two raspberries on his dish. "Okay, I shouldn't say this, but I trust you, so don't repeat it. Eddie told me Sergio had told him plenty. The father, apparently, had a good head for business, but he ruled with an iron thumb. He could never recall ever seeing any signs of affection between his parents. His mother feared him and hated living her life keeping her mouth shut and following his orders."

Frannie laughed. "She's probably glad he's gone." She arched a brow. "Truthfully, I can't blame her."

"Me too, but think about what could happen once he died. If that woman held in all that rage for years and years, once she finally let it go, she probably exploded! In a situation like that, when all the pieces fall back together, what have you got? A monster drunk with power."

Frannie nodded and grinned. "I see your point. It doesn't explain, though, why she chose to come here."

"It was all about image, Sergio told Eddie. He said she cried and carried on something awful at the wake and funeral, but once the people cleared out, she'd turn it off like a faucet. When her children expressed their concern—their surprise, really—she admitted it was all an act. "How does it look if I don't cry? I'm his widow," she'd said. He shook his head and laughed. "That struck me so funny. But anyway, that's why she came, primarily. She had never traveled anywhere and grabbed the chance to come to America with her son while the rest of her family handled the restaurant."

"And in her eyes that would look good 'for the people' I suppose. Like she was too upset to work and had to get away to grieve."

"Something like that, I imagine."

After Tony left, Frannie put on a good front for her remaining employees, but inwardly she battled her emotions. She didn't know whether to cry or scream. At the moment, a part of her hated him. No matter what was going on, she deserved at least a phone call.

But the other part of her was devastated by the total blatant rejection. The more she thought about it, the more livid she became. By the time she closed up, she needed to vent in the worst way. Instead of driving home she drove straight to Amore Evenings, specifically to Glory's apartment above the restaurant.

* * *

161

Danny was in his mother's arms when Glory opened the door. "Oh, thank God, you're home," Frannie said, "I'm furious and I need your ear. Are you alone?"

Perplexed, Glory stepped aside to let her in. "Of course I'm alone. Who would be here besides me and Danny?" *Damn, I'm doing it again.* "He just woke up."

Frannie reached out for her godson. "Give him to me. I love the taste of his skin when he wakes up. Maybe that sweet face will calm me down."

In her living room, Glory took a second look at Frannie. "Your face is all blotched up again. What happened? Spit it out."

Frannie handed the baby right back to his mother and collapsed on the sofa. She covered her face with her hands and sobbed.

"Oh geez, I'm afraid to ask what's wrong. Lately it seems that one of us is always in tears." She lifted Frannie's chin, then put Danny in his playpen and joined her on the sofa. "We're reversing roles now; it's your turn to talk." Glory said it with a half smile and Frannie returned one. "He's here, Glory. He's been here a week and never called me. Can you believe that?"

Glory avoided her gaze. "Unfortunately, I can." She wanted to tell her it's time to give up that impossible dream but decided it would be too cruel to say it bluntly. Her friend, who was admired by all for her keen sense of judgment and strength of character, was falling apart at the seams. And why? For a guy who probably wasn't worthy of her anguish.

Frannie shot her a sideways glance. "You don't believe he ever cared enough, do you?"

Glory threw her hands out. "How can I possibly know? I barely remember what he looks like and we never met, so I can't really pass judgment. I never had a chance to form an impression."

"But I did," Frannie said, pointing a finger. "You have to trust my judgment on this, Glory. I've learned to separate the good guys from the bull throwers."

Glory cocked a brow, said nothing, leaving Frannie to rethink that one.

Frannie slapped her forehead and smiled forlornly. "So okay, I screwed up big time with Wade, but I still say he *did* love me. Why would he stay with me, support two homes, if he didn't?"

Glory pursed her lips, pondered the question, then said, "First of all, he was earning big bucks selling medical equipment, you said, so it wasn't exactly a sacrifice, right? Secondly, I think some men simply can't handle commitment. No matter how much they love their wives, they get bored. Next thing you know, they're cheating." She lifted her brows and gave Frannie a slanted smile. "But they rarely take drastic steps, like bigamy, to spice up their lives. So, to answer your question, yes, I believe Wade loved you; just not enough, not *exclusively*, as it should be."

Frannie drew a breath and exhaled slowly. "That about sums it up—not enough. It helps me, though, to believe he *did* love me in his crazy way. If I couldn't hang on to that, those flashbacks of our lovemaking would be tougher to deal with. I feel like the fool of the century." She shot a long look at Glory. "And now you think I'm doing it again with Sergio, huh?"

Glory shrugged and smiled softly. "You said it, not me."

"But you didn't have to say it." She threw her hands up dismissively. "What's the difference? It's over anyway. There's no excuse for him not calling me—either from Italy or since he came back. No excuse at all."

The doorbell rang and Glory knew her conversation with Frannie would have to be cut short. "That's probably my dad, Frannie," she said, her tone apologetic. "I'm sorry.

He was supposed to come this morning, but something—or some*one*—screwed up his schedule."

Frannie put a hand up. "Hey, no problem. I have a million things to do today, anyway," she said, thinking that first on her list would be to dump those flowers she cherished, vase and all, into the trash.

When Dan came in, with one cursory glance, he got the distinct feeling he had interrupted something heavy. He kissed them both and said, "If you two were in the middle of a private conversation, I'll be glad to take Danny out for a walk in his stroller." He didn't wait for an answer, but went straight to the playpen, smiling ear-to-ear, as he lifted the baby into his arms and kissed both cheeks.

Frannie waved off his suggestion. "No, Dan. I was just leaving anyway. Enjoy your family."

"What time do you have to go down to the restaurant?" Dan asked Glory as soon as Frannie left.

"Not until five. Thank God we have Tim and Sara all summer. Those two are amazing in a managerial capacity. Without them, Frannie and I wouldn't have as much flexibility with hours. Thanks to them, we even manage to take nights off most weeks—not together, of course."

"And who's sitting with Danny tonight?" Where his grandson's care was concerned, Dan had an uneasy feeling of being swept away.

"Claire Barkley. She's great with him, and although I didn't know her or her family well, Frannie did. She claimed Claire was exceptionally intelligent and mature for seventeen, and that recommendation was good enough for me."

"How often does she babysit?"

"Well, I haven't had her that long, but the plan is she'll do Mondays through Thursday, while Marion Landis handles the weekends. So that should work out well for all concerned."

Dan paused, strongly suspecting he was among the *all concerned*. "You can still depend on grandpa, Glory. I looked forward to having him to myself those nights I babysat. And he's no trouble for me. He sleeps like an angel. I hope you didn't think he was too much for me," he said, his eyes searching hers.

"Not at all. Look, we've been through this, Dad. I just didn't want to tie you up. It wasn't just you. I felt bad for Vanessa and Wanda too. Babysitting for a working mother is a commitment. I can afford to pay sitters, so why should I impose on family?" She avoided eye contact with her father and took Danny from his arms. "I just want to change his diaper."

"I'll do that," Dan said gladly. "I love to watch those chubby legs kick."

While Dan played with his grandson, the silence between him and his daughter hung heavily. He put the baby in the playpen, then went to Glory who busied herself polishing the chrome in her already immaculate kitchen. He placed his hand gently on her shoulders and turned her around, forcing her to look at him. "Sweetheart, this is all about Jessica, isn't it?"

Her face went taut, her voice edged with impatience. "What do you mean *this*? I'm trying to be considerate; simple as that. Maybe your own conscience is making you imagine things that are nonexistent."

Dan let go of her and stepped back. He felt as if she had struck him in the face. "My *conscience*? How can you say that?" He threw his hands to his temples as if he wanted to block her words from his memory. "Since Louise died, everyone—including you, Glory, encouraged me—begged me—to get a life. But God forbid that should include one special friend who happens to be a woman!"

Glory rolled her unsympathetic eyes, crossed her arms. "First of all, Dad, I told you that before Alex died. It's a whole different scenario now. And secondly, I get the feeling the 'good doctor' is more than a friend. Or if she isn't yet, she will be."

Dan was so dumbfounded by this radical personality change in his daughter that it left him stunned and silent for a few moments. More importantly, it scared him. He had to suppress an urge to lash back at her; to demand an apology, to explain that his love for her was not threatened by his relationship with Jessica. But he feared any further discussion now would escalate into an argumentative discussion. He'd have to tread gently with Glory or he'd lose her and his grandson.

"Would you mind if I took Danny for a walk around the cove for a half hour or so? I think you can use some time alone."

"Oh, don't worry about that," she said, her expression veiled with bitterness. "I get plenty of time alone. But go ahead, take him. He loves a stroll around Perkins Cove."

"Okay, but we still need to talk," he said cautiously.

"What more is there to say? We've discussed the situation ad nauseam."

"Ad nauseam? Is it that repulsive to you?"

Glory relented a bit and gave him a weak smile, although she spoke with a disparaging tone. "I didn't mean for you to take the expression literally, Dad. I meant what I said. What's there to discuss? You're entitled to make your own choices and form your own opinions, and I'm entitled to mine, right?"

"And you've already formed an opinion—a negative opinion—about Jessica, haven't you?" he asked, trying to keep the rising anger out of his voice.

She lifted her eyebrows. "Not really. Jessica Branson is a fine doctor. In that capacity, I have nothing negative to say about her."

"But on a personal level, you feel differently, don't you? You see her as some kind of rival for my attention."

Glory rolled her eyes. "I wouldn't use *rival,* but something like that, yes," she admitted.

"But that's where you're wrong, Glory," Dan pleaded. "She's my friend and yes, maybe something stronger will grow out of our friendship, but that in no way threatens my relationship with you and Danny or any of my children. You can't equate the two types of feelings. You don't stop loving your family because someone else entered your life."

"No, I'll agree with that," she said, "but you can allow your family to fade in the background a bit. And when I say *you*, I mean that in the plural sense—"

"But you think I fall into that category, don't you?" He threw his gaze and hands up to heaven. "Dear God, Glory, on the basis of what? What the heck did I do to turn you against me like this?"

Her eyes welled with tears and her voice broke when she spoke. "Nothing, I guess. At least nothing I should object to. I want you to be happy, Dad, really I do." She looked at him with eyes half pleading, half remorseful. "But I feel so abandoned. You've been like my father, my brother and my friend all rolled into one, and now with her . . ." She couldn't speak.

Dan took the few steps towards her and held her in his arms. "I'm still all of those things, Glory. Look, I don't know what's up ahead for me and Jessica. It could all fizzle out. I hope not, to be honest, but right now it's good. I feel alive again. What could be wrong with that?"

"For you nothing, for me, everything. It took me thirty-five years to find you, Dad, and now I have to share you? Can you blame me for being upset? I feel like my world is falling apart. Starting with Jason, then my parents, then Alex and now you. Everyone I love I lose. And how about Danny? Think about it. My baby lost his daddy and now his time with grandpa will be sharply curtailed."

"That's not true! Why do you think it would?" Dan's gripping frustration weakened his control.

"Because that's the way a lot of women are—no, I should say people, not women, because men are often guilty too. They pretend to be perfectly amenable to sharing you with your family; they'll give you plenty of freedom until they hook you into marriage. Then they think they own you. You live by their calendar, not your own."

Dan stood there, perplexed, studying her face. "I can't believe you're so cynical. Is that what Jason did to you all those years you were married?"

She nodded, then gave it more thought. "He took complete control of my life. Every free moment was planned by him. Oh, I could suggest, of course, but everything was subject to his approval."

"So when you told me how much you loved him, you weren't being truthful, were you? Not that you owed me the truth—not when it came to your marriage."

"But that's the weirdest part. I was so damn naïve; I never realized what was happening. He was a good husband; considerate, affectionate, attentive . . . all those attributes that supposedly constitute the perfect husband. He was fine as long as he had me at his side whenever he wanted me there or tucked away at home when he wasn't. But he'd be highly insulted if I wanted to spend time alone with anyone else. That was unheard of! Not even my parents. He didn't dislike them, but we only visited them when both of us could go. There was no such thing as mother/daughter lunches or that sort of thing." She smirked and shook her head. "What a jerk I was."

Dan frowned at her story. "That's insane, particularly in this day and age. Why did you allow him to control you like that?"

She threw her hands out. "Who knows why? As I said, I was young and naïve. It became a way of life and I just accepted it. It wasn't until he left me, when I found myself enjoying this newfound freedom that I realized what I had been missing. I never realized I was nothing more than a possession to him." Her brows furrowed and she waved it off. "How the heck did I get on that? We were talking about you and Jessica."

"You were talking about manipulative people, suggesting that Jessica was one of them."

"I did not!" she said defensively. "I was generalizing."

"Maybe so, but Jessica was the crux of our discussion."

"Okay, so maybe I was generalizing with her in mind. I'm not accusing her; I'm just saying you should keep your eyes wide open."

"They *are* wide open, and I can say without reservation that there's nothing negative about her. She's kind, caring, dedicated and fun to be with, and I'm sorry you don't see her that way because she's become very special to me."

"Well, good. If you're happy, I'm happy," she said with a smile that belied her words, then closed the subject. "If you're going to take Danny out, you'd better go now. He'll need dinner and a bath before I go to work."

"I'm going," he said, taking his grandson in his arms. "But do me one little favor, Glory? Think back to what you were feeling when my family turned their backs on you. Remember how much that hurt you to be rejected like that?"

"That's not a fair comparison, Dad. I was *family,* your *daughter.* Jessica is a stranger who just walked into your life when you were too vulnerable to resist."

"And you were a stranger too when we met. But I loved you instantly."

She gave him a *give me patience* eyeroll.

He stopped once more on his way out with Danny. "Give her a chance, Glory. If you love me, please do it for me, okay?"

With a *we'll see* shrug, she nodded and turned away.

# Chapter Twenty-eight

"It'll be either a late lunch or an early dinner, whatever you want to call it," Tess Oliveri told her daughter. "I checked with Suzanne and she's working six to closing tomorrow night, so I thought three o'clock would be good. You'll have a chance to go home and change after closing Amore Breakfast, with plenty of time for daddy's birthday dinner before you go to Amore Evenings."

"That should work," Frannie said. "Who's coming?"

"Who would you expect?" Tess said as if mocking the question. "Just us, your uncle Jerry and Suzanne, Aunt Josie and Uncle Andy," she answered. "That's all the family we have here, right?"

Frannie laughed. "I'm not complaining, Mom. I had no one else in mind. Family is all we need," she said while silently wishing she could include both Sergio and Rob in that picture. "How is Uncle Jerry these days? I haven't seen him for weeks."

"Oh, don't waste your worries on him, he's doing great. The good Lord must still have a hand over him. Since he started with AA, he's like a new man. Your father is so proud; he says he feels like the brother he lost came back to life."

"Thank God, but I do worry about him slipping again. Suzanne needs him now more than ever since she and Rob broke up."

"Yes, that's so awful. I had no idea until I called Suzanne to invite them to daddy's dinner. Then she had to tell me. What's that all about, do you know? Those two are crazy about each other! What could have happened?"

"Who knows, Mom? It's their business and we can't ask questions. If Suzanne wants to talk, she knows where to find us."

She hated lying to her mother or even being evasive, but sometimes she had no choice. She only held back when she wanted to spare her hurt or worry, or if she was sworn to secrecy, which was the case here. "Okay, then. I'll see you on Thursday. I wish I could come earlier to give you a hand, but—"

"Don't bother to explain. I wouldn't dream of asking you. With your busy schedule in the summertime, I don't know how you can keep your head on straight."

"We all find time to do what we like to do, Mom, and I never take on more than I can handle, so don't worry about me."

"I don't really. You seem to thrive on that hectic pace. It's amazing how you can keep up with it. But anyway, I'll be fine. Aunt Josie and Uncle Andy are coming earlier, so she'll help me. You know how she is, my sister, she can't sit still."

She hung up smiling, comforted by her mother's voice. Although she'd always avoided dumping her problems on her parents, it was good to know they were close by again and she could if she felt the need. Several years before, friends of theirs had convinced them to move with them to a magnificent adult community in Vermont. The spacious condo and all the amenities that came with it were too tempting to resist. But after giving it a try, her parents soon discovered that neither its active lifestyle nor luxurious surroundings could supersede their family and roots.

During her conversation with her mother, Frannie had ignored the bleep of an incoming call. With a yawn, she tapped out the numbers to retrieve the message.

Her legs went numb as she listened.

"Cara mia, I so sorry . . . so disappointed not to hear your voice. I wish I could tell you to call me, but that not possible. If I get chance, I call you again."

Nonplussed, she stared at the phone in her hand as if it might offer her an explanation. *Not possible?* What in heaven's name is going on in Eddie Pisano's house to prevent him from calling?

Her frown dropped and she drew a deep breath. At least he called, she mused, breaking into a smile. He still cares, she was sure of it. She had heard it in his voice. Although Glory had alluded to the fact that theirs was just a fleeting romance blown out of proportion, Frannie strongly disagreed.

Instinctively, she started to call her, but changed her mind. She thought maybe it would restore her faith a little. Poor Glory seemed to be digging her hole of depression so deep Frannie feared she might never be able to climb out. Somehow she had to help her. But when your own spirits are so deflated that you need a hand yourself, where do you find the strength to help someone else?

She put aside all thoughts of Glory, allowing herself to bask in the hope Sergio's phone call had generated. She gave up trying to guess her way through his mysterious message. She listened to it a few times more and concluded that whatever the problem, it circled around his mother. Even if she had reluctantly assumed a subservient position all her married life, she might be exploding with power now that her husband is dead, as Tony Gerard has surmised. Or maybe she's crying her eyes out, using the grieving widow image to manipulate her children.

In any event, Frannie's thoughts did not conjure up images of the stereotyped sweet old Italian woman whose sole purpose in life was to please her family. No, Philomena Giannetta, sight unseen, had already become a formidable foe. She had to be the reason Sergio hadn't contacted her before sending the flowers and until today's phone call.

And as much as she didn't like to entertain the thought, she strongly suspected she had fallen in love with a mamma's boy.

# Chapter Twenty-nine

Dan was determined not to let his troubles show on his face tonight. The last time they were together, Jessica had seen beyond his forced smile and questioned him about it. He had a hard time convincing her that he wasn't harboring dark thoughts.

They had a romantic dinner at Clay Hill Farm, where the tables weren't cramped together. They sat at a window table where soft lights from the outdoor gardens twinkled in the darkness. They could relax and speak intimately without fear of being overheard. In a quiet moment, they held hands across the table while they sipped their wine.

"You're staring at me, Dan." Jessica fanned her fingers before his eyes. "What are you thinking? You look so deep in thought again."

He nodded and smiled softly. "I apologize. Yes, I was deep in thought, thinking about your profound effect on me. I'm crazy in love with you, but you know that, don't you?"

Jessica lowered her eyes and brushed a feathery finger across his hand. "Yes, I guess I've known for sure since that afternoon on the beach." She lifted her gaze to meet his. "But it's nice to hear anyway. As a matter of fact," she said playfully, "feel free to say it as often as the urge strikes you."

Dan put his elbows on the table and leaned closer, unaware how the flickering candle illuminated his aging, but still ruggedly handsome face. "I love you, I love you, I love you. And it feels *so-o-o* good to say it." He sat back, squared his shoulders and grinned. His expression needed no words once he lifted his brows questioningly.

Jessica laughed. "My turn, huh? Yes, I course I love you, too," she said, then lowered her voice. "Do you think I would have invited you to my bedroom if I didn't?"

Dan stared at her for a long moment, as if marveling at the intricacies of a masterpiece. "All of a sudden it's not food I hunger for," he whispered.

She smiled suggestively. "I know the feeling, but relax. We have all night to satisfy all our hungers. We'll start with food."

\* \* \*

They got through dinner feeling giddy and euphoric now that they had openly professed their love. It wasn't until much later that their mood went somber. They lay sated in her bed, snuggled together and wrapped in a patchwork quilt.

Jessica laced her fingers with his. "I still think something's bothering you," she said. "I sense something, Dan . . . like, you know how much we love each other and you're glad we finally shared the words, but now where does that leave us? What do we do about it? Talk to me, sweetheart. If there ever was a time for honesty, it's now."

He stroked her hair and brushed a kiss on her forehead. "There *is* something on my mind, Jess, but I'm not sure this is the right time to discuss it. And if I'm really lucky, it might all blow over or maybe I can work it out myself without worrying your pretty head about it."

The little kisses he blew at the back of her neck had been working their magic again, but she managed to fight them off. She wiggled herself out of his arms first, then the quilt, and sat up. She propped the pillows behind her and crossed her arms.

He looked up from the position he had been enjoying and when their gazes met, he knew their cuddling time was temporarily over. Although she still had a loving smile on her beautiful face, it was clearly shaded with that *We need to talk* expression.

Dan reluctantly sat up next to her. Jessica was ready to listen and from the determined look on her face, trying to stall her would be futile. He introduced the sensitive subject with a question. "Jess, how are your children reacting to our relationship?"

"Oh, okay, so it's family stuff, huh?" She asked the question lightly as if it were a common problem which they'd have to struggle through. "It's to be expected, Dan. When children lose a parent, it's like God died. They don't want to see anyone walk in his or her shoes." She turned to search his eyes, then asked, "Are your children giving you a hard time about me, Dan? Now don't lie or give me a washed down version. I need—we both need—the truth. Maybe if we try together, we can win them over."

"Why? Are your kids against me too?"

She pursed her lips. "I wouldn't say against you personally. I do think, though, they'd be relieved to hear that we broke up. Up to now there were only a few subtle hints, like, 'I don't want to rain on your parade, Mom, but Dan Madison—or any man—might get tired of being pushed aside by the demands of your profession.'"

"That's not true. I'm real proud of what you do. I can handle it."

"That's not the point. They're just trying to pile up the negatives in case our 'friendship' goes beyond the boundaries they would deem acceptable."

"Are they both against us or is one worse than the other?"

Jessica couldn't give the question a quick yes or no answer. She gave it some thought first. "Maybe, maybe not. Carole has always been more vocal about everything. Richard seems to hold back mostly, but every now and then he lets a few words slip out—very few—but rife with hidden messages or warnings."

"Like, for instance?"

She tried to dismiss it. "Do we really have to get into that? I'd really rather not repeat his words. I might have misinterpreted his meaning and I wouldn't want to cast shadows over him, in your eyes particularly."

He threw her a sidelong glance. "C'mon, Jess. Weren't you the one who wanted total honesty? And after I thought about it twice, you're right. How else are we going to fight their opposition if we don't join forces? You know, 'United we stand, divided we fall,' right?"

She shot him a critical look. "Gee, don't make this sound like we're at war with our own children!"

"I'm not, not at all! We just have to *prevent* war with our children."

"Seriously," she continued, her voice softer, "it's alienation we want to avoid. That would kill me." She cringed at the painful thought of losing her close relationship with her son and daughter.

Dan merely nodded, but her words had tugged at his conscience. He took her hand again, and stroked her fingers while he ruminated a few moments. "It would kill me, too. Not only if it happened to my relationship with my children, but God forbid, you and yours as well. That would be a big price to pay for either of us. And trust me, no matter how much you love me now, you'd hate me later for driving a wedge between you and your children."

She wrinkled her nose. "No, don't say *hate*. It's too strong a word. And I doubt that you'd ever intentionally do anything that remotely resembles 'driving a wedge.' I think I know you well enough to say you're not capable of hurting anyone, no matter how slight. You'd bow out gracefully before you let that happen." She threw the quilt aside and started to get off the bed, then swung her legs right back in. "But wait a minute. We got sidetracked. This conversation started about your children, not mine. You never elaborated. What's been going on?"

Dan heaved a sigh, not knowing what to respond, how much and how truthful. With total honesty he could lose her and he wasn't about to take that gamble. "Okay," he began, "First of all, your assessment of my character is flattering, but I'm not as unselfish as you might think. Frankly, if my family were to express strong objection to my relationship with you, that wouldn't stop me from seeing you. No way! It's my life, my decisions to make. I certainly don't have to answer to my children. I haven't always agreed with their decisions and choices, but I've always respected that their lives are their own, and I expect the same from them."

"And you would feel no guilt for hurting them?" She didn't wait for an answer, but scrunched her face for another question. "And speaking of guilt, do you get occasional guilt attacks for loving me? Does it make you feel unfaithful to Louise?"

Dan sighed again, thinned his lips and decided to go for the whole truth. "The only thing I feel guilty about is not feeling guilty."

Jessica arched her brows as though his answer surprised her. "That's amazing," she murmured.

"Why?"

"Because that's exactly how I've been reacting. I actually *try* to feel guilty, but I can't."

Despite the serious nature of their discussion, Dan had to laugh. "Now why would you want to punish yourself like that?"

Her brows furrowed. "I'm not sure myself. It's crazy, I know, but I feel as if I should suffer in some way. It doesn't seem right to embrace this newfound happiness as a result of Doug's death."

Dan threw his hands up. "You're absolutely right, you *are* crazy! I can't believe someone as intelligent as you would make such an insane comment. What we have together is not a result of Doug's death. How the heck did you draw that conclusion?"

Jessica laughed, aware that her comment did sound ludicrous. "I worded it incorrectly. Naturally, it's not a *direct* result of Doug's death, but we would never be here, like this," she said, circling a finger around the bed, "if Doug and Louise hadn't died."

"So you *do* feel guilty?"

"No, that's my point. Like you, I feel that I should, but I don't." She threw a forlorn gaze upward as though apologizing to Doug for her uncontrollable feelings.

Dan lifted the quilt with an invitational smile. "In that case, why don't we both shut up and savor the moment? Life is too short to let guilt or lack of guilt stand in the way of our happiness."

Jessica relaxed with a giggle. "Words of wisdom, my dear Mr. Madison. I couldn't have said it better." She cuddled herself in his arms again, feeling content and thankful that Dan Madison had walked into her life.

# Chapter Thirty

Frannie had to psych herself to appear relaxed and happy at her dad's birthday dinner. Sergio's call had stirred up her hopes again, but two days had passed and she hadn't heard a word since he left that strange phone message.

She pulled up in her parents' driveway still feeling anxious, but the moment her dad greeted her at the door and kissed her, he looked so happy and healthy that her anxiety melted away.

"I left your present in my trunk, Dad. I never got around to wrapping it, so I'll bring it in when we have your cake, okay?"

"Of course it's okay. I hope you didn't spend a lot of money again," he said, wagging a finger at her. "Your mother and I feel bad when you buy us expensive presents."

Mimicking him, she wagged her finger right back. "You're preaching again, Dad. I'm perfectly capable of handling my own money. If I couldn't afford them, I wouldn't buy them." She laughed inwardly anticipating how he'd react when he opened this year's present. She had gone overboard and bought him a complete set of expensive golf clubs. For sure, he'd scold her first, but he'd be thrilled.

She joined her mom and her aunt in the kitchen while her dad and uncle relaxed in the den.

"Suzanne and Uncle Jerry should be here any minute," Tess said. "She called when she left to pick him up."

Frannie was hoping she'd get a chance to corner Suzanne and ask if she told Rob about the baby's father. God, she hoped not. There was no way any good could come from that revelation, but Suzanne had disagreed. When she arrived minutes later with Heather in a pink sundress with a matching hat, the two-year-old grabbed everyone's attention. Her grandpa, Frannie's Uncle Jerry, was holding her, beaming with pride. It still blew Frannie's mind to watch him in this new role of loving daddy and grandpa. Until he committed to life under the watchful eye of AA, he expressed neither love nor interest in anyone, not even his granddaughter. It wasn't until his daughter's accident, when he almost lost her, that he secretly vowed to God. He had promised that if He'd spare Suzanne's life and free her from the threat of a murder charge, he would fight his addiction with all the strength he could muster.

Frannie kissed her cousin hello and sneaked her a hooded-eye look. "Hey, what's new, Suzanne?" she said casually, but the big question was in her eyes.

"Nothing. Everything's the same," Suzanne said, meeting her gaze. Her answer sent a clear message that allowed Frannie to breathe a sigh of relief.

It wasn't until after the cake was eaten and the gifts opened that the older folks retired to the den again, taking Heather with them. Suzanne and Frannie had gladly volunteered to clean up so they could talk privately.

Frannie turned to her cousin the moment everyone was safely out of sight. "So you didn't tell him, right?"

"No, not yet, anyway. I'm not sure I ever will. I picked up the phone several times with that *whatever happens happens* attitude, but I always chickened out."

Frannie put the melting remains of the ice cream birthday cake in the freezer while Suzanne continued to load the dishwasher. "I wouldn't call that chickening out, Suzanne. You made the right choice."

Suzanne nodded with a dubious smirk. "Yeah, right. For everyone but me."

Frannie clenched her teeth, trying to release her frustration without raising her voice. "Let it go, Suzanne. If you don't, you'll open a door for a lifetime of heartaches, not only for you but your daughter as well."

"That door is open no matter which way I go."

Tess took them by surprise when she walked in. "What's the big secret between you two?"

"What secret? We're just talking, Mom," Frannie said, her tone a little too casual to be credible.

Tess returned a knowing smile, shaking her head. "No, you can't fool me. I heard you guys when I came out of the bathroom. You were whispering like two thieves in the night." She made the chat-chat-chat gesture with her fingers.

Frannie relaxed with the assurance her mother hadn't picked up any of their conversation. If she had, she wouldn't be teasing them. She threw Tess a piercing gaze, though, silently asking her not to push it.

Tess suddenly realized she had walked in on a serious discussion. Her face sobered and she walked off with a hand wave. "Okay, I'll leave you two alone," she said.

Frannie drew a breath and blew it out fast. "Look, Suzanne, there's no sense rehashing it. You know how I feel. I can preach till I'm blue in the face, but that won't change the fact that the decision is yours alone to make. Just promise me you won't make any impulsive moves without considering *very, very carefully* the ramifications of your decision."

"Don't worry. I've become a hopeless insomniac doing just that."

# Chapter Thirty-one

Kim Haggarty peeked into the bedrooms of her two children. Satisfied that they were asleep, she joined her husband out on their screened-in porch. Crickets were singing their song in the darkness while Greg was glued to the TV screen in rapt attention. He was watching a political debate, listening to one of the candidates vying for The White House. The presidential hopeful gave myriad reasons why his opponents should not hold the office, but so far Kim hadn't heard anything to convince her that this one should.

She sat quietly until the last of the candidates had spoken, the political analyst had wrapped up, and the station went to commercial. Greg then got out of his recliner and stretched his arms and legs. "I'll go pour our wine now. What kind do you want tonight?" he asked routinely. They had fallen into the habit of enjoying a glass together after their children went to bed. Like a reward at the end of an exhausting day, Kim had said.

She wrinkled her nose, as if she found the suggestion of wine unappealing. "None," she said, but she couldn't stop that cat-that-ate-the-canary smile from creeping up her face.

Greg tilted his head and looked at her quizzically. "None? That's a switch. You always look forward to your nightly glass of wine." He shrugged his shoulders and started to walk away, headed for the kitchen and the wine.

"Come back, Greg. I need to talk to you," she said, then brushed it off. "No, on second thought, you'd better get your wine. You'll need it."

He peered at her, then took a longer, more analytical look. "You're grinning like you're dying to tell me something. So I guess it's nothing bad, right?"

Kim clasped her hands. "Right."

"Some juicy gossip going around town? Is that what you can't wait to tell me?"

"Wrong!" She blew a breath. "Will you just go and hurry back 'cause you'll never guess."

Greg came back with his glass of cabernet sauvignon and sat in the chair facing her. His wife's smile was infectious and he found himself laughing, though he had no idea why. "Okay, you have my ear now. Spill it out; I'm listening."

Kim's smile weakened. "I hope you'll still be smiling after I tell you." Her gaze fell to her lap for a moment. When it lifted, their eyes locked. "The stick showed a plus sign."

A dozen wrinkles rippled his forehead. "What the heck are you talking about? What stick?"

"The stick that comes with a pregnancy test."

Greg stared at her, bewildered. She couldn't mean what he thought she meant. "A plus sign means positive, right? *Whose* stick?"

Kim threw her head back and rolled her eyes. "*My* stick, stupid! Who else would I be talking about? I'm three weeks late, so I took the test this morning. I was in shock too, so I waited for tonight to tell you."

Greg left the club chair and moved to the sofa. He held her hand and stared at her, still in disbelief. "Sweetheart, I hate to see you get your hopes up like this, but that damn thing has to be wrong. I'm sure you remember what the doctor said way back when."

"Yes, I remember the grim prognosis, but I also remember when I said 'Never?' and he answered, 'I'm not God. I can never say never.'"

"Sure I remember that. But he was just trying to soften the blow for you. I caught the hopeless smirk he threw me, like I would have to help you accept the fact that we couldn't have any more children."

"But the fact is, he was right—he's not God. And God decided that the Haggartys should have a welcome addition to their family. At least I hope it's welcome." She gazed at him hopefully.

Greg burst out laughing and hugged his wife. "Honey, if we can trust that stick, then I'm thrilled! For you, for me and for the kids. I'm shocked out of my mind, but I couldn't be happier, believe me."

Kim exhaled the breath she had held too long and allowed her tears to spill out. "That's all I needed to hear, Greg. Now I can be thrilled too. But let's not tell anyone— not even our parents—not until I go to the doctor. That'll make it official."

* * *

Kim was snoring softly in Greg's arms while his mind raced with pleasant thoughts about the baby. He kissed her gently while she slept, thanking God for giving him a wife as precious as Kim. He didn't deserve her; that was for sure.

He cringed as the memory of his one night of infidelity filled his mind again. One passionate night in New York with Suzanne Oliveri. The night that left him with sickening waves of guilt he'd never been able to shake off and never would.

It wasn't until after he dozed off that he shot up in bed, his eyes wide, like searchlights in the darkness. It hit him like a bolt of lightning. He had a flashback of how shocked everyone was when the news broke that Suzanne's live-in lover, Tyler Keaton, the creep she was later accused of murdering, was not the father of her baby. At the time there was much speculation and plenty of wagging tongues, but Heather had been conceived while Suzanne lived with

Keaton in New York, so no one knew for sure. Even Greg wondered who the guy was, never considering himself in light of his sterility. His *assumed* sterility.

*Stupid, friggin' jackass!* he thought. All he had to do was count the months from his night with her in that round bed he couldn't erase from his mind, and the day Heather was born.

*My God, she's mine! That beautiful child is my daughter!* He got out of bed, glanced back at his wife, who slept peacefully, probably with happy dreams about their unborn baby.

By the time he reached the bathroom, Greg was crying silently. He sat on the lid of the seat, his head cradled in his hands. It was then that his eye spotted the stick in the wastebasket. He jumped to his feet and raised the lid. The wine he had drunk suddenly wanted out.

# Chapter Thirty-two

Frannie noticed the black Lincoln pulling into a parking space, but nothing about it captured her attention. Cars came in and out continually from the moment Amore Breakfast opened until shortly before it closed. She focused exclusively on the hungry people around her, all of whom waited patiently for tables. Ordinarily, she loved chatting with them and answering their questions about local spots of interest. But not today, not at this very moment.

She stopped a conversation midsentence when three passengers emerged from the Lincoln. Her heart went into fast forward while her legs went rubbery. She had been proud of herself the past few days, having made a diligent effort to sweep Sergio from her thoughts. With perseverance she'd eventually get him out of her system, she kept telling herself.

Her resolve diminished when Sergio's gaze locked with hers. He was walking directly toward her with a rail-thin fortyish man she assumed was his cousin, Eddie Pisano. The elderly woman at his side would need no introduction. She was short and round with salt and pepper hair twisted into a bun at the nape of her neck. *Attitude* was clearly defined on her face. In one fleeting glance anyone could glean that this was no *Aunt Bea from Mayberry U.S.A.* Ironically, the resemblance between mother and son was startling; the only difference being Sergio's face was strikingly handsome, softened by the gentleness of his personality. Conversely, his mother's face looked stiff as concrete; the defiance permanently etched in her masculine features.

At Amore Breakfast, nine o'clock on a Friday morning in July was certainly an inopportune time to handle a personal crisis, but there it was, only footsteps away. Frannie steeled herself and tried to hold a smile, albeit unsuccessfully. She got away with it, though, since she immediately offered her condolences.

When Sergio introduced Eddie and his mother, Frannie melted a little at the sound of his voice. Its gentle tone, romanticized by his Italian accent, had endeared him to her initially and its charm was still working. He explained to his mother that he had done gardening work for her until the news came about his father's death.

"You can speak Italian, Sergio," Frannie said. "I speak it myself and I'm sure it's easier for her."

Sergio never got a chance to respond. "English easy for me, too," Philomena snapped back complacently. "We get plenty Americano tourists. I learn fast."

"I'm sure you do," Frannie answered with a tight smile. She quickly put them on her waiting list and excused herself. She returned to the dining room, glad she had wormed herself away from the obnoxious woman. What troubled her more was Sergio's demeanor in the presence of his mother. He was a big, muscular guy who looked like he could take on the world, but today he impressed her differently. Like a snail wishing it could curl back in its shell.

But that snail still managed to arouse her sensuality.

Later, when she finally seated them, she was tempted to stop at their table for no other reason than to get another long look at the face that monopolized her dreams. But if he had been nothing more than her gardener for a brief period, why would she single them out for casual conversation?

It was Sergio himself, the drop-dead gorgeous snail, who gave her the opening. She had felt—or maybe imagined—his eyes on her since she walked away from them in the parking lot. He raised a finger now, with that familiar *Check, please* expression.

"Oh, I'm sorry," she said. "Do you need your waitress? I'll send her right over."

"No, not yet, please. My cousin and I, we take little more coffee. But I want to say, I sorry I leave you big headache with gardens. I come back if you like."

Sergio looked at her with puppy dog eyes. While his mother sat next to him with crossed arms, he tried to communicate what he really wanted to convey. There was very little gardening left for him to do now, but that fact carried no weight since his offer was nothing more than an excuse to see her.

"Well, naturally, some spring planting couldn't wait and I handled it when you left, but if you could spare the time, I could still use some help around the property. Why don't you call me any afternoon, before I go to Amore Evenings, and we'll work out a convenient time."

Philomena arched her thick eyebrows and sneered. The blatant gestures easily conveyed that her son should feel no obligation to honor his previous commitment. His father's death should have negated that responsibility. But she said nothing, as though it weren't important enough to concern herself.

A short time later, on their way out, Sergio offered Frannie a polite thank you for their excellent and hearty breakfasts. Philomena's silence made her stubborn statement in opposition, but Frannie suspected that hell could freeze over before this woman would offer any complimentary words. She had noticed, however, that Philomena's plate looked as if it had been licked clean by a cat. *Well, maybe it was.*

While Sergio walked his mother to the car, Eddie remained to pay the bill, then lingered, waiting to speak to Frannie. "I want to apologize for my aunt," he said. "She's a tough, cantankerous woman, and to tell you the truth, I can't wait till she goes back to Italy."

Frannie laughed. "Oh, you poor thing. I had only a short dose of her but that left a lasting impression. If I were in your shoes and had to put up with her 24/7, I'd probably be pulling my hair out. How long do you think they'll stay? Is there an end in sight?"

Eddie shrugged. "It's hard to judge. A few weeks, I think. It's my own fault. I felt sorry for my aunt after my uncle died. But you have to understand that I never knew her—I had a whole different image, believe me. She's the most overbearing woman I've ever known. Today, for instance, we made an excuse to get away from her. We told her to forget breakfast, we'd grab something out, but she insisted on tailing along." He raised his eyes to heaven. "My cousin, God love him, has the patience of a saint."

"And maybe that patience is the heart of the problem. It allows her to manipulate him. Maybe he ought to try dishing out some tough love." Frannie could no longer ignore the two women behind him waiting to speak to her. "But hey, that's his business, not mine. Thanks for coming in. Hope to see you again."

"Oh, you will! Now that I've been here, I'll definitely be back."

As she spoke to the two women, she watched the Lincoln pull out. Anticipating Sergio's next call, her stomach rumbled, but a rush of troublesome thoughts filled her head. Where could this lead—to a temporary love affair whenever he could get away from that witch? To an affair that would leave her brokenhearted?

All day long, the sensible part of her sent warnings that throbbed her temples.

But the other part was rapidly taking command and a shoo-in to win the battle.

# Chapter Thirty-three

Jerry Oliveri arrived at his daughter's apartment with a bag of groceries. He pulled out a dozen eggs, an onion, a plastic container of fried zucchini slices and a loaf of French bread.

"Why did you bring food, Dad? I'll be back in an hour, tops. I'm only going grocery shopping. I could have picked up lunch for us."

"What's the big deal? A zucchini and onion omelet is better than anything you can buy and it takes only five minutes to cook."

Heather came running in at the sound of her grandfather's voice. "Poppy! Poppy!" she called, arms outstretched and giggling.

While Jerry played with her, Suzanne watched with a soft smile, still amazed that he had made the commitment to stop drinking and attend AA meetings regularly. If he hadn't, he'd never be playing with his granddaughter now. It was almost as if he had been reborn the day he made that promise to himself.

"What are you staring at?" he asked his daughter.

"Nothing in particular. Just that I'm so proud of you, Dad. We're all proud."

His face went grim. "Don't be too proud. It hasn't been easy, that's for sure. Sometimes the temptation is stronger than you are." He kissed Heather on the forehead and the smile crossed his face again. "But this little angel keeps me going. I want her to be able to depend on me. Especially now that Rob's not around." He looked at her through squinted eyes. "Are you sure you can't tell me why you two broke up?

You never know, maybe I can help in some way. I hate to see you hurting like this."

"Like what? Who said I'm hurting?"

He gave her a rueful smile. "Since I found sobriety, Suzanne, I see everything a lot clearer now. So don't bother trying to fool your old man."

The gentle plea in his tone had reached its target. She broke down and sobbed.

Jerry didn't hesitate. He put Heather down, dragged a chair next to his daughter. She had covered her eyes with her hands and he gently peeled them away. "What's going on? Even if I can't help, it's always better to get it off your chest."

It took Suzanne awhile to speak. She didn't know whether it was her consuming problem with Rob, or her father behaving like a father, that brought on the rush of tears. She wiped them with a napkin, then blew her nose. "He wants to adopt Heather." She saw her father's eyes widen with unexpected pleasure. "No, before you get excited, Dad, it sounds good, but it's not. He can't adopt her without her real father's permission. And that's not going to happen. *Never.*"

"Look, Suzanne, whoever the hell the SOB is, if he hasn't given a damn about her for two years, what makes you think he wouldn't sign a release?" He made a sudden sour face. "I'm not sure I want to know this, but do you think he'd be looking for a payoff?"

"Absolutely not!" she snapped back.

Suzanne's indignant tone did not pass unnoticed by her father. "You sound like you're defending the guy. Suzanne, you know I've never asked you any questions about Heather's father. I was hoping you'd come to me some day and talk. Then I decided the less I know—"

Suzanne put her hand up but Jerry ignored it. "No, wait. I admit that when you came home from New York pregnant, I was in no shape to listen—"

"Or care," Suzanne interjected. Remembering his constant mortifying and repulsive inebriation, she hadn't been able to hold back the biting remark, but she went instantly contrite. "I'm sorry, Dad. You didn't deserve that. I know what a struggle it's been; how hard you've been trying to stay sober. And I know you're doing it mostly for me and Heather." She leaned forward and gave him a quick hug and kiss.

Jerry's eyes glazed over, but he didn't cry. He swallowed the lump in his throat and continued. Now that she had opened up, he didn't want the subject to drop. "What makes you so sure he won't give her up? As far as I can see, he shows no parental responsibility at all. He doesn't support her and he's probably never seen her. Am I right?" He watched her carefully, searching for the truth in her eyes or body language. As it turned out, it was her three-second pause that revealed the answer to his question. "No, I'm wrong. He has seen her, hasn't he? And how much do you know about him other than what he told you? Can he be trusted with her?" Jerry's imagination escalated his fears for his granddaughter's safety.

Suzanne cast her gaze downward and offered no response. All her life she had wished her father would have shown some interest like this, but now it was like trying to catch a runaway train. No matter how you chase it, you can't ever catch up.

There was only one way out of this, she decided. A half truth was better than none.

"First of all, Dad, get it out of your head that her father is some deadbeat bum I dragged off the streets of New York. He's a law-abiding, highly educated decent person, who earns a good living. Believe me, if he had any idea I had a child from our one night together, he would have helped me financially."

"You mean you never told him? That could cause you a lot of trouble down the road, Suzanne. He has a right to know his own child, especially if he's this Mr. Wonderful you describe."

"He is, Dad," Suzanne said, unable to face him. "But no one is infallible. We all have our moments of weakness. You see, Mr. Wonderful made one tremendous mistake. He had a brief infatuation with me. And I'm not being selfish denying him his daughter. I wish for Heather's sake as well as his that they could know each other. But that, unfortunately, can't ever happen either." She paused, aware that their conversation had gone too far already. She took a deep breath and spoke slowly so that she could choose her words carefully. "As I said, Heather's father has no idea he made me pregnant. Even I thought it was Tyler's child—after all, I lived with him. But I don't want to rehash what Tyler put me through . . . I was so vulnerable back then. So when this Mr. Wonderful came by, he was so different from Tyler, that I liked him instantly. I was able to relax and enjoy our conversation. He had a good sense of humor, listened to all the silly things I had to say, and in general, made me feel good about myself."

"So good that he managed to get you pregnant, huh?" He cringed when he unintentionally spoke his immediate thoughts. He bit down on his lip, angrier at himself for neglecting her so long. If she'd had a father's guidance during those formidable years, she probably would have never met Tyler Keaton or this guy who made her pregnant.

"I know it hurts you to hear it, Dad, but the plain truth is I offered no resistance. And the worst of my sin—and his—is that he told me right up front that he had a wife and two children. I went up to his hotel room anyway. He was from Oklahoma," she lied, "and we both knew we'd never see each other again, so what harm could it do? His family would never know."

Jerry's conscience reminded him that he had been no paragon of virtue himself, but it killed him to know his daughter had drifted into a life so far removed from the teachings and examples set by her mother. "I hope your mother can't hear you right now. She had tried so hard to raise you with some sense of morality, but if you see no harm in sleeping with a married man, I guess she failed, didn't she?"

"I hate to keep throwing it up, Dad, but maybe if you hadn't left the entire parenting responsibility to Mom, I might have developed different attitudes. But it wasn't until after she passed away and I lost you to the almighty bottle that I gave up. I was bitter and angry with God for taking both of you away from me."

Jerry blinked his moist eyes and his breath caught in his throat. She was absolutely right, of course. By the time she had reached her teen years, alcohol had become his number one companion. He had little time for his daughter's problems. Her mother had grabbed the reins and that was fine with him. What could he say to her now? Not a damn thing could undo his past mistakes.

"I'll go to my grave regretting those years—for you and for your mother. I was selfish and turned a deaf ear on both of you. After awhile your mother couldn't depend on me for anything. Oh, I took out the garbage every night and cleaned the garage now and then. Everything else—and I mean everything, even you—I dumped it all on her." His eyes teared up again and this time he let them fall freely.

"Forget it, Dad. You have enough of an uphill climb battling your alcoholism. Don't burden yourself with regrets. Mom loved you in spite of your weaknesses." She shrugged as if to say she couldn't understand why. "She was forever making excuses for you."

"I know. That's what makes me feel worse. She was so damn good and I treated her so badly sometimes."

Suzanne laughed, trying to break the mood and drift away from the subject of Heather's father. "Well, I'll agree with you on that one," she said.

He neither laughed nor smiled with her. Instead he studied her silently a few seconds. "So it's because of his family that you never told him? To protect them?"

"Yes, And Heather too, in a way. Think about it. Even though he's a decent guy, what difference does that make? He could never be a real father to her; not when he already has a family. So why cause everyone so much pain? And think of Heather. How do you think she'd feel knowing how she was conceived?"

"Someday she'll be asking her own questions. How will you answer her then?"

"I haven't figured that out yet. Don't think it won't haunt me, knowing that day will come eventually. I gave a lot of thought to telling Rob, though. It's been agonizing trying to make that decision. I knew what *not* telling him would cost me, but I came to the conclusion that if he can't accept us as we are, then our situation is hopeless. Better to break it off now rather than have it looming over us after we married."

Jerry nodded, wishing he could disagree, then asked, "Is it all about his adopting Heather or is it just that he needs to know who her father is?"

"Probably both. He feels there should be no secrets between us, but I strongly disagree. I can understand why he wants to adopt Heather, and believe me, there's nothing I'd want more, but not if revealing her father is the price I have to pay." She waved her hand and shivered, as if the thought chilled her.

"So you gave him up instead, didn't you? It was your choice?"

Suzanne shrugged. "He gave me no other choice."

Jerry stared ahead, focused on nothing while he pondered all she had said. Finally, he drew a breath and said, "On second thought, Suzanne, your mother didn't need me. She did a hell of a job raising you."

# Chapter Thirty-four

A whole week had passed since Tim and his daughter had dined at Amore Evenings. Emma had teased him about his noticeable reaction to Glory English. He had to admit that initially he was stunned by her good looks, but it wasn't until after Frannie had introduced them that he began to feel like a schoolboy with his first crush. They had exchanged only a few polite words but her voice and her smile had captivated him.

All week long that mesmerizing smile had invaded his thoughts surprisingly often. Under different circumstances, with such an immediate attraction, he would not have hesitated to make a move, but with Glory, he wrestled with indecision. He wasn't sure he wanted to get involved with someone in love with a memory. Stiff competition. And even if he did decide to call her, he suspected she would approach a new relationship with extreme caution or avoid it completely to spare herself any more pain.

On Sunday morning Tim was driving towards a local eatery where he usually met friends for breakfast after ten o'clock mass. But impulse made him pull over. He reached for his cell phone and called Frannie Oliveri.

"Frannie, I know it's a bad time to call," he said apologetically, "but I was thinking about driving down for breakfast. And I was wondering if you'd have time to talk to me later today. Just for a few minutes; it's personal."

"Is anything wrong, Tim?" she asked, curious and slightly worried. She couldn't imagine what was on his mind or why he chose her to confide in. Yes, they were friends, but not as close anymore now that Suzanne was no longer under his constant care.

"Nothing's wrong," Tim answered, starting to feel foolish. "I'll explain when I see you. I just need a little help with a minor decision."

"Wow! Now I'm really curious! Why don't you drive down, have breakfast, and if you're not in a hurry, you can hang around until I close. We can talk uninterrupted then."

"Perfect. And in between I can always browse around your charming village or sit by the beach."

"Strange . . ." Frannie mumbled when she turned off the phone. Curiosity put an eager smile on her face, but she was too busy to give it much thought. She went out on the porch to call the next people on her waiting list.

* * *

Frannie was ready and waiting when Tim returned from his "browsing" trip around Ogunquit. His arms were overloaded with shopping bags from Revelations, a gift shop also located on Shore Road a short walk from Amore Breakfast.

She lifted a brow and smiled. "I wouldn't call that browsing."

Tim laughed. "They have a fantastic stock in there. Really different and interesting stuff. I couldn't resist doing a little early Christmas shopping." He put the bags in his trunk and they both re-entered the restaurant, now cleaned up and quiet.

"This is a little embarrassing," he said, noting Frannie's anticipatory grin. "Am I allowed to change my mind?"

She took a long pull on her water bottle. "No," she said. "You kept me in suspense too long and since I know it's not bad news, I want to hear it now." She folded her arms and waited with the same determined grin. Her mind was already racing. She knew Tim Quinlan was long divorced and his ex-wife had remarried, but if this was going where she thought it was going, it was definitely too good to be true.

Tim gave her a sidelong study. "Why do I get the feeling you know why I'm here?"

"I have absolutely no idea why you're here," she said, trying to hold a benign expression. "What you might see on my face is my own romantic imagination at work; hoping for exciting news," she said, but didn't dare describe the scenes her mind had conjured up.

Tim drew a breath. "Okay, here goes. I wanted to ask you about Glory—"

Frannie slapped the table. "Yes! I was hoping she was the reason you came to see me. So shoot. What do you want to know?"

"Well, actually it was my daughter Emma's idea to talk to you first. She teased the hell out of me that night about my attraction to Glory. I didn't realize it was plastered all over my face." He laughed. "I probably made a real fool of myself." Once he got the introductory words out, he rambled on in that same *how do I get out of this* tone.

Frannie thought it was adorable and wanted to spare him. She patted his hand. "Don't be embarrassed. She turns plenty of heads. The woman is gorgeous and the best part is she's totally oblivious. There's not a trace of conceit in Glory English. Believe me, if I had that effect on the opposite sex I'd put it to good use." She lifted her eyebrows and giggled.

"Don't sell yourself short, Frannie. I'm sure you turn plenty of heads too."

"Yeah, well, let's put it this way: If they were to cast Glory and me in a movie, she'd end up with the male lead and I'd get his best friend."

Tim laughed at the analogy. "Sometimes the friend is the better choice. From what you told me about her jerk husband, he was no prize."

Frannie's face sobered. "He hurt her big time, Tim. She never had a clue that he was planning to leave her. I certainly knew the feeling well. It was the commonality that made our friendship click. We were both burned so badly by our husbands." She waved it over her shoulder. "Well, that's water under the bridge. Let's get back to Glory. I was about to say that after her husband took off with another woman, she lost all confidence in herself. She doesn't see herself as the mega-beauty everyone else sees. If it wasn't enough to hold Jason, she figured, why would her face and body impress anyone else? Then along came Alex Howard—" Again, Frannie waved it off because there was no need to repeat that tragic story. "But let's get back to you, Tim. You want to ask her out but don't know if she's approachable yet. So what is it you want, my opinion or her phone number?"

Tim twisted his lips. "I'm not sure what I want, that's the problem. If she's still clinging to her memories of Alex, I'd probably be wasting my time. I'm also hesitant about calling her. I don't want to take her by surprise. I might scare her off."

"Are you suggesting that I intercede? Feel her out and break it to her gently? Tell her that you're interested and get her reaction?"

Tim sighed with relief. "Would you?"

Frannie laughed, thrilled at how well this could work out if Glory was receptive. An instant flashback of their recent "pajama party" gave her renewed confidence. She had admitted that a boyfriend in her future might be welcome. "Loneliness is a bitch," she had said.

"I've been thinking about Glory's problems long before you entered the picture, Tim." She paused, wondering how much to tell him, but decided he deserved to know what he'd be stepping into. Glory had been on an emotional seesaw a long time. And now with this profound jealousy of her dad's relationship with Jessica Branson, her emotions were particularly shaky. Did she want to throw her friend Tim into this quagmire? Would that be fair to him? On the other hand,

Tim Quinlan might be just what the doctor ordered—the doctor himself.

"Okay," she said, nodding. "My final analysis and advice to you is this: I say Glory is ready for someone else in her life. She actually *needs* someone, and I'll get to that, but in my opinion, you should call her directly. I'll give you her home number and tell you the best time to catch her. You're right, though; your surprise call could scare her off. You know how it is, Tim, with many grievants; they feel an obligation to honor the memory of their lost love. But I know Glory better than she knows herself, so if she turns you down, let me know. That's when I'll jump in."

Tim listened quietly but his troubled facial expression was clearly indicative of his thoughts. He wondered if he should forget the whole idea.

"No, wait, hear me out, Tim. It gets worse but there's a silver lining out there."

He laughed forlornly. "I'm not sure I'm up to the challenge of finding it!"

"Let me finish with the negative stuff. Then I'll help you look for it," she said with an optimistic smile that soon faded. "But in all fairness, I need to make you aware of another problem Glory's been experiencing lately—a self-imposed problem."

Tim drew a breath and was almost ready to accept defeat and leave but she had piqued his interest again. "To be honest, Frannie, I'm thinking maybe this is a bad idea."

"No, don't give up, Tim. It isn't an incurable problem. As a matter of fact, if she accepts you in her life, her other problem may disappear completely."

His look was even more quizzical than before. "That needs an explanation, Frannie, not a conclusion. And secondly, when you say 'accepts you in her life,' understand that I don't want to look that far ahead. I admit feeling a strong attraction to her, but I'm not thinking long-term commitment. If it happens, it happens, but right now all I'd like is some pleasant female companionship. Simple as that for now."

"That's perfectly understandable. But let me explain her other problem. It concerns a budding romance between Dan Madison—that's Glory's dad—and her obstetrician, a Dr. Jessica Branson."

"Oh, geez! I think I know what's coming. Glory's not happy about that, is she?"

She shot him a look that answered his question. "Not at all," she said ruefully. "Let me tell you what's been happening . . ."

Tim listened while she told him all about Glory's recent behavior; her bouts with self-pity and depression and her abnormal reaction to her father's relationship with Jessica Branson. His memory of Glory English clouded as Frannie spoke about the real person behind that magnificent smile. Inwardly she was at war with herself, she explained, despite her efforts to hide it, particularly among her Amore Evenings guests.

He understood Glory's inner turmoil and was more than sympathetic, both professionally and personally. But he wasn't looking to shadow his life with someone else's problems. He was looking to sprinkle his own with a little sunshine. When he met Glory his hopes had soared. She had struck him like an oasis in the desert or sunshine breaking through a dark sky. But realistically, in the romance department he had been starving for years now, always looking for that someone special, so maybe it was his own loneliness that made him overreact.

Frannie kept right on talking while Tim ruminated, although he did a convincing job of pretending to be attentive. She had created a clear picture, rife with subtle warnings. And yet she spoke with such enthusiasm and hope that he didn't have the heart to disappoint her. She was fighting to lift her friend out of her depression. *And I'm the vehicle that can get the job done.* He laughed to himself at the irony. He had thought Glory English could be *his* personal cure-all.

Frannie extended her hands and shrugged. "And that's about it, Tim. I laid it all out on this table so you can't say later I didn't warn you. So what do you say? Are you still interested?" She grimaced as if expecting his negative response.

Tim threw his gaze upward looking for guidance. But God was probably too busy with bigger problems and left Tim to decide for himself. He took a deep breath and exhaled slowly. "I hope I don't regret this, but give me Glory's number."

Frannie was so excited that she slid out of her seat and kissed him. "Don't look so glum, chum. I've got good vibes about this. You made the right decision. Trust me."

"I *do* trust you so I'll think positively." He gave her numbers for his home, his cell, his office, the hospital and his e-mail address.

"You believe in covering all the bases, don't you?" she teased.

Tim relaxed and laughed with her. "A home run would be great, but I'd gladly settle for first base."

"I'll see what I can do," Frannie said with a twinkle in her voice. "Keep your fingers crossed."

She felt uplifted and energetic as she drove off. During her entire conversation with Tim Quinlan, Sergio had been tucked away in the back of her mind. Yes, she realized, you *can* find strength to help someone else when your own spirits are down. As a matter of fact, it's great medicine for depression.

# Chapter Thirty-five

Catherine Butler's call woke her son at 8:45 Monday morning. Still in a deep sleep, Rob wanted to ignore it but gave a one-eyed peek at the caller ID and jolted upright. His mother never called him in the morning, knowing that he never got to bed before the wee hours.

Something had to be wrong.

"I'm sorry I woke you, Robbie, but I had no choice. I'm at work already and I can't reach Daddy. He doesn't answer his cell. I called his office but he didn't get there yet."

Rob got a queasy feeling in his stomach but he kept an even tone. "What time did he leave? Should he have been there already?" Rob struggled to get his prosthesis on. From a physical standpoint the routine of putting it on every morning had become effortless, but the alarm in his mother's voice had him fumbling.

"It's not Dad I'm worried about. It's Grandpa. I always give him a fast call in the mornings before I leave for work. You hear so many stories about old people living alone—"

"So what happened? You didn't get him? There could be a million reasons for that. Don't panic," he said while panic began to creep in on him too. "Let me go, Mom. I'll call him myself and get back to you."

"No, Rob, I called a few times and still no answer. If he's in the bathroom or out in the yard and misses my call, he always calls me back."

Rob's stomach rumbled. And it had nothing to do with hunger. "Okay, hang up, Mom. I'm on my way. I'll call you as soon as I get there."

* * *

To many people Dennis Butler would not be considered old by today's standards. But that depended on who was counting. To those who were also pushing seventy they liked to think he still had plenty of good years ahead; to those who hadn't reached their fortieth birthday, Dennis had one foot in the grave.

Dennis, whose cup was always half full, had strongly disagreed with the latter opinion. He felt fine, he said, and still had plenty of living to do. In October he would celebrate his seventieth birthday and party plans were already in motion. But as Rob drove towards his grandfather's house, his fears snowballed. The little knot that had formed in his stomach when his mother called now felt like a concrete basketball. Nausea was setting in rapidly at the thought of what he might find.

He pulled into the driveway hoping to see his grandpa standing in the doorway with his usual wide smile, waiting to hug him. But unfortunately, wishful thinking doesn't create reality. Rob checked the rear property, just in case he was working back there—or God forbid collapsed—but Dennis was nowhere in sight. His car was parked in the driveway, which was not a good sign. When he walked up the back deck stairs, his stomach plummeted. The door was ajar, pushed back against the kitchen wall. Another bad sign. Even if he had walked somewhere, his grandpa would never leave the door wide open.

He had to be in there.

With a totally dry mouth, Rob called his name; gently at first, then with more urgency. He punched the screen door handle with more force than necessary and stormed in, his heart thumping. When he crossed into the living room headed for the upstairs bedrooms, Rob froze in his tracks.

Four startled eyes stared back at him. No one budged an inch and no one uttered a sound for what seemed like an endless moment.

A rush of tears from one of them broke the silence. "Oh, my God, Dennis," Dora Malanski cried. "This is so-o-o embarrassing!"

He sat down next to her and patted her hand, but didn't even try to console her. With a sigh, Dennis went through the formality of introducing her. "Rob, this is my friend, Mrs. Dora Malanski. She's the widow of Dr. Peter Malanski, our dentist who passed away three years ago."

Dora found her voice, and although it was still shaky, she pleaded her case to defend her honor. "We just had breakfast. Your grandfather was in the mood for blueberry pancakes, he said, but didn't want to bother making them for himself. So when he called and offered to pick me up . . ." The sound of her own babbling embarrassed Dora even more. Nothing sounded credible or excusable, so she just waved it away as though continuing would be senseless.

The color returned to Dennis' cheeks, somewhat redder than his natural complexion. He glanced down at Dora, who was now seated on the couch with her face buried in her hands. Dennis knew she had blurted out all she intended to say, so he'd have to carry the ball. "We really did have blueberry pancakes, Rob." He extended a hand toward the kitchen. "See for yourself. The dishes are all in the dishwasher."

His grandfather's expression was so endearing to Rob that it tugged at his heart. It begged for forgiveness and understanding as if they had committed some capital crime. For Rob, the shock of the unexpected scene was finally diminishing, allowing reality to set in. And humor. He burst out laughing and hugged Dennis. "I'm sorry, Gramps. I'm not laughing *at* you. I'm laughing with relief. I was so damn scared driving here. I had all kinds of crazy thoughts in my head. Why the heck didn't you return Mom's call? You could have spared all of us this . . ." He circled a finger and left the rest unsaid.

But Dennis said it for him. "Embarrassment, yes. A stupid oversight on my part. I meant to call her but I just plain forgot." With tightened lips, he tapped his temple in an empty-head gesture, then stole a quick glance at Dora. Her sudden outburst of tears had quickly subsided but she was still upset by the shock of being "caught" and the humiliation that followed. From the tense and angry look on her face, Rob suspected she was busy reprimanding herself for accepting his grandpa's invitation in the first place. She was probably equally mortified that Rob might find the story amusing and repeat it to his customers at the bar.

Rob decided to make an effort to quash her anxieties. He stooped slightly but remained standing. He spoke softly and made a concentrated effort to sugarcoat his words. "Mrs. Malanski, I'm sorry my barging in here this morning caused you discomfort, but there's really no need to be upset. He looked up at his grandfather as if delivering a dual message, then scolded him with squinty eyes. "Right now I could kill him for not calling my mom. If he had, I wouldn't be here, but the point is, please don't feel embarrassed or uncomfortable." He smiled warmly, then shrugged. "I think if you two are friends . . . well, that's just great!"

Dora exhaled the breath she held and returned a weak smile.

"We are friends, Robbie, good friends." Dennis said and realized he was glad Rob had made the discovery. His secret was out and he could relax once the whole family knew. He placed a hand on Rob's shoulder. "And thanks for taking it so well. I know it's a shock—especially to young folk like you who frown on this sort of thing. They think we're over the hill and romance at our age is ludicrous."

Exasperated, Dora let out a rueful sigh. "Oh, don't say *romance*, Dennis. I'm not ready to let that word get out. For now we're friends and that's enough."

Rob struggled to hold a serious expression. "Please, Mrs. Malanski, let me put your mind at ease. You can rest assured that neither the word *romance* nor the incident itself will be repeated to anyone—not even my parents." He turned to Dennis again. "That'll be up to him, whenever he's ready. And my guess is they'll be delighted."

"I hope you're right," Dennis said. Pessimism lined his face momentarily, but he soon brightened. "Now that you know, Rob, I think I'm going to tell them soon. Maybe tomorrow. Better to face it than worry yourself sick."

"That's the right attitude, Gramps. Now I'm going to take off, but make sure you call Mom—like right now. I'll leave it to you to make your excuses."

He took another moment to say good-bye to Dora. She looked a hell of a lot better now. That look of resignation drained the tension from her face. She had amazingly good skin for her age. Sure it sagged here and there, but its silky flawless texture peeled years off her age. She smiled wide now for Rob, revealing teeth too perfect to be real, but what the heck, he thought; Grandpa wore dentures too.

He drove off in a giddy mood, smiling all alone like an idiot. It gave him such a kick to think of Grandpa Dennis *in love*. Silly images crossed his mind and he laughed out loud when he remembered their dentures. Would they share the same glass at night? Is that *love?* Are dentures still put in a glass?

As he drove, he found himself humming Dean Martin's old mega-hit, *That's Amore*. It seemed amore was everywhere except in his path. The blues dragged him down again. He missed Suzanne so badly he ached. She was always in his mind but there seemed to be no solution to their problem. Little Heather too had wrapped herself around his heart the very first time he held her. He felt like a father whose wife suddenly took off with his child. But it wasn't that way at all. It was he who had caused this separation, although for good reason. He still strongly believed that his demands were justifiable.

*Demands.* The word itself stirred his conscience. Did he have a right to make demands? Suzanne was adamant about protecting the secrets of her past life. *And wasn't I the one who told her let's not look back, only forward?*

She loved him as much as he loved her. He had no doubt about that. And she felt blessed, she'd said, that he loved her daughter as well. So why then would she give it all up if not to protect Heather from her lowlife father?

Do I have a right to interfere with that decision?

And if I choose not to interfere, can I live with my decision?

The answers to both questions never came to him no matter how many times he battled with them. He forced the thoughts out of his head and tried to think of something pleasant.

Today that was easy. All he had to do was think back to the scene at his grandpa's house. After his mother's call he had tortured himself driving there, imagining heart attack, stroke, a fall down the cellar steps, a slip and fall in the shower that left him unconscious . . . After all that worry, to find him with that guilty but childish look—like a kid caught with his hand in the cookie jar—well, that kind of fright followed by relief had to make you stop and count your blessings, Rob mused.

But these days he didn't have as many blessings as he used to. He could if he wanted to, he knew, but he couldn't bring himself to make that call. He didn't know if he could handle never knowing the truth and never being able to adopt the child he had grown to love.

# Chapter Thirty-six

Frannie was in a fairly good mood all day Sunday after Tim Quinlan's visit. She was excited that he might call Glory if he didn't lose his nerve or give it too much thought. Perhaps she had given him more information than necessary, but since he had asked for her advice, she felt compelled to be honest.

All of Sunday night while she and Glory worked together at Amore Evenings, she had been tempted to tell her about Tim's visit and his interest in her, but that wouldn't have been fair to either one. Chances were great that if Glory were forewarned, she would decline graciously with nicely preplanned words.

By Monday, Frannie was tempted to call and ask, "What's new?" but that would have surely raised Glory's antennae. They saw each other almost every day and spoke on the phone when they didn't. Besides, she remembered Tim's indecisive look when he left Amore Breakfast on Sunday. What if he never called? Why tell Glory and subject her to feeling rejected again?

*No, I'll wait that one out,* she decided. For now she'd have to wait and see what unfolds.

Once she dismissed thoughts of pleasant possibilities between Glory and the doctor, Sergio filled her mind again. Adhering to her resolve, she refused to stress herself out or sink into depression over a man she barely knew. Crying her eyes out for any man was not her style. Not anymore. She'd been through enough with Wade. If being in love can't bring happiness, then she wanted no part of it. *An independent, tough-as-nails, successful businesswoman, that's me,* she mused.

She cast her thoughts aside and decided to go shopping for something frivolous. Tonight was her turn to cover the first dinner crowd at Amore Evenings, but she still had two hours to spare and she'd put it to good use. Shopping never failed to lift her spirits—especially if the trip was fruitful. It was certainly better than sitting around and pining about Sergio. Since his surprise visit at Amore Breakfast on Friday, she had been more annoyed with herself than him. With his mother in tow, his demeanor that day had drastically diminished his macho image.

So why couldn't she shake him out of her head?

And then it came. The long-awaited phone call from her fair-haired, gray-eyed Italian hunk, complete with cleft chin, who melted like a marshmallow in a bonfire in the presence of his sour-faced mother.

She glared at the name on the caller ID. Edward Pisano. Sergio was obviously calling from his cousin's home. So where was mamma? She wanted to ignore the ring and let it go to voice mail, but the Frannie Oliveri who had inexplicably fallen fast and hard for the charismatic Italian lacked the emotional strength.

She clicked the talk button, allowing the simple gesture to turn on more than the phone. Her heart raced immediately and seconds later other body parts came to life with surges of warmth and tingling sensations.

"Cara mia," Frannie heard and gasped. She sat down. "Yes, I'm here," she said, realizing she hadn't said hello or made a sound when she answered the phone. Then, as if she'd been poked in the shoulder, she shifted into her *tough-as-nails* mode. "What's going on, Sergio? I was on my way out."

"Uh-oh, you mad with me. I can hear. And you have somewhere to go. I sorry I pick bad time, but this good chance for me to talk. *Tutta la case e per me.* I have all house to myself."

"No, Eddie, no Mamma?" She stressed the *mamma*, her tone intimating that his freedom surprised her.

Sergio heaved an audible sigh, acknowledging her irritable mood. "Ah, my dear Francesca, you no understand. I have much to say—"

Frannie's heart continued to pound away, but her blood was boiling too. "Don't call me *Francesca.* This is America, not Italy. My birth certificate says *Frances,* not *Francesca."* She grimaced at her own words as they spilled from her lips. They completely belied her true character. Is this another one of the pitfalls of love? she wondered—becoming a cranky, nasty bitch? Yes, she realized. Hadn't Glory too unleashed a bitchy streak fighting for her father's love?

"Okay, Frances, Frannie, whatever you like, cara mia." Despite her attitude, Sergio maintained his gentle tone. "Please give me chance to see you. I come now if you have time."

Her blood settled down to a simmer. "Oh? Are you sure you can manage that or would you like to bring your mother?" Her face soured again, hating the sound of her biting tongue. She felt like Eve White, one of Joanne Woodward's characters in *The Three Faces of Eve.* As the meek Eve White, she was totally helpless to stop her alter-ego, Eve Black, from slipping out like a snake and taking control of her mind and body. Frannie wished she could shove her own alter-ego back inside and bury her, but knew that couldn't happen until she listened to Sergio's excuses and had her chance to vent her anger.

He didn't bother to answer her sarcastic question. "I be there twenty minute? Is good with you, cara mia?"

She had snapped when he called her *Francesca,* but every time she heard "cara mia"—*my dear*, she melted.

"Okay. Twenty minutes, Sergio, but I don't have too much time. I have the early shift at Amore Evenings tonight."

When she clicked off, she took a chance and called Glory. "Hey, it's me. Look, no big deal if you can't, but do you think we can switch hours tonight? I need an extra hour. Something came up. Something important."

\* \* \*

Frannie had no time to waste. He'd be there in less than a half hour. She jumped in the shower, pulled clothes out of the closet and flung them on her bed. She had chosen a black pinstriped pants suit and a white silk blouse. Her hair required little attention. Glory was right, she thought as she fingered it into place; her new cut had worked wonders to enhance her best features, her eyes and high cheekbones. As far as her makeup was concerned, she had been blessed with good complexion and used makeup sparingly, if at all.

After she hastily buttoned up her blouse with fumbling fingers and an eye on the clock, she unbuttoned it just as fast, casting it aside with no regard to where it landed. She pulled out a cranberry red blouse instead. Sergio loved her in vivid colors, he'd said. A chill ran through her remembering when and how he had made that seemingly innocuous comment. Locked in the throes of passion one late afternoon, the first button on her denim blouse had slipped out, exposing one shoulder and half her bra—her turquoise bra—that prompted the complimentary words, replete with desire. "Even more beautiful in strong, vivid color, you are, my Frannie." His gaze then followed his finger along the swell of her cleavage while he kissed her neck. "Magnifico," he said, his eyes fixed on her turquoise bra. She wasn't sure if he was admiring the "vivid" bra or what was stuffed inside it. All she did know was that it worked like a magic key. Her mouth had opened wide and a sensual moan the likes of which she'd never heard before had escaped. Even now the vivid memory caught her breath; the erotic feeling of his fingers, the sweet warmth of his breath on her neck.

How's a woman supposed to think straight when someone you're crazy about makes you feel as if you're floating weightlessly?

She put her resolve on hold and allowed herself to bask in the memories of their few brief encounters. Reliving those fiery moments amazed her now. Whatever gave her the strength then to keep him out of her bedroom and "going for broke" was beyond her comprehension.

Maybe it was all those subtle girl-talk sessions with her mom that had taken root early in her teens. Frannie wasn't aware of it then, but her mother had been "planting seeds" during those casual conversations. She was careful not to sound preachy, aware that her daughters would have tuned her out or rolled their eyes. Tess had become a pro at it; adept at infusing her messages intermittently and in small doses. Neither Frannie nor her sister ever realized they were being sermonized or maybe *bamboozled.*

Frannie's musings were interrupted when she saw him drive up in his cousin's Ford pickup. Her knees went weak while she watched him approaching her front door. She sucked in a long breath, willing herself not to let his physical appeal temporarily knock the senses out of her.

With an uncertain smile, Sergio gazed at her as he entered the house, his eyes searching hers. She stepped aside to let him in, careful not to let her body brush with his. If not for the central air, she would have preferred to leave the door open to keep herself in check. But she was already feeling sensual stirrings rippling through her body and the air conditioning was a must.

Cautiously, he took a step toward her, his arms extended to welcome her in his embrace, but instinctively, Frannie slapped them down and fired away her angry words. "Sorry, Sergio. We need to talk first. No, let me correct that—*you* need to talk. Sure I understand that your father's death forced you to leave suddenly and I'm sincerely sorry for your loss, so forgive me if I sound insensitive, but that doesn't explain why you never called in all that time nor does it explain why you continued to avoid me for a whole week since you came back! I found out by sheer coincidence that you were here. For someone who claimed to be madly in love with me, you certainly cooled off fast! Out of sight, out of mind, huh? Or is this all about your mother? Does she still have you tied to her apron strings? In this day and age, I find that hard to believe but that's certainly the impression I got on Friday!"

Sergio waited until she ran out of steam before he responded. In his usual soft-spoken voice, he asked, "Can we sit . . . talk calmly?" He pointed a finger toward the sofa.

Frannie knew she didn't stand a chance if he got that close to her. She arched her eyebrows. "Yes, but you sit there, and I'll sit here."

He yielded to her request and sat on her rocker while she sat perched on the sofa.

"I'm listening," she said, her arms crossed.

"You have right to anger, Francesca—oh, scusi, *Frannie.* Believe me, I want very much to see you when I return to America, but my family, we have many troubles— more now since pappa die. I hope maybe good for everyone if I bring mamma here few weeks."

"Whatever those troubles are, Sergio, they couldn't have stopped you from making one phone call." Her anger had dissipated somewhat but her determination had not.

"Yes, this true, but I little afraid." He wrinkled his nose and made a wavy hand gesture that suggested indecision. "I no want to scare you . . . chase you away." This time his fingers rippled like birds in flight. "Maybe if you no like family, you no like me."

"That's ridiculous! Your family lives thousands of miles away from me. Even if I didn't like them, why should I care?"

His only response was a sigh before he cast his gaze on his steepled fingers.

In the silent seconds that hung suspended, the answer to Frannie's question rushed in like a tidal wave. Before his father's death had sent him hastily back to Italy, their relationship was merely a budding romance. Yes, they had both professed their love for each other, but nothing beyond that. They lives were worlds apart but Frannie had refused to think that far ahead. Since Wade, she'd had only two relationships with men, both of which had burned out in weeks. She had lost too much sleep during both fleeting romances worrying about whether they were right for her on a long-term basis.

Now, here was Sergio Giannetta, sitting opposite her, his expression remorseful. Excluding Wade, no man had burdened her with a heavier heart. And heavy heart or not, she knew it was time to ask the question that presented the most monumental problem. If they couldn't get past that one, there was no need to discuss any other related problems, like his sweet-as-vinegar mother and his feuding family.

"Your silence tells me plenty, Sergio. Before today, I didn't want to be presumptuous, but now I feel I have no choice. For us to continue seeing each other, we have to discuss some serious issues—one in particular." Her throat felt as if it were veiled with gauze. She paused to clear it. "In plain words, Sergio, did you believe—or assume—that if we were to be life partners, I'd leave everything behind and follow you to Italy?"

He hesitated, reluctant to meet that question head on. "You say 'life partner'; you mean marriage?"

"I wouldn't have it any other way. You know me well enough to know that." She lifted a hand and erased the air between them. "No, wait. Let me rephrase that. I didn't mean it to sound like a proposal. I'm not trying to push you into marriage, but I need to know here and now if you ever entertained that thought—me with you permanently in Italy. Because if you did, it would be senseless to go any further."

She punctuated her rambling statement with a strong nod of her head.

He studied her as though he were seeing her for the first time. "You still have much anger, cara mia. You speak to me, who love you, like we make business negotiation."

Silently Frannie had to concede that point, having heard it herself in her tone. "Well, in a way it is. It affects my businesses as well as my life in general. So please answer my question, Sergio. And answer it honestly."

He drew a breath and exhaled. "Yes," he whispered. "That my dream; is true. We have plenty property in Italy. Together we can build Casa Giannetta into palace. And someday maybe we have three or four."

Frannie felt heat rise in her neck. *Now* she was angry, not what he had seen before. All the while she had spoken— true, like a negotiator—it had been an effort to stay away from him. But she knew that if even their fingertips had touched, all sense of reasoning would be abandoned. This was too important to chance losing control of her mind by succumbing to passion. Her life literally depended on it. "That was your *dream,* you say? Is that what you found attractive in me—my business acumen? Is that what turned you on—the thought of how you could profit monetarily by hooking up with me?"

Sergio stood up and shoved his hands in his pockets. The hurt in his eyes could have melted the coldest heart. But Frannie wasn't defrosting. When he took a step toward her, she thrust her hands against his chest to stop him from coming any closer. She couldn't believe she'd done it again; allowed a man to make a Class A fool of her while breaking her heart at the same time.

"You can no believe that, per piacheri!" "How you can *say* this, cara mia? You stick knife in my heart!" He clenched his teeth as though in pain. "Yes, true, this my dream, but no my *scheme*! Yes, you have good head for business, but my family—maybe we no get along always, but our restaurant support us many years. Sometime I think to make peace I take over and buy others out. That's where my *dream* of you come in." Disappointment lined his face and he made no attempt to hide it. When she kept her gaze downward and said nothing, he continued. "What I try to say, my Frannie . . . my dream only good if you share. But in my heart I know this too much to ask."

"And if I refuse?"

He raked his fingers through his hair to stall his response. This was the showdown he had dreaded from the start. "Then you would ask same of me, yes?"

"Yes, I guess so," she admitted, then pressed on, thinking they might as well air out everything now. The results might be devastating but the issues had to be addressed. "Would you consider that at all, Sergio? Let's face it; that's our biggest hurdle to get over. There's no sense getting into anything else if we can't resolve this most important issue. So what it comes down to is which country wins, Italy or America?"

He took a long pause, then sighed. "America, if this only way I have you." He lifted a warning finger. "But I still have many responsibility in Italy to take care. Can take long time, cara mia."

"You mean your business and your family, right? Your mother mostly, I would guess. Am I right? We definitely have to discuss your mother." She tried to keep the disdain from her voice since he had made a huge concession for her but if mamma came with the package, it would take major rethinking. Keeping her eye on the prize, she chose her words carefully and spoke softly. "You have to admit, Sergio, that she was downright rude that day. Something had to be bugging her in the worst way. And truthfully, in my eyes, your masculinity took a nosedive. I was surprised and disappointed in you for not tactfully handling her."

Sergio laughed heartily. "When mamma ready to hit ceiling is like . . . how you say . . . detonate bomb! Even when she look calm, we watch; we walk on toes." He made the walking gesture with his fingers. "But no my sister Lina. Like mamma, she too have short fuse. And when you say I don't handle mamma, you wrong. I no want her to make scene in your restaurant, so I shut up like clam."

Lines creased Frannie's forehead. "I can't believe she's always that way—it doesn't seem possible that she would have no endearing qualities. For goodness sake, she has to love her family no matter how their personalities clash!"

He rolled his eyes and twisted his mouth to form a *don't ask* expression. "My mamma, she very jealous, high-strung woman." He drew a breath, obviously preferring not to get into it, but did anyway. "Today good example. She start trouble for nothing. Poor Eddie, he try be nice. Say no cook Aunt Philomena, we go eat Amore Breakfast. But he make big mistake; say something like, 'No one serve better breakfast than Amore. She go crazy. She cook for Eddie, for me, every day, and he insult her, she say." He shrugged as if he wished he could offer some explanation for her loathsome behavior, but he could come up with nothing to condone it. "Mamma and Eddie, they exchange angry words." He cringed. "I so ashamed. Eddie don't deserve. You see, my Frannie, when my father die, Eddie open his heart and his home to mamma. He say she stay long as she like. How can she turn on him like madwoman, I say. She accuse him that he take me from my responsibility; that he want me help renovate house so he get free labor." His shoulders shivered with the memory. "She so bad; so bad . . . I hurt for him . . . want to cry.

"I tell you more, my Frannie, so you understand. My cousin and his mamma and pappa—rest their souls—they help us many years ago when we almost lose business. Big money trouble. They ask no question. When you pay, you pay, they say. Do you think mamma appreciate?" He pouted bitterly. "Not even thank you! She take kindness for granted . . . like this no big sacrifice for them. They rich American relatives, she say; they no miss money. I don't see this way. So when Eddie mention his renovation plan and why he need, I jump to help. For carpentry I have skilled hands too, so this my chance to pay back. Eddie would never ask such big favor, but I make him think I want trip to America and he do me favor if I stay in his house; he family."

Frannie was beginning to think that Philomena Giannetta would take the prize as the mother of all mothers-in-law. From what she had heard and observed so far, she was definitely the type who ruined it for all the good ones.

Sergio threw a dismissive hand wave over his shoulder. "But this all past. We have to settle what happen now, between us." His gaze was pleading. "Whatever it take, my Frannie, we must work out. Yes, Italy my home, but without you . . ." He frowned and his voice trailed off. With questioning eyes, he extended his hands.

The fire that had raged inside Frannie only minutes before had smoldered. She lifted her hands only slightly and Sergio seized the moment. They were locked in each other's arms like two lovers reunited after years of separation.

For the moment, all their residual problems were put on hold, but Frannie felt their presence like tiny rings of fire.

# Chapter Thirty-seven

Suzanne hadn't noticed that the wrong car was parked in the Haggarty driveway. She went to the side door expecting to see Kim's smiling face. Routinely, all she had to do was transfer Heather from her arms to Kim's, along with the little pink suitcase filled with her necessities.

But Kim was not there to greet her today. She was surprised to find only Greg standing there instead. There was neither sight nor sound of their children either. She looked at Greg quizzically. "Where is everybody?"

He reached out for Heather and eased her with playful words. She too seemed disappointed not to see Kim and the children.

"They'll be here soon. The kids had a birthday party this afternoon and they were having such fun, Kim said, that she didn't want to rush home. Since I came home early, she asked me to take Heather." Greg noticed her slight hesitancy. "She'll be fine with me, don't worry," he said assuringly.

He had misinterpreted her expression. She wasn't the least bit concerned with his competency but it chilled her to see her daughter in her unsuspecting father's arms. A nervous laugh escaped. "Oh, no, I wasn't worried at all. It was just that I know how Heather always looks for the kids. She loves playing with them." She heaved a dismissive sigh. "But anyway, she's already had her dinner. Her snacks, along with everything else she needs, are in here." She handed him the suitcase and left abruptly.

Greg was watching her walk back to her car when he was struck by an irresistible impulse. "Suzanne, wait!" he called out. "Can you come back a minute?"

She looked at him curiously but his smile was relaxed and she assumed he had a question about Heather's care since he was temporarily in charge. "What do you need, Greg? Did I forget something?" she asked when she was back inside his kitchen.

There was no trace of the relaxed smile he wore seconds ago. "Yes, I need to know something and I need the truth." He looked at Heather, then at Suzanne. "Is she mine?"

The question fell on her like a bomb. A wave of dizziness consumed her. Her mouth went instantly dry and she fought for the courage to meet his waiting gaze. "You know that's not possible, Greg. What makes you ask a question like that?" She cloaked her response with a disparaging look as if she considered the query ludicrous, but her heart was playing war drums again. Someday she'd have to deal with Heather's inquiries, but she had years to work out her fictitious story. This, however, was a scenario she never anticipated. She was totally unprepared.

"But it *is* possible, Suzanne. And don't try to put on a false front because I can see how nervous you are. Your hands are trembling."

She waved it off with a fake laugh. "Oh, don't judge me by that. I have a lot going on right now."

"Who's her father, Suzanne?"

"I'm not sure," she lied, her self-degrading implication crystal clear. "Certainly not you, Greg. I don't want to get into the sensitive subject, nor do I have the time, but you're the one who explained why that's not possible."

"Suzanne, let me get to the point. Not a soul knows this yet, but Kim is pregnant."

The news shocked Suzanne but came as no surprise. Heather was living proof that the mumps had not denied him the ability to impregnate a woman. She smiled at him amiably. "Well, congratulations. I'm sure Kim is thrilled, but I really have to leave, Greg. My boss is a stickler for punctuality."

She reached for the doorknob to escape his probing, but he grabbed her arm. "Suzanne, she *looks* like me! I can see it myself!"

At the door, Suzanne steeled herself to look and sound convincing. "Greg, I think your guilt about us is making your imagination run wild. I'm happy for you and Kim, considering what you told me about how the mumps affected you, so count your blessings that a long shot came through. But the chances of a long shot coming through twice are remote."

Greg glared at her. "Remote does not mean impossible."

She reached for Heather. "On second thought, Greg, tell Kim I didn't feel well and decided to call in sick because—"

The growling sound of SUV doors opening stopped her. Kim and her children were getting out. Heather wiggled with delight and reached out to Kim, who took her from her mother's arms and kissed her. Suzanne got sick to her stomach and thought she might vomit. She couldn't get away fast enough.

"Perfect timing, huh, Suzanne?" Kim said.

"Yes, perfect timing is right, Kim."

# Chapter Thirty-eight

For the fourth time that day, Dr. Tim Quinlan began dialing Glory English's number. Again, he clicked off before completing the call.

"This is ridiculous!" he said aloud as he paced. "I make life and death decisions every single day, and I can't decide whether or not to ask a woman to dinner!" Aside from all he had learned about her fragile emotional state, he couldn't fathom how they could work out a mutually convenient time even if she *did* accept. She co-owned a successful restaurant open seven nights a week, had a baby to care for all her free hours, and wrote a weekly column that was syndicated all over the country! How does a trauma surgeon who works long exhaustive hours coordinate a date with her?

A sudden thought swept away his skepticism. He remembered Frannie telling him the story of Glory's father and his romantic relationship with her obstetrician. If they've been managing to work it out, why can't he and Glory?

With that in mind, he tapped out the numbers for the fifth time. What the hell, he concluded, she may give me a fast and polite brushoff, so why worry about coordinating our schedules?

He was still having second thoughts when he heard the first ring of her phone, but as he visualized her answering his call, all the reasons that stopped him before were suddenly insignificant.

"Hello?" Perplexed, Glory noted the caller ID and couldn't imagine why Dr. Timothy Quinlan would call her.

Tim heard the questioning tone in her greeting and laughed. "Yes, it's me, Glory, Tim Quinlan. Did I catch you at a bad time? Can you talk now?"

Glory glanced over at her dad, who was playing with Danny out on the deck. "My dad stopped by unexpectedly. He's captain on a tour boat that runs out of Perkins Cove and had an hour to spare before his next cruise."

"Oh, then, don't let me keep you. Maybe I can call again at a more convenient time."

"No, it's okay, Tim. He came to play with his grandson mostly, so I can talk a few minutes. And frankly," she said, infusing a slight laugh, "I'm curious as to why you're calling—and who gave you my number."

"Oh, geez. I hope I didn't cause any trouble. Frannie gave me your number. I went there Sunday for a late breakfast and we had a nice talk once the place emptied out."

Glory was about to ask what brought him all the way to Ogunquit for breakfast, but it was none of her business, so instead she said, "Oh, how nice! Frannie probably enjoyed your visit. She never mentioned that you'd been there," she said, then realized that sounded slightly insulting—as though a surprise visit from Dr. Tim Quinlan hadn't been worthy of mention. "Now that I think about it, I can understand why. Frannie and I may see each other every day, but that doesn't mean we get to talk conversationally. Amore Evenings is so busy at night there's never time for small talk." Glory winced at her second blunder, then laughed apologetically. "I'm sorry, Tim. I didn't mean to imply you'd be categorized as 'small talk,' but—"

Tim laughed too and interrupted her. "Don't apologize, Glory. I'm the one who should, if an apology is in order. Frannie never told you because I told her not to."

Glory's curiosity piqued. She waited for more.

"Let me be perfectly honest with you. I was very attracted to you when we met. Even my daughter, Emma, noticed and teased me about it. Actually she's the one who encouraged me to call you." He paused, and Glory could hear him exhale. "But under the circumstances," he continued, "I didn't want to approach you without talking to Frannie first. I wasn't sure if you'd welcome my call or . . . can you help me out here, Glory? I think you know what I'm trying to say."

She relaxed him with an easy laugh. "Yes, I do, Tim, and I'm flattered, really. But I'm surprised as well, and truthfully, since Alex died, this is the first time anyone has tried to ask me for a date. I'm a little unprepared."

Tim's tone brightened. "Well, I'll accept 'unprepared'; it's better than a direct 'no.' Is there room for consideration?"

For a few seconds, Glory feared that the only sound Tim might have heard was her heartbeat. She had to say *something.* "I don't see why not. Except for the fact that I don't have much free time. Summertime is particularly hectic with the restaurant. And, of course, there's Danny. Not to mention you're a surgeon, for goodness sake! I would imagine your schedule is pretty tight too."

Now it was Tim's turn to pause and ponder what she had said. "So is that a yes or a no? Do we try to work it out or give up before trying?"

Glory eyed her father again. He sat contentedly on the glider with Danny cradled in his arms. He hadn't once glanced her way, curiously or impatiently, while she was on the phone. It wasn't his style to interfere or offer opinions unless she encouraged them, but she wondered how he'd react if she told him who had called and why.

She put the smile back in her voice and answered the handsome doctor's question. "I'd love to try, Tim. I enjoyed your company for the brief time we spoke and Frannie thinks the world of you. But again, time is a very real obstacle—for both of us. Let me ask you this: If your schedule allows, would you like to come here for a light lunch one day? Of course I'd have Danny, but he isn't walking yet so I don't have to chase him around. And he always takes a two-hour nap in the afternoon, so we can have a leisurely conversation. What do you think?"

Enthusiasm strengthened Tim's voice. "I think that sounds wonderful! Give me a second to check my calendar."

Myriad negative thoughts swirled through Glory's head while she waited, but although she had hardly thought about Tim since they met, his image grew stronger now. Those "butterflies" sailed through her stomach again. A warm and welcome feeling, she mused. She hadn't felt them since Alex had entered her life. It seemed like a lifetime ago.

Tim picked up the phone again. "Sorry to keep you waiting. If one o'clock isn't too late for you, I'm free Thursday afternoon. Is that good for you?"

"That absolutely works for me. I look forward to your visit, Tim."

* * *

"Sorry about that, Dad. I didn't want to sound rude and brush off that caller."

Dan arched a brow but asked no questions. "That's okay. I was in seventh heaven here looking at my beautiful grandson. But he's dozing off. Maybe you should put him in his crib."

Glory took Danny inside and welcomed the minute to compose herself. Her face flushed and she felt the onset of an adrenaline rush, already anticipating his visit.

She avoided Dan's curious gaze when she returned and tried to casually pick up where they had left off, but she couldn't remember what they had been discussing. Still stunned by Tim's call, her mind went blank, leaving her at a loss to start a new conversation.

"I don't mean to pry," Dan said, "but are you all right? You look a little flustered, but I can't tell if you're pleased or upset."

Glory waved off his concern and laughed. "No, no. Not upset at all. Just a little stunned maybe by that phone call." She thumbed back towards her kitchen.

Dan left the glider and took a chair opposite his daughter. "Is it something you want to discuss with me? I still have time to listen. Only if you want to, of course."

Minutes earlier Glory had no intention of telling her father anything about Tim's call. But she was still tingling inside and needed to share it. Frannie would have been her first choice, but at this hour she'd still be busy at Amore Breakfast.

She took the plunge.

"I don't think you ever met him, but do you recall ever hearing Frannie talk about the doctor who took care of her cousin, Suzanne, after her accident?"

"Yes, sure. She idolized the guy. Rob Butler was his patient too, right?"

"Yes. Well, he came to Amore Evenings with his daughter recently to celebrate her birthday. Frannie introduced us and we talked awhile. Anyway, bottom line is he later talked to Frannie to ask whether I was dating anyone yet—or if she thought I might accept an invitation from him."

Dan's excitement danced in his eyes. "I can imagine Frannie's reaction, knowing her high opinion of him, personally and professionally."

"You got it! So she had no qualms about giving him my home number."

"Good for her!" Dan said and impulsively pulled her closer for a quick hug and kiss. "So did you say yes?"

Now that Jessica Branson wasn't involved, Glory found it easy again to confide in her dad. She repeated her conversation with Tim almost verbatim. Dan digested every word with pleasure, but what pleased him most was seeing the light in her eyes again.

Before Dan reluctantly left for work, he kissed her again on the cheek and squeezed her hand. "And Glory, thanks for sharing that with me." He laughed at himself. "Thanks for sharing . . . what a clichéd line! But I mean it; it meant a lot to me."

Glory watched her father as he walked Perkins Cove towards the Finestkind tour boats. She smiled as she looked at the time. In another half hour or so, she could call Frannie.

*Should I scold her or thank her?* She opted for the latter. *If I tried to teasingly scold her, Frannie would see right through me.*

# Chapter Thirty-nine

Dan's call caught Jessica just as she entered her home. "Keep your fingers crossed, honey. There's a small chance Glory might have found the cure for her deep depression."

"Wow! That I'd like to hear and from the sound of your voice, you're dying to give me the details, but let me settle in. I just want to check my messages and change into comfortable clothes, then I'll call you back." She glanced at her wristwatch. "Or better yet, do you feel up to driving yourself here? Is it too late?"

"Not to see you. Just hearing your voice gives me a charge of energy. But it's almost nine o'clock. You must be exhausted—"

"I was. But there are different ways to cure fatigue," she said suggestively.

Dan needed no coaxing. "I'll be there in a half hour."

\* \* \*

She was wearing white shorts and a short-sleeved sheer blouse with little lighthouses all over it. The ends of the blouse were knotted under her breasts, revealing her taut and silky midriff. The busy print managed to conceal her ample breasts, but it took only one glance to see that Jessica was braless. She had been carrying two tall glasses and a pitcher of lemonade out to the porch when he opened the screen door. A small lamp on a corner table offered only enough light to find your way, but as Jessica bent over slightly to place the tray down, the lamplight illuminated her like a spotlight on a darkened stage.

Dan reached for her the moment she had placed the lemonade pitcher and glasses on the small table. They stood there for endless minutes, unable to break apart until they stumbled and fell onto the wicker sofa.

Laughter broke through their amorous mood. Both Dan and Jessica rocked with it. She had fallen first and Dan had landed in her lap like a babe in arms. Jessica was still wiping away the tears her laughter had provoked when she was finally able to speak coherently. "Too bad we couldn't have captured that on camera. It would have been a classic, like an old slapstick comedy."

"I imagine Katharine Hepburn and Cary Grant might have done it better," Dan joked.

"I imagine you're right!" Jessica said. As their laughter subsided, she poured them each a glass of lemonade and sat next to him. "But you haven't told me yet about Glory's so-called depression cure. That certainly sounded promising. What's that about?"

Dan sipped his lemonade and gave her a cautious smile. "I'm trying not to get too excited, but if this develops the way I hope it will, it'll be quite a breakthrough for Glory. And I'm more than confident she'll get over this fixation she has about us as a couple being a threat to her and Danny."

"Well, don't give me your conclusions before telling your story. Start at the beginning."

Dan laughed. "You're right. But it's not really a story. I'm just hoping it will be; one with a happy ending, of course."

Jessica rolled her eyes and blew an impatient breath.

"Okay, okay, here's all I know so far . . ."

After hearing the scant details, Jessica's eyes lit up. "So she's going to see him Thursday? *This* Thursday?"

"Yes." He lifted a hand and crossed his fingers. "I'm afraid to be too optimistic and I certainly don't want to see her hurt again, but I plan to do some heavy-duty praying."

"Me too," Jessica said eagerly, but like Dan, part of her prayers would be self-serving. If Glory and her doctor can develop a friendship that moves on to romance, well, then Jessica would have to agree with Dan. It could be the cure-all that would positively affect them as well.

She looked up at him with an optimistic smile. "We'll just have to wait it out, Dan. But it sounds like a great start. Just the fact that she said yes to Tim Quinlan is hopeful. I wish I could meet him. I'm curious."

"Let's hope you get your wish." He brushed a strand of hair away from her eyes and kissed them both gently. He pecked at her nose next, then her lips. "So where were we before I told you my happy story?"

Jessica grinned. "Actually, you had fallen into my lap."

"Well, that would never have happened if we had more room in the first place," he whispered in her hair.

"My dear Mr. Madison. How ungracious of me! You're absolutely right." She laced her fingers with his and walked him into the dark and quiet house. In her bedroom, she flipped through a stack of CDs. Let's see, we've had Frank Sinatra, Dinah Washington, Dean Martin and Ella Fitzgerald serenade us the last few times. How about Nat King Cole tonight?"

"Sweetheart, I wouldn't care if only crickets and night owls sang to us."

Jessica's giggle stopped abruptly. The velvety voice of the immortal Nat King Cole had filled the room and she felt the warmth of Dan's lips on her neck. "Yes, you certainly are unforgettable," he whispered.

# Chapter Forty

After three weeks, Rob had given up—not that he had expected to hear from Suzanne. Whatever the story, whoever the father, she was adamant about taking that secret to her grave in order to protect her daughter. And maybe her daughter's father.

No, he had resigned himself to the fact that if reconciliation still had a fighting chance, he'd have to make the first move. And, more importantly, he'd have to prepare himself to concede to Suzanne's wishes. He could never adopt Heather; only love and protect her while living in fear that someday her real father would show up and claim his parental right.

What kind of life would that be? The thought sickened him but the alternative was worse. These past weeks he'd had only a small taste of life without them and couldn't imagine how he could ever heal the hole in his heart. He longed to hear Suzanne's voice, her infectious laugh. A rueful smile curled his mouth imagining how she would have enjoyed hearing the amusing little story about Grandpa Dennis and his lady friend, Dora Malanski.

"Hey, what the heck," he mumbled and impulsively reached for the phone, praying she hadn't left for work yet. He breathed a sigh of relief when she answered. His tension drained like sand trickling down an hourglass. The surprise in her voice was not unexpected, but on second thought, he realized, it was more like shock. "Hi, I'm glad I caught you. I just wanted to know how you both are and to remind you that if ever you need my help with anything, I want you to call me, okay?"

Suzanne's mind went numb and her heart reacted. "I always need you, Rob. *We* need you, but Heather's young, thank God. She'll forget you."

Rob winced at her stinging words but it was the bare truth. "And you?"

Her voice stiffened. "What I need or want is immaterial; Heather is my only concern. Why did you call, Rob— really? It's not that I don't appreciate your offer to help if the need arises, but you already gave me that assurance before we parted."

Rob exhaled. "Okay. The truth is I missed hearing your voice, but besides that I had a cute little story to tell you about my grandpa Dennis. At the time it happened I wished I could call you so we could share a laugh at least."

"So tell me. I don't do much laughing these days."

"For whatever it's worth, it's been hell for me too, Suzanne. I've been—"

She cut him off. Sharing miseries was a dead-end street, so why bother? "Tell me about Grandpa Dennis, Rob."

As Rob told the story, embellishing it with added humor to stretch their conversation, her icy tone instantly defrosted. "That's absolutely adorable, Rob! Good for him— for them! So how did your parents react when he told them? I wish I could have been there to enjoy that scene!"

"I wasn't there myself, but my mother was thrilled. Grandpa said she jumped out of the chair and hugged him. My dad wasn't that demonstrative at first, but once the shock settled he was happy, especially since they've both known Dora Malanski for years. They say he couldn't have chosen a nicer woman. As a matter of fact, my mom is having a family dinner for them to officially welcome her. She made it for Tuesday night, when I'm off."

"That's my night off next week, too," she said without thinking of its implication.

"Well, with your rotating schedule, that's too good to pass up. I'm sure you and Heather would be welcome if you'd like to come."

Suzanne took so long to respond that Rob thought they had been cut off. "Suzanne—you there?"

"Yes, sorry. I'm just thinking. It's very tempting, but I'm not sure accepting your invitation is a wise decision. Let's be honest, Rob, our breakup wasn't the result of an argument. It was an amicable agreement to part because there's no solution for us. If I were in your shoes, I'd make the same demands. But trust me, if you were in mine, you would have made the same choice too, no matter how painful."

"Look, Suzanne, there's a part of me that loves and respects you more for denying your own happiness to protect Heather." He heard her gasp and knew she was crying. "No, please listen, sweetheart, and try not to cry. It kills me to hear you and not be able to hold you in my arms."

She sniffed, then blew her nose. "I'm okay. Say what you have to say."

"If all I had to deal with was knowing there were several men before me, I won't play it down and say it won't bother me, but I can psych myself to only look forward, not back, as I've always preached to you. But when it comes to Heather, I'm so afraid of the future. I already love her like a daughter and keep having horrible visions of this guy showing up out of the blue one day. I'd be devastated!"

"That'll never happen. I told you that. Not unless her life depended on it."

Rob took another pensive moment. He wanted so much to believe her. Finally he said, "Okay, Suzanne, so should I tell my mother she'll have two more guests?"

"Yes!"

Suzanne's spirits were still soaring when she hung up. But she worried about Greg now. Had she put his suspicion to rest with her curt response? Had she been convincing enough? The more she thought about it, the more benign it seemed. Greg *wanted* to be convinced that Heather wasn't his, so he'd never risk pursuing it. And even if he *did* find out, what could he possibly do about it that wouldn't cost him his wife and children?

Nothing. Nothing at all, she concluded, then put it in the back of her mind and convinced herself to heed Rob's advice. *Look forward, not back.*

# Chapter Forty-one

To her own surprise, Glory was a nervous wreck. It seemed ludicrous that she could oversee the meals served to hundreds of guests in her restaurant night after night, but to prepare one simple lunch had her all thumbs today.

Of course, it wasn't the *what* she served; it was the *whom.*

She arranged her lobster salad on a bed of Boston lettuce and garnished it with red pepper slices, lemon wedges and black olives. In her oven warmer, she had a mix of pumpernickel, French bread and a few small rolls. A ridiculous amount for two people, but she wanted to offer a choice.

With a critical eye, she stepped back to look over her table setting. Had she gone too far with her quest for an informal presentation? She hadn't wanted a showy, professional look, but rather a homey one; a casual lunch for two casual acquaintances who might become friends.

But with the bread in the oven and dessert in the refrigerator, her table looked pathetically bare.

Her queasy stomach brought back a sharp memory that filled her with a sense of foreboding. Everything about this "casual" lunch date seemed disconcertingly similar to her first date with Alex. The one difference for which she was grateful, though, was her physical reaction—or lack thereof. When Frannie had introduced them at Amore Evenings, she had admired Tim Quinlan's good looks and his amiable demeanor, but once she had left his table, she hadn't given him more than a passing thought. He was just another one of the many warm friendly people she had met since she became a restaurateur.

Alex, on the other hand, had walked into her life when she couldn't have been more vulnerable. His attention had done wonders to boost her self-esteem which her husband Jason had destroyed in one flat statement before dumping her. Up until Jason left, Glory had never desired anyone but him, nor did she ever fantasize about someone else. In the aftermath of their breakup, she refused to look twice at any man. With the exception of her father—Steven English, the man she believed to be her father—she trusted none of them and had begun to hate them all collectively.

And so it was somewhat unsettling when she found herself sexually aroused by Alex's presence. After his death, she often thought that besides Alex's love for her, his greatest gift was not only restoration of her self-esteem, but she was able to look at men again without disdain. There were plenty of good ones left; you just had to know how to weed them out.

Her eyes kept darting at the wall clock. She wished the minutes away so she could get through those first few awkward moments. Danny was overdue for his nap but still in a good mood. Glory watched him as he sat in his playpen chewing his toys and making those lovable baby-talk sounds. He looked so adorable in his nautical seersucker sunsuit; she couldn't wait to show him off to Tim. With a forlorn smile, she ran her fingers through his blond curls, wondering and worrying what the future had in store for him, her beautiful fatherless child.

Tim Quinlan arrived ten minutes early with an apology spread across his face. "I'm a little early—do you mind?"

"Don't be silly. Of course not," she said, ushering him in. She lifted Danny out of his playpen, wiped up his dribble, and introduced him proudly. "This is Danny, my pride and joy."

"Well, I can certainly understand why! He's a cute little guy. Does his personality match his looks? If so, you're a lucky mother." He winced, realizing *lucky mother* was a poor choice of words. "I'm sorry," he mumbled.

"Don't be, please. That's a typical example of what puts distance between me and almost everyone I talk to. I know they mean well, but pity won't help me heal. No one talks to me normally; they're afraid to complain. Even Frannie kept her troubles to herself thinking it would be insensitive to tell me her troubles when none of her problems could parallel mine. And as a result, she had lost her best friend and I had lost mine until we finally got to talk it out. Our friendship is back on track now, thank God."

Tim hadn't even sat down yet and Glory had already given him a good sampling of her emotional despair. He covered his face with his hands, then fanned his fingers to allow his contrite smile to break through. He pointed to the door. "Why don't I go back out so we can start again? This time I won't put my foot in my mouth, promise." He raised his hand to seal it.

Glory burst out laughing. She covered her mouth and looked up at him contritely. "I feel like such an idiot. I wouldn't blame you if you left and didn't come back. What a terrible way to greet a guest!"

"No, not at all. I'm glad you got that out. Now if I slip again—which I'm bound to do—we'll simply let it pass, okay?"

Her smile stretched wide. "Okay! Let's start again. Why, Tim Quinlan! It's so nice to see you again. Are you hungry? I don't have much variety, but I made a huge lobster salad."

"I absolutely love lobster salad!"

"That's a relief. I wasn't sure. I don't know anyone who doesn't like it, but some people are allergic to shellfish. Then I remembered that you and your daughter had ordered baked clam appetizers that night." She still had Danny in her arms when she opened her refrigerator and reached for her carafe of lemonade.

"Here, let me do that," Tim offered. "You have the baby."

"He's going right in for his nap. I stalled him today so you could meet him. Let me put him down, then we can eat without interruption." She started to walk away, then stepped back and handed him a cutting board, a knife and a bread basket. "We can eat faster if you slice up the bread. It's in the oven."

"Now you're talking!"

Glory returned minutes later to find the counter clean, the cutting board hanging in place, and the warm bread piled high in the basket.

"Wow! That was fast and efficient. Want to work part time at Amore Evenings?"

They both laughed and sat down to eat. She handed him the lobster salad platter and he helped himself to a generous portion. "I hope you don't mind eating inside, but it's a little unbearable out there today."

"No, this is great. With all this glass, you have an unobstructed panoramic view here. It's like being outside without the heat."

Glory looked it over with an appreciative eye. "It *is* great. It's funny how you get used to what you live with, but I do love it, especially at night with all the lights twinkling on the ocean. The sights and sounds are mesmerizing. And boy! You can't beat the convenience of living only steps away from your business. Not only for the convenience—I don't even have to step outside in bad weather—but it gives me such peace of mind about Danny. God forbid there's a problem or he gets sick suddenly, I'm right here."

She noted that Tim hadn't eaten a bite yet, probably to be polite while she chatted away incessantly. Anxiety had stolen her appetite, but for his sake, she forced herself to eat.

"Here, try one of these flaky rolls," she said. "They're so delicious, they'll melt in your mouth."

Tim dipped his head and gave her a playful smile. "I confess I already sneaked one when you went to put Danny down for his nap. So I'll try this now." He helped himself to two slices of pumpernickel bread. "It smells wonderful."

The way his gaze locked with hers made Glory wonder if he was talking about the pumpernickel or her perfume.

"So, do you miss New York, Glory? It's certainly an exciting city; so much to see and do. I've been there many times for business and pleasure, but I barely scratched the surface."

Glory gave his question serious thought. She hadn't thought about New York for a long time. "I guess everyone misses what's 'home' to them. I'm no exception. But, first of all, I never lived in Manhattan, so when I did go there, I was like a tourist too. I'd actually enjoy a vacation there and *really* see it. And secondly, as you probably know, I was married twelve years before my husband and I split. Knowing what I know now, I don't miss those years at all, but I have wonderful memories of growing up in Brooklyn. When we moved upstate I was twelve and it took me a long time to adjust. Eventually I did, though, but nothing—and I mean nothing—could compare with Brooklyn as I knew it. Unfortunately, everything changes."

"Nostalgia is a bittersweet feeling for all of us, but some changes are welcome; they improve the quality of our lives. I'm one of four children and my parents struggled financially when we were kids. We lived in a low-income Boston neighborhood where you had to toughen up to survive. But when my father decided to turn a hobby into a business, he became a successful cabinet maker. It wasn't long after that we moved from that small rented apartment to a small house in a much nicer neighborhood. So there 'change' was certainly welcome."

"And now you're a surgeon—how wonderful! Your parents must be so proud. Are they alive?"

"Yes and healthy, but they live in Connecticut near my sister. I visited them last month, for Father's Day."

Glory took another bite of her half sandwich and realized she was hungrier than she thought. "Is Emma your only child, Tim?"

"No, I have a son, Adam, two years older. He'll be starting med school in the fall; wants to be a heart surgeon, God love him." He shook his head as though his son's decision still amazed him, but pride sneaked into his smile. "Talk about change! You had to know my Adam. As a teenager all he ever dreamed about was to become a race car driver. Not exactly what parents want for their child. But miraculously, soon after he started college, he made a complete reversal and decided to shoot for heart surgeon! Can you imagine?"

Glory laughed, feeling more relaxed with her guest. "Now that's what I call another positive change!" She sipped her lemonade and refilled Tom's glass. "I didn't mean to give you the wrong impression. I too made positive changes. Moving to Ogunquit was one of them. Going into business with Frannie is another. Monetarily and socially, they were both good moves . . ." She paused, then forced the smile back on her face.

Tim noted her uneasiness. "It's okay, Glory. I understand what you were thinking; that Alex died in your restaurant and maybe he'd still be alive if Amore Evenings never existed."

She nodded. "Exactly."

"But you've got to put that out of your head. If God decided to take him home, it would have happened anywhere. Nothing you could have done or not done would have stopped it. Do you believe in God—or fate?"

Her laugh was edged with cynicism. "Oh, I believe in Him all right, but I admit to being very angry with Him for a

241

long time after Alex died. I'm better now; not totally healed, but better. It's hard to feel sorry for yourself when you see all the horrific sufferings all over the world while you're enjoying all the comforts of a free country."

"And knowing that our freedom comes with a very high price; so many wars, so many young lives."

Glory wiped the air. "Sorry, Tim. I didn't mean to get morbid. Let's talk about something pleasant. Like Emma and her ambitions and yours as well." She put a hand up before he could answer. "No, I shouldn't say your 'ambitions'; I think you've already realized your dream." She lifted her brows and beamed at him as though in awe of his profession. "How about traveling? Do you get much time to explore other countries?" She smiled pleasantly but wondered if he traveled alone. *What kind of fun is that?* No, she decided, Tim Quinlan would have no trouble finding attractive, intelligent female traveling companions.

"Oh, sure. I love to travel. Most recently I've been to France and Spain, but I'm always looking ahead to the next trip." He was about to ask her a similar question but caught himself. Even though she'd have the time to travel during the winter months, where could she go with a baby and really enjoy herself? It made him ask himself what the heck he was doing here with Glory English. But while he sat there, looking at her face and listening to her voice, he couldn't think of any place he'd rather be.

She answered his silent questions. "Ideally, I would love an extended European vacation, but I don't see that in my immediate future. I am considering, though, joining Frannie and her friends on a cruise this winter. People have been so unbelievably nice since Alex died. They barely know me, but you know how it is—when tragedy strikes, everyone's heart opens up."

"And I'm sure you would do the same. So you're going, right? You'll have a great time; everyone does."

"I'm thinking about it, but I don't know if I can leave Danny. I'll miss him terribly."

"He'll be fine. And you should take advantage of the opportunity now while he's still a baby. The older he gets, the more attached he'll be, and you'll really hate to leave him."

Glory nodded in agreement, then laughed. "And once he reaches that two to three stage, those babysitting offers might dry up."

Tim pointed a finger. "That's another consideration, so I say go for it now."

"I love your positive attitude. Is it contagious?"

Tim shrugged. "I guess with a little 'exposure' it could be. Maybe we should give it a try."

With a soft smile, Glory looked at him, unsure of how to respond, but after a few seconds, her hesitancy was awkward for both of them. "You're very pleasant company, Tim," she began. "It's no wonder Frannie admires you so. And it's not that I wouldn't enjoy seeing you again, but I want you to understand the kind of friendship we'd share—a limited one, to say the least." She paused for a breath and avoided his eyes. "This is terribly embarrassing for me but it's important that I make myself clear. I wouldn't want you to waste your time. I'm not ready, Tim, for anything beyond friendship. And truthfully, I could use a male friend; someone I'd feel comfortable with; someone who'd boost my spirits when I'm down; someone who might lessen my periods of depression."

"And someone who might drag you away from your apartment and restaurant once in a while. Not that they're depressing places to be," he added, spreading his arms and gaze in admiration, "but everyone needs a change of scenery and good conversation with someone you actually *like*. I often accept invitations from people I'm not crazy about, just to get out and not spend the evening alone. But I'm not sure it's worth it."

Glory gave him a knowing laugh. "I couldn't agree more. I've done that myself a few times. I used to love sitting right here with my father. Sometimes we'd just share sob stories about dealing with our grief, and sometimes we'd drift away to other stories and find ourselves laughing. There's still so much we don't know about each other . . . all those missing years." She lifted her gaze and forced a grin. "But now he has this woman—my obstetrician, believe it or not—and truthfully, I feel sort of left out."

"Does he make you feel neglected in any way?"

"Not really. You might say he makes sure he fits us into his busy schedule, but I don't think Danny and I are number one anymore. And that scares me."

"Why? If you don't mind my asking."

She made a sour face. "I'm not sure. I feel this separation between us; I can't talk to him the way I did before. I feel that he might discuss all our conversations with *his Jessica.*"

"That isn't necessarily true, but if it bothers you, why don't you simply ask him not to repeat any of your conversations to anyone?"

With twisted lips, she gave him a sidelong glance. "Oh, yeah, right. Like I can be sure he won't."

"Forgive me, Glory, if I'm being intrusive, and you don't have to answer me if you don't want, but is there something that particularly irks you about Jessica? Or is it only that she's stolen some of your dad's time and attention? And I shouldn't say 'stolen' if he gave it willingly."

"Well, willingly or not, she has more of it now and I have less."

Tim found himself speechless. In his estimation, Glory's jealousy was even worse than Frannie had described. He looked far beyond her good looks and desirable body now. He knew deep down he might be inviting trouble, but felt an inexplicable need to help this beautiful misguided soul.

"All right, Glory. If a friend is all you want right now, a friend I'd like to be. I think we'd be good company for each other. Now what did you say about dessert?"

Glory brightened. "We serve a fantastic cheesecake in our restaurant, but this morning I decided to pull out one of my mother's old recipes and made my own." She went to her refrigerator and placed the cake dish on the table. "Presenting Amanda English's incomparable New York style fudge-swirl toasted almond cheesecake!"

Tim went wide-eyed and grabbed the cake knife. He cut them each a piece while Glory went for the coffee. "We've only just begun our friendship, Glory, and I already love the fringe benefits!"

Now that the ground rules had been set and accepted amiably, Glory relaxed. He steered her away from the delicate subject of her father and Jessica Branson and they enjoyed a long and animated conversation. They laughed and talked nonstop for another hour until Danny's cries interrupted.

# Chapter Forty-two

Frannie was beginning to wish she and Sergio had never met. Contrary to the words that guided her when judging people, *Magnify the good, suppress the bad,* for the past few days she had been reversing that order. If she were to write them down, undoubtedly the reasons against a lifetime commitment with Sergio would far exceed those in favor. He had called her once since Monday afternoon when he came to her house, but she had missed his call and hadn't heard from him since.

Maybe he'll call late tonight when I get home from Amore Evenings, she thought, when his mother would be asleep and not apt to interrupt.

She was out in the yard giving Benny a long overdue bath when her house phone rang. Surely it had to be Sergio. Although he had her cell number now, barring emergencies, he agreed to call her only at home where she had total privacy. Leaving Benny tied up and coated with soap suds, she ran to the porch where she had left the phone. Slightly breathless, she grabbed it, expecting to hear his voice, but the caller ID immediately deflated her spirit.

Glory. Frannie's disappointment came with a rush of guilt. Conversations with her closest friend, whether business or personal, were always welcome. But today she was waiting and hoping to hear from Sergio.

Her eyes widened when she was suddenly struck with the realization of why Glory was calling. *Dear God! What's wrong with me lately? How could I have forgotten?*

Grateful that she remembered just in time, she brightened. "Hey! I've been dying to call you, but I was afraid he might still be there. How did it go?"

"I was a wreck before he came, regretting that I had invited him—"

"Stop right there! What's there to regret? It was just a damn lunch—what's wrong with that?"

"Well, to begin with, let's think realistically. True, I have a beautiful home here, but I'm sort of confined to quarters, you might say. Who would want to come here on a continual basis? It would be ridiculous for Tim to drive all the way from Portland to sit here with me for a couple of hours while Danny naps."

"I'm sure you could get a sitter for a few hours if necessary. You just met the guy, Glory. Don't take a defeatist attitude from day one. Just go with the flow; see what happens." Frannie laughed to herself listening to her own preachy words. All day she had been nurturing a defeatist attitude—not that it had worked yet. "First tell me what happened—with all the details. But before you do, I need to know, how did it end? Are you going to see him again?"

Glory heaved a sigh. "Yes, but on a friendship basis only; I had to make that clear."

Frannie rolled her eyes and grinned, glad Glory couldn't see her reaction. "Was it necessary to get into that?" she asked, imagining the discomfort Tim might have endured.

"You're right, Frannie. He's a really great guy, so I wanted to put my cards on the table and give it to him straight. Then if we continue to see each other he can never say I misled him."

"How honorable of you!" Before Frannie could stop it, she exploded with laughter.

"Why are you so hysterical? I'm dead serious!" Glory said, although she felt a smile tugging at her lips. It was

247

difficult to stay serious listening to Frannie's laughing fit. "You always do this to me! You crack up when I least expect it."

"I'm sorry, Glory," she said, wiping her eyes. "Let me enjoy it. It feels so good to laugh; a welcome respite from all the headaches and heartaches lately. But sometimes you get so dramatic, that I couldn't help it. As you spoke, I was imagining poor Tim cursing me out while listening to your speech, or lament; whatever it was."

"It wasn't either! And Tim didn't seem the least bit uncomfortable. He kept his smile all the way through."

"I can imagine."

"And as long as he wants to see me again, my 'speech' couldn't have been that bad, right?"

"Right, I guess." Frannie was still grinning, wishing she had the nerve to ask Tim for his version.

"So how about you? Any word from your Italian lover?"

"Not since Monday. Now why did you have to mention him? I was having such a good time listening to you. So get back to you and Tim. Start with when he first arrived."

"Well, that was funny too, now that I think about it. At the time it wasn't . . . ."

They spoke for more than ten minutes before Frannie cut her off and ran outside. "Oh, my poor Benny," she said, dragging the hose. "You thought I forgot you, huh? Well, I did, but don't worry, one of these days I'll get my head on straight again."

# Chapter Forty-three

Later, when Frannie arrived at Amore Evenings, she went straight to Glory. "He called me this afternoon, only minutes after you left."

Glory gave her a questioning look. "Who? Your Italian lover—Sergio?"

Frannie rolled her eyes and smirked. "No, the UPS guy! Of course I mean Sergio. Who else would concern me these days?"

"And? What did he have to say?" Glory caught a glimpse of the large group pouring in. "Better put it on fast forward; we're filling up fast."

"He's coming tonight."

"Oh, geez," Glory said and gave her a piercing look. "Make sure you don't get pregnant," she whispered.

"No way!" Frannie answered and walked away with an ear-to-ear grin.

*No way she won't get pregnant or no way she won't sleep with him?* Glory wondered. Either way, she didn't like it. Maybe she was being too judgmental. After all, she didn't know the guy, but she didn't like the way Frannie was obsessing over him. She had bad vibes about their relationship. It was fraught with problems and she feared Frannie was headed for heartbreak. Again.

As busy as they were, the hours were dragging for Frannie. She had told Sergio not to come until ten o'clock since there was little chance she could leave the restaurant before nine. That worked for him, he said, because his mother was always sound asleep by nine and he wouldn't have to tolerate all her questions.

Well, Frannie thought, she had one more question herself. *Who gets mamma?*

By 8:30 the rush was winding down. The tables were still full, but the last name on their waiting list had finally been crossed off. Frannie was working in her office when her cell phone rang. Her first thought was Sergio calling to cancel. Maybe Philomena had other plans for her boy tonight. She heaved a sigh of relief when the caller's number appeared until she realized her cousin would never call her at work unless it was important. "Suzanne? Is anything wrong?"

"No, we're fine," Suzanne assured her. "I'm sorry to bother you, but I wanted to catch you before you went home."

Frannie heard her voice crack and bolted upright in her chair. "Something *is* wrong. Tell me, Suzanne. I'm alone in the office so I can talk."

"I can't; it's too complicated. I just called to ask if you could come here straight from work. This is my only night off and I really need to talk . . ." Her sobs drowned her voice awhile until she managed to say, "Can you come here, *please*?"

Panic widened Frannie's eyes. "Now? Tonight? Why?"

All she heard in response was a muffled cry. "Suzanne, you can't call me here crying without telling me why! Answer me!"

"Greg knows."

Frannie went numb. Her first reaction was anger; she felt justifiably selfish. Struggling to handle her own problems along with two businesses seven days a week was stressful enough. Getting tangled in everyone else's problems was taxing her patience. Especially when there were no simple answers. Pile them all up on your shoulders and you're bound to collapse, she admonished herself.

*Maybe I should divorce myself from them and let the pieces fall where they may.*

But that was before Suzanne had uttered those two words. *Greg knows.* She felt as if someone had struck her over the head with a sledgehammer. With a deep breath of resignation, she locked up her paperwork, mumbled a hasty goodnight to Glory, and left.

She pounded the steering wheel with both fists. "Why tonight of all friggin' nights! I can't even call him! What the hell are you doing to yourself, girl, getting involved with this mamma's boy? What are we—two kids who have to sneak dates? I don't need this crap. I really don't!"

She rambled on as she drove, expunging all the frustrations that had been tormenting her since the day Tony Gerard came in and casually mentioned his friend's Italian house guests.

It was 9:15 when she pulled into her driveway to let Benny out before facing Suzanne's crisis. He would be there in forty-five minutes. Would he wait? Would he worry? She considered taping a note to her back door but he'd probably never see it anyway. If he doesn't see her car, why would he get out of his? Besides, she had a sudden flashback of the night she came home and found little Heather—an infant at the time—with a note from Suzanne taped to her diaper. A chill ran through her remembering all the frightful events that followed. She wasn't the superstitious type, but tonight something about a note rubbed her the wrong way.

Suzanne looked like hell when she opened the door for Frannie. Her hair was a tangled mess and she obviously hadn't bothered to wash her face. She was dressed all in black and with mascara smeared under her bloodshot eyes, she looked haunting.

Frannie's gaze was unsympathetic. "How in God's name did Greg find out, Suzanne? You told him, didn't you?"

"No!"

"You had to tell him! How else would he find out? If I'm the only one who knows, I surely didn't tell him! And as far as he knows, he can't impregnate a woman anymore, so—"

"Kim is pregnant!" Suzanne pulled out a kitchen chair, folded her arms on the table and cried into them.

Frannie sat next to her and listened to her sobs for a few silent seconds while she digested the shocking revelation. Gently, she pulled at her hair. "Sit up, Suzanne. Tell me what happened. How did he make the connection?"

Suzanne grabbed a paper napkin and wiped her eyes. The mascara had now drizzled down her cheeks like ink splashes. "Frannie, once he learned he wasn't sterile, all he had to do was count. He knew exactly when we were together and when Heather was born." Another wave of sobs rocked her shoulders. "He even said she looks like him and he's right—she does!"

"Tell me what happened. From the beginning," Frannie said. She had completely abandoned her earlier selfish attitude and embraced the love and sympathy she had for her cousin and her child. True, she had made her own bed, as the saying goes, but she had come such a long way from the person she was then to who she is now. Still, she couldn't rise above it.

Frannie listened just for the sake of listening. There wasn't a damn thing she could do about it except show that she cared. Suzanne needed someone's constant love and support through whatever might lie ahead. It wasn't the kind of trouble she could share with her father. Their relationship was certainly better but the missing years had left irreparable damage. More importantly, she needed Rob. He was her best friend, the man she loved.

After awhile Suzanne chased her out. She apologized repeatedly for dragging her there after working day and night. They had resolved nothing except to hope and pray that this crisis would pass. As her cousin had said, maybe he'll believe her because he wants to believe her. What would happen to his family if he chooses not to?

She wasn't more than five hundred feet away from home when she spotted the pickup truck driving away. He had waited all this time for her. She had neither the energy nor the will to get out of the car when she pulled up in her driveway.

"Now it's my turn to cry," she mumbled, and shed her tears on the steering wheel.

# Chapter Forty-four

An hour later Frannie was sitting in her living room staring into space. She hadn't turned on the television or her lamp, although she had intended to distract herself by glancing through her latest *Time* magazine. The room was too cool for her shortie pajamas, but she was oblivious to the chill.

This is going to be another one of those sleepless nights, she thought, but she was so keyed up she couldn't bring herself to get into bed. She fought to keep Suzanne's dilemma out of her head tonight. The magnitude of that problem, should it explode, was so far-reaching that she shivered just thinking about it. Her own troubles paled by comparison. Finding love and losing love were commonplace heartfelt situations experienced by most people. It hurts like hell but life goes on.

After sitting there awhile motionless, the air conditioning penetrated and chilled her. She got up to reach for her throw blanket but made an about-face toward her liquor cabinet instead. *Nothing like a glass of merlot to warm your bones and help you sleep,* she thought, then reconsidered. If she had to reach for the wine bottle every night she agonized over Sergio, she'd be flirting with alcoholism. She had witnessed enough of that with her uncle Jerry.

She settled for her flannel robe and headed for the kitchen to put on the teapot when the phone rang. It had only rung once when she picked it up. "Sergio, I'm so sorry—"

"What happen? I worry like crazy for you! I drive to your restaurant, don't see your car, I come back; I wait, wait, wait."

Frannie definitely heard the concern in his voice but she also detected a trace of annoyance. "Again, I'm sorry, Sergio, but it couldn't be helped. I had a sudden family crisis I had to handle."

"Someone hurt . . . sick?"

"No, but it was too important to ignore. I can't get into it. And it's not as if I could have called you," she said, but thought, *God forbid we alert your mamma to the fact that her forty-two-year-old son has another woman in his life!*

She heard him draw a breath and waited for him to respond. She hadn't spelled it out in so many words, but her message was clear.

"It late now . . . 11:30 . . . I like to come back, talk more, explain about mamma, but you have work again in morning—"

"If you're willing, so am I, Sergio. I'm not going to get much sleep tonight anyway, and although we discussed some very important problems, we haven't even scratched the surface on several others, primarily your mother. I've been very upset lately with all these issues swimming in my head. They're affecting everything I do. I'm a busy woman with a lot of responsibilities and I can't function unless we discuss and resolve *all* our problems because if we can't . . . well, I don't want to think of that 'if' now."

"You wait, cara mia. I be there."

She changed into white shorts and a pink tank top, then went to sit on her screened-in porch where she could warm up. The tranquil sounds of a summer night might relax her while she waited. And surprisingly, she did relax just sitting there listening to the birds trilling in the trees when the ocean roar didn't drown them out. But mostly it was resignation that calmed her. After her brief conversation with Sergio, she knew that tonight, one way or the other, she had to get her life back in order. She couldn't go on like this, being consumed every hour of every day with indecisive thoughts. *I love him, I love him not . . .*

Benny was in the house but when he heard the crunching sound of the pickup's tires on the graveled driveway, he went berserk. His bark was loud enough to wake up the dead, Sergio had said the first time he came to the house.

She opened the screen door for him and went to calm Benny down. "Want to sit out here?" she asked when she returned.

He shrugged. "Whatever you like, okay with me."

She had brought out two bottles of water and handed him one. "Here, I think you're going to need this. You have a lot of explaining to do."

He acknowledged her comment with a humble grin. "Yes, this I know." As always, his voice was gentle and polite, as if he were meeting her for the first time. And yet, ironically, when working in unison, his easy smile and soft-spoken voice had become powerful tools to break her down. A lamp inside the house cast a soft stream of light across his face. It was difficult for Frannie to resist touching him. She had been in his arms only a few days ago, the sweet memories vivid. Now, without the pressure of watching the clock, together with darkness and moonlight enhancing the mood, she felt herself weakening.

He dragged his chair closer so that he sat facing her, then held both her hands. His expression was rueful, as though he regretted what he was about to say. "What I say before about my mamma, I wish I could say not true. But still, she my mamma, and respect important."

"Yes, I agree, Sergio," she cut in, her tone argumentative, "but the title alone doesn't command respect. As I once said to my uncle Jerry, respect has to be earned. It isn't awarded to you just by reaching a certain age. And in my book, there are no exemptions for parents."

He looked surprised. "Your parents, you no respect?"

"Of course I do! I'm not referring to my parents. Mine are loving and considerate and never made unreasonable demands on us. So yes, they've earned my respect a hundred times over. Can you say the same about yours?"

He wrinkled his nose thoughtfully. "Sometime parent, they show love in different way. They think put roof over head, food in mouth, provide education—these things show love."

From the way he shrugged, Frannie gleaned that he didn't necessarily agree, but that's how it was growing up in the Giannetta household.

"But now these things not important," he continued dismissively. "Now it is not old problems we have with Mamma, it is new one. Bad one."

Frannie looked at him with concerned curiosity.

"I break promise to her telling you. She make me swear to God I tell no one; not even my brother and sister. Mamma have very little time to live. When I go back to Italy after Pappa die, she make me take her to doctor. She sick long time and say nothing to family. She tell me because she need me, and I her favorite." He shrugged modestly as if to say he wasn't sure why. "Maybe she favor me because I have no wife to interfere like my brother. And my sister? Forget that." He followed with a little laugh, albeit devoid of humor.

"So what is it? What did the doctor say?" Frannie asked, although she already suspected the dreaded word that looms over everyone.

"He send her for tests and they find she have lung cancer; very advanced, he say. But even if treatment can prolong life, Mamma no want; no way. She suffer more and die anyway, she say."

Frannie felt suddenly sick. Sick and ashamed of herself. Meeting Philomena Giannetta that one time had left her with such a negative impression that she had disliked her intensely. The woman was like a brick wall that stood between her and Sergio, and still was, but now Frannie had some compassion. She understood the woman's desperation. For the time she had left on this earth, she wanted and needed her son at her side. And Philomena herself needed to be needed, ergo her reaction to being dragged out to Amore that day, rather than preparing their breakfast herself. To her, Eddie's good intentions had been an insult. In a matter of seconds, the puzzle pieces were all coming together, but Frannie waited to hear it all from Sergio.

"So when she ask me to stay, take care of her, how can I refuse? I see in her eyes, the fear. If I say no, who help her?"

"Sergio, I can't believe that in a situation like this, when their mother is dying, that the family wouldn't set aside those differences and take care of her. How heartless can they be?"

His one quick laugh was rife with bitter memories. "We have Italian expression, "*I bambini imoparano cio che vivono . . .*"

"Yes, children learn what they live," Frannie said, offering the English translation.

"Well, Mamma, when she make enemy, she *never* forget. My sister-in-law, for my brother sake, in beginning she try to get along. But Mamma..." He knocked at his temple to gesture that his mother's was impenetrable.

"And your sister?"

He sighed at the question. "Lina, some years ago, she fall in love with married man. He have baby boy. Vincenzo was good man with hard luck. His wife run off with boyfriend, leave him, leave baby too. When Mamma and Pappa learn, both go crazy. Forbid her to see Vincenzo. Lina still try, he try; sometime they manage. Then after time pass, Lina can't find, he disappear. My brother and I, it hurt us to see Lina's heart break and we know Vincenzo good man. So we help, try to find, but he never come near our village again. Lina, she like dragon—breathe fire—she swear Mamma took care."

His last words widened Frannie's eyes. "You're not serious?"

Sergio laughed. "No, not like you think. We think maybe she pay him off, maybe threaten him. Is possible, but we never know for sure. So Lina too, she never forget. She too have bad streak, like Mamma."

"So in other words, you're your mother's only hope?"

"Yes, true." He kissed her fingertips and her whole body pulsated. "And that's why I never call. I try, I try very hard to forget. But I say who knows how many months Mamma have left? You here in America, I in Italy . . ." He shook his head and made a sour face. "No good, I say. This not fair. How can I ask this much from my Frannie?"

"So why didn't you call and explain all this?"

"What good it do?"

"A lot of good! At least it would have given me some comfort knowing you still loved me instead of feeling that everything you said to me—all those loving words—meant nothing to you. Didn't it ever occur to you how rejected I'd feel never hearing from you again?"

Sergio nodded in agreement through everything she said, his expression contrite. "Yes, sure I think of your feeling, my feeling, all the time. *Ti ho presente giorno e notte;* night and day. But I hope as time pass, you forget. I think now since Pappa die and Mamma sick, our restaurant have big troubles. Too much for my sister and brother alone."

"I can understand that. So since you couldn't tell them about your mother's cancer, weren't they upset when you announced you were leaving again for America and taking her with you? They would assume, and rightfully so, that your obligation to your family business should supersede any obligation you felt toward Eddie."

"I told you, Mamma give more trouble since Pappa die; she angry more, she cry all the time. Everyone surprised that she cry so much for Pappa. But they don't know she cry for herself; that she die soon too. So when Eddie say bring her, they say go, take her with you. Maybe change do her good and they get break."

Emotionally drained by what Sergio had revealed, Frannie took a pensive moment trying to sort it all out. She felt a wave of pity imagining him growing up with no affection from either parent. Were they all conceived and born for the sole purpose of devoting their lives to the family business? Was that why they were never close, had constant friction among themselves? If the old adage is true, *Children learn what they live,* then where did Sergio's gentle nature come from? Whatever the explanation, she was grateful that he had somehow escaped falling into that pit. But the more she thought about his family life, she decided sight unseen that it couldn't be totally hopeless. If the two brothers tried to help their sister years back, wasn't that motivated by love?

Sergio watched her patiently while she ruminated. He understood he had given her a lot to absorb. He also understood that although he would honor his mother's wishes, he could not impose such a burden on his Frannie.

"I don't know what to say, Sergio—about us, I mean. I suppose you'll be going back to Italy soon . . ." She couldn't bring herself to speak her thoughts. How dare she approximate a time when his mother would die so she could plan her life accordingly! Even to think it was awful.

But Sergio read her mind and understood. "Maybe we stay two week more, if Mamma feel okay. This way I help Eddie finish job."

"I was always curious about all this work he's doing on his house. Why? He lives alone, right? You explained why you want to help him, but what exactly are you and he doing there?"

He smiled uncertainly. "He want to marry woman with handicap daughter, eight-year-old. MS, I think. She need wheelchair for life so we make many changes to allow for special needs. And he want to make his woman happy; everything clean, new."

Frannie remained with her mouth open. It had taken her by surprise and she was saddened by the bittersweet news. Even though the handicapped child and her mother were two faceless people she might never meet, the story touched her. Acts of kindness always did and she admired Eddie Pisano for going overboard to welcome his bride-to-be and her handicapped child to his home.

"Wow! Now I see you have two good reasons for wanting to help Eddie. He deserves your help."

Sergio pushed his chair aside and sat next to her on the wicker loveseat. "Yes, but we must talk about us," he said, lifting her chin with a finger. "I want you in my life—forever in my life—but now, with Mamma . . . who can say how long? Then our restaurant big concern. Much to be done, much business to settle with my family. I cannot simply walk away, cara mia."

Frannie cast her gaze out into the darkness and took her time thinking it all out again. Whatever she said next would affect her entire life, but it was impossible to unscramble the myriad problems that faced them. And the thought of waiting for someone's death to open the door to your happiness was appalling. It tugged at her conscience but was an undeniable fact.

And what about her restaurants? It had taken years of hard work to achieve their success and her independence. Would marriage to Sergio jeopardize everything she had struggled to build? If their marriage went sour, it could all blow up in her face. It was a frightening thought but this was the end of the road—decision time.

When she finally turned to face him, his silvery-gray eyes were waiting, hopeful. She inhaled deeply and sighed. "Our combined problems are mind-boggling, Sergio. I hope somehow we can work them out. It'll be a daunting task, that's for sure. But for now we have to set everything aside. You have a responsibility to your mother, and as much as I'll miss you something awful, I love you more for honoring her wish. Your heart is kind and gentle, Sergio; it's the magnet that drew me to you. So let's not think too far ahead. Whatever is meant to be will be. We'll take it as it unfolds and live for the moment."

He held her face in his hands. "Yes, yes, my Frannie, and for this moment, I love you very, very much. Let me show you . . ." His kisses were passionate and relentless. Nearly breathless, Frannie pushed him away slightly so that she could look in his eyes. After a few silent seconds she stood up and clasped his hand in hers. "Yes, Sergio, come show me. We've waited too long."

# Chapter Forty-five

Jessica and Dan hadn't made any particular plan when they spoke earlier on the phone. She told him she just wanted to change into shorts and a tee shirt and do something relaxing.

"It's such a beautiful, warm night, Dan," she said when he arrived. "I'm in the mood for a long walk on the beach. I want to feel that ocean breeze on my face. How about you— any other ideas?"

He looked down at her with a smile that clearly answered her question. "Sounds like a great beginning." He kissed her forehead, then pointed to her bedroom window. "As long as it ends right there."

Jessica feigned a shy, embarrassed smile before surprising him with a long and passionate kiss. It had begun only as a playful gesture, but once they were locked in embrace, they couldn't break away. Every time their lips met, it was always one long, continuous kiss, interrupted only to breathe. Their eyes, their lips, their hands, their bodies, forever exploring the depth of their love for each other, forever searching for silent expressions of that love.

When finally their lips parted, Dan wrapped his arms around her waist while her hands rested softly on his chest. "Wow!" she said, drawing a deep breath. "Does that mean you'd rather not walk the beach with me?"

Dan laughed heartily and hugged her tighter. "No, silly. It just means I love you, in case you've forgotten. After all, I haven't told you since this afternoon when I called you."

She threw a cotton cardigan over her shoulders and tied the arms together over her chest. "Let's go," she said, reaching up to kiss the tip of his nose. "We can tell each other a million more times as we walk the beach."

Dan opened the car door for her and gave her one of his devilish smiles. "And then another million when we come back."

"Maybe not," she answered, pretending to give it serious thought. "Have you noticed how we rarely find time for conversation when we're alone in my house?"

They enjoyed their banter as he drove, laughing at each other's quips or innuendos. The light mood stayed with them until after they had walked the beach awhile and decided to take a break. "Let's sit a little closer to the shore," Dan suggested.

"No, Dan, we might get wet and mess up your car."

"I have plastic seat cushions in the trunk." He took her hand and gently pulled her down at his side. The sea serenaded them while they sat quietly; their thighs brushing, their hands clasped. They had become so close that sitting together silently was simply another way of making love. It negated the need to force conversation.

"I had an interesting conversation with my daughter this morning," Jessica said, staring into the ocean.

He darted a sideways glance. Her tone had piqued his interest. "I'm listening . . ."

"It was about us, as you probably already guessed. At first she was very cute and casual, but making remarks that alluded to the fact that we couldn't possibly be serious."

"Like what?"

"Oh, I don't remember verbatim, but they came across condescending—at least that's the way I took them. At one point I do remember her saying something like she's glad I squeezed in time for a little social life, but between my practice and my family, how could I handle that on an ongoing basis? Maybe I should be honest with you, she sweetly suggested, and why should you be left in the sidelines waiting for me to work you into my schedule?" She shot him a smirk. "And she's made a similar remark before, Dan. As if it's selfish of me to hold you back. 'Mr. Madison is a nice-looking man,' Carole said, 'and I hear he has a very pleasant personality. He could find a hundred women who have more freedom than you, Mom.'" She shook her head while worry lines creased her forehead. "The more I think about it, the more it annoys me."

Dan made an unsuccessful attempt to laugh it off casually. His feelings were hurt and it showed all over his face. "What she was *really* sweetly suggesting, as you put it, is that you politely and promptly dump me."

Jessica had to laugh at the way he phrased it. "Pretty much so. When she called I didn't have time to get into it, nor did it hit me then as much as it did later, but I'll tell you one thing . . ." She pointed a finger. "I'm going to straighten her out real fast. She's my daughter and I love her, sure, but she almost always rejected my advice, and I'm not about to accept hers. No one—not even my children—can tell me how to live my life!"

Dan relaxed again, admiring her fiery determination. "Isn't it unbelievable, all the jealousy stirred up by these 'second time around' love stories? Ours is not unique; it seems to be a common problem experienced by older people." He laughed at his frivolous thought. "Maybe we should put them all together in one big pot and straighten them out." His face sobered when memories of some of Glory's remarks surfaced. "When I think back to how my daughter Glory was hurting when my other children learned she existed. They wanted no part of her and more or less told her so. She knows well the feeling; that's why I can't fathom why she's putting me through the same treatment."

"She can't see the forest for the trees, I guess. That often happens. Some people can only look beyond their own circle, not inside. If they stopped and took a better look at themselves—really examined their own attitudes and behavior—maybe it would open their eyes; they'd have more understanding and compassion."

"Getting back to your daughter, though, when you speak to her—if you do—please don't come on too strong, for my sake and yours. If she sees anger in your eyes in defense of me, I'm in the doghouse before we even meet! And I wouldn't want to be the cause of any trouble between you. I've told you that before, and I can't stress it enough."

Jessica waved off his plea. "If I get into it with Carole, believe me, I'll be defending *myself* first, then you. No, on second thought, I shouldn't even say *defend* because there's nothing to defend. I think I'll just speak to both of them, calmly, and *tell* them—not ask permission—that we care for each other very much and plan to continue seeing each other, so they might as well get used to it."

He arched his brows. "Well, I'm glad you feel so strongly. When we first spoke about it, you were a little worried about their reaction. Remember you were concerned about possibly alienating them?"

"Yes, but I thought about it and decided to take a positive approach. In some cases, you don't *ask,* you *tell.*"

"Maybe you're right. Maybe if I talk to Glory with a positive attitude, I might get a positive reaction. I've been so careful not to hurt her and that might have exacerbated the problem." He paused to give it more thought, then lifted her hand and kissed it. "Would you like me present when you talk to them? Is that better or worse?"

Jessica scrunched her nose. "I'm not sure we're ready to 'meet the families'; let's handle our own children individually first and see where that takes us. There's no reason to rush into any formal introductions."

"I wasn't thinking formal; I just think eventually they should get used to seeing us around. Glory knows you, sure, but only as her doctor, not as the woman her father loves. But I agree; there's no hurry. As long as we don't have to contend with hostilities or sugary, condescending sermons."

"Hey, speaking of Glory, what ever happened with Tim? Has he called her again?"

"I have no idea. When I asked her how her lunch date went, she quickly corrected me, saying it was not a date. They're just friends and that's all they'll ever be." He shrugged and looked at her with disappointment.

"Don't give up, Dan. We were just friends too, and baby, look at us now!"

The sound of her giggle warmed him all over. "Okay, enough ocean for today. Let's go home, my beautiful lady."

# Chapter Forty-six

Tim had every intention of calling Lori Carpenter later this Sunday morning. He had dated her several times and occasionally enjoyed her company. More often than not, though, Lori's narcissism got in the way. Thanks to burning ambition and tenacity, her career in advertising had soared in recent years and she loved nothing better than to describe in minute detail how she had climbed the corporate ladder. She would tell him with pride how others who tried to cross her path had tumbled.

The more he recalled about their last few dinner dates, the more he frowned. Why sit across a table from her and listen to her nonstop self-praise? Sometimes as he was forced to listen his mind would drift. She'd be firing away, using the jargon of her business, while he laughed to himself wondering how she'd enjoy listening to him describe various surgical procedures, replete with medical terminology.

No, he decided, Lori might be attractive, intelligent and successful, but those positive attributes did not entice him to call her simply to fill an otherwise lonely evening. He'd rather sit with a good book.

Or Glory English. Now there was a challenge. There was something so intriguing about Glory. Although it didn't amount to narcissism, she too was self-absorbed. Despite her business success and the support of family and friends, she battled insecurity. Certainly she had been traumatized by several past events, but with determination and self-confidence, she had sought and found new beginnings, without severing the link to her livelihood. Since her move to Ogunquit, she not only still handled her *Glorious Cooking* column, but also managed a hugely successful restaurant.

He sorted out the facts about Glory's past, as he knew them, and came to one conclusion. The shock of Alex's brutal death had been unbearable for her; especially since she had just learned she was pregnant with his child. No matter how many caring people surrounded her, she felt no one would or could ever take Alex's place in her heart or replace her baby's father. She felt alone and abandoned by the men she had loved—her husband, the father who raised her, and Alex. As a result, the need for her real father's love had grown stronger until it obsessed her. Now that her father is interested in another woman—her obstetrician no less—the threat of loss looms over her once again.

Tim shook his head and a dubious smile crossed his lips. *No wonder Frannie was thrilled to have me enter the picture. She's right, though; maybe I could be the best medicine for Glory, if we find ourselves compatible. And that's a big if.*

He called her anyway with half a heart, but when she answered the phone, all those doubts were instantly swept away. She sounded like Miss Congeniality herself. No one would ever suspect her inner turmoil.

"Hey, how are you, Tim? I never expected to hear from you so soon, but I'm glad you called. You're a pleasant interruption from my grueling routine. I have so much to do, I've been chasing my tail all morning."

"Oh? Then maybe I should let you go . . . I can call again."

"No, don't be silly. I'm not so busy that I can't spare a few minutes for an old friend." She emphasized *old friend* and laughed.

"Don't laugh; it's partially true. I may be old in years, but I'm a new friend who hopes we might reach that point."

"What point?"

"To be *old* friends."

"I don't see why not, Tim. As long as you can live with what I said when you were here. Friendship is all I can offer right now."

"I can respect that," he answered with less than total honesty. He wasn't sure how long he could enjoy a celibate relationship. Old memories swiftly surfaced. It seemed like a hundred years ago when he was a young boy growing up in Boston. His parents were devout Catholics who had encouraged him to think about devoting his life to Christ. And he *did* think about it—almost constantly for a few years. But sadly, when the time came to choose, he found that he lacked the courage to enter the seminary. It was not only the commitment to a celibate life that turned him around— although it was a strong consideration. An entire lifetime is often a long, arduous road. Forever denying himself the sexual and companionable pleasures of a wife, along with the absence of children to protect and love, was too great a sacrifice.

Ironically, it was the examples set by his parents that changed his mind. They were not only devoted to their religion, but to each other as well. He had been a foolish dreamer to think that marriage to Janet could possibly offer a similar family life.

The fleeting images faded like passing clouds and he continued his conversation. "So, *friend,* now that I've reassured you that I'll respect your wishes, when can we see each other again? If you can arrange for a sitter, maybe we can work something out for an evening date. Or is your one night off usually booked?"

"Not unless you count mundane responsibilities related to the business. I spend a lot of time on the phone and computer. And sometimes, believe it or not, I spend the whole night catching up on laundry."

"Are you saying you never get out on your night off?"

Glory laughed at the disbelief in his voice. "No, I do have friends who occasionally drag me out, but not often.

And it's no big deal—I don't mind. I have a beautiful home here and it gives me a chance to hang around and enjoy it."

"But you're too young to be so socially stifled. You need to change that routine."

"Maybe so, but it's no emergency," she said, her tone edged with feigned indifference. "When something better comes along, I'll consider getting out more."

"And I don't fit into that category—something better?"

She laughed ruefully. "Sorry, Tim. That did sound awful, didn't it? But I was referring to the routine I had fallen into before I met you."

He blew a breath into the phone. "Well, that's a relief. I'd hate to think I couldn't score higher than paperwork or dirty laundry!"

They laughed together at the ludicrous comparison. "Okay, so let's get back to serious business," Tim said. "What night are you off this week and can you get a sitter? If not, that's okay too. I'll be perfectly content to sit there with you and enjoy your company."

Glory hesitated, then said. "I'm off Thursday. Does that work for you?"

"I'll make it work."

"Well, then, I'll see about a sitter and let you know. Why don't you give me another call on Tuesday, okay?"

\* \* \*

Although she hadn't admitted it to Tim, he was right. She *was* socially stifled, through no one's fault but her own. It had been easy to blame Amore Evenings and/or her son to graciously decline invitations, but she had grown comfortable with her introverted lifestyle since Alex's death. It wasn't that she preferred staying home alone, but it was better than mixing in circles where she felt like a misfit. At home she didn't have to put on any pretenses. Besides, she had nothing in common with most groups. The singles who invited her were too young for her taste, and socializing with married couples only depressed her more. When you're the only one without a partner, your grief is intensified. Couldn't they understand that? She laughed thinking that yes, sometimes they did, remembering one invitation she had been forced to accept. The host and hostess had conveniently invited a single male friend and, naturally, seated him next to her. It had been an agonizing, never-to-be-repeated evening spent being trapped by the boisterous gentleman.

She had told these casual friends—most of whom she had met through Frannie or their restaurant—that although she appreciated their good intentions, if and when she was ready for male companionship, she'd like to select her own.

It wasn't that she was ungrateful, but in most cases, these invitations were nothing more than expressions of sympathy. *Poor girl needs to get out more. All she does is work and stay home with the baby.* She didn't have to hear the words; she could see them on their facial expressions.

If she were to write a list of prerequisites for the perfect male companion, Dr. Tim Quinlan would meet almost all the requirements. But realistically, how long would he accept the "friendship only" terms she had set? Eventually, he'd want to move from "companion" to "lover."

*And so would I,* she silently admitted. But without deep love and a strong commitment, the thought of a love affair with the handsome doctor was unthinkable. *My body might be ready, but my heart and soul are not.*

For the rest of the day, Glory went through her usual motions, but she was frustrated by indecision. Finally she decided it would be best to nip it in the bud. She'd call Tim and apologize, but in the end, he'd understand.

She waited to call him until it was almost time to leave for Amore Evenings, in order to avoid a futile, prolonged conversation. Breaking away from him now, before their "friendship" developed, might be a blow to his pride, and he might be disappointed, but he'd get over it. She had no doubt if word got out that Dr. Tim Quinlan was looking, the women would line up for miles.

Feeling a little shaky about her decision, she picked up the phone to call him. He had written his home number on the back of his business card, and while it rang, she prayed that he'd answer. She wanted to say what she had to say and be done with it.

She froze for a silent second when she heard his recorded voice. With a will of their own, her fingers hit the off button without leaving a message, then tapped out another number. "Dad, it's me," she said, her voice quavering slightly. "I have to leave for work soon, but I need to ask something: Are you free to sit with Danny this Thursday night?"

A short silence hung heavily until Dan finally responded. "Would it be okay if I bring Jessica? I'm sure she won't mind sitting with me."

*No, but I would.* "Oh, if you and she have plans, then forget it. I can find someone else," she said dismissively.

Dan's voice came on strong and strange. "That's ridiculous and unnecessary," he said. "I *am* seeing Jessica that night, but we have no special plans. We'll both be there." He had originally asked if it would be okay to bring her, now he was *telling* her.

She arched her brows in surprise but his clear message rendered her momentarily silent. "Fine," was all she said, but later that night, images of Dr. Jessica Branson sitting in her home playing "grandma" would irritate her like nails scratching a blackboard.

# Chapter Forty-seven

Suzanne had spoken to Rob only once since he called, ostensibly to tell her about his Grandpa Dennis and Dora Malanski. She and Rob had been practically inseparable since they met at Maine Medical Center, but tonight, after torturous weeks without him, she was having a serious anxiety attack. Like a teenager waiting for her first date, she stayed glued to the window looking for his car.

Her heart pounded when she saw him park and enter her building. Quickly, she scooped Heather up out of her Elmo chair and went to meet him at the door. She had wondered if her daughter would remember him after this long absence, but her fears were allayed as soon as he reached the top of the stairs. "Robbie! Robbie!" she squealed, reaching out to him. He took her in his arms, kissed her playfully and tickled her silly, making a big fuss as he always did. The sight of them together again put a hard lump in Suzanne's throat.

"Hi," he said, giving Suzanne only a cautious feathery kiss. "I was afraid she might have forgotten me, but this is so great." He rubbed his nose in Heather's belly and she giggled. "Do horsey," she cried. Rob put her on his shoulders and hobbled around, neighing like a horse.

"That's enough, Heather," Suzanne said. "We're going bye-bye in Robbie's car." She could never tell if Rob was suffering any pain or discomfort. He had an amazing attitude about the loss of his foot which had necessitated the prosthesis and cane. To other amputees the prosthesis might have been looked upon as a necessary evil, but not to Rob. He said it was a blessing because it enabled him to walk and resume so many activities he had enjoyed before the accident, like playing golf with his grandfather. So knowing Rob, even if he were in excruciating pain, he'd steel himself to endure it just to entertain Heather.

No "father" could outshine Rob Butler.

Suzanne was slightly apprehensive during the car ride to his parents' home. She and Rob talked, but only amiably at first, like two friends catching up after not seeing each other for a while. Heather had dozed off in the back, as she often did in the car, but Suzanne would have welcomed an interruption from her tonight. When their conversation had waned, it was obvious to both what the other was thinking. Suzanne interrupted his thoughts with small talk. "We could have used my car, Rob, instead of switching Heather's car seat. You shouldn't have bothered."

"I'm more comfortable in mine." He glanced over at her and added, "You know that." His slanted smile quietly implied that she knew everything about him; his likes, his dislikes, his habits, his attitudes. They had shared so much, but sadly, she refused to share the one secret most important to him. It would always put a wall between them. Suzanne knew that as well as he did, which only convinced Rob more that the guy was either some worthless bum she'd never want Heather to know, or some well-known prominent man she wanted to protect—maybe a celebrity or a politician. Or maybe some ordinary guy who happens to be married; maybe someone right here in or around Ogunquit.

Would the day ever come when he could stop caring? Stop guessing?

She kept her gaze out the window, as if she were seeing the scenery for the first time, pretending she didn't notice his deep thinking.

"Do you want to talk, Suzanne—about us? We haven't really talked since I called you last week. I admit I've been avoiding it too. We still have about fifteen minutes before we get there, and since Heather is sleeping . . ."

Her quick laugh held no trace of humor. "In fifteen minutes you expect to solve all our problems?"

"We only have one problem."

"But it's a big one; unsolvable. For a while I—forget it." She was about to tell him how after their breakup she had considered revealing the name of Heather's father, but changed her mind. Why let him think her resolve was weakening? He'd only try harder until she spilled it out.

"What were you about to say? Tell me," he urged.

"Nothing important. But Rob, I hope you're not planning to work on me, a little at a time until you catch me in a weak moment, because that's not going to happen. You have to understand, once and for all, that this is not something I *won't* do; it's something I *can't* do. So either you take us as we are and promise to drop this discussion permanently or we go back to where we were these past three weeks."

"And where was that?"

"Miserable," she said, then laughed at her admission. When he laughed with her, she gave his thigh a quick affectionate squeeze.

"I don't know why we're laughing," he said. "There's not a damn thing funny about our situation."

She crossed her arms and heaved a sigh. "They say there's a bright side to everything. We just have to look for it."

"Yeah, well, there's some truth to that. And those bright sides are sitting beside me and behind me."

She blew him an air kiss. "I love you too, Rob. Heather and I both love you."

"I guess that'll be enough for me. It'll have to be."

"Oh, please, Rob, don't make it sound as if you're settling for us. We'll work it out. When two people in love really want each other, they have to make a concerted effort to make it work. I think we're worth trying, don't you?"

"Absolutely! I'm just not sure I can put it out of my head for a lifetime. That'll be tough." He paused a few seconds, then frowned. "But you know what, sweetheart? The more I think about it, the more I think I'd be much better off not knowing who the hell he is."

Suzanne blinked back the tears that welled in her eyes. Silently, she agreed with everything he'd ever said and loved him more for giving in rather than lose her and Heather. She wanted to tell him so, but she'd be bawling hysterically if she did. Instead, she pulled herself together and changed the subject. "So what did your mother say when you called to tell her I was coming tonight? Did she ask any questions about us?"

"No, I'm sure she wanted to, but she just said something sweet, like, 'Oh, what a nice surprise!'" Rob laughed, remembering. "I'm sure Grandpa Dennis will be happy to see you, Suzanne; he always liked you." He didn't tell her, though, that his grandpa also thought she should be honest with him. "And I think I like you too," he said, then reached over and cupped her chin. "A lot."

\* \* \*

Grandpa Dennis was indeed pleased to see Suzanne and Heather. He hugged all three of them, then proudly presented Dora Malanski. He introduced her to Suzanne as his "friend," but anyone could see by the light in his eyes—and hers—that they were more than friends. Dennis then sneaked a wink at his grandson and squeezed his shoulder, the latter gesture conveying his pleasure seeing them together again. "We're still on for Thursday, right?" he asked, referring to their weekly eighteen holes of golf.

"Of course," Rob answered with a grin. The twinkle in his grandpa's eyes was clear indication that he wanted to hear how their reconciliation had come about. He had been hurting too lately watching Rob's depression and not being able to help. Now Rob's company would be twice as pleasurable since they could share happy talk about the ladies in their lives.

While Catherine, Dora and Dennis were chatting in the kitchen and fussing over Heather, Jim caught a private moment with his son. "How's it going, Rob? Everything okay with you two now? I'm not asking to stick my nose in your business; you're entitled to your privacy, but I just wanted to know how you're doing."

"I'm fine, Dad. Suzanne and I just needed a break to work some things out, but I think we'll be okay now. Don't worry." Rob felt a stab of guilt because he had confided in his grandfather without hesitation, but never shared his troubles with his parents. It wasn't that they weren't close, but he had formed this special bond with his grandfather way back in his early teens. Whenever he clashed with his parents over some insignificant problem that seemed monumental at the time, Dennis would always listen. Whatever the issue, Rob never came out victorious, but after spilling out his complaints to his grandpa, his anger and frustration would dissipate.

Only Grandpa Dennis and Wanda Prewitt, his high school English teacher and now good friend, had that effect on him. He smiled remembering the wonderful Thanksgiving-style dinner she had made him the week before he was supposed to join the Army. They had talked nonstop and laughed often, but there were sobering moments as well, especially when Wanda stunned him by revealing her gay relationship with Vanessa Madison. It had been a very special night. Little did they know the tragedy that would follow hours later.

He wished he could talk to her now. If anyone could put an optimistic view on a troubling thought, it was Wanda Prewitt. The idea tempted him, but he shook it off. Why stir the pot? he decided. *You made your decision. Go with it.*

Catherine Butler's celebration dinner provided a great time for all. Catherine had fussed with the menu, which featured one of her father-in-law's favorite dishes—pot roast with caramelized onions, red cabbage and twice-baked potatoes—and two of Dora's favorite desserts, rice pudding and chocolate cream pie. But even when they could eat no more, they sat around and talked, sharing uplifting and humorous stories. It was a happy celebration for the senior lovebirds, but the presence of Suzanne and Heather as part of the family had boosted everyone's good spirits even more. Or at least that's the impression the two older couples had portrayed.

When she and Rob had arrived, Suzanne had entered the Butler home with some trepidation. After all, it was really Rob who had invited her. Once he had asked or *told* his mom, what could she say? Although she had never detected anything from Catherine and Jim Butler but warmth and sincere affection, she wondered sometimes how they truly felt. Perhaps they wished he had fallen in love with someone single and childless and without her promiscuous history. And if they did, she certainly couldn't blame them. Now that she was a parent too, she looked at many things differently.

As they were waving their goodnights at the door, Suzanne turned around to thank them all once more. "It's amazing, isn't it? We were three generations tonight—such a big difference in our ages—but I mean this sincerely . . ." She put a hand on her heart. "I can't remember the last time I had such fun. My cheeks actually hurt from laughing so much!" Then to Catherine and Jim, "And thanks again for inviting me. I had a wonderful time."

"It was our pleasure, believe me," Catherine answered enthusiastically. "And God willing, if He keeps us all healthy, tonight was only the first of many."

As Suzanne scurried off to put her sleeping daughter in the car seat, Catherine Butler seized the moment. She impulsively tugged at Rob's shirt sleeve, stood on her toes and kissed his cheek. "I'm happy for you, Rob. Don't think your father and I haven't noticed how down in the dumps you've been the past few weeks. It was such a pleasure for us to see you happy and laughing tonight. And that baby! God love her—she's beautiful. If things work out for you and Suzanne, you should think about adopting her, if that's possible." She gave him a gentle push. "But go . . . you have plenty of time to make that decision."

Rob gave her a *we'll see* shrug as if he had never entertained the thought before. But as he was closing the door behind him, he caught his grandpa's heartfelt gaze.

# Chapter Forty-eight

After a difficult five-hour surgery on a seventeen-year-old boy, Dr. Tim Quinlan took a well-deserved break. He had nearly lost his patient twice, but thanks to his skilled hands and an excellent surgical team, the boy was expected to survive. Both boys involved in the accident had blood alcohol levels that exceeded the legal limit and the eighteen-year-old driver would not be as lucky as his friend. That poor kid would leave the hospital in a body bag.

But Tim Quinlan had always been an optimist. He tried not to dwell on the ones they couldn't save, but only the ones they had saved. He sat at his desk now poring over medical journals and reports, a container of black coffee in his hand. After wolfing down a turkey wrap in four bites, he went through his telephone messages and e-mails.

One message was from Suzanne Oliveri and his smile went wide anticipating the reason for her call. He barely gave her a chance to speak when she answered. "She told you, didn't she?" He laughed good-naturedly. "My fault. I should have told her not to say anything. I just assumed she wouldn't."

Nonplussed, Suzanne stopped him before he could say anything more. "Hold on, Doc. I think we have crossed wires here. Who told me what? I have no idea what you're talking about."

"Uh-oh, sorry. Forget it. So what's up? It's so great to hear from you! Is everything okay with all you guys there in Ogunquit?" After the stressful hours in surgery trying to save the young boy's life, hearing from Suzanne had instantly relaxed him until it suddenly occurred to him this might not be a casual call. It had been almost a year since he had spoken to her or Rob Butler. Tim very rarely involved himself in his patients' private lives, but their unique love story had begun while both were hospitalized and under his care at Maine Medical Center. He had developed a special bond with the couple. "How's your dad, Suzanne—still okay?"

"Yes, thank God. It's amazing to see how ridding himself of alcohol not only helped him physically, but emotionally he's like a whole new person. He even looks younger! That nasty loudmouth you knew is totally gone— forever, I hope."

"That's wonderful to hear. Send him my regards. And what about Rob? I hope you have more good news."

Her tone shifted downward. "Rob is the reason I called, you, Doc. As far as the loss of his foot is concerned, he's doing fine—better than I ever expected he would. In the beginning he took it so well, that I thought he was in denial or something—that it would hit him later. But I was wrong, I'm happy to say." She drew a breath. "It's Rob and *me* I'm concerned with, though." She paused, feeling awkward. "I know what a busy man you are, Doc, but I was hoping—oh, I feel stupid now; I shouldn't have called—"

Tim realized his instinct had been correct. This was not a casual hello-how-are-you call. "Suzanne, if you felt the need to call me, that's reason enough. Something is obviously troubling you, so if you have the time to tell me, I have the time to listen. I have a three o'clock meeting, but until then I'm free as a bird."

He sounded so sincere and genuinely interested in helping her, if possible, that Suzanne summoned up her courage and began her story. She prefaced it, however, with a gentle reminder. "First, Doc, I know that during my hospitalization, and even after, while I was in your care, I could trust that everything we discussed was confidential; you know—the patient/doctor thing. But this is different. It concerns our personal lives—mine and Rob's. So before I tell you, I have to be sure you'll keep this conversation strictly confidential as well because—"

"Suzanne, say no more. In that respect, you have nothing to worry about."

She tried to spill out her problem as succinctly as possibly. Once she got started, she found herself surprisingly calm. She had been uncomfortable about bothering him, but his warm personality came through in a flash, reminding her of what she had loved about him in the first place. From their first conversation, she had considered him not only an excellent, dedicated doctor, but also a beautiful and sensitive human being.

She had begun her story by telling him the worst part first—she named Heather's father and explained the relationship she'd had with the Haggarty family for years. Although she listened with a keen ear for a sign of Tim's reaction, she heard nothing; not a gasp, not a sigh. Nothing at all that resembled shock or disappointment.

Even when she told him that Greg had proposed his silence unnerved her. But it dawned on her that congratulatory words would not be forthcoming, or at least premature, in light of what he had already heard.

"So that's basically it," she said, after describing their conversation the night before after his parents' dinner party.

Now came the long exhalation from Tim. "And I guess you want to know what I think about your decision."

"*Our* decision, yes."

"Well, I've got to be honest with you, Suzanne. It sounds to me that the decision was yours alone and Rob went along because he had no other option—other than to give you up. He must love you an awful lot; I hope you appreciate that."

She choked up but stifled the sobs in her throat. "I do, of course I do, and I love him too, just as much. But don't you see that I have no other options either? If it ever got out, think of the consequences! You can't build happiness by destroying other people's lives."

"I doubt that Rob would ever let that secret escape. I think he'd share your feelings. It would surely tear that family apart, and knowing Rob, he wouldn't dream of allowing that to happen."

"I considered that too, Doc. It would kill him in a way. He doesn't know Greg and Kim, but living in the same village, their paths could certainly cross someday; it's bound to happen—especially since Rob would never be able to resist seeking him out. Not to approach him, of course, but just to see what he looks like. And once he has a face to burn in his memory, can you imagine how it would turn his stomach to visualize me in bed with Greg? It would be bad enough to know I slept with a married man, but this man who now has a face and the husband of the woman who lovingly cares for my child? Her *husband's* child? No, it could never work. For Rob it would be like living with something explosive inside you; always waiting for it to blow up."

"And not for you?"

"No, I can handle it now. I had to make peace with myself; it's a mistake I can never undo. And when I look at Kim and those kids, there's no way I could ever hurt them."

Tim wanted to say, *You already did,* but could never be that unkind to Suzanne. From the way she told her story, he had no doubt that she was truly remorseful and would live with that guilt all her life. How she was going to handle it later was another story. "Someday Heather will start asking questions. I'm sure you thought about that—"

She laughed bitterly. "You have no idea, Doc, how often I think of that. But I'm forcing myself to push it out of my head. I don't mean to sound dramatic, but life has lots of bumps along the road, and since that's a long way off, I decided I should concentrate on my immediate problems. I'll have years to prepare for that crisis."

Tim was quiet while he considered all she had said, looking at the whole picture as well as he could for the moment.

"You don't agree with me, do you? Your silence is speaking loud and clear." She tried to force a laugh but it came out shaky.

"I do and I don't," he said finally. "Truthfully, I'm most worried about the fact that Greg already suspects that Heather is his—"

She cut him off. "No, don't worry—I gave that a lot of thought, believe me. I'm pretty sure I convinced him she's not his. And even if I'm wrong, I'm sure he'll never do anything about it. He'll force himself to believe it because he'll know the price he'll pay if he doesn't. Kim would be so devastated she'd take the kids and leave him in a heartbeat. And don't forget she's expecting a third child now."

With his thumb, Tim tapped repeatedly at the pen in his hand while he ruminated again. He knew she had called him hoping he'd give her some encouraging advice, or better yet, support the decisions she had already made. "No question, Suzanne, you're in a damned if you do, damned if you don't situation." He took another moment to give it more thought. "Look, my profession doesn't cover matters of the heart, and you should bear in mind that I failed to make my own marriage work, so just because I'm a doctor you shouldn't think of me as a paragon whose opinions should guide you or alter your own, okay?"

"Understood, but I have a lot of respect for your opinion. I think I realized that you were special when I first came out of that coma. As soon as you spoke, I could hear in your voice and see in your eyes that you were honest, caring and dedicated. At that stage in my life, I wasn't into trusting too many people."

Tim laughed. "Yes, now that you mention it, I remember that." He cleared his throat. "So okay, now that we got past that, let's get back to what I was about to say. I can sort of meet you halfway. I agree that Greg should never be told. I don't like that decision but I can't think of an alternative. It's a lousy thing to do, denying a father and daughter the right to know and love each other, and somewhere down the road it could cause all of you plenty of trouble and heartaches. But I'm sure you're well aware of that, so those are my feelings about telling Greg; I agree. But I *disagree* about Rob. I think he should be told. Once he knows, it'll probably hit him hard, but if his love is strong enough to forgive you, then at least you and he can begin your marriage with total honesty; a clean slate. You won't have that 'huge mountain' between you."

Suzanne blew a sigh. "I admit you're right, but it's easier said than done. It's scary for me. What if once I knock down that 'huge mountain' you speak of, he doesn't want me anymore? Then where am I?"

"It is frightening for you—and risky. But you asked for my opinion and I gave it. Still, Suzanne, you have to be absolutely sure before you make your final decision. I'd hate to have it on my conscience if I guided you in the wrong direction."

"Don't worry, Doc. I'd never blame you. Everything that's happened and anything that's going to happen is a direct result of my own actions. I accept that."

"You've come a long way, Suzanne. You've matured tremendously. From what I know about your life before we met, I think motherhood and having the love of a great guy like Rob has done wonders for you. So from now on, have faith and trust your own judgment."

She laughed under her breath. "My judgment was what got me into this mess!"

Tim laughed too. "That was the old Suzanne. The new Suzanne is a sweetheart. I think she has the strength to fight her way through all life's obstacles." He cleared his throat. "Now since you got me into this, make sure you call me again and let me know how things turned out. And if you'd like to sit and talk face to face, we can work that out too."

She heaved a sigh of relief. "I knew I'd feel better if I called you. And speaking of talking face to face, maybe we should. What did you mean before when you said, 'She told you'?"

Tim grinned and glanced at the clock. "Okay, if you still have time, I'll tell you. My problem is not as serious, but I could use some advice too. I'm sort of stuck in neutral. I assume you don't know I had a lunch date with Glory English?"

"Glory English and *you!* That's amazing! How did that happen?"

Tim didn't have to see her face to imagine her big smile and eyebrows arched in surprise. "It's not so amazing; we're both unattached," he answered playfully. "It started very innocently. My daughter was actually instrumental in making it happen . . ."

# Chapter Forty-nine

Almost a week had passed since she and Sergio made love for the first time. It was almost midnight when he had arrived again on Saturday night. Frannie usually collapsed into a dead sleep after exhaustive mornings and nights in both restaurants, but anxiety and desire had her wide-eyed and energetic after leaving Amore Evenings. He had reluctantly left after three in the morning, and although she had hardly any sleep, her energy had not waned. Memories of the night before fueled her through the next day and night. And it wasn't just the sexual satisfaction that kept the smile on her face, but the depth of their love for each other. It would take time before separation would not pain them again, but they were both willing to wait. The promise of a long life together in the not-too-distant future would sustain them for now.

In their last phone conversation the night before, Frannie had told Sergio that she'd eventually have to tell her parents and Glory about their plans. They were the most important people in her life and she couldn't spring it on them later like a sudden storm. She'd also have to explain why they can't be together for a while, she told him, but he could rest assured it would remain confidential. Truthfully, she couldn't imagine who would approach Philomena and question her about her terminal illness; no one here knew her well enough. The chances were remote, but not impossible. And anyway, she decided, a promise is a promise.

And so, after stalling for days, and with much trepidation, she called Glory from Amore Breakfast and asked if she could stop by.

"You sounded so serious when you called," Glory said when they were seated in Glory's kitchen. She tried for a quick study of her friend's eyes, but Frannie avoided her gaze. "Do you have trouble in paradise? You haven't said a word about what's happening with Sergio, and—"

"Don't be offended, Glory. It's not that I didn't want to, but you know we rarely get a chance to talk while we're working—not a real conversation, anyway. We need the quiet and privacy of our homes for serious stuff. For that matter, you haven't said a word about Tim either."

Glory waved it off. "There's not much to tell at this point. But I suspect that's not the case with you and Sergio."

When Frannie acknowledged Glory's suspicion with a nod, Glory threw her gaze up and lifted her hands in prayer. "Oh, no, don't tell me! I have a feeling I'm not going to like what you have to say." She dragged her chair a little closer, and squeezed Frannie's hands, as if the gesture might help penetrate her warning. "Frannie, before you begin, I hope you haven't made any hasty decisions—I'm begging you not to. I know the guy's had your head spinning, but you barely know him!"

"Glory, don't assume that what I feel is just a physical attraction. I've had physical attractions before and I've been in love before, and so have you. I think we both know the difference. If I just had 'the hots' for him, as you put it, my head wouldn't have been spinning all this time. Let's face it, I could have easily satisfied that urge, and he would have willingly obliged, I'm sure. And by the way, my friend—I told you I would gladly tell you when it happened—we did finally satisfy that urge—twice."

Glory leaned back in her chair, crossed her arms and sighed. For a few seconds they stared each other down, both waiting for the other to speak.

"I can't pretend to be elated about this, Frannie." She raised a hand before Frannie could interrupt. "And it isn't only our business partnership I'm worried about. We've been through a lot together and even though we've only known each other a few years, I don't have to explain what our friendship means to me—"

"And to me . . ."

"Well, friend, I just don't want to see you hurt again. After the shock of what Wade did to you, I'm afraid you'll fall apart if this romance collapses."

"Glory, the last thing I want to do is give you more to worry about. So please understand that I love you too, and I have no intention of putting our friendship aside because I have Sergio now."

Glory responded with a dubious smirk while she drummed her fingers on the table. "I do believe you, Frannie," she said, "but sometimes things change despite good intentions. It's not that you care any less, but there aren't enough hours in the day to nurture all your friendships. No matter what you feel in your heart, eventually people grow apart."

Frannie peered at her and lifted her eyebrows as high as they could stretch. "Glory, look in my eyes. Do you see indignation there?"

Glory returned a weak smile. "I see a loving friend with good intentions."

"Well, you're not looking deep enough because I *am* indignant. How can you think that little of me? After all this time, you should know me better, so yes, I'm insulted as all hell." Glory's face softened, and she was about to apologize, but Frannie was fired up and didn't allow her the opportunity. "I want you to think back a few years, Glory . . . what happened to our friendship when you and Alex fell in love? Did I fall apart?"

Glory unexpectedly burst out laughing. "As a matter of fact, you did," she said. "Maybe you didn't exactly fall apart, but you were worried too, right?" She laughed again, prodding Frannie with a pointed finger. "C'mon, admit it."

Frannie laughed too, then threw her hands up in surrender. "Okay, I do admit it. I *was* worried . . ." She smiled at the irony. "And for the same reasons you're worried now."

"Ah, see, so here we are . . . we've come full circle, huh?"

"It took me awhile to trust Alex. Let's face it, he had some dark shadows hovering over him. And from a business standpoint, I felt somewhat threatened. I was afraid he'd interfere and influence your decisions. But I was wrong. As it turned out, he was a godsend to us. So I'm glad that your faith in him lifted all that suspicion, especially . . ." She left the rest unsaid.

"Especially since he died soon after."

"Look Glory, I guess I can't expect you to have blind faith in my judgment, but I feel about Sergio the way you felt about Alex in the beginning. If you could only meet him, talk to him a little, I think you'd see for yourself what I fell in love with."

"I'd love to meet him!"

She twisted her mouth forlornly. "But that's a problem. I don't see him much and when I do, it's late, after we close Amore Evenings."

Glory's brows furrowed. "For heaven's sake, why only then?"

The baby monitor on the kitchen counter grabbed their attention. Danny was squirming in his crib, crying softly.

"Let me get my beautiful godson," Frannie said, but was disappointed that their conversation would be cut short. She still had much to say. After changing his diaper, she brought him into the kitchen, where Glory was already warming his bottle. "You want to feed him?" she asked, knowing how Frannie enjoyed little Danny.

"Of course!"

"Good, and while you do, continue where you left off. Let me put some fresh coffee on first. We can have a cup after you feed Danny."

"Good idea. Because this may take a while." She kissed the baby's forehead and smiled contentedly. "Glory, you have to be out of your mind to think for one minute that I could deny myself this beautiful baby and our friendship. Both of you are treasures in my life."

Glory choked up while she filled the coffeepot with water. She turned off the faucet and impulsively went to give Frannie a kiss on her cheek. "Ditto," she said, holding back her tears.

The two friends talked until there was no more time to spare. Both had to shower and dress for their night's work at the restaurant. But Frannie left feeling euphoric. She had told Glory every detail of her situation with Sergio and, sight unseen, Glory seemed to see him in a new light. They moved on to Glory's "friendship" with Tim Quinlan, and while Frannie listened, she knew she still had work to do in the Cupid department, but felt hopeful. Her optimism deflated a bit, though, just as she was leaving. "By the way, who's babysitting for you tomorrow night?" she asked.

Glory made a face that translated to *I'm not so sure I like the idea, but* . . . "My dad," she said.

"Great!" Frannie said, relieved to hear that Dan would be available. She knew how much it meant to Glory. "So what's the face for?"

"He's bringing *his Jessica.*"

Frannie shook her head as she went out the door, but held her confident smile. Glory's resentment of Dr. Jessica Branson was just another bump in the road. A miniscule bump by comparison. Together, she and her friend would continue to get past them all.

# Chapter Fifty

After her long talk with Frannie the day before, Glory was not nearly as apprehensive about her dinner date with Dr. Tim Quinlan. Her friend had rolled her eyes and laughed when Glory had explained the "rules" she had set. Frannie had roared with laughter. Watching her reaction had made Glory feel foolish, but she couldn't help laughing with her. In retrospect, she realized her little speech about rules had sounded ridiculous. Even now as she recalled Frannie's response, she giggled.

"That poor guy!" Frannie had said, holding her side with one hand and wiping her laugh tears with the other.

"But Tim was great, very amenable and understanding," Glory offered in defense.

"Oh, sure. I can believe *amenable,* but I'll bet he wasn't as *understanding* as you like to think. Look, why don't you forget all your damn rules. Just relax and enjoy yourself. What's meant to be will be. Stop planning every move you make! Geez, Glory, you anticipate trouble without reason. Don't you have enough problems without creating more?"

How true, Glory thought now with a broad smile. She and Frannie had often preached to each other—always with concern and affection. But when the husband you loved takes off with another woman, and the fiancé you loved even more is suddenly killed by some lunatic . . . well, you tend to approach romantic relationships with extreme caution. Frannie, conversely, lived by clichés; *What's meant to be will be; live for today; seize the moment; throw caution to the wind,* et cetera, et cetera, et cetera.

Maybe she does have the right attitude, Glory considered. After all, she was burned badly by Wade. Living with a bigamist who also has two children squirreled away is quite a shocker. And now, after Sergio finally explained his problems, she had believed every word he said and completely vindicated him. End result? She's jumping into this commitment with Sergio Giannetta, and racing full speed ahead. *And she's the one bubbling over with joy, not me,* Glory concluded.

Dan's car pulled into Glory's private parking area and her stomach tumbled.

The good doctor was casually dressed in white jeans and a plaid blouse. Pink and blue paid, she noticed, on a white background. Baby colors. How appropriate for an obstetrician, Glory mused.

She wiped the smug look off her face and went to greet them with the best smile she could manage. Without the white coat, when you took the time to notice, Jessica Branson was a stunning woman, Glory had to admit. And looking at the bright side, as Frannie would say, she could go out with peace of mind knowing a doctor was left in charge of Danny. Still, she silently wished she and her dad had never crossed paths that day in the supermarket.

She kissed her father and gave Jessica a quick handshake, then ushered them into the living room. "This is so nice of you, Dr. Branson, to give your time tonight. Babysitting is quite a step down, I imagine."

"On the contrary," Jessica answered. "It's like reaping the rewards of your labor; mine and *yours,* I should say." Her smile was warm and, with a cursory glance, Glory detected nothing unnatural in her friendly demeanor.

"Listen, before I forget, I left a bottle of wine cooling in the fridge, or if you prefer, I have ice tea and lemonade. There's also a veggie platter and crackers—"

Dan stopped her and threw her a private smile. To watch her playing humble hostess, no one would ever suspect her inner feelings. "Just do what you have to do, Glory. I know my way around. I'll find whatever we need." He smiled at her again, but added a wink to let her know he appreciated her efforts. Once his daughter was out of the house, before they had a drop to drink or a morsel of food, Dan planned to show Jessica his appreciation as well, in a much more demonstrative way. He hadn't had his arms around her or felt the warmth of her lips for days and he was feeling the effects of withdrawal.

"How great is this, huh?" he said to both of them. "My daughter is dating a doctor, and another doctor will help me look after my precious grandson. Can't ask for better protection than that."

Glory glanced at her watch and saw that she had fifteen minutes to wait if Tim arrived on time. If he hadn't allowed for a little summertime traffic, he might be late and she'd have to struggle through the strain of making conversation. "I'm sorry you couldn't get to play with him a few minutes, Dad, but he was exhausted. I tried to keep him occupied, but he conked out twenty minutes ago."

"I did want to grab a few hugs and kisses and show him off to Jessica, but maybe next time. We'll have plenty of opportunities."

Her father's remark sounded innocuous enough, but Glory understood its underlying meaning.

"Can we pick Danny up if he cries?" Jessica asked. Her eyes were bright as if she hoped he would.

She's either a good actress or she's really crazy about babies, Glory thought. And probably the latter, she conceded. Why would she have become an obstetrician if she didn't love babies? "Well, maybe just to soothe him a bit, but don't let my dad start playing with him. You'll never get him back to sleep."

Doctor number two arrived ten minutes early and Glory made the introductions. Although she had considered him an attractive man before, his appearance dazzled her tonight. He was impeccably dressed in a gray summer suit with a turquoise dress shirt open at the neck. A faint showing of dark hair on his chest added to his masculine appeal and she blinked away her flashing images. She had thought no one could compare to Alex when it came to good looks, but Tim ran a close second and was inching up fast.

"Jessica Branson seems like a really nice person," Tim said as they drove off.

She made a cynical face. "Yes, she was polite enough, but you only exchanged a few words. It's hard to tell."

"She's an excellent obstetrician; that I can tell you for certain."

Glory looked at him quizzically. "I thought you didn't know her?"

"True, but that was before you piqued my interest."

"You checked her out?"

Tim laughed. "Don't make it sound like a criminal investigation! People check doctors' backgrounds all the time."

"Yes, and truthfully, I did some checking myself before I chose her. I have no complaints about her professionally. And even socially, she was pleasant enough. I liked her, actually."

"Liked? Past tense?"

She avoided his gaze, slightly embarrassed. She wanted to get off the subject of Jessica Branson, knowing Tim disagreed with her attitude, but it was difficult to pretend the woman's presence in her father's life didn't bother her. "Well, that was before she *liked* my dad," she said, grinning now.

He darted a cautious glance. "My dear Glory, if I may give you a little friendly advice, I think you should try to accept Jessica because it looked to me like she's here to stay. I don't mean to upset you, but did you catch the way they look at each other?"

"Don't remind me," she said, throwing her gaze upward.

Smiling softly, Tim reached over and cupped her chin. His fingers feathered her for only a split-second, but Glory jumped a little at his touch. She hadn't been touched by a man since Alex, and although the gesture was nothing but friendly, it rippled through her.

"C'mon, cheer up," he said. "You should be happy for him instead of sulking. He's suffered a terrible tragedy too. I think it's wonderful that he found someone." His eyes were on the road as he spoke, but he paused to give her a sidelong glance again, hoping she picked up on his double meaning. "And isn't it comforting to know that the woman he found happens to be the person who brought your son into the world?"

Glory grinned at him. "Are you implying that should bind us in a way—make her a better candidate for the role of grandmother?"

"Actually, yes. That's pretty much what I *do* think."

Their conversation came to a halt when they reached the restaurant. She had asked him to make a reservation anywhere away from Ogunquit, hoping to avoid inquisitive eyes of local acquaintances. He had selected a charming little place in Kennebunkport overlooking the Kennebunk River.

"It lacks the elegance of Amore Evenings or Clay Hill Farm, but the food is good and I reserved a booth table overlooking the river." He laughed. "Not that it's anything special to you. Where you live and work, you have the ocean to enjoy it twenty-four hours a day."

"True, and I never get tired of looking at it and listening to its roaring sounds. It was certainly instrumental in convincing me to move from New York to Ogunquit." She glanced around and soaked in the atmosphere. "But this is special in its own way. I like this cozy, weather-beaten look. And I *love* log cabins. When I was a kid, I used to dream of living in one. I think it was *Little House on the Prairie* that inspired that dream. I used to love that show. Once in a while, I get nostalgic and catch a rerun. It still chokes me up every time."

"See? You're really an old softie."

As they climbed the steps to the restaurant's glass-enclosed dining room, Glory caught the expression on his face and easily filled in his unsaid words. Like her father, he was gently trying to infuse his message. Tim seemed determined to help her break through her hostile attitude toward Jessica.

It wasn't until their wine was served and their orders taken that Tim picked up where he had left off. "So tell me, pretty lady, how do the others feel about Jessica—your brother and sisters? I imagine it would take some adjusting for them too; maybe more so since Louise was their mother."

She pondered that a moment because she wasn't quite sure of the answer. "They seem to be accepting it better than I am, but it's possible they're acting a little, for my sake."

"They know how you feel?"

"Oh, yes!" she answered emphatically, then laughed with affection for her siblings. "They've been making a concerted effort to help me live with it, and I guess I will eventually—I hope so. But they understand it's harder for me in a different way. They had him all their lives; I didn't. And then, of course, there was Alex . . ." Another gentle laugh spilled from her lips. "Now don't say *Time heals all wounds.* That's what Frannie would say now if she were here instead of you."

"No, I wouldn't use that expression because it's not necessarily true. Time may dry up some tears and soothe the wound somewhat, but I'm not sure it ever totally *heals.*"

Glory hesitated, then asked the question that crossed her mind. "Are you still grieving your wife? Your divorce from her?"

He smiled sadly; it was an understandable assumption. "No, this is not something I'm proud of, but truth be told, I never loved my wife as I loved Belinda." His eyes glazed and went into that dreamy, faraway look; so distinctive of a person recalling memories of a love long gone, but still close to his heart. "Belinda was my college sweetheart. We were engaged and planned to marry after graduation. But one night she and her friends were out celebrating someone's birthday, and they smashed into a tree. Her three friends survived, but Belinda did not. She had been driving."

Glory's heart swelled with empathy, and though he tried to hide it, she caught him swallow hard. "I'm sorry. If I had known, I wouldn't have—"

He put a hand up and smiled wide. "No, no, don't be sorry. It was a long time ago. I should apologize for my reaction; it was unexpected. I don't know how or why I mentioned that. Once I got married, I never spoke about Belinda again—to anyone. But I'm so at ease with you," he said with a shrug, "that it just came out."

"Maybe because we have that in common . . . tragic love stories in our pasts."

"Maybe," he said, flashing his dynamic smile again. "But let's not allow them to darken our mood. We're out for the evening to enjoy a quiet, relaxing dinner, and to get to know each other better. So let's focus on now and all our tomorrows. Okay, my friend?"

"Absolutely! And Tim, thanks for your patience about Jessica. I'm not really such a bitchy brat. I'm surprised you still want to be my friend."

"Actually, I can't lie to you. I'd like more than friendship, but the ball's in your court. I won't touch it."

His expression was playful, rueful and contrite, but to Glory, it all added up to *adorable*. She couldn't resist playing along. "I did give tennis a try, but I was never good at it. Maybe someday I'll hone my skills and master the game."

Tim leaned forward, touched her hand and whispered. "Well, I'm a great tennis player, and I'd love to teach you."

# Chapter Fifty-one

Tess and Sal Oliveri were dumbfounded when their daughter broke the news. Sal was twice as upset seeing how it affected his wife.

"What the hell are you trying to do, Frannie, give your mother a heart attack?" he shouted. "Look at her—she's a basket case! How can you walk in here and tell us you're marrying some foreigner we've never laid eyes on before?"

Frannie had tried to break it gently, but knew it would shock the heck out of them anyway. She sucked in a breath, trying to stay calm. "Dad, I had no choice. He has to go back to Italy soon, and I thought you should meet him before he leaves."

"And what makes you so sure he's coming back? This guy might be taking you for a ride, my dear daughter, and I can't believe you fell for it!"

The thought of what her father was implying hurt Frannie. Although she had braced herself not to cry, a few fat tears rolled down her cheeks. Still, she understood her dad had plenty of steam to blow off, so she ignored his remark and went to hug her mother, who had escaped to the kitchen. "Mom, please, I knew it would be a shock, but this is ridiculous! You're behaving as if I dropped dead at your feet, and daddy's acting as if I had just been arrested for armed robbery! You should be happy for me, not *mourning* me!"

"I'd like to be happy, but I have the same fears as your father. Are you sure this Sergio you're infatuated with isn't after your money?"

Exasperated by the whole scene, Frannie laughed through her tears. "Mom, first of all, Sergio is not exactly poverty-stricken. He and his family own a very successful restaurant in Italy. And even if he were looking to hook some wealthy American woman, he certainly can find someone with deeper pockets than mine!"

After a few minutes alone, Sal came into the kitchen considerably calmer. He interrupted his wife and daughter's tearful conversation. "So where's he hiding, your Italian friend?"

"Dad, you don't have to make it sound like I grabbed him off a spaceship! Need I remind you that we're Italian too?"

"No, we're Americans of Italian descent. He's Italian— a citizen of Italy. Big difference."

Tess let out a gasp. "Oh, my God! I never thought of that—don't tell me he's dragging you to Italy? Dear God, you might as well take a gun and shoot me!"

"Mom, will you please calm down! I am *not* going to Italy. Get that out of your head. Sergio's coming here to live. I could never leave you and daddy, nor would I want to leave my whole life here in Ogunquit. I made that clear from the start. I agonized over it—I didn't want to lose him—but I knew I could never be happy moving to another country. And Sergio was good about it; he understood and said most women are more sentimental than men. Men can usually up and leave without looking back; women cling to their families more and all that's familiar to them."

Tess and Sal were both seated opposite her at the kitchen table, both looking drained. Frannie kept on talking incessantly, trying to convince them to trust her judgment and be happy for her. "Look, Mom, Dad," she said, holding their hands, "I know how hard this is for you to accept, especially since you've never met Sergio, but you are going to meet him—"

"When?" Sal cut in. "Why isn't he here now?"

"Tonight. And I purposely didn't bring him today because I wanted to prepare you. I knew how my news would shock you."

"You can say that again!" Sal shot back.

Tess patted her husband's hand. "Sal, stop. Getting excited won't do any of us any good. Let's wait. Let her bring him and we'll see for ourselves if he's everything she says he is."

"Oh? And if we don't like him, you think she'll just give him up?"

Tess and Sal got into an argumentative exchange, and seemed completely impervious to the fact that she was sitting right there with them. But Frannie listened with unexpected calm. Now that she had announced her life-altering decision and broken the news to Glory and her parents, she felt unbelievable relief. She hadn't realized how stressful it had been to keep Sergio a big, dark secret.

"So you're bringing him tonight? On a Friday night you're going to neglect your business?" Sal gazed at his daughter with squinted eyes, as if she had a screw loose in her head.

"Don't ever worry about Amore Evenings. Glory and I have it covered—we always do. Besides, I *am* working; just leaving early. But Sergio and I won't be here until close to nine, is that okay? I know you guys doze off early sometimes."

Sal was quick to respond with wide-eyed incredulity. "Are you kidding? We'll be wide awake, probably pacing the floors, waiting to meet your *Sergio.*"

The way her dad had emphasized *Sergio* made the name sound like a disease they had to battle or an enemy to confront. She drove away that afternoon hoping Sergio could meet the challenge of selling himself as a future son-in-law.

\* \* \*

Frannie spotted her father peeking out the living room window when they got out of the car. "I've never seen your temper, Sergio, but let me warn you—if you have one in there, don't let it out! They were pretty upset this afternoon. They don't handle surprises well, and this was a whopper!"

Sergio squeezed her hand and tried for a confident smile. "You worry too much, cara mia. I have mamma/pappa too all my life. I handle."

*Yeah, that's why your mother still doesn't know I exist and never will, if you can help it.* She wondered what excuse he dreamed up tonight to skip out before she went to sleep.

Tess and Sal were spruced up in their finest smart-casuals—outfits they saved for vacations. She grinned, thinking that was already a step in the right direction. At least they were trying to impress him too. Sergio had also made an extra effort to look well-groomed. Frannie had never seen him so formally dressed; he looked exceptionally gorgeous and extremely desirable in dress slacks, dress shirt and even a tie! That had to please her dad, for sure. Sal Oliveri was a very vocal advocate of old-fashioned principles that fell under his "respect" category. Clean and pressed slacks, socks almost always, a clean-shaven face and neatly combed hair; none of which were easy to come by these days.

So score two for Sergio, she thought. He was still one of those guys who shaved every morning, no matter what.

After Frannie introduced him, which was a totally unnecessary formality, Tess broke the ice. "I didn't know if you like brown coffee or black, Sergio, so I made both." She placed a tray of Italian pastries on the coffee table. "These are fresh from the bakery in the village," she said, bright-eyed.

Sergio wanted neither, but didn't dare refuse. "Black be fine, and cannoli too, I try." He would have preferred crumb cake or chocolate donuts from a box, but he accepted the pastry graciously. Inwardly, he was amused by their effort. It was an assumption often made; that all Italian families ate in Italy were pasta dishes, gelato or pastries for dessert, and fish on Christmas Eve.

The four of them talked about nonsense for the first ten minutes. Since Frannie and Sergio were both restaurateurs, conversation fell easily on food, which no one was the least bit interested in tonight.

Sergio made it easy for Tess and Sal. "Signore and Signora Oliveri, may I speak my mind—my heart?"

"Certainly," Tess and Sal said in unison.

"First I say—most important—that I love very much your daughter. I wish for her to be my wife. We have big problem, yes; live in two different countries. But like she tell you, I come here."

He paused and Sal jumped in. "And when do you plan to do that? Have you and my daughter discussed marriage plans yet?"

Sergio glanced over at Frannie, who hadn't said a word since Sergio took the lead. He flashed her an *Are you going to let me suffer through this alone?* look, to which she responded with a smile and a nod that said, *You're doing fine.*

Sergio's gaze returned to Sal, who waited for an answer. "Frannie tell me in the car before that she no tell you about my mamma. Because of mamma, I have no answer for you, Signore. He went on to explain about his mother's illness and his promise to keep it confidential. She wanted pity from no one, he said, and requested only that she have someone decent and trustworthy to care for her at home until she died. A home heath aide would be fine, she had said, as long as Sergio was there to watch over her and stay until she closed her eyes for good. "What can I say, Signore? She my mother; I must honor her wish. Until God take her, I must take care."

Tess and Sal looked back at him with humble faces. Frannie could tell at a glance that his scorecard had skyrocketed and realized she could boost it even higher. "Dad, I forgot to mention that Sergio is Sicilian. I'm sure that'll please you." She hadn't forgotten at all that night, but at the time it seemed irrelevant compared to their daughter announcing plans to marry a foreigner they had neither met nor heard of.

Sal's face lit up. "You're kidding!" he said, then turned to Sergio. "My family is from Palermo. I still have cousins there on my mother's side. They live in a village north of the city called San Martino della Scale. Their name is Geraci, Giovanni and Concetta—"

Sergio slapped his head and laughed with surprise. "Mamma mia! Sure I know family—their children, grandchildren—whole family. They come to our restaurant many time."

Tess and Frannie exchanged a satisfied glance. *In the bag,* it silently conveyed.

Sal was beside himself. He hugged Sergio like a long-lost son. "What a coincidence! I can't wait to call and tell them. Maybe someday we can take a trip together to visit."

Sergio's hand went to his heart and his smile was proud. "When Frannie become my wife, I would love very much to show her my country. Italy is beautiful. Yes, we all go." He kissed his fingertips and threw it her way.

"No argument from me, Sergio. As long as it's for a vacation only." There was a clear warning in her gaze which amused Sergio. "And it has to be during the winter months when the restaurants are closed."

"Whatever you like, cara mia."

They all talked congenially for another hour, but to Tess and Sal, the worst was over. Sergio had assured them he loved their daughter, he would not take her away from them and move to Italy, he would not interfere with her businesses unless she wanted him to. Monetarily, he was more than comfortable. Once he moved to America, he could take his time to decide his future here. He thought perhaps he could open another restaurant, or maybe becoming innkeepers might interest them both. He and Frannie would discuss their plans together when the time came. For now they dream.

When they were leaving, Tess said, right in front of Sergio, "Frannie, I can see why you fell for this handsome man, hook, line and sinker. Don't let him get away."

# Chapter Fifty-two

Suzanne's spirits were unusually high this afternoon. She had just returned from an afternoon visit with her father and still couldn't believe the difference in him. She still cringed remembering how, after her mother died, she had avoided him like the plague. The sight of him was unbearable, and it killed her to watch helplessly the rapid deterioration of the house that used to be home.

That was all behind them now and she never stopped thanking God and begging Him to keep watching over her father. To Suzanne, it was as though Jerry Oliveri had come back from the dead. She had her daddy back and her daughter had a loving and affectionate grandpa.

Her spirit of optimism blanketed her lately, particularly since she and Rob reconciled. She had decided that the next afternoon, when she'd see him again, she would confess the whole Greg story. It wasn't a pretty one and nothing about how she fell into bed with him would soften the blow, but it had to be done. Deep down she had known from the start that she should, but the final push came from Dr. Tim Quinlan, a man whose opinions had earned her respect.

She only prayed Rob could forgive her for her brief, but inexcusable affair. Better to face it now, before they marry, and hope for the best. If she continued to keep it a secret, it would surely torment her and shadow her life with Rob.

After putting Heather in for her nap, Suzanne was about to step in the shower when she dashed out to answer the phone. Mumbling under her breath for the annoying interruption, she answered curtly.

"Suzanne? You're out of breath. Did I get you at a bad time?"

*Kim Haggarty. Don't tell me she can't babysit!* Suzanne was already thinking ahead, dreading calling her Aunt Tess, who had offered to take Heather in emergency situations only. And that's also if you could catch her on a day when she had no other commitments.

"No, Kim. I ran for the phone because Heather just fell asleep and I run like a chicken without a head when she naps. What's up? I'm afraid to ask, but do you have a problem babysitting tonight?"

"No, not tonight, but I do have to talk to you about our arrangement."

From the tone of Kim's voice, Suzanne sensed something serious was brewing. Fear stabbed her chest for a second until common sense kicked in. Unless her husband cracked under the strain of guilt and confessed to her, there was no possible way she could know. And Kim's voice was as calm and sweet as ever. No scorned wife could ever mask her rage with such pleasantries. "Can you tell me now? You sound so serious."

"No, it's nothing earth-shattering. But the reason I'm calling is I wanted to know if you could drop Heather off fifteen minutes earlier so I can speak to you."

"I'll be there a half hour earlier. I'm a little worried. Are you sure everything's okay?"

"Everything will be, I'm sure. I'll explain when you get here."

\* \* \*

Kim was on the phone when Suzanne arrived, so she brought Heather into the den to play with the two Haggarty children. It saddened her to think these were her daughter's half-brother and half-sister, but Heather would always be denied that knowledge, as well as the love of her natural father.

"That was Greg," Kim said when she joined them. "I said I'd call him back; I don't want to hold you up." Then with her arms outstretched, she stooped down and said to Heather, "Hey, where's my kiss, buttercup?"

The display of Kim's affection to the child born of her husband's seed always gave Suzanne's stomach that sinking sensation. "What did you want to talk to me about, Kim? You left me hanging and I've been trying to guess since you called me."

Kim's smile faded. "I'm sorry, but I had to call and ask you to come earlier so I wouldn't have to spring it on you when you're in a hurry to get to work."

Suzanne merely nodded, giving Kim no chance to stall. Kim drew a breath and looked at her sorrowfully, as if about to tell her someone had died. "There's really no easy way to say this, Suzanne, so I'll just get it over with. Greg's company is moving us to Chicago within the next three months. It's a huge promotion and a wonderful opportunity that he'd be insane to refuse." Her lips quivered as she glanced over at Heather, innocently playing with the children she'd never see again. Her voice cracked when she spoke and tears soon followed. "Heather's been like part of our family. I'll miss her terribly," she said, trying to suppress her sobs for the sake of the children. "And you too, Suzanne. We've been friends a long time now. Our children are so close. I hate the thought of separating them."

Suzanne's heart hammered in her chest. "The kids are young, Kim; they'll forget."

"That's the only thing making it easier. I'm grateful they're not teenagers who'd be devastated to leave their friends. And thank God, our parents are both young enough and healthy enough to fly out for visits."

"It'll be fine, I'm sure, and I'm happy for all of you. And don't worry about me; I appreciate that you told me now. I'll have plenty of time to make arrangements for Heather. There's always day care."

Suzanne stood up abruptly, but hadn't realized her legs went rubbery. Tears streamed down her face without warning. The news had stunned her but it was mostly the sincerity of Kim's loving words that had triggered them off. *If only she knew.* She couldn't remember feeling lower or guiltier in her life, but she couldn't deny the spontaneous surge of relief that came with it; the *joy* that enveloped her. With Greg living that far away, she'd never have to face him again; never have to worry about him questioning her again; never have to see Heather in her father's arms.

Kim walked her to the door and gave her a hug. "And there is another bit of good news for us, Suzanne. We haven't told anyone yet, but I'd like to tell you, but keep it under your hat for now." She beamed. "I'm pregnant!"

"Oh, how wonderful, Kim! Congratulations!" Suzanne said and hugged her back, doing her best to act surprised.

And so, Suzanne left for work that afternoon feeling like a thousand pounds had been lifted off her shoulders. Now all she had to get past was tomorrow's talk with Rob.

# Chapter Fifty-three

Earlier in the week, Rob had suggested they try taking Heather to a small carnival in a neighboring town. Suzanne had nixed the idea at first, thinking it might be too much for Rob physically, but he had insisted. "Don't worry, together we can handle it," he had said, reading her thoughts.

Suzanne warned him again when he arrived Saturday morning. "You promise you'll tell me if it's too much for your foot?"

"I'm not as fragile as you think, but yes, I promise to tell you. C'mon, don't be a spoilsport. I'm actually looking forward to going on some of those rides. If I can't handle it, you'll be the first to know."

"Okay, but don't say I didn't warn you."

\* \* \*

Suzanne had given in to a few hours at the carnival only for Heather's sake, but to her amazement, both she and Rob actually did have fun! Watching Heather giggle with delight over every attraction, eating chicken fingers, fries and ice cream had added to their pleasure.

But although Suzanne was enjoying the outing so far, she wished they could have stayed at home. She could have used Heather's naptime to tell Rob about Greg. A carnival was certainly not a suitable locale for such a shocking revelation.

"She's getting tired, Rob, and we're both working tonight. Maybe we should start back."

"We still have plenty of time and Heather's been an angel so far."

"I know, but I want some time alone with you," she said, smiling suggestively.

"Sounds great to me, but she'll probably fall asleep in the car, so we won't have her nap to look forward to."

"But we'll still be alone. I can curl up in your arms and steal some kisses."

"On second thought, home is starting to sound better and better."

* * *

Heather did fall asleep in her car seat but never stirred when Suzanne carried her up. In the apartment, she gently placed her in the crib and hoped she would sleep long enough to get her through this crucial conversation with Rob. The stakes were high; she could lose it all, but she remained steadfast in her decision to tell all.

"Do you need to watch that now?" she asked. He had put the TV on, tuned to the golf channel.

"Not really," he said, "but why?" Her serious tone made Rob take a closer look at her. His brows snaked together with curiosity. "You look like the sky's about to fall."

"It is, Rob." She sat next to him and caressed his cheeks, then kissed him as if afraid it would be the last time.

Rob turned off the TV. "Well, I love you too, little girl," he said and returned her passion.

She broke away, but held his hand. "It's Greg Haggarty, Rob. Greg is Heather's father," she blurted out, but couldn't bring herself to look him in the eye. She cast her gaze downward and stroked his hand like a precious treasure she was about to relinquish. It seemed like a silent, but powerful storm was thundering over her as she listened to the deafening silence. Rob never moved, never pulled his hand away while his mind tried to reject her few words.

"Say something, *please*." Her voice was barely audible.

He couldn't bring himself to look at her yet and threw his gaze to the window. "I was right after all; I would have been better off not knowing."

Suzanne burst into tears. "Yes, but you *wanted* to know; you *needed* to know. And you were right. I owed you that, but look what it did to you. To us. This is what I wanted to avoid." A wail came from her lips and for several minutes her mournful sobbing was the only sound that filled the silence.

"Tell me . . . tell me how the hell that happened, not that it makes much difference now."

"But it'll be okay, now, Rob," she said through blinding tears. Her voice alone was desperately pleading for forgiveness. "Kim just told me yesterday that they're moving to Chicago. Greg's company is transferring him. In three months they'll be gone and you'll never have to worry about bumping into him."

"Well, I guess that should cheer me up."

"Tell me . . . tell me the whole story now and I never want to hear it again, understand?"

Suzanne couldn't tell what he meant. Did he mean he wanted to hear it this one time and close the book forever, or did he mean he wanted to hear it before he pushed her out of his life and would never get the chance to hear it?

"It was only one time, Rob. Neither one of us planned it . . . it all started out so innocently . . . " She went through the story again with unparalleled shame, pretty much as she told it to Frannie, summarizing wherever possible to spare him the ugly details.

She was drained when she finished and couldn't bring herself to look at him. "I guess asking you to forgive me is shooting too high, isn't it, Rob?"

He stood up, walked slowly toward the door, then answered her without looking back. "I need to be alone for a while. But don't worry; no matter what, your secret is safe with me. And I guess I should thank you for telling me."

Until Heather's cries commanded her attention, Suzanne stared into space. "So much for trust and honesty," she mumbled through bitter tears.

# Chapter Fifty-four

"Are you sure you don't mind, Tim?" Glory asked again when he arrived. His hello kiss had lingered slightly longer than what she could classify as *friendly*. She was trying to ignore the fluttery feelings it ignited. "I know you usually have breakfast with friends on Sundays."

"I *am* having breakfast with a friend, aren't I?"

She considered the question debatable, but turned away so he wouldn't see the revealing smirk tugging at her lips. "Yes, you are, but this is my whole family today. I don't want to shove them all down your throat!"

Tim laughed. "How can you say that? I thought you loved every one of them?"

"I *do* love them, and I know you're just teasing me, but seriously, Tim, I have to admit that although I've enjoyed your company tremendously, I felt a little torn trying to decide between seeing you or my family today. As I told you, Sunday brunch has become a pleasant routine we fell into. It doesn't work out every week, but we try. I didn't feel right abandoning them, nor did I want to, but when I hesitated and explained about you . . ." She laughed, embarrassed by her rambling and the implication it carried.

Tim helped her out. "So they politely asked you to drag me along, right?"

"Wrong," she said and laughed at the memory. "They actually *went nuts*! But don't mind them. No one is trying to rope you in. It's just that everyone is elated that I'm dating someone. In their collective estimation, the fact that I said yes twice is a major breakthrough."

"It is. And I'm honored that it happens to be me," Tim had gone serious for the moment but his grin resurfaced quickly. "So should I prepare for the third degree?"

She waved him off and giggled. "Oh, no. Not a chance. None of them would do that, but to play it safe, I warned them anyway. Besides, for today, Jessica is sort of the guest of honor."

"Really? That's fantastic! Now I'm looking forward to your family brunch more than ever. Speaking of major breakthroughs, how come you hadn't mentioned that before?"

"I just found out last night." She shrugged and threw him a look of defeat.

He lifted her chin. "Now *that's* progress."

"Don't read too much into my facial expressions. I haven't had a sudden change of heart. I'm still feeling the loss and that selfish part of me still wishes this could all blow over, but I know when I'm licked. With very few words, my father made that blatantly clear. And yet I was neither angry nor hurt. As much as I've been fighting it, I've always known he has a right to his own choices."

Tim threw her an incredulous look. "And you don't think Jessica Branson is a good choice?"

"I'm not saying that at all. Picking a life partner is not about piling up credentials, Tim. If it were, Jessica would be a perfect choice. In my opinion, it's about whether that person is right for you. You have to look ahead and ask whether your lives could mesh well. In their case, for instance, would Jessica's career take precedence over all else? If I have to lose my father to her, I at least want to find solace in the fact that he's happy and not sitting around feeling lonely while she runs around meeting the demands of her profession."

Tim pondered that a moment. He couldn't honestly say that issue had no bearing on the breakup of his marriage. It hadn't been the crux of their problems, but it was certainly a contributing factor. It might have been his imagination, but in one fleeting glance he had detected the question in Glory's eyes and knew she wanted to hear his views on the matter. "It can and does work when both parties cooperate. Sure, there are many times plans are disrupted, but that's life. It can happen to any couple in any profession or trade. Think about it, Glory, who would give up someone he or she loved because the other is too busy?"

She lifted a brow. "Well, if you put it that way, it *does* sound ludicrous, but I hadn't summed it up quite that way."

"And Glory," he began cautiously, "you are *not* losing your father—"

Glory felt a sermon coming on and tried to steer it off with levity. She cupped a hand over his lips and forced a laugh. "Now don't you dare say I'm gaining a mother!"

Tim rolled his eyes to heaven, then gave in and laughed with her. He lifted the hand that had covered his mouth and held it tightly. "You are *impossible,* you know that?"

"I sure do! I've been a real pain in the butt lately and I know it can't be much fun listening to me vent my fears and frustrations. Frankly, I don't know why you put up with me."

He looked down at her and their gazes locked. "Truthfully, I don't know why either. Maybe I want to stick around to see you get past this. Wouldn't it be a hell of a lot better for you to get on with your own life instead of agonizing over what you *think* you'll lose with your father?"

"I'm not sure I know how to do that. Any suggestions, Doctor?"

"That sounds like a direct question, Miss English, so I think . . ." His voice trailed off and before he realized what was happening, she was in his arms. When she didn't resist, he kissed her with a surge of longing and passion that flooded his entire body.

When they finally broke apart, they were still standing in the kitchen while Danny cooed away in his playpen. "How the heck did that happen? Believe it or not, Tim, that's not what I had in mind when I asked for suggestions."

"It wasn't what I had in mind either. It just came tumbling down on me like a rockslide." He rubbed his nose against hers. "But it was an excellent suggestion anyway, don't you think?" He pulled her closer and kissed her again until they were both so breathless they stumbled backwards.

"Up against a refrigerator door is the last place I would dream of for a first kiss," she said, pushing him away to clear her head. "I get the message and I won't deny it kind of bowled me over too, but it's too much, too soon, Tim. I'm not sure I can handle it. We talked about it."

"No, Glory, *you* talked about it. *You* set the rule, and I broke it. I never meant to, but it happened before I could stop. If you're angry, I apologize."

"I'm not angry. I wish I were so I could put the brakes on before I get hurt again. I saw it coming; I could have stopped you, but didn't. I was caught up in that same rockslide." She looked over at Danny who was getting restless. "We'd better get going." She extended her arm between them. "And please keep your distance, my dear Doctor Quinlan," she teased. "I have to touch up my hair and makeup, so do me a favor and play with Danny, okay?"

"My pleasure, Miss English," he said, bowing.

No, *my* pleasure, Dr. Quinlan, she thought and walked off with the brightest grin she'd worn in ages.

\* \* \*

Vanessa and Wanda had insisted on hosting the brunch this Sunday morning and had thoroughly enjoyed fussing with all their delectable dishes and floral arrangements. Vanessa hadn't been too enthusiastic at first; she had been battling mixed emotions since her father announced that Jessica would be joining them this week. It had pleased her to see him happy again, but like Glory, she too had hoped his infatuation would pass. Wanda had recognized her dispirited attitude the night before and immediately put a temporary halt on their preparations. After two hours of soul-baring conversation and almost a full bottle of wine, Vanessa admitted that she hadn't realized how much her feelings had mirrored Glory's. It wasn't until Wanda had brought them to the surface—when she heard her own voice, her own words spilling them out—that she realized how selfish and foolish she sounded.

\* \* \*

As previously arranged with Wanda, Dan waited for her phone call before he and Jessica left. He wanted everyone present when he and Jessica arrived so that the formality of introductions would be swift and simultaneous. Then, hopefully, they could all ease into relaxed conversation.

"You're not nervous, are you?" Dan asked when they pulled out of her driveway.

"A little," she said, wrinkling her nose thoughtfully. "I feel like a young bride-to-be on her way to a surprise shower practicing how to look surprised."

Dan laughed. "Well, that's partially true. You are a bride-to-be."

"Yes, but please, Dan, don't even hint at that today. We can't overwhelm them. Give them time to get used to me and accept that I'm not going to disappear."

"I have a feeling it'll go better than we imagined. Look what happened with your children. You were bracing yourself for an argument with your daughter and she turned out to be a sweetheart about it. Your son too; they both surprised us."

"I can't take credit for that," she said, patting his thigh. "You're an easy sell. My daughter couldn't resist your charm and my son was hooked once your conversation got into boating."

\* \* \*

Particularly this day, Dan was thrilled to see Dr. Tim Quinlan joining his family brunch. Glory hadn't mentioned him at all when they last spoke and that had troubled him. Not only was he thrilled now with the possibility of a new romance for his daughter, but Tim's presence would make it easier for Jessica.

He searched the faces of all his children as he introduced Jessica but found nothing but friendly smiles. Glory's had a trace of resignation, perhaps, but for now that was enough. If Tim Quinlan becomes a constant in her life, that resignation shall also pass, he thought.

He found a moment alone with Tim at the buffet table and took the opportunity to thank him. "I was pleasantly surprised to see you here today. And I must confess that I'm delighted, for more reasons than one."

Tim laughed as he scooped up a portion of scrambled eggs and dumped them on his dish. "I can well imagine, but don't you worry. We spoke for maybe two minutes so far but she already struck me as a warm, friendly and sincere woman."

Dan was quick to underscore Tim's assessment. "Oh, she is. She absolutely is!"

"Well, your opinion is a little prejudiced, I'd say," Tim whispered with a knowing grin, then patted Dan on the back. "Don't worry. She'll win them over in a heartbeat."

Dan shot him a dubious look. "I hope so. I'm still a little worried about Glory."

"Glory's coming around. Just hang in there; you'll see."

Tim's last comment had sounded so confident that Dan started to put two and two together in his mind. The doctor's words seemed to suggest that he'd take full charge of achieving that goal. He didn't want to make premature assumptions, but something about Tim Quinlan's demeanor told him that he had long-term plans. For his daughter's sake, the thought alone excited him.

When he returned to the dining room, he found Jessica involved in animated conversation, looking perfectly relaxed, surrounded by Wanda and his daughters. As he handed her a plate filled with fresh fruits, she gazed up at him and flashed him a wink. The simple gesture made him take a deep breath and walk away to join his son, Todd, and Mitch, Amy's husband-to-be, who had fallen into conversation with Tim Quinlan.

But he stepped away into the empty kitchen for a silent moment to thank God for giving him and his family the strength and courage to find happiness again.

# Chapter Fifty-five

Frannie had only to hear her cousin's voice that morning to know the sky had fallen on her and Rob. Too late now, she thought, but maybe she should have minded her own business from day one when she forced Suzanne into naming Heather's father. But it was Suzanne who had initiated the scene. It was she who had come to Frannie distraught and desperate.

The restaurant was too busy when she had called earlier and Frannie couldn't even get into the preliminaries. Had she told Rob about Greg? Or worse yet, had she told Greg about Heather? *A no-win situation, if ever I heard one,* she concluded.

Frannie was home only ten minutes when Suzanne arrived alone. "I left Heather with my neighbor, so I won't tie you up long, Frannie. I just needed to talk a few minutes. You know how I lean on you."

*You and everyone else,* Frannie wanted to say. "Okay, Suzanne, I'm afraid to ask, but what happened this time?"

Suzanne choked up at the question and the impatient edge in her cousin's tone. "I'm sorry. I shouldn't have bothered you with my problems. You're annoyed. I can hear it in your voice. I should go," she said and stood up abruptly.

Frannie waved her down. "Sit down. You're not going anywhere. And I'm not *annoyed.* I'm frustrated because lately everyone has problems and I can't find solutions for them. All I do is listen. Not to mention I've had a few problems of my own to deal with."

"No one expects solutions from you, Frannie. Particularly in my case, my problems are irreversible. And the funny part is, every time I look at Heather, I'm not one bit sorry, I'm grateful." When Frannie's eyebrows shot up she corrected herself. "What I mean is I'm sorry I slept with Greg, but I'm not sorry Heather was born. I'll *never* be sorry for that," she said.

"And no one would expect you to. But you still haven't told me why you're here. What happened?"

Suzanne drew a breath and sat down again. "I told Rob."

Frannie's gaze was guarded. "And?"

"And he looked like he'd swallowed poison. You should have seen him." Her mouth quivered and tears welled in her eyes, but she blinked them away. "I never should have told him. His reaction was exactly what I had feared." She repeated word for word what had transpired three days before when she told Rob about Greg.

"Well, you have to understand, Suzanne, that was quite a shock. The fact that he said he needed time alone doesn't mean he's gone forever. And he did say he never wanted to hear it again, didn't he? Doesn't that suggest something positive? Who else would speak about it but you?"

Suzanne's face soured pessimistically. "I tried to hang my hopes on that line too. But maybe the more he thinks about it, the more it'll sink in and he'll come to the conclusion he'd never be able to live with it."

Frannie considered the possibility and couldn't disagree. "Suzanne, I hope you're not blaming me because I advised you to tell him. Despite the result, I still think it was the right thing to do. And this is what I mean about my feelings of frustration. Who am I to say that my advice is sound? I don't want to be responsible for screwing up other people's lives."

"No one would hold you responsible. People *like* talking to you, Frannie; they respect your opinions, but ultimately whatever decisions are made are theirs alone to make. And my decision to tell Rob was not based solely on your advice. I too felt it was the right thing to do, but I tried to justify not telling him because I was afraid of losing him."

"Suzanne, all we can do is wait. If his love is strong enough, you'll hear from him. If not, it's better that you know it now and—" She threw her arms out and shrugged.

"And get on with my life? Is that what you were going to say?"

Frannie gave her a sad smile. "I hate that line, but yes, something like that."

Suzanne got up to leave. "Without Rob, getting on with my life won't be easy."

"Why don't you give it a few more days? If Rob doesn't call by the end of the week, then you call him. At least you won't be dangling on a string wondering if and when he'll call."

"That sounds like good advice. One way or the other, I need an answer. I'll wait until Friday." She gave her cousin a hug. "And thanks again, Frannie. I know what a pest I've been. Hopefully, once I get past this week, I'll try not to dump my troubles on you anymore."

"Don't be ridiculous! Sure I get a little impatient sometimes, but that doesn't mean I want to shut you out. Our family is small, Suzanne; we need each other."

Suzanne curled her brows. "Hey, speaking of troubles, you mentioned something about having problems yourself. Anything you want to dump on me? I could use the distraction."

Frannie laughed. "Thank God, I finally worked out my biggest problem. I'll tell you about it when you have more time."

Suzanne glanced at her wristwatch. "I have about a half hour. Is that enough?"

"I can make it enough," Frannie answered, her eyes brightening. "Maybe I should start at the end and go backwards." She smiled, anticipating her cousin's reaction. "I'm getting married."

Suzanne didn't disappoint Frannie. She reacted with a scream and a bear hug. "What are you saying? Who the heck are you marrying? And where have you been hiding him?"

"Sit yourself down again and let me tell you all about my Sergio . . ."

"Man! This is incredible! You're actually in love. As soon as you said his name it was written all over your face!"

Frannie felt her cheeks grow warm. "You're right; it is incredible. But don't say 'actually in love'; I haven't been immune to it since Wade, just cautious."

Suzanne sat opposite her and rested her chin on her hands. "So start talking and for a change I'll do the listening. I could use a happy ending story right now."

# Chapter Fifty-six

Suzanne's name never came up until Rob and Dennis were on their way home from the golf course.

"Everything still okay with you and Suzanne, Rob? You looked a little down today. I wanted to ask before but the guys were already waiting for us at the restaurant, so I never got the chance."

Rob threw him a curious glance. "Why do you say 'still okay'? Were you expecting our relationship to fall apart?" He didn't wait for an answer. "She told me, you know. She just threw it at me. It was so weird in a way. I had pushed hard for that name and when I got it, I felt ambushed."

Dennis was afraid to ask why, but considering that *ambushed* implies surprise attack, he had a pretty good idea. If Rob was surprised, it could only mean he knew the guy. "So now that you know, you're sorry you pushed, right?" He raised a hand. "And before you answer, don't tell me his name."

Incredulity crossed Rob's face. "Are you kidding, Gramps? There's no way I would ever repeat that name. From the first time I asked Suzanne, I swore up and down that I'd never reveal his identity unless Heather's life depended on it."

"So I get the impression you know him. Am I right?" His hands went up and waved like windshield wipers. "No, never mind. Don't answer. That would narrow the field. So what happened after the ambush? Were you able to get up and dust yourself off?"

Rob darted a slanted glance. "If you're asking if I was able to handle it, the answer is no. I wasn't angry, just shocked. And it might make you feel better to hear I don't know the guy. I just know *of* him. At least I don't have a face to haunt me. And that piece of information does not narrow the field, Gramps."

Dennis nodded while he processed Rob's words. "Well, that's a small consolation—the fact that he's faceless. How about Suzanne? Did she seem relieved after telling you?"

"I'm not sure. She might have been relieved to finally get it out, but she definitely wasn't happy. I'm sure she regretted it later. Truthfully, I didn't hang around long enough to find out."

Dennis winced at the image. "Oh, Rob, no. Don't tell me you split up again! When did this happen?"

"Last Saturday."

"And you haven't spoken to her since?"

"No. I told her I needed time. And I do need to sort things out."

They had reached the house. Rob pulled into the driveway and threw the car in park. His grandfather wasn't about to dismiss him yet.

"And how long do you plan to do that?" Dennis asked, his voice stronger and slightly demanding.

Rob shrugged. "As long as it takes, I guess."

"Oh. And you expect that poor girl to sit around and wait, crying her eyes out while you *sort things out*? What's there to sort out? She told you what you wanted to know, so now you deal with it! You either accept it and *bury* it or you tell her you're simply not strong enough to handle it. But keep in mind that this mistake of hers was made long before you came along. She's not the same person now. Whatever you do, Rob, do it fast. This waiting game has to be torture for her!"

"Okay, okay! Calm down, Gramps. You're right. For her sake and mine, I will make a decision in the next day or two. Don't think she's the only one hanging around in misery. This is killing me too." He squeezed his eyes closed. "But I'm having such a hard time forgiving her."

"*Forgiving her?* Who the hell do you think you are—God? He's the one who has the right—the authority—to forgive her, not you. And He will forgive her, you can be sure of that. So by you turning your back on that girl who worships the ground you walk on, you're denying God as well. Remember that," he admonished with a pointed finger.

Rob was both bewildered and surprised by his grandfather's display of anger. It was completely out of character for him. "What's going on here, Gramps? How did you get this upset? And how did God get into our conversation?"

"I put Him there because I needed His help. *You* need His help!"

Rob felt a smile tugging at his lips and tried to mask it. His grandfather was obviously in no mood. But there was something extra special about Dennis' reaction today. He cared so darn much that it endeared him more than ever. He popped the trunk for the clubs and got out of the car.

"You coming in?" Dennis roared.

"Not if you're going to yell at me," Rob answered with a mocking pout.

Dennis tried not to laugh, but couldn't help himself. Walking behind Rob towards the house, he gave him a playful slap on the back of his head. "You've got a thick head, my Robbie, you know that?" He stopped him at the garage and forced Rob to look him in the eye. "I have only one more thing to say and then I'll shut up. There's an old reliable question that works in these situations. Have you asked yourself yet if you'd be better off with or without Suzanne? Think about that long and hard, and whatever your honest answer is, let that guide you. But make your decision and call her. If you want to give up two princesses because your pride is hurt . . . well, that's your loss."

"I'll call her soon, Gramps. I promise. And either way, I'll let you know." He gave Dennis a fast hug and went back to his car. He drove away digesting and reconsidering all that his grandfather had said.

* * *

Rob never made it home. Grandpa Dennis' closing argument throbbed in his head and thundered in his heart. He didn't have to think about it long and hard, as Dennis had so passionately suggested. Rob could have answered that without hesitation way back when he and Suzanne first met at Maine Medical Center. Through all the physical pain and emotional trauma she had endured after her car went plunging down in a road collapse, coupled with a possible murder charge looming over her, Suzanne never lost her sense of humor. She never gave him one of those mournful looks draped with pity that had become too familiar after his accident. Everyone else, including his family and closest friends, had skirted the issue of his amputated foot. Oh, yes, they asked about his pain and discomfort, about what to expect in terms of therapy and any other related topic they considered safer ground, but never about his emotional suffering. Nor did they discuss anything mundane that might have interested him before, like baseball. Rob understood that their hearts were in the right places; they assumed it would be insensitive to speak of anything unrelated to his accident and the severity of his injuries. It was as though the loss of his foot had involuntarily yanked him from the normalcy of day-to-day life.

But not Suzanne. She was never afraid to ask questions that no one else dared to ask. They talked openly from the start of their friendship, sharing fears, anxieties, hopes and laughter.

A flashback came to him as he drove. The sadness on his mom's face that she could never conceal no matter how valiantly she tried. He remembered her standing at his bedside while he was still only half-conscious. Her fingers had stroked his face and he heard her voice struggling not to cry. "Try not to worry, my darling son. We have to have faith that God will help you through this. We have to believe that when he closes one door, he opens another."

He made a sharp and careless left turn off Route 1 that could have put him back in the hospital, he realized, but he had no patience for the traffic. Today the back roads would facilitate the ride to his destination.

Rob prayed that she'd be home when he got there and God came through. Just as he pulled into her parking lot, he spotted her walking towards her building, one hand holding Heather's and the other weighted down with groceries.

"Suzanne!" he called out. "Wait!"

Heather broke loose from her mother's grip and ran to him. He pulled her up and hugged her like a kidnapped child who had just been rescued.

Suzanne stayed at the back entrance to her building, frozen to the spot, hoping he had come for the right reason. But the closer he came, the wider he smiled until he burst into joyous laughter. She dropped the grocery bag down on the concrete and, with tears streaming down her face, threw her arms out and ran. But she stopped short just before embracing him. "Maybe I shouldn't get too excited, Rob. Please tell me that big, gorgeous smile means what I think it means."

He kissed her there in broad daylight, oblivious to whoever might be watching, while Heather tried her best to squeeze her tiny face between theirs for her share. "I think I loved you from the day we met, and I *know* I loved you from that day forward, and *will* love you for the rest of my life." He lowered his voice and gazed deep into her eyes. "I've been such an ass, Suzanne. It took a small sermon from my grandpa and a memory of my mom after the accident to make me see the light. I'm the one who needs forgiveness, not you."

Suzanne was still afraid to swell her heart with happiness too soon. "Are you sure, Rob, that Greg won't represent some kind of invisible monster—like an albatross you can never free yourself from?"

He cupped her chin and kissed her gently. "Who the hell is Greg?"

The words left her breathless; overcome with joy, love and gratitude. "Let's go upstairs, Rob," she whispered. "I need to hold you and never let go."

"Sounds good to me, sweetheart."

# Chapter Fifty-seven

Amore Evenings had signs prominently displayed for a week prior to October 20th that no reservations would be accepted past 7:30. The restaurant would close at 9:00 for a private party.

The true celebrant's identity, however, was somewhat nebulous. Most received invitations to a surprise celebration honoring Dennis Butler, who had turned seventy the week before. Dennis received one inviting him and Dora Malanski to celebrate a surprise engagement party for his grandson, Rob, and Suzanne Oliveri. Rob had told his grandfather that he and Suzanne received an invitation to a surprise engagement party for Sara Baisley and Tim Waite, who in reality planned to get engaged for Christmas. Sara and Tim thought they were going to Dennis Butler's surprise birthday party. And that, of course, was true.

Frannie and Glory had not only hosted the event, but had invited their own close friends, some of whom had never met Dennis Butler. Now that they were "seasoned restaurateurs," they had planned a celebration that surpassed the elegance of Amore Evening's opening.

Glory had a table reserved for Dan and Jessica, but the happy couple had no idea they would find all their children waiting to join them—a celebration in itself. Dan would be twice as pleased to see that Todd had brought Holly. They had patched up their differences a week ago, but Todd had saved the good news for tonight as an added surprise for his dad.

Sara and Tim would be guests tonight, rather than servers, and they would be surprised with the appearance of

Steve Lynch and John Weaver, his partner. Sara had been instrumental in getting them together after a long estrangement. She would be delighted to hear that the Los Angeles couple planned to spend a whole month in Ogunquit.

Frannie and Glory hadn't been sure where to seat Tony Gerard and his very pregnant wife, Corrine. They were too old for the younger crowd and too young for the older crowd. But Frannie had decided since they were practically newlyweds and expecting their first child, they should be seated with Suzanne and Rob and Sara and Tim, since both couples would soon follow in their footsteps.

Tess, Sal and Jerry Oliveri were seated with the older crowd, although a few were only in their forties. Frannie had seated herself with them to the dismay of her mother. "I feel so bad for her, Sal. She can't even have Glory for company. Glory and Tim had to sit with Dan and Jessica's families. Everyone has someone and she's stuck with us."

Jerry Oliveri leaned forward so she could acknowledge his presence. "Excuse me? She's not the only one alone."

Tess leaned over and squeezed his hand. "Don't you worry my dear brother-in-law. Now that you straightened yourself out, your day will come too."

Jerry tipped his head and smiled, as if it were a remote but possible dream.

Sal responded to his wife's concern. "She'll be fine tonight. It's not as if she has no one. Sergio just couldn't leave Italy yet, but pretty soon she'll be going home to him, not only Benny, her dog!"

"But it's been over a month since Sergio's mother died," Tess said, "and from what she tells me, he still can't give her an idea of when he's coming back from Italy."

"Doesn't matter. He'll come back and they'll have a lifetime together. In my book, Sergio is worth the wait. The guy is aces."

Tess laughed and punched his arm. "Even if he were deuces you would have loved him because he comes from Palermo."

Sal conceded with a laugh because that was partially true. Sergio had impressed him in the first few minutes, but once he mentioned Palermo and San Martino della Scale, the village where his family still lived, they were bonded for life. His face sobered as memories of his daughter's emotional pain surfaced. "I was sick to my stomach when that SOB she thought she was married to had the nerve to show up again. It's a good thing I never came face-to-face with him."

Tess squeezed her husband's hand. "We have to put all that ugly Wade business behind us, Sal. Thank God he left Ogunquit. I think if he hadn't heard about Sergio, he might have hung around and tried to worm his way back into Frannie's life."

"Over my dead body!"

"You guys better put a lid on it," Jerry said. "Your daughter's on her way to this table."

"We were just talking about Glory," Tess said to Frannie when she took her seat at their table. "Who ever thought when we talked to Dr. Quinlan every day at the hospital that he'd end up with Glory?" She threw her gaze up to heaven. "It's a blessing that poor girl deserves."

"Amen to that, Mom," Frannie said. "But let's not jump the gun. They're still getting to know each other, so let's keep our fingers crossed." She felt a telltale grin creeping up her face, but masked it with a feigned cough. She happened to know from Glory that for the past three months she and the handsome doctor were getting to know each other quite well. Although Tim had initiated it, Frannie couldn't deny feeling complacent about pairing them up.

Someone tapped her on the shoulder and Frannie jumped up to greet her dear friends, Ken Holmes and Jake Corbin who owned The Admiral's Inn. Her parents and her uncle followed, and she introduced them to the others at the table. "These are the guys who so graciously hosted a party for Suzanne and Rob when they both came home from the hospital."

Ken waved off the praise. "Hey, we had a blast ourselves. Jake and I would have done it again," he said to Tess, "but the ladies wanted to have it here. So that's fine; we have no problem being guests for a change."

"So, Frannie," Jake said, "I'm dying to meet your Sergio. I heard all good things about him. When's he coming back?"

Tess gave her husband a discreet eye roll and watched her daughter.

"No exact date yet, but soon," Frannie said with only a hint of sadness. She had been so disappointed that he hadn't been able to return in time for this celebration. She would have been so proud to show him off. "I'll bring him to meet you guys first chance we get."

She walked them to the dais to meet Dennis and Dora, and while she was chatting with them, Tim Quinlan came up to interrupt her conversation. "Can you spare a minute, Frannie? Glory needs you in the kitchen."

Both Glory and Tim had looks of concern on their faces when she entered the kitchen. Nonplussed, Frannie looked from one to the other. "What's wrong?" she asked.

"Oh, sorry, Frannie," Glory quickly said, "we didn't mean to scare you. It's just a minor problem. We have a last-minute guest that we need to seat and I wanted to get your okay to seat him at your table."

Frannie gave her a look of disbelief. "For that you had to pull me aside? What made you think you needed my approval? Of course you can. Who is it?"

A head popped up from behind an island counter. "It's me, cara mia."

Frannie let out a scream of surprise that had heads turning. Sergio laughed and opened his arms for the woman who would soon be his wife. They laughed and cried at the same time, while locked in each other's embrace. The kitchen was fully staffed and busy, but everyone took a moment to applaud and share in the joy. Glory's eyes filled with happy tears for her dearest friend and she caught a glimpse of Tim swallowing the lump in his throat. "Ah, love is so beautiful to watch, isn't it, Tim?" she said.

Tim kissed her on the forehead. "It sure is, sweetheart. We ought to know."

# Epilogue

The Christmas by the Sea Weekend had always been a heartwarming, fun-filled and enchanting time for not only the thousands of tourists, but the locals as well. The spirit of the season swelled everyone's heart and the entire village became a wonderland of happy faces spreading cheer and goodwill. This year's events began on Friday night, the 7<sup>th</sup> of December, with all the traditional festivities; tree lighting in Ogunquit Square; caroling in Perkins Cove where people sip hot chocolate or hot cider and munch on freshly-baked cookies and other seasonal treats. There was also a candlelight walk to the concert; a bonfire on the beach; hay rides; a chowder tasting competition and numerous other events. All the quaint little shops light up the village with breathtaking displays of lights and seasonal decorations and there isn't an unsmiling face to be found.

But this particular Christmas by the Sea Weekend had an extra-special event scheduled that had tugged at the hearts of everyone.

A double wedding at Amore Evenings.

Frannie Oliveri and Glory English—friends and partners for life—had endured together and survived horror and grief. Now, with Sergio and Tim, they would share the blessings and joy of marriage.

It had been impossible to get all the well-wishers inside the restaurant for the special event that had everyone teary-eyed. But throngs of people waited outside to cheer the two couples who would leave the following week for a cruise to Hawaii.

"We made it, kid," Frannie whispered to Glory as the two couples stood before a cheering crowd. "Now we have it all."

"No, Frannie, you had it all when we met. I just hung on and borrowed some of your spirit. I love you back, kiddo!"

* * *

After watching the four newlyweds being driven away in a limo, Suzanne and Rob strolled along Perkins Cove and into the village. She inhaled long deep breaths, filling her lungs with all the season's sweet fragrances and the anticipated pleasures of all the years ahead. "I'll always remember this night. I'm so happy for the four of them. I love happy endings, they're so romantic." She fingered the diamond bracelet Rob had given her for her birthday. "And speaking of romantic, I still can't believe this gorgeous bracelet, Rob. You're so good to me."

"Oh, I'm glad you reminded me." He pulled the ring out from the little box in his pocket and slipped it on her finger. "Here's something to go with it."

Suzanne eyes lit up enough to rival the village lights around her. Tears choked her voice and when it came through all she could say while she smothered him with kisses was, "I love you, I love you, I love you!"

Onlookers who witnessed the surprise engagement formed a circle around them. Everyone applauded and offered congratulations.

Later, as they continued their leisurely stroll in the crisp December air, Rob smiled down at her. "And talk about happy endings, my pretty girl, tonight is not about happy endings—not for Frannie or Glory or you or me. Tonight is about new beginnings—for all of us."

She looked up at him and winked. "Looks like Grandpa Dennis and Dora are headed in that direction too!"

Rob laughed. "He hasn't said anything yet, but I'm inclined to agree," he said, then pointed a finger at her. "But before you get romantic ideas again, don't try to talk them into a double wedding."

She lifted her eyebrows and giggled. "Hey, now that you mention it, that might be a cute idea; grandfather and grandson tying the knot with their brides on the very same day—maybe a June wedding. The more I think about it the cuter it gets."

Rob stopped in the middle of the street and interrupted her romantic musings with a kiss. "Well, don't think about it! We're not waiting six months, and as much as I love my grandpa, he and Dora are not sharing our wedding day! And what makes you think they'd want to share theirs?"

She put a finger on her chin as though pondering the question. "Good point, Rob. But what about Heather, Rob? She might want to walk down the aisle with us, so don't say I didn't warn you," she said teasingly.

He kissed the tip of her nose. "You know what I always say, sweetheart: Sounds good to me! Now why don't we go home and get rid of the babysitter?"

With her diamond sparkling, she tickled him under his chin. "Robert John Butler, you have an uncanny ability to read my thoughts."

* * *

While their husbands played shuffleboard, Frannie and Glory relaxed on the promenade deck aboard their Hawaii-bound cruise liner. "Will you hand me that sunblock, Glory? I think I need to smear myself again." Frannie turned to accept the tube from Glory's hand and did a double take. Impulsively, she lifted Glory's sunglasses. "Oh, damn, Glory, don't tell me you're crying again! This is no time for tears. We're on our honeymoons, for goodness sake! It isn't about leaving Danny, is it? I thought you were finally okay with that."

Glory sat up in her lounge chair and dabbed at the tears that welled in her eyes. "No, I'm okay, really," she said, feeling foolish and smiling. "With the whole family to spoil him, Danny will be fine. I do miss him, but truthfully, he wasn't even in my mind. No, these are happy tears, and haven't we said that happy tears are always welcome? Just think, Frannie, last year or even six months ago, who ever dreamed I'd be crazy in love again and *married*! I love Tim so much that it makes me feel a little guilty about Alex. Like maybe I should have mourned him longer. Do you know what I mean or is that stupid?"

Frannie shot her a look and laughed. "You're absolutely right. It is stupid! Why don't you just thank God for sending Tim your way? Why do you always take this martyr attitude? You have a right to be happy, so just bask in it, darn it!"

Glory giggled. "You're right, I do tend to get dramatic, but I can't help beating up on myself sometimes for what I feel or don't feel. And to be honest, I can barely visualize Alex's face anymore; not clearly. Isn't that awful?"

"No, not at all, my friend. You loved Alex with all your heart and you *showed* him that love while he was alive. If he hadn't died, Tim wouldn't have entered your life. But the reality is Alex *did* die, and the love you share now with Tim—your *husband*—shouldn't be shadowed by memories of Alex. You're a young woman, Glory, and I'm sure Alex himself wouldn't have wanted you and his son to be alone. And believe me, I don't think if you could have searched the world you could have found anyone better than Tim Quinlan. He's a gem!"

"That's for sure. He's a gem in every way possible," she said with a suggestive smile. "And Frannie, I have to admit I was a bit skeptical about Sergio before I met him. After what you went through with Wade, I didn't want to see you hurt again. But speaking of gems, you've got one too. I love that guy like a brother!"

"And I love him like a *husband*," Frannie answered, returning her friend's suggestive smile. She inhaled the salty air and shook her head. "This is all so amazing, isn't it? Like a beautiful fantasy we've been swept into. Talk about wild dreams—did you ever imagine when you walked into Amore Breakfast that day years ago that we'd be inseparable friends and successful business partners?"

"Not at that time, no. And did you ever dream that we'd end up with two princes to marry in a Cinderella-style double wedding with a honeymoon like this? It's like a fairy tale or an episode of *The Love Boat*. Remember that TV show?"

"I certainly do, but *The Love Boat* romances always had conflicts. And we already had our share of conflicts, so I'd rather stick with reality. Our futures couldn't look brighter!"

"That's what I love most about you, Frannie, you're so optimistic—always see that silver lining behind the clouds."

"That's why I have to stick to you like glue, my friend, whether you like it or not."

Glory gave her an elbow poke and scrunched her face. "I like it and you know it," she said, then flagged down a waiter and ordered two apple martinis.

Frannie spotted Sergio and Tim walking towards them looking handsome and radiantly happy. "Make that four martinis, Glory. Our *gems* are back."